APOGEE

BY BLOOD OR BY STAR
BOOK 2

TYLER E. C. BURNWORTH

Temple Dark Books

By Blood Or By Star Book 2: Apogee
First Edition

Cover art by The Structuralist, AKA Eugen Baitinger
www.ebaitinger.de

Cover design & Typesetting by Temple Dark Books
Temple Dark Publications Ltd.
www.templedarkbooks.com

ISBN (E-Book): 9781739749231
ISBN (Paperback): 9781739749224

For Brighton; because one day, you can, too.

PROLOGUE

"He's not dead," Vase said over her iced macchiato. She stirred the straw, blending the milk and coffee. "I don't care what anyone says. I know him."

Djet frowned across the table. She took a sip of foam from her own brew, exposing a small half circle of espresso the color of her skin. The shape trembled when she set it down. *An odd thing for it to do*, she thought. Coffee was a deeply personal thing. Something close to a reflection of the person ordering it. It wasn't as simple as that to most people, but Djet wasn't most people; she was a longarm. The term, a halfway clever euphemism for 'cop', originated in the streets of Vatican's *Dominicus Dorsi* district.

It wasn't Djet Rincon, former roommate at Vatican Military Institute. It was L-DET Rincon, shortened to El Dee by people too lazy to call her Longarm Detective Rincon. Vase's body language telegraphed the message her words failed to hide; this wasn't a social call. It was asking for a favor.

Djet tapped her fingernails against her cup. Her accent was an eccentric mix of Irish and Jamaican. Like the coffee they drank, it could be traced back thousands of years to Earth.

"Okay, so ya know him. How well do ya know him?"

Vase blinked several times. "What do you mean?"

"Ya make it sound like he just vanished into thin air. What about ship logs?"

Vase glared. "There's two million transits a day, Djet. That's not an option."

"Okay, fair point. What about this guy? He's a marine. What are his capabilities? Does he have violent tendencies outside of the battlefield? Does he have a motive for disappearing?"

Something passed over Vase's face. Her eyebrows narrowed and she pursed her lips, broke eye contact, resting her chin on her hand.

The barista put two cups on the counter. A man dressed in a flashy C-skin quickly scooped them up, sipping one as he passed the other to the woman at his side. His cup was free of any marks – straight espresso, most likely. The other was a cold brew with a mound of orange cream floating on top; it clung to the woman's lip.

The man stopped for a second to whisper. The woman didn't miss a beat. She pursed her lips and leaned into him. He cleaned her lip with a kiss – slightly longer than was necessary, Djet thought. They shared a laugh and left arm in arm.

A few seconds passed. Djet watched Vase stare off into space.

She's damaged. This guy did a number on her.

Djet pulled her hair back into a tight ponytail, transitioning from best friend to hard-nosed detective. She had every intention of exploiting Vase's emotions to draw out the truth, friend or not.

"If ya want him found," Djet rested her hand on Vase's, "I need to ask some questions. The usual questions detectives ask in a missing person's case. Ya need to answer honestly if ya actually want him found."

Vase slid her hand back and tucked it into her leg pocket. She leaned back in her chair and stretched her neck. "Of course," she said, like it was the most obvious thing in the world, "I don't have anything to hide. You know that, Djet."

Djet slid her espresso forward and planted her elbows on the table. It was a tactic she used to lock eyes with a suspect. Close proximity and intense eye contact would break most liars almost instantly. The times it didn't...she wasn't going to use those tactics on her old friend, but she would know if she lied.

"On the contrary, Captain Seneca, I think ya have been collecting secrets since the last time I saw ya. How long have ya known him?"

"Three years."

"What was the nature of your relationship?"

Vase blinked twice. "We were lovers."

Djet nodded, just a bit. "Ya were intimate?"

Vase broke eye contact, looking up and to the left. "You don't need to know that."

"Oh, I do. I need to know *everyting*, Vase. Every detail helps."

Vase snapped her eyes back to Djet's. Eyes covered in a shining layer of tears. Her lower lip trembled. Her words came out through clenched teeth.

"Do you need to know how big his dick is, too?"

Djet felt a pang of regret but refused to so much as blink.

"Ya mentioned in your message that he stormed off and that was the last ya saw of him. That means he was upset with ya. Could give me an idea of where he went. *Why* he was mad at ya makes the difference between him choosing to hit the nearest strip club or going off-world with the intent of never returning."

Vase scooted her chair out from under the table, metal on marble grinding, probably just like her teeth were. She flipped a dial on her belt, changing her C-skin pattern from an ambient white to the blue and gray cascade of Navy camo.

"I'm late for work."

"No," Djet leaned back in her chair until it creaked. "You're scared."

Vase flicked a lock of blonde hair off her forehead. She started checking the braids on the brown side, her eyes looking anywhere but at Djet. To the detective, the behavior matched the stacked letters scrawled in permanent marker on the side of Vase's cup. A coffee that specific could only be ordered by one of two people: an uppity coffee snob or a control freak.

Vase snapped, "I'm not scared, I'm worried. There's a difference."

Djet sipped her espresso, careful not to singe her tongue. She inhaled the wafting steam, basking in the pleasant aroma. She had enough to go on. Enough to honor the favor and start an off-the-books investigation on her free time. The whereabouts of Vase's former lover wasn't the most interesting question, though.

"What did he do to ya, Vase?"

Captain Vase picked up her coffee and turned to leave. "Let me know if you find anything."

PART 1: STARLIGHT

*"We can easily forgive a child who is afraid of the dark;
the real tragedy of life is when men are afraid of the light."*

- Plato

CHAPTER 1

The grass has blood on it.

Is it really blood? It's red. The grass is red, too.

Blink.

No, it's not blood. It's dew. The grass is covered in dew, and the grass is red, so it looks like blood.

Blink.

The grass is blood.

A scream sounds from far away. It echoes in the soft morning light, becoming louder as it draws closer. It is a cracked, throaty scream that could not possibly be human. No man or woman could make a sound like that. Not even if they were being ripped apart.

I've seen that. They don't sound like that when it happens.

Blink.

The light…it's gone.

Fading into the recesses of the tunnel – a shaft of darkness with structural supports forced into the dirt, barely visible in the dim light…the tunnel is blood…the scream fades, and he is alone.

I'm alone.

But I wasn't always alone.

I came here with…friends.

He sees them in his mind with a stark clarity that one can only experience in waking life. The marines of Raven platoon. They weren't supposed to be here.

But they are here. They didn't die.

I did not see their blood.

Her blood gushes over his hand in a deluge of forbidden heat, and it keeps…gushing.

A steady flow spreading over his hand, pouring onto the floor in a pool and it's –

Too much. It's too much blood. How can one person have so much blood?

As her blood warms his hand, she grows colder. Weaker.

In her emerald-green eyes, he sees himself.

He's covered in blood, too.

More precious than gold or digits or the galaxy's deepest, darkest secrets, that blood is leaving her, and he can't stop it. He is just a boy in the reflection held in her eyes. He's too young for this. But so is she. The image is murky, obscured by tears and pain.

"Do it," she groans.

Beside him, his friend cries, "No!"

The one friend whose face he can't see, although some dim part of his mind recognizes him. He's known this friend longer than the rest. They've grown up together.

This was the moment when all that changed.

He doesn't want to do it, but he has to do it. She *wants* him to. And beyond that, you have to honor the last request of the dying. Don't you? Isn't that how it works? Once marked for death, you get one wish. You don't get to see it fulfilled, but the knowledge that it *will* be fulfilled, even after you've died…that's enough to make the dying easier.

Easier for the person dying.

Sometimes, that blessing can be a curse.

Because of her he unsheathes the blade. As his friend's screams pelt him with tears of incredulity, he knows the truth of it. Tears are the purest form of communication, but without context, they're just scattered saline.

Her tears are of sorrow. Because she's dying.

His friend's tears are of betrayal. Because he can't stop it.

His own tears…he's not crying. He wants to – probably would if not for all the blood. The tunneled walls, his armor and his boots, his hands and his face are all blood.

Now the dagger is blood, too.

She didn't have enough. She lost too much. His friend's boiled, while his own…

He knew less about his own than he thought.

For all he knew, his blood was *not* his own.

And that scared him.

"Abraham!"

There was a thunderstorm. He didn't remember there being a thunderstorm.

Dark clouds trundled across the sky like exhaust from giant machines, the ones that churned and burned raw materials into energy with great peals of thunder that shook his chest with each angry rumble. There was no need of such machines anymore, except on Veranda.

But he wasn't on Veranda.

He was…

"ABRAHAM!"

…in Vase's apartment.

Trees with long slender leaves – they wilted like hands gone limp – billowed in a simulated breeze on the wall. Dubsteel cabinets with transparent panes held glass cups and glass plates that refracted the overhead lighting in a cascade of rainbow sparkles. The glassware spilled prismatic beauty across the swirled gray marble of the countertop. When he looked away from the dazzling trick of the light he remembered where he was, and he knew it was happening again.

Vase stared at him from the other side of the island, one hand on her hip. The skin around her eyes was wrinkled, but the glacier-blue orbs themselves were soft. Concerned. Her beauty always startled him.

"Abraham, you're doing it again. Are you okay?"

He shook his head and tried to smile. He knew he was doing it again. He also knew he couldn't hide it. Not from her. She was too smart to lie to, too attentive to miss it.

He didn't belong here. The word that had haunted him since high school floated up to the forefront of his mind.

Phantasmagoria.

He felt like his life wasn't real. The Marine Corps had changed him. The hell he survived on Duringer wasn't over for him. It may never be over. When Piebold told him about the Ghosts – eyeless demons that stalked the galaxy stealing children and who knew what else – he didn't want to believe it. But he could not forget what he saw in those awful moments of The Collision so many years ago.

The hairs on the back of his neck stood on end. A cool breeze of fear fluttered across his skin. The Shadow Man that haunted his dreams as a child was real. They had been watching him. They knew who he was.

They told him he wasn't human. Or, at least, that he wasn't *completely* human.

These thoughts came in a spark that lasted only a fraction of a second, although the beautiful woman standing in front of him, who also happened to be his commanding officer, seemed to detect it.

"Abraham." She stepped around the counter to put a gentle hand on his shoulder. As if this simple gesture would be enough to calm the torrid sea that ravaged his mental landscape. The tug of war between what was real and what wasn't.

"Vase, I..."

She put a finger to his lips. For some reason, this affected him. He sighed. His breathing slowed. Her finger was soft against his lips, and smelled strongly of onions and oil. The dinner prep was nearly done. They were just about ready to move into the cooking phase.

"Stop," she said, her voice smooth. "You can't keep doing this to yourself. You've been through something not a lot of people have. It's going to take time to work through it."

A mirthless chuckle rolled out of his throat. He took her finger off his lips and folded his fingers into hers. She squeezed his hand reassuringly.

This is real. What we have, it's not a dream.

But she knows something, part of his mind whispered as he searched her eyes for the answers. *She knows about the Ghosts. She knows about the Ghosts, and she hasn't told you what she knows. Why won't she tell you?*

"Security clearances," he thought. Her hand stiffened in his grip.

"What?" she asked, her head tilting slightly to one side.

He hadn't meant to think that out loud.

He pulled his hand out from hers and leaned back against the *fisu*. On Veranda, he would have called it a fridge. Here on Vatican – the nexus of the tangled labyrinth that had become his life – nothing was the same. Not even the icebox where people kept their food cold. When he walked the always busy streets of the *Dominicus Dorsi* district where Vase lived, he did not see cars or buses. He saw star skippers or air transports. There weren't elevators, either. They were maglifts, and there was no rumbling of gears and pulleys or the tug of gravity as the elevator ascended or descended. With a sharp cough and a barely detectible hum, the view out the window became a series of indistinct colored lines reminiscent of FTL transition he'd seen from the viewports of a dozen spacecraft.

"Vase, I need to know what's going on."

He took a deep breath and tried to ignore the dozens of past conversations they had on the subject. All the time she shot him down with excuses varying from *security clearance* to *need to know* to the very effective *can we talk about something else?* sealed with a persuasive kiss.

Try as he might, he could not fight her when she kissed him. That was the ultimate trump card she pulled to silence him, and for the last three years, he'd let her play that card. Now as he looked at her, took in her piercing eyes and the blonde-brown halves of her hair woven in intricate braids, her svelte body in her C-skin...he had to –

– blink –

– focus.

He frowned. "I need to know what you know about the Ghosts. No more secrets."

She smiled. "I know you do, Abraham."

Her hands cupped his face. She pressed herself against him, touched her nose to his. She was so close, and it felt like comfort. Warmth bloomed in his chest. The feelings he had for this woman were supernatural.

"You know I can't tell you."

"I know," he said, "but I can get the story from them."

Vase brushed her lips softly against his. Her hands slid down to his neck and, for a moment, he dared hope this would lead to more than a kiss. The hope lasted only a moment. She pulled away to capture him with her eyes.

"You can't, Abraham. They'll use you. You don't know what they are."

He pulled her hands down and took a half step back. The sliced onions saturated the kitchen air. A loaf of puffed bread, sliced and covered in a garlic smear was waiting to be thrown in the hotbox. Vegetable slices were laid next to a generous slab of meat that rested in a puddle of purple juices. All this food should have made him ravenous. It certainly tempted the part of him that hated MREs.

Hungry as he was, Abraham couldn't eat. Not right now.

He left the kitchen and the fragrant, half-prepped meal to retrieve his L-pistol from the end table by the white Terrelian leather sectional. He attached it to the magnetic clip on his C-skin belt. His pocket, a drone the shape and size of an owl, gave a hoot and fluttered over to him.

"What're you doing?" Vase asked. She threw the yellow, herb-covered bread loaves into the hotbox and cast a glance at him.

"We need to have this conversation, whether you want to or not." Abraham retrieved the spare magazines and slid them into the owl's beak and tapped his pocket on the head. It gave a tiny hoot as it sealed the items inside its body and began circling about him in a lazy orbit.

Vase crossed her arms.

He knew when she was mad, and this wasn't it. She was pretending to be mad. Abraham knew he wasn't the best at reading people, but he had spent a lot of time with Vase over the last three years. Their relationship, improper as it was between officer and enlisted, had stayed relatively secret. At least, secret enough from the people who would care to do something about it. Intimacy fosters familiarity. She wasn't angry. She was nervous.

Good, he thought.

"I meant what I said back on Juno, and what I said on Duringer, and what I've said to you a half dozen times over the last few years, Vase. I love you." A sudden itch at the back of his neck distracted him. "But I'm not going to let this go. They know things about me. Things I should know about myself. If you're not willing to tell me, or you can't because of whatever reason, that's fine. But don't try to stop me from seeking those answers on my own."

He could see the dots connecting in her eyes. She knew what he was going to do, but she hadn't given up yet.

"What about tomorrow night? The Navy Ball?" she asked innocently.

"You're not going to ditch me, are you? I was going to introduce you...there's someone I really want you to meet."

Abraham shrugged. "I don't do well with dancing."

Vase smirked. "So I've heard."

The joke had been going on so long now, he didn't even get embarrassed. The first and only time he'd ever danced was before he enlisted, and the girl he danced with...she kissed him, and he threw up. In her mouth.

Ha. Ha. It's mortifying, at first. The next thousand times people bring it up it's funny, but after that...it's just an immutable fact of history. Like a stubborn stain on the wall that can't be removed with any amount of bleach. It just sits there, an unflattering eyesore, until it becomes as much a part of the room as the knickknacks on the shelves.

"Anyway." Abraham approached the door. "I came to a decision. You're not going to like it. But it's what I want."

She approached him, her eyes questioning. "And that decision is?"

He took in a breath. It felt like the first time in three years with her that he was making a decision. Vase was used to being the one in charge. He let her lead their relationship over the years, juggling the stiff formality of officer and enlisted in public, girlfriend and boyfriend in private. Even though he desperately wanted things to progress, he didn't want to force it beyond what Vase was comfortable with. Starting now, sex was a dimension of their relationship most likely going to remain unexplored.

"I'm not re-enlisting."

Her lips parted, but she did not speak.

She's surprised. Frustrated, maybe?

Whatever she was thinking, he was sure she hadn't expected him to say that.

"If you don't re-enlist...what will you do? Vatican's not exactly hiring combat veterans to maintain bots or fly star skippers."

He smiled. "I'll figure something out."

He kissed her. She remained frozen.

She did not return the kiss, and he left.

She let him leave.

Abraham stepped into the hallway. The door sealed shut behind him, separating him from the pleasant smells of the meal. He let out the deep breath he was holding. It was more than a great meal and great company he was walking away from. He was leaving the most important person in his life behind on a whim. Chasing a chance at finding answers to the questions that kept him awake at night. Part of him knew it was crazy. Part of him hoped those answers would put an end to his waking nightmares.

It should have felt like the right thing to do.

Abraham told himself it was. No matter how many times he said it, he couldn't convince himself it was true. He shrugged it all away and started walking.

The corridor became wreathed in swirling shadows.

He came to a halt, adrenaline sizzling through his veins. His eyes darted up and down the hallway. Everywhere he looked the mysterious darkness spread like a cloud, obscuring the dubsteel walls and doors.

He sensed movement in his peripheral and whipped around, hand on his weapon. An ashy face stared at him from the shadows.

The skin was dark. Almost gray. A black bar covered the eyes, the smile beneath them familiar and frightening. He could have been a hologram, except that Abraham could neither see through him or the darkness that teemed around him like black flames.

"Abraham," Agent Smithers said in a gravelly tone.

Abraham's voice shook as he spoke.

"Smithers…how long have you been here?"

"I'm always here." He snorted. "The important question is, are you ready to take the offer? You've pissed away your life for three years, Abraham. The answers you seek have been waiting for you."

Abraham walked a few paces down the hall to put some distance between Smithers and himself. Stepping into the shadows didn't feel any different than the darkness between streetlights, but his skin crawled. He didn't want any of this conversation leaking into Vase's flat. If she heard him talking to Smithers…he didn't want to think what she would say. For the life of him, the one thing Abraham could not stand was disappointing that woman.

Why do I care about her so much?

His mind offered no answer, not at first.

A moment longer and he saw in his mind's eye the waterfall on Sepipira, the first time they both took leave to spend time together. The view from the quivarien restaurant where they both tried *schlotmiss* for the first time. Abraham didn't relish the idea of eating the worm-like anemone when it was served, until he tasted it – rich and savory, like a tangy fish. Vase had stolen his attention from the beautiful horsetail waterfall, something the locals called *Götte Blut*, or God's Blood. He asked her about that, why the locals called it God's Blood when the water was crystal clear, but she had just told him to wait for the sun to set. So they talked for hours about everything and nothing. About Duringer, the military, the galaxy and all the places they would visit, and the possibility that one of those twinkling stars in the sky would have a planet they might want to settle down on one day. They talked, and laughed, and it was good. When the sun set and both moons filled the sky like pregnant angels reflecting the wan light over them, he saw why the waterfall had earned its moniker.

As the water broke apart over the side of the shale rock cliffs, gentle moonbeams illuminated the falls, casting out rays and sparkles of every piece of the light spectrum. It was a dancing moonbow that cascaded along the dark rocks.

A breathtaking sight.

She's simple, Abraham thought. *She's got a pureness to her that I don't find in a lot of people. She's been through the same things I have and she's not the worse for wear. There's a lot of strength in that.*

A mirthless laugh escaped his lips.

A strength I haven't found in myself yet. That's why I can't let this go.

Smithers brought Abraham back to the dark hallway by clearing his throat.

"I want to know why you're telling me I have riskar DNA. It doesn't make sense, even in spite of..." *the blood, everything is blood*, "...in spite of what happened on Duringer. I don't know how to explain it."

Smithers smiled. "You have questions. I have answers. I also have a lot of other information you will find...pertinent."

Abraham nodded, but his focus wandered.

He was approaching a turning point. From the first day he joined the Marine Corps and stepped on that interplanetary vessel, he had a home. Now he was considering leaving that behind. On a practical level it didn't make sense. Why would he leave the military – the only family he ever really felt like he had – to follow a man of mystery who possessed a power he didn't understand? A power that his own eyes told him should be impossible. Did this man who seemed more than a man really know more about the bloodline Abraham abandoned?

Not knowing is too painful.

I need to know what happened.

The decision was already made.

"How do I know you won't just cart me off to a lab and dissect me?"

Smithers laughed. It sounded like old rags on a clothesline snapping in the wind.

"You don't. But if you're willing to take the chance – and let's be honest, if you want answers, this is the only choice you have – then meet me at the Olympia Space Needle in the academic sector of Dominicus Venti."

"When?"

"Three days. Time doesn't matter, really. I'll know when you're there."

Abraham looked into the black bar covering Smithers' eyes. He tried to peer through that barrier, to see any trace of humanity, but Smithers' eyes were blocked by the impenetrable umbra of that floating censor. Whether it was a trick of augmented reality or something supernatural was impossible to determine.

"Three days, Abraham."

The swirling shadows dissolved.

Seconds later, Abraham was standing in the hallway alone.

"Looks like I'll be going to the ball after all." He sighed.

CHAPTER 2

The streets of Vatican's Dominicus Venti district were quiet.

Quiet for a terra-city that never slept.

The entire planet was a cocoon of industry and intrigue. Exotic metals pilfered from far-off systems – worlds conquered by military conquests over the millennia – now formed towering skyscrapers with intersecting walkways and anti-gravity suspension bridges. The color of Vatican's surface could only be guessed at; from space, or even from the 100th level up, all one could see was infrastructure and dazzling lights in every conceivable hue.

The sky overhead was a dome of shadow. Stars twinkled like pinholes punched through a dark veil, teasing glimmers of a mystical great beyond that could never be fully brought into reality. Stargazing was a common escape from boredom.

Djet was supposed to be watching the street. She hated stakeouts.

Hours sitting in the pilot seat of the longarm star skipper tended to make her ass cramp. She was many things – daughter, detective, hand-to-hand expert in Capoeira...patient did not make the list.

Catching criminals was a rewarding line of work, but lately, she found the vastness of the galaxy more interesting. How many other worlds had detectives looking up to the stars at this moment in time? Was she making eye contact in some vague sense with hundreds, or even thousands of people who were bored out of their minds, their eyes turned up and outward with wonder at the limitless dark between them?

The cramped interior of the star skipper smelled. Her C-skin's climate controls kept her from sweating, but it wasn't body odor she detected. It was butter waffle fumes from her partner's vape cartridge.

The only things Djet liked about herself were her eyes and her lips. Her hair she had to put entirely too much work into for it to look passable. Her face was a little too round. It took too much makeup to hide the freckles that looked like coffee grounds on her cheekbones. Hailing from the industrial planet of Destin, most of Djet's lineage could be traced predictably straight back to Earth, to a rare mix of Irish and Jamaican.

She didn't like that her body was thick. Countless times as a teenager she had stared in the mirror, pressing her stomach in as hard as she could, wishing against hope that she would be skinny one day. Her mother had told her early on that the Rincon women were known as 'knockouts'. The term was a street one for curvy women whose 'tits a man could rest his head on after hips and ass knock him out'.

Diet wasn't interested in men, though.

She preferred everything to be in its right place. If she was going to knock a man out, she was going to use her bare-knuckled fist, or the ball of her foot and fifteen years of Capoeira to do it. If she was going to pursue a man, well, that was another matter entirely. She had been there and done that a few times, but in her experience, men didn't like to be chased and conquered the same way women did.

Ever since the first few weeks of college six years ago, Djet had realized something was different about her. It took her meeting Vase to realize what it was, and even then she stewed over it in consternation for a year and a half before working up the courage to drag those feelings into the light.

Vase – beauty queen and social dominatrix that she was – didn't feel the same way. But that was okay. Because Djet didn't love her, not really. She didn't want to be *with* her so much as she wanted to *be* her. Short and thin. Sensible proportions of 'tits, hips and ass'. A charming laugh and a cold stare, each given when needed, nothing held back for anything. Vase was as close to a free spirit as anyone Djet had ever met.

The thoughts that had once ran through her mind, churning her blood until it burned hot in her veins like firewater, came rushing back in like a dam bursting open.

"Djet, how long can you do that for, huh?"

Her partner, Cesar "Blaze" Cisneros, stole her wandering thoughts.

Diet shifted in her seat, trying to stretch her sore hamstrings.

"Blaze, mind ya business, yeah?"

"I don't care how you pick it or whatever, just don't touch the stick with that hand."

Djet wiped her nose – and the embarrassment – from her face.

She was scratching an itch, not picking it. That was a losing argument, so she leaned her back against the security cage that separated the rear compartment and didn't bother replying. The longarm edition sky runner was an air vehicle small enough to zip between the three hundred and forty levels of Vatican terra-city and still park on the ramps without impeding the never-ending flow of foot traffic.

A squad car, for all intents and purposes.

Blaze, having made his point, wrapped himself in a cocoon of silence. He stared down the walkway, puffing on his vape stick, mood pensive. Her partner was always pensive. Most detectives were.

Vatican is a strange place, Djet decided for the thousandth time.

When she thought about the capital world of the galaxy's largest superpower, she wanted to envision gold-paved streets under a crystal-clear sky. Rainbow rivers gently bending through lush gardens every shade of green in the spectrum. She could picture herself walking down that golden path barefoot, the sun blanketing her skin with warm, tiny kisses while she drank in the radiant perfumes of the heavenly flora. People of all kinds would be there, enraptured by the same zen-like aura that came naturally from the splendor that surrounded them. In a place like this, everything would be simple and calm and beautiful. A relaxing walk at dawn in a place like this, an hour could pass in a second.

Places like this, of course, did not exist.

Not for humanity, and not for any of the Nine Nations.

Civilization followed the same pattern no matter what corner of the dark sea of space in which they arose. Humanity's origins were lost to that darkness somewhere between the beginning and the end, if there ever would be an end. If the end really mattered. Djet was not a student of history. She did not spend time philosophizing on the past, or the future. She did wonder at the state of the Human Collective, because *who wouldn't*? Strange things had been happening on the news.

No, it wasn't that *things* were strange...the news itself was strange.

Politics had seeped into the everyday news cycle and it made her sick.

She didn't care about the Riskar War. She was glad it was over.

But it wasn't really over. Something was different about that war. Ever since The Collision, things were different. Was it a tragedy? Sure. Did the destruction of an outer rim world affect her? No. The Collective declared war on the riskar, sent in their troops and glassed their worlds into oblivion. The loss of Milune and Veranda were tragic. Tens of thousands of humans died. But humanity did what it always did; flexed its military muscles. The riskar were nearly wiped off the galactic stage, and the galaxy didn't even blink.

None of that had anything to do with Vatican.

So why did she have to hear about it every day, three years after the final battle at Duringer? Because the Nine Nations were so busy dividing up the riskar resources amongst themselves, they didn't seem to mind humanity being branded as an imperialist society.

Which is ridiculous, Djet thought. *All we did was defend ourselves.*

Anyone who called it revenge was either a conscientious objector or an entitled autocrat; both slices of society deemed themselves morally superior for turning their nose up at the thought of war, as if words solved everything.

But there, Djet thought, *there is the core of the problem. Words are no panacea. If they were, we wouldn't need politicians to argue on our behalf.*

And, another part of her retorted, if politicians were actually good at their job, they would have figured out effective diplomacy centuries ago. Maybe that way, their constituents wouldn't have to race off to distant worlds to die. Every life lost nothing more than a punctuation mark to the endless epithets of the elected ruling class.

All those deaths, in Djet's opinion, proved the futility of the system.

A system that did not allow for gold-paved streets and rainbow rivers.

For countless centuries, human futurists and artists had speculated on the idea of a planet-wide city. It wasn't until the seventh millennium when a string of mostly dead planets had been discovered out in the depths of space that here humanity had decided to put down roots. A cold, red, lifeless world was transformed into the first Terra City by the ninth millennium.

The entire planet cocooned with a spiraling haze of industry and steel towers and interconnecting suspension bridges that was the stuff of futurist daydreams five thousand years ago. On Vatican, they had made it a reality. The finishing touch had been the completion of the first Dyson Sphere.

A white dwarf star was the center of orbit for the dead planets. About the same time as the last square inch of landmass had been covered by the base of colossal buildings, the supermassive beryllium rings started spinning around the white dwarf. Vatican was bathed in the pale white glow of Starlight forevermore.

Vatican was different than Earth had been. Different than Djet remembered learning about in school, anyway. Earth had seasons, and weather, and the yellow dwarf star called Sol that lit the surface. Vatican had Starlight. Someone on Earth who visited Vatican for the first time might have thought they were in New York City, and that someone had replaced the moon with a giant LED light bulb and a fancy mobile around it.

The air was hot, though. Wireless electricity towers were stationed at the corners of buildings and every so often along the walkways and bridges. They looked like barbed spheres atop thin poles, surrounded by cylindrical glass tubes with purple light arcing within. It was an expensive and antiquated way to power a terra-city, and to make sure electronic devices stayed at a constant full battery charge.

"You see the news?" her partner asked, spewing more fumes.

Djet shook her head. "Nah. Anyting interesting?"

He shook his head, scratched his stubbled hair.

"No. Just more of the Navy's bullshit about The Collision."

"Why bullshit?" Djet asked.

He shrugged her question off like it wasn't worth answering.

Blaze was an older man, not too far from her father's age. He was close to retiring. Old Blaze had only been stuck on this surveillance detail because he was her partner. In effect, Djet had been a detective for five months and was dictating the life of a man who had about thirty more years of service than she did. It was the kind of gravitas you had when your name meant something.

Blaze inhaled his vape-stick for a long five seconds, held his breath for two and sighed a cloud of butter waffle fumes. The sweet aroma settled on the dash like fog. Tiny particles danced against the windshield, evaporating in sections until Djet could see the street clearly again.

The duracrete walkway stretched for half a block before branching into a T. The northbound section held her attention; just over the curb and the safety glass, one level down was a parking apron. A hodgepodge of run-down civilian sky runners nestled between an apartment tower and a twelve-level liquor emporium.

"I don't believe any of those pass their weight and balance inspections," Djet said, referring to the basic yearly requirement for air vehicle registration.

Blaze's jaw dropped. He slowly turned his head toward her, eyes wide like he'd seen something he hadn't expected to see.

"Should we call it in?" he asked.

Djet felt a wave of embarrassment rush over her again.

She lightly punched him on the shoulder and said, "I'm just saying. Look at the state of those things. That one's missing a few panels, and there's – what is that, coolant or hydraulic fluid? – something's leaking from almost all of them."

One of them was not missing panels or leaking, though.

It was parked at the east end of the lot, like it was too good to be clustered with the run-down skippers. The smooth, gleaming yellow fuselage was covered in green flames that danced hypnotically across the surface. The twin engines were polished chrome covered by aggressively angled nacelles. Clearly, it was designed for one thing: punching holes in the sky.

Even Djet had to admit it looked nice.

"How much ya tink that cost?" she asked. When Blaze didn't answer, she asked again, "The motion flames on the paint. How much for someting like that?"

Blaze shrugged. "Seven large. Easy."

Blaze was old. He didn't play into her conversations as much as she would have liked. After ten straight hours of surveillance, the skipper compartment felt like it was shrinking in on them. A more uncomfortable way to spend a night she could not conceive. It took her by complete surprise when he cleared his throat and launched into a story, eyes fixated on the sky puncher and its green inferno.

"Your daddy was the best of us, Djet. You know that. It's why you're following in his footsteps." A phlegm-filled rattle shook the old man, deep in his chest. Djet knew him well enough to recognize this as a laugh. "Yeah, Warin and I go way back to the beginning. We were the youngest, dumbest pair of recruits to walk under the C-wire and into the Third Watch station. That was almost forty years ago."

Djet let her eyes drift back to the street as Blaze took a hit from his vape-stick. He talked as he exhaled, his smoke-filled voice an octave lower, his eyes glazed over with memories.

"Your father hasn't changed much over the years. He's always been a great longarm. The best. I'm not the only one who thinks that way. First week of the academy he had the patrol manual practically memorized. Hard to compete with someone like that. Not that I ever aspired to be Chief of the Watch or anything, myself. No, Warin had that locked in from the beginning. When you were born, the party we threw... *whoo*, that was some serious shit. I think we were drunk for forty-eight hours straight."

Djet chuckled. That would be her father, all right. Warin loved his hookah and his alcohol. She didn't care much for drinking, but she liked a fresh nicotine cake and a good bubbler to just sit back and relax.

Blaze continued, tapping his vape-stick on the dash as his exhaled cloud evaporated.

"You remember when Singularity happened. The only time I ever saw your father off his game. Whatever happened then, it must've been bad."

"He never told me about Singularity." Djet wrinkled her brow. "What was that?"

Blaze cast a sidelong glance at her.

"He never...the big investigation he was called onto? NCIS even ran an inquiry against their own leadership staff about it. Latreaux, that navy admiral, was even caught up in it. It was Warin's last case as detective. No one knows the particulars – other than the explosion and the near-total loss of personnel on the station – but... no, I guess he wouldn't want you knowing about that. It's still classified."

Djet frowned. "If it's classified, how do ya know all this?"

Blaze averted his eyes with a sniff.

"All I know is, whatever went down there, your father was put through the grinder on it. Must've handled it all right, though, because he became Chief of the Third Watch a couple months after the case was closed."

Wonder why he never told me about this, Djet thought. *That's not like my Fatti to keep secrets.*

Warin was the most open and honest person Djet knew. Countless times when she was growing up, he had shown her case files and let her try to work things out with him. His very first case, involving the shocking murder of a young girl, was still unsolved. It had become a yearly thing between the two of them; on the anniversary of the murder, Djet would return home and they would spend an hour or two walking through the crime scene together. It always ended in frustration and the same dead ends.

Djet went to ask Blaze more about Singularity when he sat bolt upright.

"There," he said, nodding his head toward the parking apron. "He's stocking."

Finally.

Djet vigorously popped the door seal and stretched the stiffness out of her legs. Her C-skin was an unassuming swirl of gray clouds with the occasional spark of lightning running across it. For some reason it was one of the more popular clothing themes in this district. It was supposed to help her to blend in.

Down on the parking apron, a young man was carrying a large white crate down to the back of the yellow puncher. His lack of facial hair put him at mid to late teens, his pale skin marked him as most likely a Vatican native. The hatchback raised automatically as he approached.

Djet sealed the skipper's door and checked her Pulse. It was almost midnight.

Detectives work all hours, Djet, day or night.

Her father's voice, half-heartedly trying to talk her out of the job. That was years ago, and she hadn't listened. Long nights were hard, but she couldn't imagine herself doing anything else.

"Djet, hang back," Blaze said, checking his pistol.

"What for?" she asked, checking her weapon, too.

"Cover. I'm going into the flat while he's out."

Blaze started walking.

"Wait," Djet said, following him. "Don't we want to catch him making the delivery?"

Blaze stopped and stared with such intensity her feet automatically planted on the street.

"Your daddy is one of the best longarms I ever knew, girl. Doesn't mean you're him. Your skin ain't black, sister. It's green. You don't know what you're doing. Hang back and keep your teeth shut until I radio you in."

A hot spike of rage bit her in the back. Goosebumps walked down her skin. Djet wanted to reach out and slap the back of his head for talking to her like that.

She couldn't do that without compromising her job. Warin Rincon's name was worth a lot in the law enforcement community, but it had its limits.

She nodded and did as she was told.

A part of her was indignant, knowing she could handle it. Another part knew she hadn't reached the inner circle of trust with the good old boys' club. And she hadn't seen enough yet to know how to react to every situation.

Djet leaned over the railing to keep the parking area in view.

The kid was gone, but the hatchback was left open. The crate rested on the ground in front of it. Closer now that she was out of the sky runner, she could see a symbol on the side, two bent arrows pointing straight up inside a circle. It didn't look familiar. She wrote it off as a shipping company logo.

She waited over a minute. No sign of the kid, or more boxes.

Something wasn't sitting well in Djet's stomach.

Blaze told her to hang back, but what could be taking so long? It was a test of her nerves. A lot of things could go wrong between here and the front door of a drug dealer's flat. If Blaze got in over his head, she might not know until it was too late.

A crowd of mixed species teenagers passed by, muttering to each other in several languages Djet couldn't understand. She recognized two riskar, a half dozen humans and a short, furry mammal that looked like a teddy bear whose genus and species she couldn't remember. She acted bored, heaving a sigh and watching them in her peripheral as they passed.

Nah, she told her shaky nerves, *Blaze is a professional. He knows what he's doing.*

Nearly all of the vehicles in the parking lot were sky runners, meant to skip around on Vatican. Local sorties concerned more with positional thrusters than anything with significant speed. Nothing that could crack the exosphere and taste true vacuum. Except for that sky puncher. What was it doing here? Sky runners were the hallmark of the lower income side of the terra city. The people who lived here frequented other parts of the world but had no desire or reason to leave.

So, who in this ghetto needed to break atmo regularly?

Her Pulse chirped.

"Rincon, Sisneros. Two in custody. Fall in and watch for strays."

Damn, she thought. *He's good.*

"En route."

She took her finger off the device and drew her L-pistol, careful to keep the barrel pointed down. Her boots clicked on the walkway as she hurried under the overhang and entered the stairwell. A man and a woman were arguing at the bottom, hands waving vigorously.

"Longarm entering the stairwell," Djet projected her voice from the lower, guttural part of her diaphragm. "Clear the area."

The man looked up at her, his nose wrinkled. A red bruise on his neck, partially concealed in the crook of his jawline, drew her eye for a split second before he grabbed the woman by the arm and pulled her out of the way. They both put their hands up as Djet descended the stairs.

She eyed them close. No visible weapons.

"For your safety and mine, I'm going to have to ask that you sequester yourselves inside for the time being," Djet said.

"Sure thing, miss," the man said with a wooden smile.

She glanced down the hall underneath the stairs.

The flat in question was open, but there was no sign of Blaze or the two suspects he had arrested. Djet took slow and deliberate steps toward the flat. She heard a door open behind her, assumed the couple was going back inside as she'd ordered, and came to stand up alongside the entrance to the drug dealer's flat.

At the threshold she could smell the funk of a drug den.

It was a miasma of wet blacktop and fragrant, rotting moss. Something tingled in her nostrils like cinnamon. One of the occupants had probably been lighting up some of their supply. The tingle, she remembered from narcotics class at the academy, was a cross-species similar to hashish. She loved the smell but hated the sensation produced by inhaling it. Never used the stuff herself, but a part of her still wondered why so many chose to devote their lives to its consumption.

Djet tapped her Pulse, sending a single click over the bandwidth. She waited, pistol by her head, hoping to hear the return click of Blaze acknowledging her.

Five seconds went by with no response.

Her heart starting thudding – not faster, but *harder*. Adrenaline made her weapon wobble slightly in her grip.

"Blaze, you aight?" she called.

The hair on the back of her neck stood on end.

A laser blast screamed through the open door millimeters from her face.

Djet's instinct was to drop to her haunches, but if it had been anything directed at her, she would have already been dead. She peeked around the doorframe and back in, less than half a second of exposure.

In that moment, she saw enough.

The flat was a standard twelve-by-twelve living area with an adjoining suite at the rear. Pale light revealed yellowing carpet that probably wasn't that color when the tenant first moved in. The blast had come from the room beyond the living area. She could see ruddy carpet pockmarked with cigarette burns, and dark stains from spilled alcohol or blood that had never been cleaned. The kitchen area to the left was covered in food wrappers and the rotting scraps of leftover meals. The air circulation vent between the suite door and the couch hung limply on a single warped hinge. A leather sofa sat in the living room with the cushions flattened almost completely into the frame, covered in viscous yellow liquid that reminded her of mucus.

Another strange detail was the mirror on the ceiling above the couch.

She spoke from her diaphragm, squeezing as much authority and anger into her voice as she could manage. Adrenaline made it come out a bit higher than she would have liked, but it stayed just firm enough not to crack.

"Longarm Detective entering flat two zero one. Lay down ya weapons and come out with your appendages raised or ya will be shot on sight!"

Djet heard the footsteps in the hallway before she saw who was making them. Something set off a warning in her head, and she followed that instinct for what it was worth. She hustled into the apartment, dove behind the sofa's tall arm and glanced into the mirror above.

She saw the top of his head as he took a step into the flat.

The man from the hallway arguing with the girl.

He was holding a sawed-off shotgun. It was no soft-point slug thrower, either. It was of alien make, something closer to a plasma launcher than a shotgun.

"I know you're in here, bitch. You stumbled down the wrong path b–"

Djet popped up and shot him in the throat.

He lowered the weapon, offhand flying up to his neck.

She put two more bolts in his chest.

C-skin threads and flesh cauterized as bright plumes of blood scattered from his back in wide clouds like puncturing a can of aerosol paint. The alien shotgun hit the carpet just before his body did.

The smell of burnt flesh filled the air.

A warbling vocal run ushered from the back room.

Djet kept her eyes on the mirror, but she could only see the kitchen area and the other side of the couch. The entrance to the back door was past the mirror's reflection.

"Todai! Mir lokai," an alien voice gurgled.

Djet dropped her heat sink and swapped it out. She latched it in slow.

"Ya boy's dead!" she shouted. "My offer still stands. Drop ya weapons, come out with your appendages –"

A ball rolled into the room, hissing and spinning on its axis like a bowling ball, blue smoke seeping out of it like the end of a hookah pipe.

Djet realized her mistake.

The ball was between her and the front door.

The hissing named it a grenade before the word could pop into her head.

She ripped the couch away from the wall, put her back against the wall and kicked it with all her strength. The couch skittered across the carpet and tipped over on top of the grenade. Blue smoke curled around the leather arms for a fraction of a second before it detonated.

Foam and leather fragments and tendrils of mucus blew out.

Plastic molding cracked and rained down on her.

The heat was like picking up a hot pan on the stove – all over her body.

Djet's ears pinched, hard. She felt a scream tear through her throat. A high-pitched ringing echoed inside her skull. The carpet ripped and caught on fire. Blue smoke mingled with black. Her visibility went to almost nothing. Her left side, arm, and neck felt burned. She blinked and squeezed her diaphragm a few times, finally forcing a sip of air into her lungs.

Rage boiled in her again.

Where the hell is Blaze?

She stumbled and pulled the crook of her elbow up to her face, trying to keep her smoke inhalation to a minimum. Scorched mucus cracked under her boot, emulsifying into the carpet. The left side of her body hurt. Djet shuffled over the debris, clearing the threshold of the backroom's door. She tried to call out for her partner but fell into a coughing fit instead.

Smoke was filling the room so thick it was like a wall.

Djet's vision narrowed. Her thoughts blurred together until her brain felt like it was melting. She knew she had to get out, but she couldn't take the chance that Blaze was incapacitated inside the apartment. She stepped on something fleshy. When she tried to move it with her foot, it didn't budge.

Kneeling and probing the darkness with her fingers, she felt liquid. Hot, sticky.

She couldn't see, but if it was Blaze, he was already dead.

She turned and made for the hallway.

CHAPTER 3

The bar was a dive, but it came by the title honestly.

People frequented establishments like this because they *wanted* to be in a dive bar. They came for cheap drinks and dishonest conversations and expected other patrons playing different versions of the same game. It was like an arcade machine in the economy class section of every spaceport. Drop a few digits in, hit the right combination of buttons long enough, maybe you score. Do it well enough, maybe you beat your own personal best.

Humans and humanoids alike partook in tobacco and various other substances of questionable legality from pipes, bulbs, or accordion-hosed implements. Great clouds of smoke whorled about the darkness until Vatican's two-third G force gently guided the misting particles to the ground. Abraham didn't have to guess why his boots squeaked as he stepped up to the bar.

He gave the packed dance floor and its prancing lights a wide berth.

The smell of the smoke was terrible. Abraham had smelled scorched ozone and cordite on several worlds. Carbon scoring. Riskar waste. Vase taught him to appreciate the pleasant relief of a skillfully cooked meal. An unintended side effect was the increased sensitivity in his sense of smell. The smoke, and the breath particles exhaled by the smokers, was one of the worst. He swore these odors were the result of otherwise pleasant things like vanilla and sugar that underwent a gain-of-function test in a lab with the intent of weaponizing them to inflict as much pain on the olfactory senses as possible.

Or you're just being dramatic, he chided himself. Vase was always getting on him for having intense views on mundane topics.

He found his oldest friend drinking noisily from a bulbous glass at the bartop. Larry Poplenko might have been the only person in the bar not looking for intimacy; which was for the best, as he was currently shoulder to shoulder with a torind and another marine from Raven Squad.

That designation, after what happened on Duringer, was revived when they'd joined the 209th Marine Extrasolar Force. Captain Vase, newly promoted after the devastating events that led to the defeat of the Riskar Royal Navy and the end of the Riskar War, was given the honor of naming her company. She'd selected Falcon Company, and named the three squads Eagle, Raven, and Raptor, the former two in honor of the fallen on Duringer.

It chapped Abraham's ass that his best friend had never recovered from the horrors of that event. Losing his short-time girlfriend had left indelible scars on his psyche.

The wounds of war, his drill sergeant had said, *sometimes those don't heal*.

Larry slapped the empty glass on the counter and belched.

The marine next to him erupted in laughter at the display.

She was Sergeant Savony Raelis, Raptor's squad leader. Abraham was surprised he didn't recognize her by her short, tight-curled hair and broad shoulders. She patted Larry on the back, and when he raised his hand to call for another round, she pulled his hand to the bar top with a shake of her head.

"Ham!"

Abraham turned.

There was only one person who would refer to him by such a ridiculous name. Corporal Alan Piebold, a soft-spoken giant of a man whose huge grin was clearly amplified by drink.

"Glad you could make it, brother."

He shook Abraham's hand and clapped him on the back with a little too much enthusiasm.

"Good to see you again, Alan. Is Larry still trying to get his ass kicked?"

Piebold snorted, jostling the dregs of his pint-sized mug.

"I've been trying to talk him down for an hour. He's running up a tab high enough for a whole squad. You know him," he said with a shake of his head, "he won't listen to anybody."

They both looked in Larry's direction.

Larry was holding a tall cylindrical glass, half-filled with a neon blue liquid, staring at it like he wanted to bury his face in it and never come up for air. His nose had gotten bigger, his cheeks a bit puffier. His face showed a red tint that proved his major food group was any variety of alcohol.

Abraham patted Piebold on the back and took a step toward Larry.

Piebold stopped him with a meaty hand on the shoulder.

"Hey, Ham, watch out for that guy." He pointed. "The one with the weird C-skin pattern, looks like an optical illusion on a loop. He's been eyeballing us all night."

Abraham nodded and approached his oldest friend.

"We're almost done with our first four years," Abraham warned Larry. "If you're not re-upping, at least don't go out on a bad note."

Larry swallowed the remaining half of his drink and slapped the glass on the counter. He sucked air through his teeth, flicked his eyes toward Abraham. The whites of his eyes were riddled with red veins. His lower eyelids were dark.

When's the last time he slept? Abraham wondered.

"Fuck off, Abraham."

Abraham shrugged off the verbal punch.

"You're too drunk to be lamenting in public. Let's get you home before you do something you'll regret."

Larry stopped Abraham with a hand on the shoulder.

"You didn't hear me, Abraham. I don't care. These last few years I've been asking myself why. *Why* this, *why* that? Then I realized, *why* anything? Nothing matters. And when I realized nothing matters, I also realized I regret *everything*. Shit I did. Shit I didn't do. What's one more? A drop in the fucking bucket."

Larry waved his hand at the bartender for another round.

Abraham waved her off. She froze mid-stride. She let out a surprised yelp as the tiara slipped from her head.

"Larry, I'm cutting you off. She wouldn't want you like this."

Larry's face whipped around, eyes filled with murder.

"Do. Not. Talk about her," he said through clenched teeth.

"Larry, it's been three years. I know you loved –"

Stars exploded in Abraham's eyes.

His pocket screeched and flitted out of the way.

It happened so fast, he didn't realize Larry had hit him with his glass.

Not until the pain washed over his skull and a rivulet of blood trickled down his neck. Dribbles of blood and blue alcohol ran down his C-skin, unable to find purchase on the hi-tech material.

Abraham staggered back, his hand instinctively touching the wound.

When he pulled away, his palm shimmered in the reflected dance-floor lights. Glass slivers were embedded in his palm, traced with thin red circles of blood.

Blink.

The pervasive odor of smoke and alcohol was overtaken by a mossy stench of rotting wood. The dance beat became the thundering rhythm of his heart. Drinkers became red-leaved trees and the drunken laughter sounded more like the howls of a brutal enemy on the hunt.

Pain lanced into his shoulder.

A jagged glass projectile protruded from his body like a thirty-centimeter blade.

Panic gripped him. He tried to pull it out.

Fragments broke off, embedded in his hand...

I'm hit! Not bad, though. I'll live.

Blink.

The memory washed away.

He could smell the smoke again. Heard the dance beat and the pockets of laughter around him.

Larry was not laughing. He stared without remorse.

"Okay boys, that's enough," Savony said from beside him.

The bartender leaned over the counter, her exposed skin pressing through the tattered gaps in her shirt, and pointed toward the door.

"Take that shit outside!"

Larry crossed his arms and threw his chin at the door.

"You heard her, Zeeben. Get gone."

Piebold appeared at Larry's side. He made eye contact with Abraham and gave him a nod.

"We're all leaving. Now," Abraham said, and looked at Savony. "Get us a sky runner, Sergeant."

"Definitely," she said, swiping her Portal over the counter to settle both her and Larry's tab. "You're paying me back for this, Poplenko."

"I'm not – hey!"

Piebold helped Abraham grapple with Larry until they each had an arm and carried him out into the street. Larry struggled, but he was no match for both of them. He screamed and cursed at Abraham, contorting himself like a child throwing a tantrum.

Purple lights dangling from the level above cast a pallor over the street as the cool air of high-tier Vatican greeted them. A few people rubbernecked as they passed, but no one stopped. It was an unwritten rule of the terra-city that you didn't stop unless you wanted to get involved. So no one did.

They set Larry down on the curb outside the bar.

He put his face in his hands, shoulders shaking.

He was crying.

"I can't, guys," he slurred into his hands. "I can't do this shit anymore."

The street was surprisingly empty of people. The two-meter-high security rail, a duraglass wall that prevented citizens from slipping to a hundred-plus-story plunge to their deaths, was ten meters away.

Abraham opened his mouth to offer some comforting words when Larry bolted straight for the wall.

Larry covered the distance in seconds.

Abraham was right on his heels, Piebold just a few steps behind.

Larry jumped up and halfway over the wall. Abraham caught him by the ankle and yanked.

Larry held firm.

Piebold grabbed Larry by the belt of his C-skin and ripped him off the wall.

Larry curled up into a ball on the street. He cried and slammed his fist against the duracrete. The lanky marine that had once been the cool kid in high school Abraham looked up to…he was gone.

"Fuck you guys!" Larry shouted. "You don't know what I'm dealing with!"

Piebold gave Abraham a look that said *not this again.*

"Larry, bro, we were all there. We do know what you're going through," Piebold said.

"No!" Larry wailed.

Abraham tried to put a hand on his shoulder. Larry slapped it away.

"No, Zeeben. You killed her. You didn't have to *do* that. I don't care if she wanted you to, you shouldn't have *done* that!"

The sobs ended in a shuddering breath a moment later.

He murmured weakly, "*I* should have. It was supposed to be *me*."

Floating close by, Abraham's pocket gave three short hoots.

Piebold looked at the owl-shaped drone, then back over his shoulder.

"Ham," he said in a crisp voice. It was a warning tone.

The same tone Abraham had heard the big man use countless times in the field.

The blue-haired kid with the optical illusion pattern on his C-skin had left the bar. The same kid Piebold said was eyeballing them all night.

Blue Hair walked toward them, two torinds behind and a few paces to each side. The squid-like humanoids' tentacles quivered in a hand-washing gesture. Brackish moisture glistened on their aqueous membranes, through which a skull and internal organs were visible.

Abraham knew how dangerous these aliens were. He did not know why they were in cahoots with this kid.

Blue Hair spoke in a high octave that would have been comedic under different circumstances.

"You space jockeys picked the wrong corner of Vatican to disrupt."

Piebold took a deep breath. His massive shoulders swelled with anticipation. "You and your mudsuckers there better turn around and disappear. I'm not saying it twice."

Blue Hair made a melodramatic expression of incredulity. He blinked a few times before saying, "Don't you know who I am?"

Larry sat up and sniffed. He eyed Blue Hair warily.

Piebold shrugged. "I don't really care who you are."

"I'm Thalex Coup De."

Abraham and Piebold shared a look followed by a shrug.

Thalex huffed. "My mother runs Vatican. Kind of like the Madame Executor of the Human Collective. That ring a bell?"

Abraham and Piebold stared.

"Holy shit, guys, come on!" Thalex threw his hands about, clearly frustrated. "My mother is in charge of everything and everyone, and since she's not here, that means I'm in charge of everything and everyone. You guys gotta pay for causing a scene back there."

"Look, kid," Piebold put up a hand, "you don't wanna do anything stupid."

Larry hopped to his feet and put a hand on the duraglass. He opened his mouth to say something and then charged full speed at Thalex.

"Dammit," Abraham said, drawing his L-pistol.

Larry bowled into Thalex and took him to the ground with a thud. He was already slamming fists into the kid's face when a crack split the air. The torind on his left attacked.

A blue-gray tentacle wrapped around Larry's neck. It turned a dark purple as it squeezed with binding torque.

Abraham shot the alien in the head.

Water and black ink sprayed from the exit wound.

Larry paused to cough up brackish water, then punched Thalex again.

The torind on his right moved in, a menacing gurgle of foam bubbling between its mouth tentacles.

Piebold stepped between the torind and Larry as the tentacles snapped forth.

The big man caught the first blow on his wrist. Another slammed into his face with a wet slap. Piebold grabbed the offending appendage and ripped it off with a grunt. The dismembered tatters of flesh coiled on the ground for a few seconds, then stilled.

The sound of tearing membrane reminded Abraham of Vase deveining a prawn.

Piebold kicked the torind right in the flesh skirt. The alien wrapped its remaining tentacles around his torso. He grabbed the skull in his large hand and slammed the creature to the ground, where he finished it with a curb stomp and a spray of brackish ink, water, and blood.

CRACK!

Abraham felt a slight pinch in the back of his neck.

He spun on his heel, weapon up.

A translucent red shield floated in the air a meter away from him. A soft-point slug, flattened against the shield, dropped to the ground with a tink. The red shield dissipated like it was never there.

A third torind stood a few meters back. It looked at the pistol in its hand, head turning at an angle.

Abraham fired two shots.

Plumes of ink and blood erupted from the alien's back.

The rounds tore through the tender flesh and smacked into the duraglass railing behind the alien. It collapsed to the ground, pain-laced moans becoming gurgles. Vital fluids pooled around it like a small oil spill, and the gurgling stopped.

"Okay! Okay!" Thalex cried, palms up in a vain attempt to ward off Larry's punches.

Abraham didn't recognize Larry.

He knew he was looking at his oldest friend, but the maniac he saw pummeling the blue-haired kid from the bar did not look like Larry at all. The dead torind's tentacle was still suction-cupped to his neck, the corpse twitching with every blow Larry landed on Thalex. Oily ink-blood covered Larry's face and neck. He bared his teeth and let out a howl filled with primal rage.

Piebold yelled in his gruff, commanding voice, "Poplenko, enough!"

Abraham helped Piebold pull Larry off the kid. They shoved him against the duraglass, pinning him by his shoulders.

"Let me go, Zeeben!" Larry fumed.

"Hey!" Thalex lisped through blood lips, "I'm suing you guys! This is bullshit!"

Piebold unwrapped the torind corpse from Larry and tossed it in a heap next to Thalex.

"Think twice before you pick a fight with marines, kid."

Abraham got in Larry's face. If consoling wasn't going to work, maybe he needed a more military approach.

"Lance Corporal Poplenko, lock it up!"

Larry stiffened.

"Stow this shit. Right now. You could have killed that kid."

Larry went limp. He was defeated and he knew it.

"Piebold," Abraham said, "where the hell is Savony with that atmo skipper?"

"I'll ping her," Piebold said, retrieving his Portal from his C-skin pocket.

"Oh, shit." Piebold tilted his chin up. *Check your six.*

Abraham craned his neck.

A large cooking pot rose from behind the security railing.

It was nearly an exact replica of the one in Vase's flat...except for the blue corona at the base. The pot swiveled on its axis. As it floated overhead, Abraham's instinct was to shoot it.

Before his finger could touch the trigger a bright beam of light emitted from the face of the floating pot.

A spotlight.

Stamped in red block letters on the bot's side was the designation: *Vatican Zany News Network, Reporting Unit Z-017.*

"Great," Abraham groaned. "Now we're really fucked."

It took entirely too long to get Larry and Piebold back to their flat.

The atmo skipper ride was filled with awkward tension as Larry alternated between tear-laced blubbering, doubly incoherent due to his intoxication, and periods of almost catatonic silence until he finally passed out, face smearing a line of drool over the window. Even the turbulence of the ride jostling his skull against the duraglass didn't wake him.

Once they swiped into Larry and Piebold's shared flat, the big man dumped Larry onto the couch without ceremony. Abraham gave Piebold a fist bump and a quick "thank you" before he took off at a dead sprint for the orbital lift.

Abraham hopped off the lift thirty minutes later, tension gnawing at his gut.

He was late but kept himself in check by ignoring the time on his Portal. He dabbed the cut on the side of his head, depositing a blood-soaked wad of bar napkins in the waste receptacle at the tram section.

Starlight was the most beautiful thing he'd ever seen.

Sometimes he still felt like that boy who lived on a homestead in the middle of a tobacco field on a backwater planet. New sights, particularly in terms of technological advancements, always managed to elicit wide-eyed wonder.

The rings rotated at different speeds, akin to scientific magic maintaining a pseudo-atmosphere. He transitioned from the lift station to the Starwalk, a bridge that connected two opposite points of the innermost ring. One could be convinced of the absence of gravity all the way up here, just outside of Vatican's atmosphere. He spun the dial on his belt to increase the magnetism on his boots. He cranked the thermal settings on his C-skin up a few notches – space was cold, and as far as he could see, the only barrier between him and the void was the meter-and-a-half high duraglass railing on either side of the Starwalk. Plumes of oxygen poured steadily out of vents set every three meters. The excess mist pooled on the floor, thinning as it wafted upward. It smelled like the mist from a sprinkler, another flash of memory from Veranda.

None of this makes any kind of scientific sense to me, Abraham thought. *But* damn *is it cool.*

A small crowd of navy and marine personnel gathered around a podium, everyone in C-skin mess dress patterns. At a distance they looked like a sea of blue and red cells vibrating, shifting without moving. Abraham wormed his way into the crowd to take a spot closer to the podium just as Admiral Latreaux took the stage.

Apparently I missed the cocktail hour.

He searched the crowd. No sign of Vase.

The grizzled old admiral hadn't aged a bit. The last time Abraham saw him was when he presented the medals a week after the catastrophe on Duringer. The admiral carried himself as if he were the most important human alive. His stern features were like those of a bulldog: squared shoulders prepared to charge at any moment, jowls that made his head look more square than it should have been. He cleared his throat gruffly. His Pocket – a simple orb textured to look like a small moon – floated a few centimeters under his chin to act as a microphone.

"Welcome to the Navy Ball."

Cheers. Applause. The vibe wasn't the stiff military formality Abraham had expected. It felt more like a late-night pool party at a luxurious resort. The only thing missing was the music.

"As you all know, we've had a very successful campaign against the aveo, and I'm proud to announce that the actions taken by brave men and women like you have put an end to that conflict."

Cheers. Applause. Abraham wanted to forget that 'campaign'. He still didn't understand why the Corps stepped in to stop the aveo from reclaiming a string of planets the torinds had stolen from them during the Riskar War.

"I have the distinct honor and privilege to promote four outstanding performers this year, and I'd like to get right to it. I will read the names now, please hold your applause until all names have been read. Senior Chief Petty Officer Kellie Kalty, promoted to Master Chief Petty Officer. Lieutenant Commander Duran, promoted to Commander. Vase Seneca, promoted to Captain. Major Fallon promoted to Lieutenant Colonel."

Cheers. Applause.

That's *why I couldn't find you*, Abraham thought.

Vase took the stage, looking every bit as regal as she always did.

The four promotees each took their turn saluting while the admiral touched the center chest of their C-skins. The ranks materialized under his fingers. He saluted them and they exited stage right. Once the newly christened lieutenant colonel had left the stage, Latreaux turned to address the crowd once again.

"Stay vigilant, people. We are kicking ass for humanity. It's in our job description. Scuttlebutt throughout our forces is saying that there is something big going on behind the scenes. The fallout from Duringer a few years ago is still very much on everyone's mind."

The admiral paused in dramatic fashion as scattered whispers ran through the crowd. More than a few eyes turned to stare in Abraham's direction.

He winced a little on the inside.

These people can think and talk about it all they want, he grumbled to himself. *I wish I could forget it.*

Latreaux silenced the crowd by clearing his throat.

"It's not the first time an entire planet was destroyed, we all know that, but it did make an unintended statement that has been a thorn in the Navy's ass ever since. I will never dress down a sailor or a marine for making the choices that keep themselves and their comrades alive. You won't hear me say those human lives we lost were necessary losses."

Latreaux took a moment to pass his thousand-yard stare in a slow sweep over the crowd.

Abraham saw right through the political maneuver. Manufactured sobriety. Once you attained a certain rank in the Human Collective's military, it didn't matter that you still wore the uniform. You were a politician playing soldier. He wondered if the admiral's charge of the Riskar War included the actual battle planning.

He doubted it.

"However, we do need to start making better choices as a force," Latreaux said.

"I have one final announcement to make. This comes from our folks at intel. We have been directed by the Collective to continue monitoring the situation in what was formerly known as riskar space. To do this effectively, we will be working closely with our best research and development firm, Mandrake Enterprises. I want to make it clear this is a purely precautionary measure. As of now, nothing ominous or foreboding is brewing in that system. That being said – as we all know – energy signatures of the magnitude required to destroy a planet often draw the attention of newcomers to the galactic stage. So, I refer to my opening statement. Stay vigilant, people."

Latreaux descended the stage to a cascade of applause.

Abraham felt the atmosphere change.

Budding conversations raised the volume to a level more commonly associated with a party.

Who needs music when you have an ambience like this?

It was odd, because he always found officer types to be stiff and formal, or awkward and squirrelly, but that wasn't the case here. Officers and enlisted alike commingled, taking drinks from Pocket-carried butler trays and swapping stories with vigor. He realized he couldn't detect an odor beyond the cold humidity of venting oxygen, but sound seemed oddly unaffected despite the fact they were, for all intents and purposes, standing in a walkway in space with no sealed structure around them.

He found Vase standing by stage right.

As he approached, her face wrinkled like she caught a whiff of something offensive.

He looked over his shoulder, before turning his attention back to her, realizing the look was intended for him. He fought the reflex to touch the cut that still burned on the side of his head.

This isn't going to end well.

"You're late." She took a ball-shaped glass from a floating tray, popped the lip-seal and sipped it.

Abraham shrugged.

The crowd was mostly officers or high-ranking enlisted personnel. He estimated an eighty-twenty split, which meant he was one of the lowest ranking people here. He tried to calm himself with the idea that he'd be a civilian soon, meaning he'd technically outrank everyone in the military. But he knew better. It was a quiet lie he whispered to himself to try to diffuse the tension he felt. It might have also been the after-effect of getting into a shootout in public that had him on edge.

"Vase, I need to speak with you...alone."

Vase gulped the champagne down to half and shivered. Negative energy billowed off her in waves.

She walked past him without saying anything, her glass at shoulder height. Little things like that reinforced Abraham's understanding that Vase had a privileged upbringing far different from his own. Abraham followed her to the railing, where they both stood and looked down at Vatican.

The terra city was the apex of human ingenuity, the perfect marriage of art and function. Forty billion permanent residents, and something like twenty million transients on any given day. The railing was a slate gray that shimmered in the faintest light, indicating it was probably beryllium. The most common metal in space-worthy construction. *Why does my brain fire off with this random crap when I'm nervous?* The pseudo-atmosphere was cool, like standing in a walk-in freezer, but the smooth metal of the railing was neutral to his touch.

He cleared his throat.

"Vase, I can explain –"

"Why you're late? Why you have a battle scar on your head that's still bleeding?"

Braided hair framed her head like a crown. Her icy blue eyes stared laser beams at him. He could feel her disapproval, commingled with something like incredulity. It was like a punch to his gut. He hated disappointing her.

"Yes," he said, touching his head. It burned.

When he pulled his hand away, a thin line of blood clung to his fingers.

"About that. There's going to be a story on the news. Larry had himself another incident, and...I *may* have had to use deadly force. It was all self defense, though."

"Deadly force?" Vase spluttered. "You *killed* someone?"

Abraham put his hands up.

"No! Well, not exactly. A couple of torind thugs tried to pop our heads off, so I uh...I shot them."

"Abraham!" Vase fumed. "What the hell is wrong with you guys?"

"It wasn't on purpose," Abraham muttered.

Vase blinked. "What, you shot them by *accident*?"

"Well, no, but...they started it!"

Vase dropped her voice an entire octave.

"Larry's done. He's getting a dishonorable discharge. You're getting a reprimand at the least. We can't have shit like this going on. On our home planet, nonetheless! It's just a bad –"

"A bad look?" It was his turn to interrupt her. "No shit, Vase. We've already established he needs help."

A barking voice intruded on their conversation. Abraham's hackles rose instinctively.

"Captain Seneca! Sergeant...Zeeben, right?"

Abraham locked to attention. He went to fire a salute before the admiral waved him down.

"At ease." Admiral Latreaux gave a forced smile. As he spoke, his eyes constantly shifted left and right, sifting the crowd. "This is a celebration. No customs and courtesies rendered here, Sergeant."

"Thank you, Admiral," Abraham replied.

Three long seconds of awkward eye contact followed.

"Very motivational speech today, sir."

The Admiral huffed. His face remained the default mask of cold indifference. Abraham thought the huff was supposed to be a laugh, but he wasn't sure.

Latreaux turned to Vase and asked, "So, how's it feel?"

Then he gave her a hug.

She hugged him back.

"It's nice. Did I really deserve it, though? I don't want people to think..."

Latreaux shrugged and patted her cheek. The gesture should have been grossly inappropriate, but it didn't feel that way. It felt...familiar. Familiar in a way that left Abraham confused.

"People talk, Vase." Latreaux shrugged. "You can't change that. To answer your question, though...yes, you deserve it. Your actions have distinguished yourself from your peers. You handle all your assignments with aplomb – regardless of strains on resources and personnel, I might add – and you have repeatedly demonstrated sound tactical decision-making under pressure. I didn't promote you just because you're my daughter."

Abraham's mouth went dry. He realized it had fallen open.

"Daughter?" The word just fell out.

Latreaux spun on his heel, smiling. This time, it wasn't forced.

"Of course. I allowed Vase to have her mother's last name, after the…er, after her mother passed away. Terrible thing. Inspired me to ensure the armed forces never let another massacre happen again."

Abraham's knees felt weak. He tasted betrayal on his breath.

"You uh...what about Milune, sir?"

Latreaux clapped a meaty hand on Abraham's shoulder. His knees tightened under the force of the gesture.

"That was, ultimately, *my* failure, son. I can't be everywhere at once. What a story to attach to your family legacy, though, eh? You got those bastards back. Gave 'em what they deserved. I disagree with your methods – detonating the weapon and all – but you did save a lot of lives. Bit of a political shitstorm in the aftermath, but that's for me to handle."

Abraham felt numb. He managed a polite nod.

"Permission to be dismissed, sir?"

Vase glared at him.

"As you were, Sergeant."

Vase grabbed his arm and spun him around.

Caught off-guard, his knee buckled as the magnets kept his feet in place for a moment. He pivoted into the awkward movement, leaning on Vase for balance. She stood him up and put her hand in his.

"I wanted to introduce you –"

Abraham yanked his hand out of her grip.

"Vase, stop."

His words went over like an airlock blowing a seal. Admiral Latreaux arched his brows. Several bystanders stopped their conversations, eyes pivoting toward him. For the first time in his military career, he didn't care about the ranks of the people who saw him acting out of turn.

He ignored all of them.

Vase gave him a blank stare. He could see the conflict in her eyes. She was hurt, but she was in public. She didn't want anyone to see it.

He didn't care.

"Anything else you wanna tell me?" Abraham shouted. "You know more about the…" Latreaux's mask of indifference was back, with the exception of his flexing jawline. "…other stuff, too, don't you?"

Her eyes went wide. A blush bloomed in her cheeks. She remained silent.

Silent because she knew exactly what he was talking about. That, and more. She didn't just know something; she was *hiding* it from him.

She knows more about the Ghost Society than she's ever told me. She's known the whole time. She's lying to me, and I don't know why.

"Abraham," she said shakily.

He held up a hand to stop her.

"I'm gone."

He stormed off for the orbital lift.

"Abraham!" Vase called. "Abraham, come back here!"

He didn't look back.

CHAPTER 4

Djet sat in the hallway with a blanket wrapped around her shoulders. Her lungs felt bruised, her throat raw. The right side of her C-skin was in tatters. Exposed sections of the skin on her right arm, shoulder and neck were a swollen, angry red.

A first aid probe hissed as it danced around her, swiveling unsteadily on a tiny green plume of propulsion. Slots on its body emitted needles and probes that pricked her skin every so often with soft-tip sensors to assess her state.

"First-degree burns. Minor," it remarked in a tinny, disinterested voice. It could have been someone transmitting a radio call from a restroom stall. The probe swiveled to expose a small straw-like appendage with a notch in the end.

"Exhale for six seconds."

Djet bit down and exhaled into it for two seconds before breaking off into a coughing fit.

The probe chirped. "Carbon monoxide levels twelve percent. Recommend –"

Djet continued to cough as she swatted the machine away.

A few patrol longarms from her department moved around her, canvassing the scene. A recorder drone washed the area with its wide-band green laser, meticulously photographing and storing every square millimeter of the flat. The drone would compile the data into a realistic holographic reconstruction and upload it to the Third Watch database. Detectives assigned to the case could then download this reconstruction and enter the rendering with a virtual reality interface to explore the crime scene without disturbing any potential evidence. This was all standard procedure. She had spent countless hours in crime scene renderings herself. Most of those hours on the Casey Benton case – the one her father hadn't been able to solve for thirty-five years.

Djet caught her breath, tried to rub the itchy dryness out of her eyes. The last hour was a blur. The image of the man with the shotgun in her sight picture, the discharging of her weapon and he dropped…it played over and over in her mind. The grenade, barely a meter away from her. She could hear the hissing of the burning wick.

A shiver wracked her shoulders.

I can't just sit here.

In total disregard for protocol, she stood up, brushed herself off, and approached the flat's door.

"Oi, El Dee, you can't be in here right now."

Longarm Rugard, barely nineteen and a relatively new addition to the force, held up a hand to stop her. His chiseled jaw might have been considered classically handsome, but his blond flat-top looked ridiculous – as did his other hand, which rested on his L-pistol.

It was a small thing. Hardly more than a rookie reflex.

It told Djet he always did this when addressing people on the street.

Probably hasn't made him any friends.

Come to think of it, this was the first time Djet had seen Rugard outside the walls of the department. She noted his perfectly polished boots with an internal scoff.

Kid's so new he hasn't yet got his boots dirty.

"Back off, Rugard," Djet coughed as she shrugged past him to stand at the threshold.

He let her pass for the same reason she stayed put when Blaze told her to: in the subculture of law enforcement, seniority is part of the rule of law. She was a detective. Rugard was a rookie. Rank is important, but there's no substitute for experience.

Carpet cracked under her boots. The place was a mess.

It looked like the aftermath of a battlefield as much as a crime scene. Spiral fissures and holes ran across the floor like cauterized wounds. A crumbled husk of marble fragments covered in ash and dust was all that remained of the kitchen counter. Cordite and melted flesh percolated in the air. The effluvium sent her into a coughing fit.

That was when she saw the dead man at her feet.

The asshole with the alien shotgun.

Seeing her handiwork up close put her in an odd state of detachment.

It wasn't the first time she'd fired her weapon in the field. It was the first time she'd killed a suspect, though. Wounding someone, knowing they were stopped but they'd see their family again, even with bars between them, was different. Whoever this guy was, the people who knew him were never going to see him again.

I did that, she thought. *I took him away from you.*

His eyes were milky. They didn't seem to hold light the way eyes normally did. His pale skin was ashen. The holes in his chest were black rings with dark red centers. Signature indications of laser blasts. She knelt to look at the neck.

Her bolt had penetrated the bruise, singed the surrounded flesh...now that she was looking at it up close, she could see it was a tattoo. She could barely make out the tips of what looked like arrows escaping a circle. She had seen it before.

The package in the back of the yellow sky puncher.

Djet spun on her heel. She was out of the flat and down the hallway before she remembered to breathe. Shouldering her way through a few longarms, she shirked the blanket she forgot she had over her shoulders and coughed until she grasped the railing at the edge of the block. She caught her breath long enough to look down at the parking apron.

It was exactly how she saw it an hour ago…

Except for the empty parking slot on the north side.

The spot where the yellow sky puncher had been.

"Detective Rincon. Turn around."

Djet's gut tightened.

Her boss joined her at the walkway railing.

Longarm Captain Barica Spitzen was a hard woman. Her face was made of rough age lines. Strands of gray ran through her once-black hair. She was tall, thin, and pear-shaped. Her body weight accumulated in her hips and lower half in a way that made her upper body appear like a thin tree sprouted from a large, thick cluster of roots.

Her slanted eyes narrowed, but it didn't necessarily mean she was pissed. Djet picked up on this cue during her first interview. Street longarms spent a lot of time interacting with the dirty lower crust of society. Drug dealers, skin traders, petty criminals and gangs. It was necessary to learn how to read body language and facial expressions with an intimacy that bordered on reading someone's thoughts. That was the idea. In common practice, it really just told you if someone was getting aggressive or agitated; if they were actually listening to what you were saying. If you paid enough attention, you could usually detect if a suspect was lying or not with a reasonable degree of certainty.

If Djet was reading her right, Captain Spitzen was not pissed. She was concerned.

"Detective," her voice lilted up half an octave, "what went wrong?"

The question was like a punch in the face.

"*Nut*teen went wrong, Captain. Blaze took the lead, I backed him up. Procedure was followed to the letter. Somebody just likes killing longarms."

A few wrinkles bunched together as Spitzen pursed her lips. When she made to speak again, they disappeared like sand bars sinking beneath ocean waves.

Djet read that as *calm waters ahead.*

"Blaze is all right."

Djet breathed deep. It felt like she had spiderwebs in her lungs, or something hard, like strands of hay stuck inside. She coughed again, trying to clear out some of the carbon monoxide from her lungs, regretting the deep breath. The coughing didn't help. It took her a minute to get it under control. Spitzen waited patiently for her to gather herself enough to reply.

"That's good," Djet said. "I thought I stumbled over his body in there. The fire was –"

"Blaze set the fire. There was a biohazard concern, and he had to contain it."

No, Djet thought, *it was a grenade. Of alien make.*

She distinctly remembered that in the moment she thought she was going to die, she saw a grenade. She could hear the hissing in her memory, clear as if it were sitting on the ground next to her. That picture was indelibly etched into her brain.

Ya don't forget the moment ya come face to face with your own imminent death.

Djet let the puzzlement show on her face.

The captain gave a stern nod.

Her lips were a firm, straight line. A few tiny wrinkles quivered at the corners of her eyes. The resolute nature of her expression combined with her unblinking gaze communicated clearly what she would never commit to words.

Captain Spitzen wasn't informing Djet of what happened.

She was telling her what to remember.

A chill snaked down Djet's spine like a rivulet of ice water. She clenched her teeth to avoid shivering.

This did not sit well with her.

The average detective relies too much on their gut, her father always said. *Ya gut ain't no substitute for ya brain.*

Djet's brain was telling her Captain Spitzen expected her to lie on her report. She had already talked to Blaze. Now she was talking to Djet. Making sure everyone had the story straight. No loose ends, no hotshot detectives running their mouths at the Watch about what they saw or what really happened.

It didn't make sense. Djet wasn't sure what she saw. What could be so concerning that it needed to be buried?

The symbol...the arrows escaping the circle. It was on the crate. The man she killed had that same symbol tattooed on his neck.

What was it? A company logo?

This was all to keep a lid on bad *press*?

"You took in a lot of smoke, Detective," Captain Spitzen said flatly. "Take a minute to collect yourself."

Her vision was starting to tunnel. The smoke inhalation, or the surrealism of her captain's disregard for facts...something was making her lightheaded. Djet blinked a few times, leaned heavily on the guardrail. The captain was setting it up for Djet to have an excuse for forgetting this entire conversation.

Ya have me confused wit someone who bends the law. I'm not that person.

"What about the crate, and the yellow –"

"The crate..." Captain Spitzen's eye contact was almost physical. It was like her eyes emitted a tractor beam, locking Djet's whole body into paralysis. It was psychosomatic, but Djet couldn't deny the intensity. To the captain, this was deadly serious.

"The crate," Spitzen said, "burned up in the fire. It contained a biohazardous material, and Blaze destroyed it before it could leak and spread. It's gone, Detective."

Spitzen placed a thin-boned hand on Djet's shoulder. It was like the hand of death. Skeletal and cold. The skin was stretched almost translucent over the tiny bones, but the grip was tight with barely checked pressure.

She leaned in to make eye contact with Djet, nodding slowly.

"You both saw the same thing. I expect to see that reflected in your VF-5. Now get your ass home and rest up for a few hours. I want the report by the end of the day."

Djet spent a long time in the shower, reflecting not only on the incident in the flat, but also on the surprise meeting with Vase that morning. She was listening to an acid punk reggae mash-up in the hope it might help her mood.

It didn't. It just made her more pissed off.

The plucky guitars, double-bass drums, angst-laced vocals delivered in accented yells – rather than serving as an outlet for her rising anger, they created an echo chamber for her emotions. She let the water cascade down her body until the stream went cold. She stayed in the chilling stream until her teeth began to chatter. When her jaw started to ache, she'd had enough. With a voice command to her Pocket, she shut off both the offensive spray and the music.

Djet caught a glimpse of herself in the mirror as she dried with a towel and wished she hadn't.

Her curves were staring back at her with a defeated slouch, like her breasts and belly were slouching with bad posture. No amount of working out was going to change these curves. Her abs were there. They were just under a layer of skin or fat or something that hid them from view. She turned to the side and slid her hand into the curve between her butt and her hamstring. She wanted a distinct line there, separating the two parts of her anatomy, to give her a more cut figure. When she let go, the cheek bounced against the hamstring and the angled line was replaced by an overlap of flesh.

She glared at her reflection, toweling off her neck-length, bone straight hair. The burns were already gone, wiped away by the medical bot before she left the crime scene.

"I squat two hundred eighty pounds and my ass still looks like a waterbed. The fuck am I doing wrong?"

Part of her after-work routine included weighing herself on the scale and spending a half hour doing her hair and makeup, putting herself together to somewhat resemble the way she actually saw herself. Right now, she wasn't up for it. Not after the day she had.

Djet threw on a nightgown. Black threads with a pattern of different colored shapes. One of her previous girlfriends had called it 'thrift-store fashion' but it was what she had grown up with. Destin, her home world, was the ugly stepchild of Vatican, lost in the shadow of humanity's capitol. A light-year and a half away, but a different world, figuratively and literally. Traveling on the Mag Rail Accel/Decel Loop, it took about an hour to get there.

The travel was why Djet only went home on weekends. Once she made detective, she even gave up the weekends. If she got a call when she was back home, it would take her an extra hour and a half just to get back to Vatican – not including transit time to the crime scene or Longarm HQ – and she hated rushing. She felt good about following in her father's footsteps. Earning her own share of the honor that Warin had given the Rincon family name. Continuing her father's legacy, not so much. She hoped that she would be a healthy parallel to it, someone who merited her own achievements but also stood alongside the sterling image of the first Rincon to make Chief of the Watch.

She fell back onto the lovesack, so-called because it was a plump square, more like a bed than a couch. The purple cushions gave her a light hug as she sank into them, her muscles loosening enough for a pleasurable sigh to slowly pass through her lips. She stretched her arms and legs, sliding them back and forth as if she were making a snow angel. Her Pocket floated up over her with an inquisitive *meow*. It was a cat's head with a sporadically quivering vestigial tail. The programming caused it to tilt its head slightly when it detected eye contact.

"Night light," Djet sighed.

The Pocket blinked.

The lights retreated to a gentle moonlight silver.

Djet let her thoughts drift on a current of emotion and intrigue. Her flat was the only place she felt safe enough to drop her mental shield and think unhindered. *It was good to see Vase again*, she thought. Of course, the meeting hadn't been anything more than her ex best friend calling for a favor, but Djet couldn't expect someone who wasn't into girls to requite her affections. That was a lost cause.

It doesn't pay to be a hopeless romantic, Totti, her mother's voice echoed in her mind.

"Yeah. It costs me," she answered the thought aloud.

Her eyes stung with a burning pain when she finally shut them – a lingering effect of the exposure to smoke and the common phenomenon of dry eye induced by Vatican's elevated temperature. But it was also the building angst at the lack of accomplishing anything today; and the pain of a kiss that had nearly ended a friendship so many years ago.

She rubbed a finger on her lips. The tingle under her skin was a burgeoning hope, an animalistic impulse crying out for reciprocation she knew could never be. Would never be.

The feeling swelled in her chest and spread into her legs. Blood pulsed in tiny spasms over her body. This feeling wasn't going to go away on its own. She wasn't going to get any sleep until it did.

"Pulse."

The Pocket gave a *meow* and darted into her bedroom.

It came back out a moment later to deposit her device on the cushion next to her.

Djet scrolled through her list of contacts, fingers hovering over Vase's name. She wanted so badly to put the connection through, though she didn't dare. She'd had enough disappointment for one day. Her finger scrolled down to Emily's name, the one with a black heart icon next to it. Her finger hovered over the name.

A red diamond flashed on the screen.

Djet opened the priority message with a frustrated groan.

It was from Blaze. No subject, no text.

She thought it might be him telling her how to copy his report, but it was just a link.

Vatican Zany News Network. A new report.

She opened the link and swiped the feed up to her viewing wall.

"Oiyo, Vaticanners! Dis be Minchen Sinco of Vatican Zany News and holy shit-balls do we have a story for you tonight!"

Djet muted the reporter but kept the feed playing.

The camera panned up over the lip of a security railing. Purple lighting washed over the camera lens.

Looks like it's in the upper levels, Djet thought. *Hardly anything newsworthy goes on up there.*

The lens adjusted, filtering through the glaring lights to bring the scene into full view.

A group of three humans was engaged in a stand-off with another human and two torinds.

That's a rarity. Torinds don't frequent Collective worlds without good reason.

One of the men was slamming his fists into the face of another man. Djet would have written it off as just another citizen fistfight out of her immediate jurisdiction, if not for the alien wrapped around the man's back.

It flailed with each punch the man threw, but it didn't drop to the ground.

Those suction-cupped tentacles had a death grip on him...but the alien was clearly dead.

She sat up on the lovesac.

Murder always got her attention.

The video continued. Another man, a meathead body type with a close-cropped haircut, curb-stomped another torind. Brain matter splattered onto the pavement. The buffoon slipped on the gore and dropped to his back.

The flash of a weapon discharge came from the corner of the camera followed by a glint of light in the air. A man in the background of the shot turned and fired twice. The third torind collapsed in a puddle of ink and water.

The image cut to a close-up of Thalex Coup De, face bruised and bloodied. This must have been an interview after the fact. His mouth was moving, his expression rage and disbelief. Djet hit the unmute button.

"...these fucking Marines think they're above the law. This shit has gotta stop! An unarmed citizen, minding my own business, and they jump me because of who my mother is. I'm filing a lawsuit against the military."

Djet muted the feed but replayed it to see the action again. She watched it three times. She reversed the video until the individual in the background was pivoted toward the camera, weapon up. She uttered voice commands to zoom in and adjust the pixelation for clarity. She double-checked the date of the newsfeed.

"Blaze," Djet laughed, "you lucky bastard."

He may have just been sharing some news. Maybe he saw a conspiracy in it. Maybe it was just one detective sharing a clip of an incident that was sure to get the Watch caught up in a media firestorm.

Whatever it was, he'd dumped her first clue right into her lap.

Abraham Zeeben had been on Vatican two days ago.

The tingling urge Djet had been so bothered by a moment ago was gone.

In its place was a block of ice in her gut.

She had a starting place now.

"Cabbage cone," she said to her Pocket.

To her Pulse, she said, "X-ray, facial recognition."

Her Pulse responded, running a scan on the faces of the individuals in the video. The Pocket meowed, ruffled around in her fridge for a second, then floated in and dropped a cone-shaped cabbage into her hand. It was stuffed with peppers, pineapples, coconut shavings, and drizzled with a honey lime dressing. She bit into the top of it with a crunch. The explosion of tangy sweetness from the dressing and the fruits danced with the gentle spice of the peppers.

As she took another bite, four headshots replaced the video frame:

Zeeben, Abraham. Sergeant, Human Marine Corps.
[DISCHARGED, HONORABLE]

Poplenko, Larry. Corporal, Human Marine Corps.
[DISCHARGED, GENERAL]

Piebold, Alan. Sergeant, Human Marine Corps.
[ACTIVE DUTY]

Coup De, Thalex.
[AFFILIATION: *Madame Executor Thessaly Coup De of Vatican*]

Djet looked at the faces, studying them. Committing them to memory.

"Can you locate any of these individuals?" she asked the Pulse.

"Subject Piebold is on world. Subject Coup De is on world."

"Damn," Djet huffed.

She looked back and forth between Piebold and Coup De's headshots. How did these two individuals end up at the same bar? Really, Thalex shouldn't have been anywhere without a Centurion Security detail. That was puzzling. She needed to talk to both of them, see if they had any idea where Abraham could have gone.

"So do I start with the muscle or the hustler?"

Both, her mind answered.

She did a quick search on the Human Collective's global address list, found them and fired off witness interview requests, digitally signing each with her Longarm Detective encryption keys. She took her last bite of the cabbage cone. The dressing dripped across her fingers and down the back of her hand.

Djet wiped her hand on her nightgown and opened a message window to her mother:

"Oi, Mutti, how are ya? I'm going to be coming home tomorrow for a visit. Ya have plans for dinner?"

She sent the video message and opened a separate window to type up her VF-5.

A response blinked in her mailbox.

It was Alan Piebold.

"That was fast."

He agreed to meet her, but not at the station. His choice of public meeting place made her raise an eyebrow.

She *was* doing this off the books. Probably better not to do it at the station, anyway.

She sent an acknowledgement to the corporal and hurriedly typed up her report.

Her report, not the one Captain Spitzen wanted her to write.

That'll be enough for some punitive admin leave, she thought before falling into the comfort of sleep.

CHAPTER 5

How had she managed to keep her father's identity secret for four years? And what was she hiding about the Ghosts? It was like a fissure erupted in their relationship, separating them on opposite sides of a gaping chasm.

One that she created with her betrayal.

He couldn't shake the thoughts, the pain of the lies cutting at his brain like a hacksaw. It bothered him the whole lift ride back down to Dominicus Dorsi. It shouted inside his skull when he walked under the blue lighting and past the two-story ritzy shops with large sheets of transparent duraglass showcasing the most expensive wares humanity had to offer.

Who cares about the new Call of War game? Why am I supposed to get the new Lemon Portal? Are people really beating down the doors of the Vatican Sky Mall to pre-order the newest sky runner? I hate advertisements.

He shrugged off the glaring lights and the holographic commercials as he walked.

He was choking on the doubts of his feelings about Vase when he took the maglift down forty-four floors to the pale yellow lighting of the Dominicus Ventra area. By the time he crossed into the middle-class flats and found his way back to Larry's flat, his breathing was calm, but his mind still raced.

He pounded on the door until Piebold let him in. The smell of raw meat hung in the air. Abraham wasn't in the mood to ask for an explanation.

"The fuck is wrong with her?" he spat.

It wasn't how he wanted to start the conversation. It just came out before he could filter it. He had been very careful over the last four years to keep their relationship as private as possible. The last thing either of them needed was their embarrassing domestic disputes repeated by the people they worked with.

The people they fought wars with.

"I dunno, Ham." Piebold sighed and plopped back down on the couch. He was so big his neck rested on one arm, his calves on the other. He tucked his L-pistol into the cushions and slapped a piece of raw meat over his left eye.

Corporal Tayla ParTerre and Sergeant Savony Raelis were in the kitchen, drinking something bubbly and yellow, whispering to each other. At first glance the nature of the conversation was a high school gossip session, until he saw the Portal between them. Video call, probably family. Seeing them like this, they didn't look like the fierce warriors he'd fought with on a half-dozen worlds far from Vatican. Tayla was short, her skin a natural caramel tan, and unlike Savony she kept her hair long. When they weren't deployed, she even painted her nails.

These two had been assigned to Raven Platoon for the last two years as replacements when Tar and Juke were transferred.

Someone must have moved Larry, Abraham thought.

The lanky marine was passed out on his bed, a glorified king-sized inflatable mattress. Abraham's outburst got him stirring and groaning until he stood up and chugged water from the kitchen sink with cupped hands. He sat down on the floor and rested the back of his head on Piebold's ribs. Anyone who didn't know better would read more into the men's close proximity; anyone who hadn't been through what they'd been through. It wasn't the closeness of lovers; it was the closeness of brothers who entrusted their lives to each other on the regular.

The couch was a felt-lined loveseat they inherited with the apartment. An alien had lived here before, though they didn't know what species. The loveseat was barely twenty-five centimeters off the floor. It almost looked like Piebold was on a pallet, rather than a couch.

"What's going on?" Piebold asked, sounding only half-interested. He adjusted the large slab of raw meat suctioned to the side of his face and scratched his chin. His C-skin was unsealed, looking baggy and unkempt in its static gray color of powered down.

"You got bitch problems, Zeeben?" Tayla asked.

"This is more of a guys-only conversation, ParTerre. Fuck off."

"Ooh, somebody's crotch-rocket needs a tune-up," Savony said.

Abraham growled, "Jealous bitches. If your love lives were a movie, it'd be *Lake Flaccid*."

The girls laughed. The razzing died down.

Abraham set his pistol on the orange and gray countertop. His Pocket perched on the edge and chirped. He tapped its head to put it to sleep and unsealed his C-skin but kept it on.

Abraham told them the whole thing. How he and Vase had trusted each other beyond anything, how they never lied to each other, and how he had just found out one of the very first things she'd ever told him had been a lie. One of omission, sure, but a lie nonetheless. And it hurt. It was like he'd been distracted by a kiss and stabbed in the back.

When it was all over, Larry shrugged.

"I mean, she's an officer, bro. Fuck her."

Piebold snickered.

"He already did that, Larry. You should try to talk to her and see if she'll come clean."

Abraham tried not to let his embarrassment show. Everyone

assumed it, but it hadn't happened.

Now it definitely won't, he groaned inwardly.

Tayla pulled her long black hair into a pony tail.

"No," she said, "you should walk away. Seneca's too far out of your league, Abraham. No offense, just honest."

Larry massaged his temples. He had a black and blue ring around his neck. It looked painful, not that he seemed to notice. The bar incident was only a few hours ago, but he seemed to be sobering up. At least, partially.

"Nah, man. She's sexy as hell, I won't deny that. But if you can't trust her, you should be quitting her, ASAP. Think about it tactically, bro. We always talk about operational security and all that horseshit, right? So, start applying it to your life off-duty, too, Abraham. You can't trust her, you can't be with her."

Savony added, "She's his first, Larry. He's gonna have a hard time walking away."

Piebold yawned. "Whatever the hell you do, I'm taking a nap."

Abraham sighed, steeling himself. He had kept up the lie that Vase and he had...gotten to that step, mostly because he was embarrassed that they hadn't, but also because he wanted the constant virgin jokes to stop. He blinked, shifting gears in his mind. He had already come to a decision, but he didn't have to make it alone. There were no secrets between fireteams. He had told them all about Smithers and the Ghosts long ago. They were in the know about that. What he was about to tell them...he wasn't sure how they were going to take it. He had intended to tell Vase, but she just cut herself off by lying to him. Now he just wanted his friends to know.

"I'm breaking up with Vase. And I'm taking Smithers up on his offer."

That got everyone's attention.

"They want me. Bad. I'm in a good position to demand whatever I want at this point. So here it is." He gestured an arms-wide-open sweep with his palms. "Anyone who wants to come with me, now's your chance."

Larry shook his head and scoffed.

"You're a crazy bastard, Abraham."

All eyes in the room turned to him.

He shrugged. "What? Of course I'm in. What do I have to lose?"

Piebold shoved Larry off and sat bolt upright. He peeled the steak off his face, ruffled through the couch cushion for a moment. When he brought his hand up, he was holding his L-pistol. He held the steak out with one hand and pulled the trigger. The Vatican-legal soft-point round shredded the raw meat with a *snap!* Flakes and bits of bloody steak spattered the apartment wall. The bullet pierced the plaster drywall, pinging against the bulkhead plating behind it.

The sound was muffled somewhat by the meat. Piebold's narrowed eyes were anything but subdued.

He was pissed.

"You wanna throw in with the Ghosts? This is what'll be left of you."

The stringy remnants of the steak flew toward Abraham. He instinctively caught it, more to keep it from hitting him in the face than to prevent it from falling on the floor. His fingers ran through the striated fibers of what had once been a living creature but was now just a pound of dead, mutilated flesh.

Mutilated animal flesh that tasted pretty good when Vase had made him Steak Diane that one time. He looked at the ruined meat in his fingers. *What a waste of good steak*, he thought.

Abraham saw the way they were all looking at him. The shock in their eyes. The way Savony's mouth gaped open, and Tayla covered hers with a hand. They were less concerned with Piebold's firing a gun in the apartment. Somehow *that* wasn't as shocking as Abraham's declaration of joining the Ghost Society.

He did the only thing he could do.

He doubled down.

And tossed the steak on the floor.

"I'm going. If anyone else wants to come, be ready in an hour."

Piebold cursed and rolled over to put his back to Abraham.

"Never figured you for a traitor, Ham."

"I'm not a traitor, Alan. I want answers. They have them."

Smithers' words coming from his lips.

He hated himself for it, but it didn't change his mind. This was the only way he could find out what was going on with him. Why he had some innate ability to summon invisible shields that constantly saved his life. Why he fought a war against aliens whose DNA he shared. He didn't say any of this. Didn't have to. The people in this room were the closest to him. They already knew why he was doing it. They just hadn't realized he would actually do it.

He walked into Larry's room, where they all kept their bug-out bags – no packing required. He plopped down on Larry's sleeping bag mattress and put his head in his hands.

Father, forgive me.

The old man's weathered face rose in the darkness of his mind. It was a youthful face for a man his age. Tired eyes emanated sorrow that covered the sting of betrayal. This not from a lie, but from a failure to properly communicate. If the old man knew anything, he just never found the right time to say it. The image of Obadiah seemed to nod, but in typical fashion the expression conveyed nothing. An empty gesture. Just another way to keep a person at arm's length from the thoughts and feelings inside the man.

He gritted his teeth and spent the next hour trying to talk himself out of it.

After an hour of self-reflection that left him with no reason to change his mind, he left the apartment.

Larry, Tayla, and Savony followed him.

Abraham still couldn't believe they were going with him.

They took a sky runner thirty minutes south of Dominicus Dorsi, leaving behind the wealthiest section of Vatican. The lights changed colors several times as they sailed across the atmosphere, weaving between spires, electrical bulbs and avionics towers. Plumes of flame lanced across the sky, vessels from every corner of space coming and going from the technological heart of the universe.

The sky runner docked on a landing pad at a public transit stop with yellow dotted lines over a black square. Abraham led the way down the walkway into the Academic Circle. It was his favorite part of Vatican, one he often visited when Vase was taking care of local political concerns that came along with her job. Not the college area, but the rooftop gardens. He knew this area as well as you could know a public park.

Larry and Tayla to his left, Savony on his right, they walked through the Hall of Education on their way to the Olympia Space Needle. He felt like an asshole for breaking up two of Falcon platoon's fireteams. Of course, Vase would be pissed. The thought of her scowling actually made him smile a bit on the inside. She was so used to having everything the way she wanted...she probably didn't know what to do with herself now.

It wasn't that he wanted her to be pissed.

He still cared about her. Still loved her if he thought about it long enough.

Don't, he told himself. *You're not staying. You can't.*

"You really think he's gonna go for this?" Savony asked.

Abraham took a few more steps before he worked up enough confidence to mask his doubt.

"Of course."

He could feel the side-eyes from the three of them at this, but he marched on, determined.

The duraglass was so clean it confused the eye into believing it wasn't even there. The green and black hallway was ornate to the point of grandiose. It was an unnecessary excess that Abraham had come to recognize as a style unique to Vatican. Not all parts of it – the seedy under levels were their own kind of legend – but the Academic Circle was known to have some of the most advanced architecture in all of human-controlled space.

The floors and ceiling were deep black. A hint of silver rippled in waves across the material. His eyes told him he was walking across a slow-moving river of metal, but his brain knew better. An effect like this was probably achieved by painstaking alignment of each individual molecule, seamlessly linking each section with an A.I.-controlled machinist.

It was beautiful.

Abraham had spent the last forty-five minutes trying desperately to think of a way to talk himself out of selling his soul to the Ghost Society. The constant questions pinging from his friends weren't helping. It was like they were reading his mind, speaking aloud the doubts that teemed within. He couldn't reconcile how they were crazy enough to leave their military contracts in pursuit of something none of them really understood. He doubted it was his leadership qualities and his charisma. It had to be something base, something instinctual on their part. The need for understanding, the nagging itch of the unknown that would only intensify if they turned down an opportunity to explore it.

Or maybe it was that gut-level instinct to peek behind the curtain.

The curtain that separates the perceived truth from the objective truth.

There are three types of people where the curtain is concerned.

The first is the person who doesn't even know the curtain is there. Out of touch, consumed with the business of life, or simply naïve, this person carries on with no concern for the curtain. They have accepted the world around them as immutable fact, assuming their position in society without question.

The second type of person sees the curtain and understands why it's there. This person knows some great and powerful mystery is being withheld from them, but they accept it, because...the curtain is there for a reason. Whoever hung that curtain must have done so because the mystery is too much for the average person to handle. This person clings to the safety offered by the curtain – they *want* the curtain.

The third type of person – Abraham included himself and his three friends in this category – wanted to tear the curtain down. To face the great mystery regardless of the consequences. After all, who decided to put that curtain up in the first place? Why did one person, or a group of people, think it was their privilege, or responsibility, to determine the truth for everyone else? For these people, the fear isn't what lies beyond the curtain; the fear is in never penetrating the fog of lies that keep the curtain in place.

That was why they were going to join the Ghost Society.

Because knowing is better than not knowing.

Even if the truth is a desolate, miserable wasteland, it's better than a beautiful castle of lies. No castle stands the test of time. No king, no man, is perfect.

It is absurd that one man should rule over another, who cannot rule over himself.

Something his brother said once. David had a knack for digging up ancient texts and boring him to death by reciting long passages from them. Sometimes, one or two lines would stick with him, though. A pang in his chest told Abraham he missed his brother more than he would have thought possible just a few years ago.

Before the Riskar War and all the hell that came with it.

If I turn back now, I'll never know.

He blinked, realizing Savony had asked him a question.

"Like I said before," he told Savony, trying to refocus, "they want me bad enough, they'll accept any demands I make."

Savony crossed her arms. They were slender but knotted with muscle. She was the only woman Abraham knew whose passion for weightlifting was the defining aspect of her life. And he knew a lot of female marines. Cardio? Sure. Calisthenics? Check. Power lifting? Most could do a little bit, maybe dabbled here and there, but Savony...she took a sharp breath, which caused her trapezius to swell impressively.

Yeah, she's obsessed. Makes her a damn good marine.

Savony asked with a sigh, "And you're sure they're gonna be okay with you giving them orders on your first day?"

"They'll go for it," Abraham said with more confidence than he felt. "Smithers has been harassing me constantly over the last few years. Yesterday he gave me the impression they weren't taking no for an answer. Trust me. It'll be fine."

Larry walked with his head down, C-skin boots scuffing against the deck with every step. Abraham didn't envy the weight he carried. He felt heavy enough having to deal with his own shit. The idea that his buddy was never going to get over Duringer had been a part of his daily thought regimen ever since the funeral. Leaving the military was, perhaps, an additional positive. A change of scenery would be good for Larry.

They exited the college tower through a spiral staircase that led up to the rooftop gardens. The open air was filled with the loamy scents of hydroponics and fresh-growing plant life. It was a welcome switch from the filtered air inside the college.

The viridian-tinged glass of the archway led to the uppermost level and a sprawling field about ten square kilometers stuffed with clusters of trees and rows of plants sprinkled with flower bulbs of every color. As he walked deeper into the garden, Abraham brushed his fingertips against blue tulips, caught a pleasant whiff of white and pink lilies. When they reached the hydrangea section, he pivoted to the west. A black spire with a snaking spiral staircase split the gentle illumination from Starlight above. The building was something Abraham's father could have designed on Milune. Unbroken panes of viridian glass, each a story tall, cascaded down the exterior with a few meters' gap between them. The exposed rebar and handrails in the gaps gave the building an artsy but intentionally incomplete sort of look that spoke to Abraham on some internal level. Starlight's illumination spilled over it like a glass waterfall.

"Pretty," Larry muttered in a way that meant he knew it should be but didn't see it that way.

Savony almost swooned at the sight, stretching each word into a sentence: "I. *Love*. This."

They entered the base of the building and ascended the stairs, marveling at the unfiltered view of the Vatican skyline. Abraham started to feel the binding in his knees when they passed the threshold to the roof. He ignored the chattering conversation the girls were having about Vatican. Vase gave him the grand tour three years ago, and he spent most of his time between deployments here.

In his mind, it was high time they moved on.

The rooftop was a large slab of duraglass. The innards of the tower could be seen below, the crisscrossing staircase and the exotic metal rebar. It looked like the inside of a clocktower, but somehow more grandiose. The fact that such opulence was given to a college observatory was testament to the enormous wealth concentrated on humanity's capitol world.

Oxygen vents spilled a healthy waft of fog across the floor, rising up like steam from hot springs in the dead of winter. The first layer of space was only a few kilometers up. Starlight was close enough to see the Starwalk below the light source. Abraham felt heady. If he lost his balance over the edge...it was a long way down.

Without warning, a red bolt of lightning struck the center of the platform.

It was not a violent thing, just a beam of light. It was there for a blink, and then it was gone. Gasps shook the three behind Abraham; he felt the surprise gnaw at his own gut. He knew it was Smithers before he saw him; he had seen the man use the same mode of transport at Camp Butler on Juno during basic training.

"Abraham," the Ghost spoke through swirling shadows.

"Smithers. You know why I'm here."

It felt good to throw the man's words back at him. A giddy jolt of glee fluttered in his stomach, tamed by the fear of the unknown. There was no going back after this. Larry's face had grown pale. Savony and Tayla were looking at each other with wide eyes and tight lips.

"You did not come alone."

Abraham shrugged.

"I have questions, you have answers, right? I'm here, but I'm not going alone."

The Ghost smiled, ashy skin stretching thin over sharp cheekbones. The black bar rose slightly over his nose. Was that because he raised his eyebrows, or just a glitch?

"You think the Society accepts just anyone?"

"You made me an offer. Now I'm making a counteroffer. Take it or leave it, Smithers."

His smile faded, leaving a flat expression that could have been the resting face of a dead person. The swirling shadows parted slightly as he stepped forward, entering their personal space. His breath was cold and smelled like a clogged air vent.

"This is a one-way street." He turned his head left and right, regarding the gathered ex-marines. "If you open this door, it shuts behind you."

Savony spoke up, a tremor in her voice. "I'm down for anything."

Larry crossed his arms. "It's all of us or none of us, dead man."

Tayla bit her lip and shot Larry a warning look.

Smithers jerked his head at that comment. The bar covering his eyes shrank almost to a square. Eyes narrowed in anger, maybe.

"Very well."

He held out his hand, palm up.

Confused looks passed among them for a moment. Abraham was the first to put his hand on Smithers'. Larry added his, then the girls, one at a time.

"Word of advice," Smithers' creaky voice intoned. "Hold your breath."

Abraham took a sharp breath.

The world around him exploded.

Silence clamped around him like a vise. It was like plunging underwater. Or like someone hit the mute button on life itself.

The cold emptiness of space rushed past at breakneck speed. Stars skimmed by, centimeters from his body. No friction. No rushing air. No crack of the sound barrier breaking. He floated in the red void of a power he didn't understand. His body felt nothing, but his brain was telling him he was a hair's breadth from dying. He fought the urge to grab Smithers' hand with both of his for fear of falling away into the emptiness of space.

The sensation died before he got hypoxic. It had to have been ten seconds. Maybe less.

He felt solid ground under his feet.

Abraham stumbled away from Smithers, blinking against the harsh light of a sun that wasn't there a few seconds ago.

Grass brushed against his ankles. A breeze carrying the smell of saltwater washed over him. The sky above was lit by an orange ball of fire smaller than his fist, but intensely bright. Heat attached itself to his skin, instantly producing sweat that ran down his back. A series of rocky cliffs jutted up from a half kilometer away and disappeared on the horizon.

He breathed deep and ruffled his hair.

Larry looked like he was going to be sick. He put his hands on his knees and started panting. Savony twirled on her heels, spinning wide-eyed to take in the sights around her. Tayla fell to her knees, feeling the grass like it was her first time seeing it. As far as Abraham knew, it was.

"What the hell was that?" Larry asked between breaths.

The swirling shadows were gone. Smithers stood before them in a mirror-black C-skin. The tight fit of the material shifted without crinkling as he took a step away from them and pointed to a gray and black building just a short walk up a dirt road.

"This," he said, "was Earth. We're taking that orbital lift up to Spectre."

Abraham realized he was holding his breath again. He fixed that, blinking away the stars and clouds of hypoxia.

Earth was a dead world. Everyone knew that.

For thousands of years it had been classified as a...

Ghost Planet.

A pit opened up in his stomach.

What the fuck have I gotten us into?

The orbital lift was a glorified metal box with what Abraham surmised must be the standard Ghost décor. White bulkheads with black accents, the construction formed so well the seams in the paneling were barely a millimeter wide.

It smelled like it had been recently sanitized.

The elevator lurched violently. It issued a creak and a groan that made Abraham think of a nature documentary about blue whales and the noises they made. He wished he'd spent his time more wisely prior to this journey; Smithers' words about the shutting door stood very tall in his mind right now.

I wonder how many people have blown chunks in here, he thought.

The view through the window made his mind go blank.

Grass fields stretched out for hundreds of klicks in every direction. The higher the elevator took them, the better he could see the coastline in the distance, then the smooth blue of the ocean. The waves seemed still. Calm, like a photograph. Clouds washed over the window, moisture coiling against the glass until it cleared, and then all he could see were clouds. They were high enough now that the horizon bent, the curve of the planet growing sharper and darker.

The stars appeared low at first. A shudder rocked the elevator.

Abraham steadied himself with a hand on the wall, absorbing the impact tremors with his knees. The pull of gravity on his body was starting to get to the point where he wasn't sure if he could remain standing. Just when he thought he was going to collapse to hands and knees, everything started to feel lighter.

The pressure on him released. He felt the effects of vertigo in his stomach. Then he felt nothing at all.

Gravity became a memory.

Larry shouted an obscenity. His head bounced against the roof, three meters up. Savony and Tayla were holding hands and spinning in a circle. Smithers had his feet planted, red glowing light bent over them. His arms were crossed, and he seemed to be making a conscious effort to ignore the giggles coming from the girls as they took turns kicking off the walls and free-floating across the open air.

Of course, Abraham thought. *Something as simple as zero G wouldn't bother a freak like him, either.*

He looked down at his own boots, which were also covered in a red glow.

So, he didn't know *how* he was part riskar, but this involuntary manipulation of gravity was certainly contributing to its confirmation. It was a large part of the reason he'd chosen to take Smithers up on his offer. If he were able to learn more about his genetics, it might answer questions about his parentage.

Smithers spoke. His voice made Abraham's skin crawl.

"That," he pointed at Abraham's feet, "is going to be one of the first answers we get you."

Abraham blinked. "You can see it?"

Smithers shook his head. "Regardless of what you think, I am one hundred percent human."

"But you're doing it, too."

Smithers shrugged and patted his belt. "Technically."

"Did you reverse engineer riskar tech? Is that what you're saying?"

"Careful," Smithers said. "You're suggesting the Riskar War was a front for stealing their technology."

Abraham felt a tightness in his chest.

"Wasn't it?"

Smithers smiled but said nothing.

The elevator shuddered one final time as it docked with Spectre. A hiss of air whined through the seals on the door as the pressure equalized between the box and the station. The doors slid aside to reveal a long hallway whose white walls were trimmed in black and cut every ten meters with large glass panes that showed the endless void of stars swirling in the sea of nothing that was space.

This is it, Abraham thought.

Abraham was, by this point, used to the backdrop beyond the glass. He'd spent the last four years travelling the stars with the Marine Corps. He'd seen planets and star systems he could never have imagined as a boy on Milune. It was the stuff David talked about endlessly over the years while Abraham worked the tobacco farm. Alien worlds, human settlements light years apart from each other, trade disputes and government feuds over trivial things that didn't concern simple farmers like the Zeebens.

Maybe you should have been a marine, and I should have stayed on the farm...or maybe not, because then we'd both be dead.

Now, stepping onto the Ghost station, Abraham felt like each compartment was a different room in the same home. He hadn't caught a glimpse of the station from the outside, but he was developing the idea that it was double the size of Starlight. This again made him think of how many Ghosts were stationed here, and how many more were riding the red lightning across the galaxy to do whatever they did.

"Follow me," Smithers said, walking ahead of them.

As they walked, Abraham stole glances at the planet below. Earth was abandoned thousands of years ago. He wondered if the Ghost Society had been around back then. If they had orchestrated the destruction of the planet, or faked it because they wanted to claim it for themselves. That brought up a sea of questions.

"Smithers," Abraham said, "how many of you are there?"

Savony coughed uncomfortably. Tayla rubbed a hand on her back.

Smithers said, "You'll find out."

"I'm just thinking," Abraham said as they turned a corner, "if every planet designated as a Ghost Planet is yours, you've got to have people on them, right? That's like...twenty-five planets."

"Thirty-three," Smithers said under his breath.

"Whatever."

They entered a large room with a long black table in the center. Chairs were situated at appropriate intervals around it, enough for twenty people, but the room was empty. Abraham felt the heat in the room, tasted the musty smell of air that had been recycled from every other part of the station. Unpleasant, but familiar.

Smithers exited the room through a door at the back. It slid shut with a pneumatic hiss. Abraham pulled out a chair and sat down. The gravity here felt no different from what he'd felt down on Earth.

Still hard to believe I've been to Earth.

"Just make ourselves at home, huh?" Larry chuckled, pulling out his own chair.

"Dude, this is like, *hardcore* shit." Savony plopped into a chair next to Larry.

"It feels so...alien," Tayla said, leaning back against the bulkhead with her arms crossed. She waved a lock of hair from her face and rested her head on the bulkhead. Abraham had seen her tired before, and this wasn't it; she was stressed.

They all were. It had been a long four years in the Marine Corps. This was the first time they were stepping out of that umbrella, the protection and surety of a life in the military. It was going to be uncomfortable in the same way that all new things were, at first. Abraham wondered if being a Ghost was going to be as interesting as he hoped. He was a foot soldier, his office the battlefield. It would be a disappointment if he was relegated to running errands and making surprise appearances to scare people into doing what the Society wanted.

No, he thought. *It's gotta be more than that. They're no different from everyone else. They have an agenda.*

The door slid open. A very pale, very tall man entered the room. His Ghost Bar covered his eyes, the same as Smithers, but he wore the navy wings and fire-plume pin on his C-skin denoting him as a Navy pilot. The stranger was a half-meter taller than Larry with a strong build. The muscles fitting his frame made him look proportional.

Perfectly combed blond hair topped a chiseled chin and pronounced jawline. He might have been a classically handsome dude if he had some color to him. In the typical fashion of the Ghosts, they seemed to avoid the sun with religious fervor. This individual was no different.

But then, he *was* different. It didn't hit him until he spoke.

Abraham recognized him.

Larry made a choking sound.

The Ghost said, "Abraham Zeeben and Larry Poplenko. I never thought I'd see you boys again."

Savony slapped Larry's shoulder.

"You know a Ghost and you never told us?"

Larry's jaw hung open. Wordless breaths of air spilled out.

Abraham felt his guts tighten in a vise. He couldn't take his eyes off the man.

"I'm Agent Lannam, Ghost Society."

"Myles Lannam," Abraham said. "That's...impossible."

Myles' smile changed him. He was no longer the childhood hero from Veranda. Now, he was something else. Something different. Pronounced dead six years ago, he couldn't be physically standing here in front of them. It didn't make sense.

He's not here, Abraham thought. *He's just another Ghost.*

CHAPTER 6

The crystal garden was Djet's favorite spot on Vatican.

Rock formations rose into the sky like monoliths, glittering in the pale glow of Starlight. She followed the walkway up to a quartz zirconium spire that was particularly eye-catching. At six meters tall, the fancy rock looked like a half slice of pomegranate; instead of seeds, facets shimmered in the crevices. The air was humid, with an odor of sulphur and brine. If she closed her eyes, she could picture herself on a wharf by the sea on some far away planet. Some place that wasn't a series of interconnected boxes stuffed with too many beings out to take advantage of one another.

Gaseous oxygen coiled around her feet and snaked up her person. It was already cold this high up. The breathing accommodations forced her to dial up the thermal settings on her C-skin. The gathering storm clouds she wore flashed with forked lightning.

She considered the crystal rock before her, tracing the depression in the center, following the cracks down to the meta-steel deck where it was embedded. The deep purple – almost ruby – of the precious mineral was supposed to have some sort of medical properties. How people living in the height of technology could still be made to believe those things, Djet would never puzzle out.

There were some mysteries that weren't meant to be solved.

"Like, where the fuck is this douchebag?" she continued her thoughts aloud.

Condensation clung to the crystal. It probably felt wet. Or maybe just slightly slick. Djet stuck her finger out to touch it.

"I wouldn't do that, ma'am."

Reflexes kicked in. She yanked her hand back like a child caught messing with the cookie jar. She spun on her heel and steadied her hips against the guardrail.

"What took you so long, then?"

Alan Piebold crossed his huge arms and leaned the small of his back against the guardrail next to her. Not that anything about this man could be called small; the tight fit of his C-skin made him look like a Silver Age superhero. Smooth skin on his bald head caught a glint from Starlight and held it.

"I told you I didn't want to do this. This isn't my usual hangout."

He narrowed his eyes. A muscle twitched in his neck. To his credit, he didn't glance around or put his hand to the weapon on his belt. He just stood there, leaning against the rail and breathing slow breaths.

He's a surprisingly controlled man, Djet thought. *These are the really dangerous kind.*

"Ya mean a twenty-four-year-old single man doesn't normally spend his midnight hours in a crystal petting zoo? Alan, I'm surprised."

He snickered.

"No, you're not. You're surprised I responded so quickly. And now you're wondering why I chose to meet here. I'm going to tell you what I know. Then, you're going to leave me alone."

"What's with the hostility, Alan? Ya boy's not in trouble. I just got someone looking for him. I'm not gonna arrest him. All I wanna know is where he's gone off to, and if he's okay."

Piebold shook his head and gave a snort.

"I don't know where he's at. I doubt he's okay. I do know who he left with, but you're not going to believe it. I'm serious about the no contact thing. Don't try to message me, because I'll block you."

"Ya find that necessary? Ya don't strike me as the rash type, Alan."

"You've got me wrong, Detective."

The big man took in a deep breath, swelling up his chest and shoulders. He stretched his neck. It cracked a few times.

"If I strike you, I don't stop till you're dead. I know something that can point you in the right direction, but I want to be left alone after this. I'm shipping out soon and I don't want anything screwing with my career."

Djet let him have his moment of grandstanding. She played into it.

"Absolutely understandable. I wouldn't ask you to sacrifice yourself or your livelihood just to get me some information. I appreciate anything you can give me, though."

She sidled along the guardrail, halving the distance between them. As she moved, she lowered her voice to a little above a whisper.

"How do you know where he went?"

Alan shrugged and laughed. It started as a snort, but after a moment his shoulders were rocking and his face was red. He shook his head, pulled a Pulse from his pocket and tapped it on the shimmering crystal behind him.

"Now you know everything I know. Just don't tell them you got it from me."

He turned to leave.

Djet pushed off the railing, gently, and stepped into his path.

"Now, wait, Alan. I appreciate the information, but I need some answers."

Djet was trained in Capoiera, no stranger to martial arts. She knew to expect some kind of movement here, but Piebold was *fast.* He had her wrist crushed in a death grip before she could counter. Her metacarpals creaked against each other in his grip.

The big man looked at her, really looked at her for the first time. His eyes passed over her face, down her body and hovered at her belt for a split second, passed down to her boots and flicked back up to eye contact.

Was that a weapons search, or did he just check me out?

It wouldn't have been creepy if he did. She was more creeped out by the fact that she couldn't tell. Piebold had a dichotomous presence. His physicality screamed *ready for violence*. The air of nonchalance he broadcast didn't match.

It wasn't haughty; it was confident.

His breath smelled like spearmint and rosemary.

"Do not ever contact me again."

Djet smiled. "You are a strange man, Corporal."

"You get me?" he asked.

"Not at all, if I'm being honest," Djet said, keeping her voice light despite the pain in her wrist, "but I'll figure you out."

He released her arm with a snicker and walked away.

Djet rubbed the joint, heat collecting at her face.

What's wrong with you? You should have kicked his ass!

Yeah, but then I'd never get anything else out of him.

Djet opened the message on her Portal. A red border overtook the screen, indicating it was encrypted. She touched the Portal to the rock crystal, same as Piebold had done a moment ago. The border flipped green as the encryption cleared.

My name is Alan Piebold, the message displayed. *I was born on Vatican. Moved to Veranda when I was eleven. Over the last thirteen years, I've been looking for my sister. The Ghosts took her. I know how this sounds, but it's true. They took her right in front of me. And now that's where your missing person is. Only they didn't take him.*

Djet's jaw dropped. Her gut clenched. She read on:

"He went to them."

Djet chewed on that for a moment. Were these Ghosts real? Alan's uncorroborated statement that they were…that wasn't enough to confirm anything. Hadn't Vase mentioned something about a secret society? The name was different, though. No, this was completely separate from the shit her old best friend was peddling.

Coming up with nothing, she returned to the message.

There is something big going on in the Human Collective. In the Liberty House itself, if you ask me. I'm just a grunt, I don't know what all that is. Honestly, I don't give a fuck about it, either. I'm earning a paycheck. Putting days behind me. I didn't meet with you for any other reason than this...after you find Abraham, I want you to find my sister.

Djet would have broken the Portal against the crystal if it hadn't been so expensive. This was the last thing she needed. Not a guilty party. A guilty organization. Not one missing person. Two missing people, one of them a cold case.

Two clients who weren't paying her shit.

Her Pulse chimed.

Priority message from Vase. It contained two sentences.

Face to face when you can. Navy shipyard, dock 49 Bravo.

For Djet, it was the final straw. Mysterious enterprises that operated in the shadows were not her forte. Since when did Vase become so...secretive? And why was Alan acting exactly the same way? None of this made any sense, especially this request from Vase. What new information could she possibly have? Was this a meeting with Vase, or...something else? No, Vase wouldn't be going anywhere for a few months.

At least, that was what she had implied.

Unless she took leave and did some investigating on her own.

Fair point.

Still...Djet wanted to visit her father. She needed his advice. She wanted to walk the Third Ward for the first time in several months. She had walked those plates many times in her youth. She remembered the shops, the eateries and the food stands, the quasi-business district which was really just a metals emporium. None of which she had even glanced at in her last few trips there. *I'll get with Vase after*, she told herself. *Doesn't hurt to wait a day.*

Oh, but it could hurt. Vase had a way of cooking up trouble. She liked to think of herself as a master web weaver, like a black widow, but really she was a shit-stirrer who always fell into the pot. She never seemed to catch any real-world consequences for her mistakes, though.

To her credit, she never made the same mistake twice.

Concentrating on the woman conjured up an image of her in Djet's mind. She was standing with one hand on her hip, the other pressing a finger over her lips.

"That's not enough," Djet said aloud to herself. "If I walk in on you in the thralls of some cult ritual, Vase, I'm going to be pissed."

This is humbling. I'm supposed to be a detective, but it feels like I keep getting cheat codes from my intel officer friend. Curiously emphasized cheat codes. Like she's leading me along a familiar path.

So, Djet asked the image of Vase in her mind, *have you seen this path, or have you walked it?*

The Vase in her mind waved her finger and smiled obnoxiously. Then she vanished.

Djet pocketed her Pulse and headed for the elevator lift, waving her hands and talking to herself. The consensus of her thoughts was negative, but she felt a tinge of excitement, too.

She was going to talk to people who might have answers. But first, she needed to take care of something personal.

Djet let the tingles finish crawling up and down her skin, enjoying the sensation that lessened with each beat of her pulse.

Emily lay under the sheets next to her. She was falling asleep.

After that display, she's earned it.

Her Pocket, which rested on the counter in the kitchen flicking its tail every so often, meowed as it adjusted the overhead lights to night mode.

The bend in Emily's neck, where her shoulder started, was bare. Her thin face was soft, perfect features that caught the eye and held it. She was the kind of woman who drew attention, who demanded a second look from people. Whether they were attracted to her or not, everyone who met her for the first time had the same two- or three-second delay before greeting her as their brain processed her natural beauty. It might have been the perfect symmetry of her face, or the gentle smile she always wore; whatever it was, Djet had fallen for it at first sight.

She was a stickler for the law, but when it came to morality...what was morality, besides a social construct? Arbitrary rules of right and wrong, codified by social consensus? She didn't give a damn about social consensus, or about society at large, really. She just wanted what she wanted, and she knew how to get it. Life was simple when you looked at it that way. Far less stressful than trying to adhere to or live by unwritten rules under the assumption that most people agreed on them without ever putting them into writing or voting them into law.

No, Djet thought, *that's not right. I have a moral compass. It's just ingrained with the saying* Memento Mori. *Remember mortality. Remember you're human. That's a free pass to make mistakes, learn from them, and probably make them a few more times before learning enough not to make those same mistakes again.*

That made sense. Life was a journey, where failures and successes worked together to forge a complete person. She had experienced many of both in her time. Enough to know who she was as a person. She was a damned good detective. A great friend, and an insolent daughter.

Why, then, do I feel so empty?

Her body felt fine. More than fine. She really needed this. The problem wasn't in her head, either.

Her mind was sharp, agile, analytical to a fault. The problem was that in-between space, the place she didn't like to linger – her heart. Her emotional nexus was a no-man's-land in more ways than one. She did not know why her exterior self could portray full-fledged emotions that she did not feel. She did not know why she felt the need to convince others that she was emotionally connected to them, even when she was not.

Her eyes drifted to Emily, to her auburn hair, tracing the sinuous waves down to the soft, pale flesh of her cheek that flowed to rose-colored lips. She radiated beauty in such intensity it was a physical boon to Djet's eyes, something that sparked that tingle under her skin and quickened her pulse...but the sensation died there. It was like a waterfall, dumping a deluge into an endless abyss. It worried her that she was more interested in figuring out someone like Alan Piebold than in carrying a conversation with the angel that lay in her bed.

She didn't understand the way her mind worked sometimes.

"Emily," Djet shook her shoulder.

"Hmm?" Emily responded with a smile.

Djet got up and slipped into her C-skin. "Time to go."

Emily sat up, ran a hand through her hair, shielding her nakedness with a tight grip on the blankets. "You're not coming to sleep?"

"Sprout chips," Djet said. Her Pocket meowed in response.

"What?" Emily asked.

Djet sank into the cushions of her couch with a satisfied sigh. She pulled up her Pulse and swiped the screen, throwing a projection of the Zeeben video into the air between her and Emily. Emily glared at her through the translucent image. The Pocket meowed and dropped a bag of sprout chips into Djet's outstretched hand.

She opened the bag noisily, scooped out two or three of the fried sprouts and popped them into her mouth. They tasted like salt and rust, but they were healthy, so she tolerated them. As she chewed noisily, she started the playback on the video. A few frames in, Emily was still glaring at her through the translucent video feed.

"Door's right here." Djet indicated to her left.

Emily tossed the blankets off in a huff. She threw her C-skin on, snatched up her purse and gave a violent toss of her hair as she walked past Djet. She placed her hand on the open switch and cast a glare.

"Djet?"

Djet didn't look at her, barely heard her. *Why was Abraham at this dive bar in the first place?* she wondered.

"You're a cunt," Emily spat.

Djet sighed. She didn't want to, but she was going to have to track down and talk to this kid, this Thalex Coup De. He probably didn't know anything, but writing him off wasn't a good idea. She had yet to get a response from him, but she had only sent the message yesterday. The sprout chips were a bit saltier than she remembered. She shrugged; she was still going to finish the bag, and probably have a protein smoothie with something citrusy in it. Sweet would wipe the excess salt from her palette.

Engrossed in the video and her own thoughts, she didn't hear the door shut after Emily left.

CHAPTER 7

Myles Lannam cleared his throat.

Abraham still couldn't believe it was him. He recognized him, even with the Ghost bar covering his eyes. He looked exactly the same minus the pale, ashy complexion that seemed to be a prerequisite for being a Ghost.

Myles opened up a map on the table. The universe sprang to life in holographic form. Millions of stars and planets as motes of light in the air, spinning and orbiting in slow motion. He touched one system, zooming in and bringing up several windows of text. A few windows popped up showing riskar vessels.

The last window showed a small planet and a forest moon.

"Your first briefing, then," Myles said, "is knowing who we are and what we do. This is the Ghost Society. Historically speaking, we're a bunch of people who were in the right place at the right time. That's the short version. The long version...let's just say that you guys aren't going to hear that until your clearances go through."

Savony leaned over to look at Abraham.

"Clearances," she asked, "as in, they're going to be interrogating our families?"

Abraham shrugged. "I don't have a family anymore."

Tayla crossed her arms and leaned back in her chair. She tried to kick Abraham, but her legs were too short. She stubbed her toe on the underside of the table.

"Abraham, you're the exception here, not the rule. Did you know this was part of it?"

Larry put a hand on Tayla's shoulder. "Tayla, don't worry. Security clearances are interviews, not interrogations. Your family is going to be fine."

Abraham felt like cold water had just been dumped down his back. Larry hadn't been much for comforting people over the last few years. He went through the stages of depression associated with grieving, but he had not yet rounded out to the acceptance part. Seeing his old best buddy being a positive force toward anything was like a memory of a time before the military.

It was oddly...normal.

Myles cleared his throat.

"All right, if the emotions are running high, that's understandable, but I do have a briefing to get through, and you all have a lot to do before you can begin anything resembling training. So, back to the simulation."

Myles pointed at the forest moon and tapped it. The planets started moving.

It was at that moment that Abraham recognized it for what it was.

Four riskar vessels were attacking Milune. One large ship, a carrier or something along those lines, hung back in the empty darkness of space. The riskar fighters chased their plumes of red that was their strange reverse-propulsion system. They painted the surface of Milune with laser blasts, leaving glowing white craters of glass in their wake.

Abraham's breath caught in his chest. He was glad there wasn't any sound. No close-ups of the planet's surface. It could have just been a model, a re-creation of the event. It didn't have to be the actual laser blasts he saw as a kid. This didn't have to be the real footage. If Myles zoomed in far enough, they would *not* see the death of Abraham's mother.

It didn't have to be real.

Larry tapped his fingers on the table, eyes roaming about the room, looking anywhere but at the simulation.

A tendril of red energy like a laser beam erupted from Milune and spiked upward to Dajun, the forest moon. In moments, the two celestial bodies collided. Shortly after was a clouded scene of rocks and flame that had been Milune. Dajun, looking like an apple with a bite taken out of it, spun off into the darkness where it became a cloud of large rocks.

The riskar ships docked inside the carrier. The carrier and the three cruisers lit off, tracing a red pathway out of the frame.

"We've all seen this, Mr. Ghost," Savony said. "It's The Collision."

Myles nodded sagely.

"Indeed, you have seen clips of this event over and over again. And that's why this is your first assignment. Something here is not right. You each will be issued Portals with this re-creation loaded on them. I want you to examine and re-examine this footage until you can tell me what you and the rest of humanity are missing."

Larry was suddenly fixated on the frozen image of what had once been Milune. He asked a question, words falling from his mouth like he was fighting them.

"Are you...saying the riskar...*didn't* do this?"

Myles smiled.

"That's your first assignment, Mr. Poplenko. Tomorrow, this time, you all should have the answer."

He turned and opened the door, stopping at the threshold for a moment.

"One last thing," he said, "this isn't the Marine Corps. There are no standards. No units, no companies or platoons. Becoming a Ghost means you are a company of one. An individual capable of achieving the impossible. Everything we do – every mission, every time – everything is No Fail. Your exams are not graded. It's strictly pass or fail. If you're not ready for this, just say the word and we'll get you back to where you belong."

He shut the door.

Abraham and Larry stared at the wreckage of their home planet, facing the question that had haunted them all their lives:

What happened on Milune?

Abraham woke a few hours later to the noise of tapping fingers.

The dorm room was slightly larger than the four-man bunks he was used to on most navy vessels. It had two beds, two wall lockers and two terminal stations. A shower unit and restroom were attached to the far end by a compartment seal that always remained open. The scent of mineral water filled the entire room. That was the first thing Abraham did when he left the briefing room – shirked his C-skin and hit the shower. When Myles's voice came over the intercom to announce chow was available, he dimmed the lights as Larry opted for the shower next. He ignored the grumbling in his stomach, pulled on a pair of black shorts and a black shirt – apparently the Ghost's PT uniform – and passed out on the bed.

Until the typing woke him up.

Larry was staring at the video, eyes glazed over. The dimmed lights washed his face in the glow of the terminal window. His fingers worked at the keyboard and his Pulse, simultaneously manipulating the window and taking notes. There was no way to tell what he was feeling. Only that his mind was deeply locked in on the screen.

"You figure that out yet?" Abraham asked.

Larry shrugged.

Abraham scratched the back of his head. He hadn't gotten a cut since first returning from Feldscar. Military regulations being what they were, he'd had close-cropped fades for the last four years. The lengthy fibers tickling his ears were foreign to him. He sat up on the bed, swinging his legs to distract himself.

"They call it The Collision. Dajun was forced, through some kind of gravity manipulation technology...Dajun was forced into Milune. Like a bowling ball thrown into a glass window."

Larry chuckled. "You think that's what this is?"

Abraham stiffened. Nothing about this was funny. They both lost people that day. Larry both of his parents, and Abraham his mother. He still thought about her sometimes. Mostly when he was alone, or felt alone. Nothing like being trapped in the same room as a friend you were once close to, who could laugh at watching the deaths of the people closest to him on an endless loop.

"Rictor told me the riskar didn't do it. I know they have their ideas about honor and integrity, same as any other race. But their belief system allows for them to lie to another species with a clean conscience."

Larry paused the replay. A beam of red light paused halfway between Milune and Dajun. Larry pointed at it with a knobby finger.

"This is what no one has figured out. It's right here, right in front of our faces, and no one has ever said anything about it."

Abraham stared. The beam was reaching out toward Dajun. From Milune.

"It wasn't a ship that did this..." The words fell from his lips even though he didn't want them to.

The Shadow Man. The red glow in his hand.

"He wasn't pushing Dajun away," Abraham breathed, "he was *pulling it in.*"

Larry raised an eyebrow. "What, now?"

"Remember the Shadow Man I told you guys about in basic?"

Larry crossed his arms. "Abraham, that was four years ago. I don't..."

He didn't need to finish. Abraham heard the rest, even if Larry didn't say it.

I don't want to remember.

Abraham wished he had that luxury.

"I saw a man. An adult man, with a glowing red hand. I can see gravity when it's being manipulated, same as the riskar."

"Yeah, I know. Because you are one."

"Because I'm partly one." Abraham gritted his teeth. He hated to admit it. Still struggled to believe it. "I can see it, but I didn't realize it at the time. I was nine years old, bro. I didn't know what the hell was going on."

"But now you do," Larry pressed.

Abraham nodded.

"We need to get the girls in here. Now."

Savony blew a raspberry and laughed.

Tayla's jaw dropped.

Several tense moments passed before anyone spoke.

The girls' PT uniforms were sports bras and shorts. Standing next to

Savony, Tayla looked like she had just graduated high school, although she was the same age as Abraham. They either brought their own soap with them, or the Ghosts had provided something that reeked of wildflowers. The smell they brought into his dorm room reminded him of the grassy area around Stony Ridge High.

Larry played the clip again at half speed.

Like a contrail from a spacecraft, the beam rose from Milune, reached out and touched Dajun. A few frames later, the planet and moon collided. Milune fractured like a snow globe dropped on the floor.

"This is what we were supposed to find," Larry said matter-of-factly.

Tayla pulled her hair into an updo.

"This is too obvious. Why hasn't anyone else – not even conspiracy theorists – come out with this? We're marines, not scientists or video analysts. How did we find this when no one else could?"

Savony wrapped an arm around Tayla and said in a soft voice, "Because we were told to look for it."

Abraham shook his head. "No. That's not it. Myles said this was a simulation. A re-creation. That means it's a representation of what happened. Not exactly what happened."

Tayla asked, "Do we have access to the newsfeeds?"

Larry grunted and started typing at the keys. The simulation slid to the side. Larry keyed up the newsfeed, the one Abraham had seen a thousand times throughout his childhood.

They watched it three times, each time noticing the same thing.

The real-world footage was missing the red beam of light.

"They're screwing with us!" Tayla shouted. "They messed with the simulation to throw us off."

Savony patted Tayla on the head. "I don't think so, Tayla. It's more like they gave us a hint."

"Not a hint," Abraham said. "They're telling it straight out. I should have seen it before."

"Seen what?" Tayla asked.

Abraham laughed with self-deprecation. "How could I have been so stupid?"

Savony crossed her arms, one eyebrow shooting up.

"Is this gonna be a long conversation with yourself, or are you going to let us in on what you're thinking?"

Abraham stood up in a flurry. Inspiration struck – he had to act fast. The rest of them wouldn't understand what he was about to say unless they saw it for themselves.

"You know," he said, ripping open the drawer under his bed, "anything about what happened on Duringer?"

"I know the official story, and a few rumors." Savony shrugged.

Tayla flopped down on Larry's bed, exasperated. "What's that got to do with this, exactly? And what the hell are you looking for?"

Abraham dug through his belongings until he found his L-pistol. He checked the magazine. Still loaded with Vatican-approved plastic rounds. Lethal, but useable on spacecraft and stations.

"Larry." Abraham tossed the weapon to him.

Larry caught it like it was a live spider. He looked at it, looked at Abraham, and raised both his eyebrows.

"The fuck is this, Zeeben?"

"You know what needs to happen." Abraham swallowed a lump in his throat. "Shoot me."

Tayla made a choking sound.

Savony blew a raspberry and said, "Now I know you've lost your mind, Zeeben."

Larry laughed. "You really want me to do that?"

Abraham shrugged. "Just do it."

"Absolutely not!" Savony reached for the gun.

Larry jerked it out of her reach, but made no move to point the weapon at Abraham.

"What's this supposed to prove, exactly?" Tayla asked.

"Don't you want to, after everything?" Abraham goaded him. "After Duringer?"

Larry's nostrils flared. He shook his head and put the handgun on the desk.

"Larry, it won't hit me. You know it won't."

Savony recoiled like she'd been slapped. "It won't hit you? What're you talking about?"

"How many times have we been in enemy fire, Savony? How many times have I been hit, or even sustained an armor impact?"

Savony looked at him like he was speaking riskar.

Tayla tapped her chin a few times, thinking out loud. "You know...he's right. His ID signature has an infinity symbol by his name. That's a security clearance I've never even heard of." She cast suspicious eyes at Abraham. "I just thought you were related to someone and lied about it."

"You have me confused with our former commanding officer," Abraham deadpanned.

Larry picked up the handgun and handed it to Tayla.

"If you're so confident, put your tits where your mouth is."

Tayla took the weapon reluctantly. "This is stupid."

"It's not, though," Abraham insisted. "I can talk about it until I'm blue in the face, guys. Seeing is believing. The reason I have that clearance is because of what I can do. It's why I'm here. To get answers. I need you to believe me."

Abraham looked at each of them in turn. "All of you."

Larry laughed darkly. "You're completely insane, Abraham."

Savony shook her head. "This is the dumbest idea I've ever heard. Discharge a weapon in a dorm room to prove a point? Come on, Zeeben. I've seen you on the battlefield. You're crazy. But even you aren't stupid crazy."

Abraham approached Tayla and flicked the safety off the pistol.

"Come on. Trust me."

"You sure about this?" she asked, her face etched with indecision.

Abraham took a few steps back. "Of course I am. Just do it."

Tayla shrugged. She pointed the weapon at Abraham and pulled the trigger.

Savony screamed.

White hot pain bit into him just below his clavicle.

Abraham fell back onto his bed, too surprised to scream.

Momentum bounced him off the bed and onto the floor.

He turned his head to see Larry put a hand to his forehead and heave a sigh.

He smelled it before it he saw it.

Blood. The floor was blood.

Blood seeped from Abraham's back, pooling under his cheek.

"What the fuck!" Tayla cried, looking frantically from Abraham to Larry. "You said – he said – what the fuck?"

Savony shrieked, "Abraham, you dumbass!"

The room got very cold and dark. Abraham closed his eyes.

CHAPTER 8

Djet transitioned on foot from Destin's mag lift to the airship yard, still reeling from the bone-jarring launch and recovery that was the Accel/Decel Loop. The science was too much for her to comprehend, so she saved her brain power for thinking about Abraham Zeeben. And *not* thinking about Alan Piebold and his missing sister. She accepted the three days of administrative leave without pay as a small victory badge. It gave her some time to dig into her off-the-books investigation.

She intended to maximize every hour.

Great blimps sailed over the gray sky, every size and shape imaginable. Djet had grown up here, only spending the school terms away on Vatican. Destin was an industrious society, lead producer of metalworks for the human military. The population density was a little high, the economic standards on the lower end, but still above the poverty line. The only non-humans here were a small population of navites – short, furry bipeds with a knack for theft and a propensity to wear human hand-me-down clothes. Embedded in the metalworking force were a few Grand Pleiades, humanoids over two meters tall with pale skin stretched over physiques like the Greek gods of old, but they were few and far between.

Djet booked passage on an airship from the Interplanetary Transit Depot to the Third Ward. Her old stomping grounds. The teenage boy who worked the counter looked like a bag of skin and bones. She paid a generous tip, hoping the boy would use it for a meal for himself. Her Pulse updated with the registration code, which opened the gate to the loading ramp. She breathed in the sulphur and smog of the air, relishing the nostalgic miasma. It may have been subliminal and all in her head, but she could feel the contaminants swirling inside her lungs.

It gave her a heady sort of high.

Djet entered the airship cabin, holding her Pulse against her wrist with her offhand as she squeezed through a pack of navites. The instinct was a natural one. The chittering aliens didn't make an attempt to swipe it from her. They could tell a local with situational awareness from a clueless transient. She walked to the bow of the cabin and stood at the railing, staring out at the massive, interconnected plates of the First Ward. They reminded her of air vents she'd seen in every flat on Vatican. The same concept wrapped in a dome with the top cut off like a plateau, except for one swooped and angled wind-buffer that could be rotated to preserve the open-air top level of the city.

Abraham Zeeben was an itch she couldn't scratch.

He was on Vatican just two weeks and a day ago. Out of contact with

Vase for a week. Disappeared from the planet seven or eight days ago. That narrowed her search window considerably.

The longer she went without discovering anything, the harder it would be to find him.

Statistically, Djet should be looking for his body after the first forty-eight hours.

Her gut, the most important tool a detective had in their line of work, told her this case was an exception to the rule. It was something about the link Blaze had sent her. Something in that vid told her Abraham wasn't one to go looking for trouble. Or if he did, he was probably capable of handling himself.

So the question of *where he was* could be answered by first discovering *why he left*.

This was why she needed to speak to her father. The grizzled old Longarm Chief would have much better insight into a case of this nature. He'd worked dozens of disappearances over the years.

She took a seat near the railing, the open-air deck affording her a splendid view of the industrial architecture below. In less than an hour she'd be back home.

Always a bittersweet feeling, going back to see her mother.

Ksara greeted her with a loud clanging of a pan on the stove and the shuffling of feet across carpet.

The door opened to an old woman with gray-streaked hair who greeted her with a powerful hug. The wafting scent of shrimp jambalaya and jerk-spiced chicken spilled out of the condo.

"Totti, it's so good to see ya!" Her mother looked down the walkway, left and right, then released the hug. "No man wit ya this time, either, huh?"

Djet slipped past her mother and entered the conjoined living room and kitchen. She plopped down on the fuchsia sectional, eyes roaming over pistachio-colored drapes framing the windows and red end tables. The walls were stained a pallid yellow from her father's constant hookah use. The device, like a miniature medieval tower, dominated the red plastic coffee table. A nicotine cake rested on the top, fresh and unburned.

"Fatti hasn't returned yet?" she asked.

"He's on his way. Ya know your Fatti, he thinks himself too important to ever be on time."

Djet laughed. "That's him, ya."

“So,” her mother drawled, stirring a cloud of pleasant-smelling steam from the pot, “how’s the job?”

Djet scooted back and forth to sink further into the couch, taking comfort more in the nostalgia than in the actual material. It stuck to the skin on the back of her neck, but she ignored it.

“Job’s fine, Mutti. I got to talk wit Vase the other day.”

The lack of response from the kitchen was expected.

Djet drove the wedge further, elaborating on how Vase still looked the same at twenty-three as she did when she was sixteen. That it would take more than combat and a rogue lover to put wrinkles on a woman like that. It was a delightful irony, and a double entendre at that; Ksara hated her daughter’s lack of interest in men. While Vase didn’t return Djet’s affections, her barbed remarks toward her mother was a passive aggressive tick that served no purpose but to pull Djet into an emotional tug of war between the humor of chafing her mother and the unscratched itch that was Vase Seneca.

The table was set and the cooking finished when Djet finally gave up the charade and let the room dissolve into silence.

As if that was his calling card, Warin Rincon entered the flat.

“Fatti, ya late!” The couch made a suction noise when she bolted up to her feet and crushed the old man in a hug.

He smelled of hookah and vermillion spice. Probably had a late lunch. The smell was from a fast-food joint somewhere in the First Ward. He returned the hug, took a step back to look Djet up and down.

“Oh, Totti, ya been slinging the iron, ya? Lookit ya, prime state of a proud longarm if I ever seen one!”

Djet relished the pride her father took in her following in his footsteps. She batted her eyelashes and let out a rolling gut laugh.

“Blaze has been telling me to slow it down. He says I have to eat a horse for dinner every day to stay as built as I am.”

Warin guffawed. “Blaze is still kicking? The grizzled old bastard ought to be retired by now.”

Warin dropped his briefcase on the counter and seated himself at the table. He slapped both palms on the table and said in an elevated voice, “Ksara, the man of the house is starving!”

Djet seated herself across from him. Tiny twitches in her nerves were building. It was all she could do to stay still. She wanted to launch right into a tirade over the events in the flat. Dispel any rumors that may have circulated up to her father about her being a screw-up. The way he had greeted her suggested he hadn’t been told anything.

Hopefully that was a good sign.

Ksara bumbled into the dining area, steam and delicious vapors of shrimp and expertly spiced chicken commingling about her. She set the food down on the table, placed one hand on her hip and hefted a serving spoon in Warin's direction.

"Now, Warin, I know ya ain't gonna be sassing the madame of the kitchen in her own house, ya? So ya eat ya food and be grateful. So starving is ya that Mutti didn't even get a hello kiss?"

Warin groaned facetiously and half stood to plant a kiss on her cheek.

"Plate it up, woman!" he said with a devilish grin.

Ksara slapped a mound of jumbalaya on his plate, grumbling in a good-natured sort of way.

Djet's chest felt warm and soft. She could feel a tenderness behind her mother's eyes. Not the kind that would cause tears; the kind that left light-ringed memories in the mind. This was a great moment. There had been several dinners just like this one, but something about the family being together after her near-death experience in the flat made this one extra special to her.

Once the food was served and they were well into devouring it, Djet thought the pleasantries had been observed long enough. She swallowed a zesty bite of chicken – Mutti always used the perfect balance of zing and sweet – and waved her fork at her father to get his attention.

"Fatti, I got a question for ya."

Ksara frowned. "Not at the table, Totti. Shop talk is for the patio. Why don't ya tell me something good that happened to ya today, instead?"

Djet scowled. "No, Mutti, this is important. I need advice on a case I'm working."

Ksara glared at Warin, who intentionally did not look over at her.

"Go on then, Totti. Let's hear it."

Djet, consciously aware of her mother's eye-rolling, spilled the whole story. Everything about the flat, Blaze nearly dying, how she filed her report – truthfully – how she was on administrative leave following the incident. She glossed over the part where she was trapped in the room with an alien grenade, but made sure to hammer home the point that Blaze had her back about the report, as a good partner should.

She had just gotten to the part about the video her partner had sent her when Warin held up a hand to stop her.

"Djet," he said, face soured like he'd ate some bad chicken, "if this is about an off-the-books case, we need to take this to the patio."

Ksara was already taking her and Warin's empty plates to the kitchen. With her back turned, Djet couldn't read her mother's reaction.

"Sure thing, Fatti."

The smoke from the hookah smelled like turpentine. Her father used grain alcohol in place of water to cover the bottom of the bowl. The odor from the steam made Djet's eyes water. It had been well over three months since she'd last smoked one of these things, and now her lungs and eyes screamed with each puff.

Djet held her thumb over her hose to preserve the suction.

Warin took a drag on his accordion hose, then covered it with his own thumb. Cloudy tendrils of mist escaped his nostrils as he stared over the balcony. The streets were lined with lanterns that popped to life as the orange sky succumbed to the gray of twilight. Djet watched him for a few moments, until the peaceful milieu was swallowed in a cloud of acrid gas as Warin exhaled.

Five minutes of total silence followed. Warin pursed his lips a few times, working himself up to say something he clearly did not want to.

"Lookit heeya, Djet," her father said, not looking at her, nor gesturing with his hands – a thing he did only when he was being deadly serious – "I ain't no saint. Ya know that."

Djet refrained from taking another hit of the hookah. Her eyes were still watering from the first.

"Ya, I know that. But Fatti, I need to tell ya –"

Warin nodded, eyes fixated on the orange-becoming-gray glow on the horizon. Something in his gaze stole the words from her before she could say them.

"Good." A hollow smirk spread across his face. "So I'll tell ya the story of what I saw. I'll tell ya what I did, and why I have to do the tings I do now. And, där," he placed a hand on hers and gave a gentle squeeze, "ya *will* think differently of me after this."

Djet squeezed his hand. She could have told him no, she wouldn't, but she didn't want to lie to him. There was an unspoken rule in their relationship, one that had been in place as long as she could remember. It was the *honesty and trust are paramount* rule, and she had never deviated from it. Was he worried about telling her this because he had violated that rule? Or was it just something he was embarrassed about, like rookie mistakes?

Fear turned a knot in her gut. She did not like seeing her father this disconcerted. It was starting to make *her* disconcerted. She hated that just as much.

"All right. So. The incident on Singularity. Ya remember?"

Djet nodded.

"I was called in to investigate. I was new to the longarms. They wanted an 'impartial inquiry', is what they called it. I got cleared, briefed, and read in on some tings I still wish I didn't know. I ain't telling you all that stuff, that's not what this is. I am telling you that I did not get to investigate *shit*. Not until much, much later in my career."

"What're ya saying? That the longarms were contracted to give a clean report when that wasn't the case?"

"I'm saying that they pulled me in – a detective so green I hadn't even completed a case – and had me write up a report the way they wanted me to. Unofficially, I saw more than I should have. I did more than I should have. But all those findings stayed with me and my partner."

"Larson? Your first partner who..." She didn't say 'committed suicide'. Just let her words die off, because she didn't need to speak them aloud.

He nodded.

"Djet, där, I don't want you in the longarms anymore. I don't want you trying to tie up my loose ends."

Djet stiffened. Her father was telling her something. But why was he being so cryptic? And what the hell did any of this have to do with a question she hadn't even asked yet?

"No, no, Fatti, I'm not getting myself in over my head, here. I take after you, not Mutti. I'm ready to do great tings, just like you. Ya been rambling so long, I didn't even get to ask ya advice!"

Warin produced a small notepad, lifted the top sheet without tearing it, and slipped his pulse underneath it. He pulled the sheet back down over the pulse, produced an ink pen from his pocket and clicked it. Whatever this was, he was taking extreme precaution to make sure it didn't transfer a depression onto the pages beneath. He scrawled over the paper for a few seconds, tore the sheet and held it up for her to see. It was a shape. A symbol. Djet had been through the recognized gang symbols in the Third Watch database a hundred times in her line of work, but this symbol jumped out at her for two reasons: it wasn't in the database, and she had seen it before.

It was on the neck of the man she killed.

It was on the crate in the back of the yellow sky puncher.

"Fatti...what is this?"

His eyes were wide, his lips a tight, thin line. He shook his head but shoved the paper to her.

"That's a question for ya friend, Totti." He squeezed her hand, so tight her joints creaked. "And only for her. Do *not* get caught with this, ya understand?"

Her throat was dry. The spices from the meal were suddenly irritating her esophagus. Reflux chewed at her stomach. This was new territory for her, seeing her father this disturbed. For the hundredth time since that last conversation with Vase, Djet found herself asking the same question.

What the hell is going on?

"Of course," she told her father, though she did not understand why it was necessary.

"Good." He slapped his knee and stood. "Now let's get in there and visit with your Mutti a little while before you go."

Djet stood, grateful to be abandoning the hookah. It was hitting her a lot harder than she was used to, and she feared any more would make her throw up. Something clenched her gut, but it wasn't the hookah. She had one more question for her father.

"Fatti…?" she asked in a small voice. The voice of a child who had just woken from a nightmare and wanted to be told everything was going to be okay. She hated herself for it, but she couldn't stop herself.

He smiled at her.

"Do you know anything about the Ghost Society?"

The smile faded. Maybe it was never there in the first place.

He placed a hand on her shoulder and held her gaze with sad eyes.

"Djet, där," he said with a sigh, "don't ask questions you already know the answer to."

CHAPTER 9

Abraham tried to open his eyes. He winced at the intense fluorescent lighting. A chill gripped him on the inside, like ice water flowing through his veins. Disinfectant, or something like it, stung his nostrils. A steady beep close by told him he was in the medical wing. The bed creaked when he tried to sit up.

"He's up." Smithers' voice.

Where...

Oh yeah. I told someone to shoot me. And they did.

"Good. I was worried," Myles replied. It was strange, recognizing the voice of someone you thought was dead.

It wasn't supposed to work that way, though. Why didn't my gravity shield come up?

Am I broken? Did I use it up?

"Worried?" Smithers grunted next to Myles.

"We spent a lot of time and money bringing him in. And his friends." Myles' C-skin crinkled with a shrug. "It'd be fraud, waste and abuse if he died before we learned anything about him."

Smithers chuckled. "You're right about that, Agent Lannam."

Abraham fluttered his eyelids until, by degrees, he was able to peer around through a determined squint. Smithers was standing at the edge of the bed with his arms folded in front of him. It was the same pose of his old drill instructor, Staff Sergeant Hinton. He'd always stand like that, his death stare meticulously examining recruits for the smallest flaw. If he found one, that statuesque pose would transform into a bone-chilling knife hand and a thorough dressing down straight from the diaphragm.

Guilt washed over him.

Bloodstained glass. The face of a legend, twisted in pain.

I'm dyin' here...Ain't nothing changing that.

The whine of an alien weapon. The flash and the crack of glass penetrating bone.

The loudest sigh...

"Zeeben," Myles stepped up to the edge of the bed. His blonde hair so pale it was almost gray. "You feeling better?"

Abraham shrugged the memory away. He grimaced at the pain, dull and throbbing. Probably kept at a distance by whatever cocktail was being piped through the tube embedded in his arm.

"That will serve as a yes," Smithers offered. "I had expected competitiveness amongst the candidates, but I did not foresee attempted murder. At least, not this early."

Myles glanced at the heartbeat monitor with a frown.

"Try to relax." He turned his Ghost-Bar-covered eyes to Abraham. "We already have the story from your cohorts. I don't need to hear what happened. I need to hear you explain *why* it happened. Rather, why *nothing* happened."

At least, Abraham thought, it had been Tayla that shot him. If Larry opted for it, the bullet would have found its way into his skull and the lights would have never come back on.

"I don't know how to answer that," Abraham said. "You guys seem to know more about me than I do."

Smithers nodded. "That's partly why you're here. We're going to get to the bottom of your family history, but we need to have the conversation about your…abilities, now."

Abraham scoffed. A pressure was developing inside, below his intestines.

"Great. I can't get five minutes to take a piss?"

A trickling sounded from behind his head.

Abraham turned to see a triangular vial bubbling with yellow liquid. He followed the line from the top of the glass, where it routed underneath the blanket draped over his hips and legs.

Red hot embarrassment stained his face.

"You guys put a catheter in me?"

Smithers smiled.

"You did it personally, didn't you?"

Smithers balked at that. "Of course not."

Myles pulled a Portal out of the pants pocket of his mirror-black C-skin and swiped a window into the air between them.

"If you guys are done flirting, I'd like to go over this sooner rather than later. The dining facility closes in forty-one minutes."

Silence descended upon the room like a light being dimmed.

Myles swiped at the air. The window shifted from Abraham's vital signs, all nominal, to a double helix of many colors. Myles' pale fingers touched two strands and expanded them.

"These are the abnormalities in your genome, Abraham. You have about twenty-one percent riskar DNA. The rest is human. Nothing out of the ordinary."

"That's it?" Abraham asked.

"Yes," Myles said. "So the obvious question is, how well did you know your parents?"

Abraham fell inside himself, like a sea creature seeking refuge in its shell. He didn't know how to answer it. His whole life, the seventeen years prior to the military, he thought he'd known his life story. His father was a successful architect on Milune. His mother was the daughter of a jeweler.

His parents had met at a Christmas party two years before he was born. Judging by appearances alone, Obadiah and Kellina were both undeniably human. Weighing all of this, he realized he had no reason to lie.

"I don't have the answers."

"That's not good enough," Smithers said.

It happened slowly, but when it lit off, it was a lightning strike:

A drop of cold water rippled in his gut. It spread like the surface of a freezing lake, tendrils of pain and anger knifing into his nerves. So quickly it bloomed that it completely ensnared him before he could recognize it.

Before he could control it.

Abraham ripped the IV out of his arm. Blood spurted from his inner elbow.

He ripped the catheter off, grateful it was a condom-style, planted his feet on the cold tiles of the floor and kicked his bed against the wall. Standing there clothed in nothing but pure rage, he charged at Smithers, going for the throat.

A wave of red light slammed into his chest. His back hit the bulkhead, forcing the wind out of his lungs. He collapsed to his knees and fists, panting. The room was swirling around him. The drugs in his system teemed with the swirling. He felt like the fluid in his body was operating at high tide, eroding his sense of space.

The wound by his collar bone burned. A trickle of fresh blood seeped through the bandage, tracing his ribs to patter on the floor beside him.

"Don't do that again." Smithers wiped imaginary dust from his shoulders.

It happened without conscious thought. A pulse of red anti-gravity billowed out from Abraham. He could see the distortion before him, like a heatwave. Smithers was lifted off his feet and thrown into the bulkhead four meters back. He was pinned to the wall, feet half a meter off the deck.

"Abraham!" Smithers said through gritted teeth. "Put me down."

The click of the gun in his ear didn't register until he felt the barrel against his skull.

"Abraham," Myles said in a soft voice, "stop. We'll figure this out, I promise."

"How?" he growled, spit collecting at his lower lip. "How are you going to figure it out, Myles? You can't tell me my parents weren't human. Or that I'm not their son. I wasn't fucking adopted, I wasn't *stolen*. I'm not a fucking lab experiment, as much as you want to make me one!"

Smithers' boots hit the deck. He did a good job of acting like he knew it was coming, barely moving his hands to balance himself.

"Okay." Myles lowered the handgun and holstered it to his magnetic belt. "Now we can talk."

He picked up a pair of PT shorts and threw them on the floor.

"After you're dressed."

Abraham pulled the shorts on and spent a few minutes in the lavatory splashing water on his face.

The blood had clotted on his arm, but the throbbing was getting worse. A purple and black bruise had shown up already, but he couldn't take his eyes off his reflection.

The stubble on his cheeks and chin, the longer hair, the paleness that was already starting to show on his skin...he had been in Ghost control for less than a week and he already didn't recognize himself. He peeled the bandage off his shoulder. It crackled and tugged at the wound, but once he removed it, he saw a slit across the bullet hole.

They had to dig it out, he realized.

He let the bandage fall to the floor. There was still some dried blood on one of his feet. He looked in the mirror and followed the trail up his left side, over his ribs to the wound near his clavicle. He spent a few moments scraping it off with a fingernail, washing the remnants away in the sink. A knock at the door stopped him from finishing the job.

He hustled over to it and hit the panel.

The door slid open. Larry was standing in front of him, looking sheepish.

"Hey, buddy. You doing all right?" He scratched the back of his head.

Abraham nodded. "Yeah. What do you want?"

Larry leaned in. "Look, Tayla's upset about this whole thing. She's around the corner. We just want to make sure you're doing all right."

"You care how I'm doing, Larry? You sure about that?"

Larry's eyebrows drew together. "Look, Abraham, you're not my favorite person in the world, but I don't hate you. You're still my best friend."

Abraham shook his head. He couldn't stop the ill-bore smile from painting his face incredulous.

"Larry, I'm you're *only* friend. You think anyone else would put up with your moping around for this long?"

"Abraham, I –"

"No. Stop. You're my best friend, Larry, but that hasn't stopped you from being a whiny bitch. I'm tired of babying you. I didn't kill Amory, Larry. I put her out of her misery. Because she *wanted* me to."

Larry's face froze at the mention of her name.

And then it melted. Not into a blubbering cascade of tears. Not sobs and hugs and collapsing into a wet puddle of emotion. He wilted like a tree that had gone without water for months. His face sagged and his shoulders rocked with an explosive sigh.

"I know."

Abraham put a hand on his shoulder. "You know I didn't want to do it."

"I know."

"Then look at me and tell me this is over. Whatever the hell..." Abraham waved a hand, "*this* is. We're in uncharted territory here, Larry. We have to look out for each other. You know I have your back. I've held you up. I've carried you this far. I need to know you got my back, too."

Larry nodded, his gaze fixated on Abraham's wound.

"Larry. Look at me."

Larry made eye contact, and it was the look Abraham had been looking for ever since he plunged that dagger into a young woman's skull four years ago.

Understanding. Shared pain.

Forgiveness.

"I know all this, Abraham. I just...I miss her, you know? It's fucked up."

"It is fucked up. *We're* fucked up. But we have to move on, or her sacrifice doesn't mean anything. You know that, too, right? She died so we could get out of there. It's not the way anyone wanted it, but it's the way it had to be."

Larry nodded.

Tayla appeared behind him, her hands crossed in front of her. Her short, trim body was completely at odds with the little girl mannerisms that saw her tuck a lock of hair behind her ear and clear her throat.

"ParTerre, don't bother apologizing," Abraham said. "I'll live. You did what I told you to. No hard feelings."

As if she had been holding her breath, Tayla exhaled, long and low. "Oh, okay." A moment later, she added, "So, uh, what now?"

Abraham walked back to his bed and plopped down in it. He waved them in. Savony joined them from the hallway.

"Now," he said, "we're going to get interviewed by the Ghosts, and I have to come up with an explanation for why I am the way I am. Problem is, I've got no fucking clue what's going on."

Savony said, "We could start with asking you questions. Interview you about your childhood. Treat it like The Collision simulation. Maybe you're overlooking something."

Tayla nodded. "Yeah, something that someone who isn't you would be able to figure out."

Abraham sighed. They were right.

That didn't mean he wanted to do it this way.

Between the girls' shoulders, he saw Smithers in the hallway, leaning against the door jamb.

He took a deep breath to fight the ripple of goosebumps that assailed him. He started with the ice cream on Milune. He told of the fire in the sky. The screams of people dying as buildings collapsed. He stumbled over the part of his mother dying in a flash, of seeing the Shadow Man with the glowing red hand –

"Bro," Savony cut him off. "You saw a dude with a red hand? Didn't you say that you seeing red means gravity manipulation?"

"Yeah. And clearly this Shadow Man was a Ghost. I've put that much together. But he was pushing Dajun away when –"

Tayla chimed in. "Pushing it away? How could one person have enough power to move an entire moon, Abraham? That sounds impossible."

Larry slammed his fist on the table. Everyone turned to look at him.

"Did you have something to add, Poplenko?" Tayla asked.

"That beam of light. The one in the news clip. Did you see it, Abraham?"

Did he? He tried to remember.

"Yes. Didn't you?"

Larry played the simulation and the news clip side-by-side at one quarter speed. The beam appeared on the surface of Milune, inching its way up to Dajun in both clips, as far as Abraham was concerned. The moment it touched Dajun, the forest moon began its descent.

"Girls?" Larry asked.

"I'm only seeing it in the simulation," Tayla said.

Savony wrinkled her brow. "Same."

Lead dropped in Abraham's gut.

Rictor was right.

Larry nodded emphatically. "You know what this means."

Abraham's throat was dry.

Tayla's mouth hung agape.

Savony breathed, "The riskar..."

Abraham interjected, "Didn't do it. The Ghosts caused The Collision."

Savony crossed her arms. A creak issued from her teeth grinding.

"And we sold our soul to 'em."

CHAPTER 10

Djet stood outside the docking yard of the *Veritas*, her father's symbol etched in her mind. She had, of course, followed his paranoid instructions to the letter, but that didn't do anything to dissuade the nagging feeling she had that something terribly sinister was at work, and that her father knew about it. She'd committed the symbol to memory, shredded and burned the scrap of paper her father had given her. Standard procedure for destroying classified materials.

The open hangar showed the endless sea of stars that stretched out to forever and beyond. Starlight wasn't anywhere to be seen. It was the middle of the night in Dominicus Venti. Pale LED lighting cast a pall over the bulkheads of the docking bay like a permanent snapshot of a lightning strike. She leaned back against the maintenance crew lockers, trying to ignore the gritty odor of grease, electrical burn and musty body odor.

It ain't me, she thought with a sniff. *Damn mechanics, I guess.*

She didn't have to wait long enough for the smell to make her nauseous. The ramp to the stealth ship slid open and Vase stepped out far enough to wave. She was in her C-skin, the pattern dialed in to a blue smear of pixelated light that pulsed every few seconds.

"Come in," she said.

Djet stepped up the ramp, her boots making less sound on the ramp than she felt they should. The inside of the ship made her think of the inner workings of an environment plate on Destin. Nothing had been painted with any kind of aesthetic. It was designed to be a very difficult ship for enemies to board. She passed through a labyrinthine pathway with constant turns that defied any kind of logic. She could see seams in the wall panels, but no way to open them. Every ten paces she crossed the threshold of an open airlock.

Holy shit, she thought. *This ship is impregnable.*

"Fancy assignment you have here, Vase."

Vase shrugged. She didn't speak again until they were in her quarters. It was a large space for a ship, twelve meters by twelve, with a desk pulled out of the wall at one end, and a bed at the other. Djet felt a jolt of electricity run through her heart when she saw the bed was big enough for two. She blushed, as if Vase might read her thoughts.

"What've you got?"

She took the chair at the desk. Vase sat on the bed.

"All business, ya?"

Vase pulled her hair back into a ponytail but kept her eyes on Djet. There was something there. Something Djet's instincts told her was fear. A tightness at the corners of her eyes. Vase's breathing was shallow, but soft. She was definitely scared, but was it fear of being caught with a longarm on her ship, or did she already know what Djet was going to ask?

"All business, then," Djet said after a moment of silence. "I found something, but I don't know where to go from here. This whole thing is off the books, but the trail I'm on has the potential to open up a can of shit we can't close. It's gonna get out at some point. Knowing that doesn't change anything for ya, though, does it?"

Vase shook her head. "You know it doesn't."

Djet leaned back in the chair, rested a forearm on the desk.

"Ya got paper in here, somewhere?"

She pulled out a notepad and pen from the desk, drew the symbol her father had provided her. The same one that Blaze had seen on the man she'd killed in flat 201. When she showed it to Vase, the lack of recognition was telling. If it had been a shock, Vase was damn good at covering it with a blank stare.

"What is this?" she asked, innocence in her tone setting off alarms for Djet.

Djet handed her the paper, studying Vase as she studied the symbol.

"That's what I wanted to ask ya. I'm not one for conspiracies, Vase. Stakes have raised. I was doing this as a favor for ya, but now I have my own reasons for doing this."

Vase bit her lip. Djet smiled.

"It's...not something I'm supposed to talk about."

Djet let her voice drop to barely more than a whisper. She leaned forward on the chair.

"Whatever that is, my father thinks it's related to your lost soul. I never seen a reaction like this from him before. What could this thing be that my Fatti drew it on paper? Why is the damn *Chief of the Longarms* too scared to draw it on his Portal, Vase?"

Vase gently took the pad and pen from Djet, looked at it for a moment, then promptly dumped both items into the shipboard recycler as if they were contaminated with an infectious disease. They were atomized in moments, but the sound was sealed away in the heavy plating of the ship. She patted the bed beside her.

"Sit."

Djet's chest fluttered. She complied, sitting on the firm cushion of the mattress. She wrapped an arm around Vase's waist, struggling to keep her focus on the questions she was asking and not on the smell of Vase's hair. The pull this woman had on her was supernatural.

"Look," Vase turned and took Djet's hands in hers. "I know how you feel about me. I don't want to talk about it. You know why. But I'm here for you in every other way you need me."

Djet closed off her emotions. Her face must have shown this, because Vase wrapped her arms around her and rested her cheek against hers. She whispered with intensity, a sound barely audible even in the stark quiet of the shipboard environment.

"Pathfinders. Destin, Third Ward. The green door. Start there."

Djet rubbed her hand on Vase's back, her breath heating up. It was a cruel torture. But it was more than that. It wasn't Vase trying to entice her into doing what she wanted. It was Vase apologizing for getting Djet involved in something that could very likely end with her body in the streetside recycling gutter. She savored the moment, an equilibrium of love and hate so intense it was like warm summer rain falling from a clear sky.

Djet pulled out her Pulse, the one she'd dropped an entire paycheck to have hacked.

"This is slaved to only one other Pulse." She let the irony slip between her teeth as she broke the embrace and stood to leave. "I'll be in touch."

Djet reported into the precinct on time, irritated that she had to work when her off-the-books case had completely derailed her focus and embroiled her in something even more complex. She walked the halls to the briefing room, ignoring co-workers, not seeing the gold and black digital paint on the walls or the pictures of the chain of command with her father at the second highest position, only under Thessaly Coup De, Madame Executor of Vatican. She wanted to interview Thalex, the kid who got his ass kicked by Abraham and his buddies. She needed to get back to Destin and check out that green door lead Vase had given her.

For now, she needed to report to work. Everything else would have to wait.

This was the first time she'd been on administrative leave without pay. The stares she got when she waltzed into the detective briefing room was a new feeling. Everyone seemed surprised that she would even return to work after filing that report.

Djet owned it with a smile. On the outside, anyway. Inside, she was fighting against the feeling of coming apart at the seams. Thoughts battled in her head.

I didn't leave toothpaste stains on my pants today, right? – Are they laughing at me, or are they proud I stood my ground? – Am I going to get my ass ripped in front of the whole room? – Neal is staring at my ass again – Why is that light still not fixed? – I'm pretty sure –

"Detective Rincon, take a seat."

Captain Barica Spitzen stood at the head of the room. Djet blushed and headed to the open seat next to Blaze. He was sitting back in his chair, hands behind his head. The look on his face was boredom. Just another cop ready to get a dressing down. He'd seen it a million times over the years, or so his demeanor suggested.

Djet took some small relief in that.

"Stick it out, sister," Blaze whispered into the back of his hand.

The room was in a stranglehold. It was so quiet she could hear Blaze breathing next to her.

Captain Spitzen clapped her hands together once, commanding attention.

"Everyone's here, so no need to take roll. We're still looking into the situation in flat two zero one, but that's been elevated to our Special Interest Investigators, so this department has officially washed our hands of it."

She paused, staring laser beams at Djet.

Djet rocked her shoulders to let out some tension but kept her face straight.

"Now that that's understood, I'm moving to our first order of business. We have had more reports of petty crimes in the dockyards in Dominicus Dorsi. Seems that the local gangs are using the high traffic area as a cover for their deals. Densin and Elyria will take that assignment. Gibbons and his team are still investigating the possible suicide in the Business Square. The rest of you have open cases, so pursue them with all due diligence. I'll need to see Rincon and Sisneros after. Dismissed."

The detectives filed out in a hurry. No one wanted to linger behind to hear Djet get dressed down. She felt that was a pretty good sign of respect, if nothing else. Once the room was cleared and they were alone, Djet settled in for the rant she knew was coming.

"Welcome back, Detective Rincon."

"Thanks, ma'am...?"

The captain stood over the edge of the desk. Her knuckles turned white. The ceramic creaked under her fingers.

"I don't want to have to say this twice. You will follow established policies and procedures. You will uphold the tasks placed upon you from here on out, or you will be fired. Is that clear?"

Djet bit her lip, wished she hadn't, then pulled her teeth off it. Her lips were dry.

"Crystal."

Spitzen tapped a few times on her Portal, lips moving but not speaking as she thought her way through whatever it was she was doing. After a moment, she swiped up and Djet's Portal chimed.

"Those are your new operating instructions. You are not to do anything without your partner observing. Your newfound disdain for authority has you on the babysitting program. Abide by those regulations for a few months and we'll revisit your lack of loyalty. Maybe even forgive you."

Djet felt the anger in her clenched teeth tight enough to make her jaw ache.

Blaze patted her on the back.

"Good to know you're still with us, sister."

Spitzen pocketed her Portal and clapped her hands together.

"Unless there's something else?"

Djet shook her head.

"Good. Now get to fucking work."

"We aren't supposed to discuss what happened, you know."

Djet inhaled some of the residual butter-waffle fumes from her partner's exhaled hit. Back in the longarm sky runner, staking out another drug trafficking area...she was excited to still have a job, but the frustration threatened to sour that sentiment. She had never considered herself one to take on the system, but now she found herself at the bottom of a barrel, drowning in shit. Blaze trying to comfort her was somehow only making it worse.

"We're gonna talk about it or I'm turning in my badge right now."

Blaze smiled, salt and pepper stubble crinkling as his face stretched. He leaned back in the seat, tapping his knuckles on the window. The view beyond him was a bustling throng of people and aliens stopping by luggage carousels or frequenting the merchant stands. The smells of so many different foods blended into a grease-tinged assault on the sinuses. It was a far cry from the comfort of Destin.

"I thought ya was dead, Blaze."

The old man chuckled. "I still got a few tricks up my sleeve, Djet. Your father taught me a great many things. Surviving was one of them. Grenade-proof vents required by district code in all living areas was another."

"So what happened when ya went in there? Ya saw a grenade and ya dove for cover?"

"I'd rather talk about the vid I sent you. What did you make of it?"

Djet let him dodge her questions. Blaze was old, and he probably didn't have much of a mind for a younger detective blasting him with questions that would seem obvious to a veteran like himself. Still, she made a mental note to bring it up to him at another time. He wasn't going to get out of this without explaining himself to her.

"You ever heard of the Pathfinders?"

Blaze recoiled like he'd been punched.

"Are we talking about the same vid, here, sister?"

She shook her head.

"The man I shot had a tattoo on his neck. It was a symbol for some group that calls themselves Pathfinders. I talked with Captain Seneca about this, and she confirmed it. My Fatti drew that same symbol. He knew it – knew what it was, and he was scared of it. Who the hell are these people?"

Blaze put a hand on her hand. Physical contact between them was such a rarity, it actually stopped Djet's vocal spewing like a valve cranked to off. The stare in his dark eyes was deep.

"Djet, the Pathfinders are the worst kept secret society in space. Everyone knows about them, apparently except for you. What a lot of people don't know, and the part that makes them scared to talk about them, is that they aren't an exclusively human group."

Djet kept her expression flat. He wasn't telling her any earth-shattering news, here.

Blaze paused to take a drag on his vape, exhaling sweet clouds of mist into the cabin.

"Look," he said, tapping the window again, "there's a reason we share and trade technology but don't integrate species for the most part. Especially in a scientific capacity. When science types get together and start looking into what makes organic life tick, it always leads to the same end. Comparing and contrasting at first, experimentation next. Some things just shouldn't be done."

Djet felt a wave of panic wash over her. She was beginning to understand now.

"They're doing gene splicing?"

Blaze shrugged. His lack of eye contact all but confirmed it. But how could he know?

"No one on the outside of that organization knows for sure. But there's a long, tired history of such things. You just have to know where to look."

"Un-fucking-believable."

"Right?" He gave a wicked smile. "Eugenics and the like have been a big problem for us as a people for a long time. I don't know if you can feel it or not, girl, but there's a big push by certain groups to get the ball rolling. There's three sides to this thing. The people who want it, the people who don't, and the people who can't be bothered to pick a side. I let the Liberty House sort out the politics, but this isn't going away."

Djet bit her lip. "What are you saying? There's gonna be a war? Between who, the military and the Pathfinders?"

Blaze shrugged, took a hit from his vape stick.

"I'm not saying anything. Just thinking out loud."

"There hasn't been a civil war in...a thousand years? The Liberty House may be corrupt, but they at least know enough to keep humans from killing each other. Most territories are settled, Blaze. Any disputes are interspecies, and that's not going away. My Fatti always said the two tings people will always fight about is territory and money."

Blaze nodded. "Yeah, your old man is wise to say that. I'm too old for this shit, Djet."

She leaned forward. "Oh, yeah?"

Blaze nodded. "I might as well tell you now. I'm retiring."

Djet blinked. She knew her partner couldn't work forever, but she thought he still had a few more years in him. A pang of regret hit her stomach. If she knew he was calling it quits this soon, she would have been nicer to him.

"Shit, Blaze. Ya serious?"

"It's time." He stared into the distance. "Well past time."

Djet sat back. She didn't know what to say.

"I saved myself a nest egg, you know, after things didn't work out with my old girl. I'll spend a few years on Sepipira, and then...who knows?" He laughed.

"And then," Djet said with an ironic edge to her voice, "you'll have to figure out what to do with all the illegitimate children you produced over those years."

"Sepipira is more than just strippers and casinos," he said defensively.

Djet waved a hand dismissively. "Nah, not much more."

They shared a laugh.

The orange and yellow haze of the sky was obscured with thick, acrid layers of smoke.

The air tasted hot and metallic, a hallmark of Destin's metalworks industry. The skyline to the south and west was lined with thick smokestacks from the refineries and smelting plants on the lower levels. Due to the unpredictable and near-constant high winds, most of the cities looked like a bastardization of man-made plateaus and incomplete buildings. Girders and beams ran in an endless array that looked like prison bars, or a giant bird cage. Two plates per section made for three layers of infrastructure, the first being on ground level and reserved for the mining, refining, and other forms of metallurgy. Living spaces and shops were on the second level, sporting arenas and airship launch pads on the uppermost level.

Djet stepped down the platform at the edge of the MagLev drop-off station and turned the corner to the airbus ticket counter. Atop the slate tiles of the ticket stand, a thin metal pole protruded a few meters up, a purple sock dangling limp at the top of the pole. As she glanced at it, the same way someone might look at a clock in a public square on any other world, a vesper surged forth, whipping her hair. The purple sock stretched out its wrinkles and changed direction from north to north-northwest. She stopped walking and grabbed a handrail by the edge of the MagLev drop-off, saw others doing the same.

A speaker system clicked to life and a gritty voice boomed.

"Third Ward, wind direction shift. Zero three. Repeat: wind direction is now zero three, prepare for plate shift."

Djet heard a series of gravelly shouts from the control dock next to the station. The ground shook under her feet. Pneumatic thundering like a jackhammer started pounding away on the inner drive tube of the plate; she could feel the slamming pistons as the gears churned and locked, churned and locked. The metal clanking became a groan, and the sky began to slowly move in front of her.

It wasn't really the sky moving, though. It was the Third Ward's upper level. At an elevation of about ten thousand feet, the upper level was exposed to the pervasive wind streams that blew across Destin; the planet was smaller, newer. At least when speaking relative to the universe's timeline of billions of years. New planets spin faster than old ones, and Destin was no exception; the days and nights were about six hours a piece, which led to the Destin schedule: workers put in a twelve-hour shift, one full day and night, and then got one day off, another twelve hours of downtime. This was how Djet encountered life, until she moved to Vatican where there was no downtime. That terra-city was operating at peak activity all day and all night no matter what.

The Third Ward plate rotated into the wind. A large lip, like a mountain with the front and middle carved out, was repositioned to block the gale-force gusts. The wind roared into the lip and was diverted around and over it. Coils of black smoke acted as tracers for the wind path, carving sinuous lines across the sky.

The PA system sounded a tone for five seconds, and then a voice said, "Plate shift complete. Repeat: plate shift complete."

Everyone let go of the handrails and resumed their travels.

Djet did the same, got into the line for the underside of the Third Ward plate. Up top was a nice view, but the shops and the businesses were underneath the plate. She grew up there, on the Third Ward. She inhaled the oil and smoke until her skin tingled. This place, as underdeveloped as it seemed after spending time on Vatican, would always be her home.

One by one the people in front of her stepped onto the covered escalator. She checked her Portal twice, starting to get impatient until it was her turn. She rode the escalator down and entered the market level of the Third Ward. The streets were a perfect grid, designed long ago by studious workmen who favored right angles, and with extra thought given to gainfully employing every bit of real estate. Every room was occupied, every sales stand staffed and packed with trinkets; purses and knick-knacks, pots and pans and blades ranging from simple pocket-knives to hand-forged longswords. Djet grew up with a fascination for blades, although her father had always coached her that they were tools rather than weapons.

She passed all these stands, including a few food stands that sold some savory spiced meats, one in particular lathered in a dark sauce that tempted her, but she reminded herself why she was here. It wasn't a vacation to visit her family, and it wasn't a nostalgia tour. She needed to find answers. It was a fortunate coincidence that the answers were in her backyard all along. Between an iron art stand and a utility bot spare parts warehouse, Djet saw a green door. She had walked up and down this same road hundreds of times in her childhood. She did not remember ever seeing a green door. Now that she was looking for it, it stood out as suspicious now.

She slipped through a huddle of four chittering navites. One of them kicked at her shin as she walked by, but she ignored it. The furry little things were troublemakers, and she was likely to get into a scuffle with them if she tried to tell the pint-sized bastard off.

The bronze door handle was cold to the touch. When she tried to turn it, it clicked. Locked. She pounded a fist on it, casting a casual glance up and down the road. People continued to meander along, no one paying her any mind. After a minute, she heard movement behind the door.

A slot in the top slid open. Large, dark eyes looked back at her.

"Wrong place, lady."

Djet made a flustered face.

"I don't understand, sir, they sent me here and I don't know why you would just turn me away without knowing who I am."

The eyes didn't blink. They just stared.

"What line of work are you in?"

Djet sighed. "I'm looking for someone. This guy, he just disappeared, and no one knows anyting about it."

"You looking for someone?"

Djet nodded emphatically. "Yes, sir. I'm looking for a marine who disappeared about two months ago."

The slat shut rapidly. Djet held her breath, until the door handle jiggled and opened. The man waved her in.

"Watch your step. There's critters in here, and they don't take well to being stepped on."

He refused to give her his name, but that wasn't the weirdest part.

The room was dimly lit with candles and an old book on a wooden table. The candles smelled like soap and sandalwood. Window slats at the top of each wall were full open, letting in a draft that made the flames atop the candles sway rhythmically. Creeper vines snaked up and down the walls, covered in droopy leaves. Tiny blades of loose grass skittered across the concrete floor in the breeze. He wasn't lying about the critters, either.

A spider the size of Djet's foot crossed her path when she was two steps into the room. Covered in spiny green and yellow fur, it watched her with eight white eyes on a dark cephalothorax as it creeped past her. Further into the space a cluster of a hundred or more insects the size of her little finger huddled in a corner, leather-like bodies squeaking as they quivered in the faint light. Several strange pods grew from the ceiling and hung down, almost like hunks of meat she'd seen at the vendors outside, except there were no hooks holding them up; there was a strange sort of muck that kept them attached to the ceiling.

The smell was awful. The soap and sandalwood of the burning candles did not mask the rotting moss odor these creatures gave off. Or maybe it was the man himself. Djet wasn't sure. He wore tan shorts and a button up sand-colored shirt. Brown leather boots that scuffed as he dragged his feet across the floor. Resting atop his head was a white wide-brimmed hat with a chestnut-brown leather strap around it. He looked like an explorer, a safari man. What the hell was a guy like this doing on a planet like Destin? And where had he gathered up all this nature? You couldn't walk a city block and find as much as two scrap-beetles...How had he gotten all of this into this room, high above the ground where such things grew, and sustained it with minimal sunlight?

He waved a hand at the spider. "Stippy don't bite unless you step on him, so don't do that. These," he indicated the nervous looking pile of smaller insects, "I wouldn't care if you stepped on these, since they're just food for Stippy, but they void their bowels when they die, and you do not want to smell that."

Djet felt her skin crawling. It took everything in her to resist the urge to pat herself down and scratch at her forearms. This place was disgusting. She was going to throttle Vase the next time she saw her. How dare she send her to a rotting pit like this. What could this degenerate possibly know that Vase didn't?

"Ah, no complaints here," Djet said, "I'm just looking for information. You have a, uh...a lot of friends, I see."

The man guffawed. "Of course I do. Better company'n most people." The man opened a small fridge and pulled out a glass jar without a lid. It was halfway full of a reddish liquid that smelled like fruity alcohol. As the man leaned his back against the wall, two crisscrossed vines sidled out of the way to avoid being crushed under his girth, and he drained half the liquid in a prodigious gulp.

He wasn't a large man, maybe six feet tall and was probably once in shape. He had a large belly and a stocky chest, arms and legs that looked like he used to work out but had recently given it up. Djet marked him at two hundred pounds. He wiped his lips with the back of his hand. "So, who're you looking for?"

"A marine. His name is Abraham Zeeben. Are you sure you can help me?"

The man laughed obnoxiously again. Djet wasn't sure if he was drunk or just a loud person. He was difficult to get a read on, which was probably intentional.

"Really?" He laughed again, slapping his knee this time. "You keep mentioning that this kid was a marine like it should mean something to me. Do I look military to you? You think I know every marine there is? That name doesn't mean...did you say Zeeben?"

Djet nodded.

The man pointed at her and laughed. "That's a dumbass name."

Djet frowned. "What's your name, then, sir?"

He shook his head. "Nuh uh, lady. Point of fact is, you can't afford to ask me that question." He raised an eyebrow. "You don't need to know what you don't need to know. I'll answer your questions, try to help you figure out your little mystery you've got going on here," he waved a hand to indicate he was talking about her and drained the rest of his beverage. He gestured at her with the glass, prompting her to speak.

"Okay, what do you know about the Ghost Society?"

The man's face changed instantly. The at-ease manner became much more sober, and he glared at her with narrowed eyes. As far as Djet was concerned, that was a bullseye of a question. He didn't answer her at first. He moved over to the hanging cocoon-like sack of whatever it was and peeled back a layer, exposing a row of red balls. The balls looked like a candy that was popular on Vatican, small spheres with sugary liquid inside that kids would put in their milkshakes. He ran his finger down the length, dropping the row of fifteen or so balls into his cup and replaced the flap on the cocoon.

"What do you know about 'em?" he asked, swirling his glass. The red spheres congealed into the liquid he had just drank, filling the cup up to almost full.

Djet found herself at a loss. This was a sensory overload like she wasn't used to. She felt she'd stepped into some weird trans-dimensional portal and ended up in a world entirely different from her own. Nothing in this room made sense. Everything was disgusting. This guy – whoever the hell he was – was the strangest person she'd ever met.

"I, uh...that's why I'm here," she stammered, crossing her arms to stop herself from scratching at phantom itches. What she hoped was phantom itches. "I don't know much. Other than...they like to abduct children."

The man continued swirling his glass. "No, that isn't their style. Least it wasn't fifty years ago. Hell, I don't know a whole lot of what they're into nowadays. I've been..." he gestured at the room, "shall we say...out of contact...for quite a while, now."

"Holy shit," Djet couldn't stop herself from exclaiming, "you were a Ghost?"

"Well, yes and no. But that was a long time ago." The old man grinned. "Or it wasn't."

"If you were," Djet took a step toward him, narrowly avoiding one of the little bugs that left the quivering pile to roam the floor, "then you have to know what's going on. Why would a marine want to be in the Ghost Society? What do they do, who are they?"

The old man took a swig of his beverage, set it down on the table in between candles, and produced a tin from his pocket. He tapped it a few times with his finger, then cracked it open. Smells of molasses and toothpaste – *it's not toothpaste, that's spearmint...or wintergreen* – emanated from the can. Djet watched him scoop into the can and stuff whatever it was into his lip.

He gave a satisfied sigh, sealed the can with a pop and returned it to his pocket. The whole time he did this, he never broke eye contact with Djet, and it made her feel like he was studying her. Not her body language, because he only looked at her eyes. For some reason, that gave her the creeps more than all the insect activity in the room.

"Let me ask you a question, lady." He paused to spit on the floor, drawing a dozen or more of the small insects over to the impact site.

"Why are you trying to find this kid?"

Djet frowned. "Did I say he was a kid? He was a marine, age twenty-two. That's hardly a child."

The man smiled, his lower lip bulging so it looked like his mouth was open. The stuff from the can clung to his teeth. It looked like dead insect legs caught between them.

"Secret's out, lady."

Djet's blood ran cold. She suddenly felt the urge to piss her pants.

"What?" she asked in as level a voice as she could manage.

"I know who you're looking for, and I know where to find him."

Relief flooded her chest. "Okay, good." She sighed. "So where –"

"Nuh uh," the old man held up a finger. "I know who you are, too, and what you're after. I'm not going to tell you what you want to hear. I'm going to tell you what you need to hear."

"What is this bullshit?" Djet grumbled. "I'm a detective with the longarms on Vatican, I don't have time –"

He cleared his throat and spat again. "No, you don't. That's why you need to hear this, and you need to high-tail it out of here, right now. Because I can't stay here much longer. Not now that you've led them here. So, listen good. I'm only saying this once."

"Led who here? What are you talking about?"

The old man got quiet, and suddenly the whole room did, too. Stippy, the disgusting spider, put all its appendages on the ground, all eight of its eyes fixated on the man. The quivering bugs in the corner of the room stopped shaking. The window slats did not shut, but the wind died. All but two of the candles stopped burning. They stopped burning with no wispy trails of extinguished flame. It was like they were never lit.

In the near total darkness, she could no longer see the man's eyes. His mouth moved, and she watched his lips as he spoke.

"The Pathfinders have a cell on Aldebaranzan. They've been stirring the pot for a while now, and they're about to kick things off here, soon. That's what you needed to hear."

A blinding red light filled the room, like a solar flare right in front of her.

Djet stumbled onto her back, arms flailing. She was blind. All she could see was red. Bright, solid red. A giant sunspot had completely usurped her vision. Suddenly cold concrete was under her back. She was lying down but didn't feel like she'd fallen. Something wet squelched loudly under her arm. She flipped onto her stomach and got to her hands and knees.

The red dimmed, slowly fading to black. Her eyes were open, but she couldn't see anything. A noxious odor assaulted her sinuses, and she retched. A streak of light split the shadows in front of her.

"Is he in there?" a gruff voice called out.

"No. Just a girl."

"A girl?" The man scoffed. "This isn't the right place."

"Bad intel again?"

"No, he was here. We know where he's going. Let's get moving."

"What about her?"

"He wouldn't have talked to her. He likes his women with scales, tails, or wings."

The two men laughed. The laughter grew softer until it disappeared.

Djet ran her hands down her arms, found the remains of a crushed quiver bug on her shoulder, and swatted it off with a shriek. The smell was in her throat. It felt like it was crawling its way into her gut. She clamped down with her abs, vowing not to puke.

Her vision was hazy and she was disoriented from the fall, or maybe the rank odor, but she managed to see one of the men's faces in the crack of light when he peeked his head in the door.

He had a pale face, and his eyes were covered with a thick black line.

That was enough to get her panic meter pegged to twelve.

PART 2: SPECTRE

The first and greatest victory is to conquer yourself.

- Plato

CHAPTER 11

Abraham spent a lot of time thinking. As the days on Singularity turned into weeks, he began to feel like a fish stuck in a bowl, cut off from the ocean he'd once swam in with no limits. Now, he was relegated to a tiny space, unable to leave and under constant surveillance.

Sweat collected in his hair. It created a halo effect of cold on his skin. As he moved, individual beads of sweat flung off his head. His muscles burned with a different kind of fatigue than he was used to. In the Corps, Abraham was either in the field, on a starship, or on Vatican, and when he was any of those places that wasn't the field, he frequented a gym for at least a few hours per day.

After the first month on Singularity, he had started to become used to a few things he never thought he would. The first was the spin gravity generated by the station, which offered only one third G, or thirty-three percent of what was considered optimal for human biology. Perhaps fittingly, the gym was kept at a full G through some technology that, when Abraham had asked Darin, the resident Ghost fitness manager – an appropriately snarky meathead – had simply shrugged and said it was some magic bullshit that was above his paygrade.

Abraham settled the bar on the hooks above the bench. His chest muscles ached with a tight pinching. He was very close to overdoing it. He didn't have to pay attention to biology classes to know that weightlifting caused micro tears on muscles, and that the body repaired these micro tears with more muscle fibers, which increased both their size and strength. He knew overworking them would lead these micro tears to become actual tears, and that would be an injury. It was never a good time for an injury, but doubly so while he was in tryouts for the Ghost Society.

Abraham slid out from under the bar and swapped places with Larry so he could serve as spotter.

Larry had gone through the most drastic physical change Abraham had ever seen. The spindly boy with the goofy smile was gone for good. He took a moment to get his hands situated just right on the bar, then popped it off and started knocking out reps with alacrity. The motions were smooth, controlled, but quick. Much quicker than Abraham's had been.

"Damn, Larry, slow down, bro. You're making me look bad!"

Larry breathed in rhythm with his reps until he hit eighteen and racked the bar. He hadn't needed Abraham's assistance at all. He sat up, pulled his shirt off and wiped a line of sweat from his forehead.

"I'm into this shit, Abraham," he said, resting an elbow on his knee. "I feel like I belong here."

"That's good, bro. You do belong here. I think we all do."

Larry took a swig from his water, gulped it down and said, "Yeah. I wanna do some secret squirrel shit, man. Topple a government, or assassinate some alien monarch. The shit that you think you're going to do in the Corps, because that's how it is in the movies. When we were boots, we just dropped in, shot up a town and pulled out. I had to watch the damn news to figure out if we even solved anything after a deployment."

Abraham massaged his chest, weighing the thought of another set. He decided against it and motioned Larry to follow him to the free weights. He picked up a set and started some standing curls.

"You know," he said between reps, "I feel the same way. Like, the Corps was prepping us for this."

Larry grabbed the next heavier set of free weights and started his set. "Fuck the Corps, man. I'm dead inside already."

The mornings were filled with awkward, disjointed conversations between Abraham and his friends, and plenty of hard stares. He realized he was the catalyst here, the thing that brought them all into the hands of the Ghost Society, but he had good reason for doing it. At least, he told himself he did. In his mind, the Ghosts had the answers; working with them wasn't a choice. It was the only way to resolve the questions that had plagued him ever since The Collision.

Piebold's sister was snatched up by them years ago, he thought. *There's something going on, and I've got to find out what it is. Why would they abduct a child? And why are they so interested in me?*

The Ghosts didn't officially exist. They operated outside the normal parameters of the Collective. Abducting people, especially children, showed they operated with a different moral compass. Or perhaps without one at all.

Still, he thought, *too late for second guessing.*

The days were made up of long hours of classroom instruction on technical aspects of espionage. How to conceal yourself in an environment, how to observe a target without being seen, how to bypass security measures on ships and in buildings. Abraham found the whole thing ironic. If this had been a group of private citizens, they would be liable for domestic terrorism charges.

This was how he began to see the Ghosts for what they were: the

Navy's pet terrorist organization. Plausible deniability. Perhaps even whitewashed personnel performing military functions in a civilian capacity. This way the Navy could keep its reputation clean of nefarious imperialism while benefiting from nefarious imperialism.

How much does the Navy really know about what the Society does? Or the Collective, for that matter?

Vase had known the Ghosts were real. This meant that her father, Admiral Latreaux, also knew. And if the highest-ranking member of the Navy knew about them, it was practically guaranteed that they communicated regularly. Did that also mean the Navy was collaborating with the Ghost Society? To what end?

The four of them sat at a table in the dining facility, eating and not making much conversation. Savony was running her fork through her potatoes, twirling a curl of her hair with a finger. Larry and Tayla had finished eating but remained quiet.

Say what you like about the Ghost Society, but their dining facility is on point, Abraham thought, relishing his first bite of steak that emulsified in a swirl of butter and medium-rare juices.

Despite Abraham's wound having healed enough for him to return to the gym, he was still sore from getting back into his routine – but it was a good sore. Apparently, the few weeks of downtime had done his body good. The Ghosts had not yet implemented physical exams, but he knew they were coming.

He rubbed his forehead. Too many thoughts jumbled into a mishmash, a never-ending spiral of questions. They promised answers. Dangled that carrot over his head constantly. In the past few weeks, he hadn't gotten so much as a nibble on that carrot. The sinking feeling in his gut intensified. It was starting to give him a headache. Ever since he joined the Marine Corps his life had been a wild spiral of adventure laced with misery.

"Abraham, you better eat," Tayla said. "Your stomach's going to be growling in an hour and it's going to distract me when I'm trying to take notes."

Abraham dropped his fork on his plate. The steak rested on the table, missing only a single bite.

"I know everyone's pissed at me. I understand why. I just know that this is the way we get answers. So yeah, it sucks that we're locked in with the Ghosts – assuming we pass the training – but it also puts us in the know."

Larry chuckled. "In the know about what?"

Abraham glared at him. "In the know about what the hell is going on with me. You know, you could have stayed on Piebold's couch."

Larry shrugged. "This is more fun. In two months, we'll either become boogeymen or we'll be dead. The suspense is already killing me."

Savony said, "Larry, that's not helping."

Tayla narrowed her eyebrows. "Larry, what's going on with you?"

He flashed his best smile. "What are you talking about, girl?"

Tayla kept her expression frozen and blinked her eyes a few times. "You don't feel like you've been creepy lately?

Larry blew a raspberry. "Me? Creepy? Absolutely not."

"You have been unnaturally happy since we got here," Savony said.

"Oh, right." He clapped his hands and rubbed them together, like he had been waiting to say something, after all. "I'm finally peeking my head out of the stream of shit I've been drowning in, and you're upset because I'm acting different? I'm not happy, not even close. I don't know if I can be happy ever again. But, for the first time since..." He trailed off, the silence saying the words he had not yet worked up to speaking out loud. "I've got a purpose, now. I'm gonna be a Ghost. And I'm gonna be damn good at it."

Abraham held out a fist. "Hell yeah, brother."

Larry bumped it. "We're here. Let's make the most of it."

Savony rolled her eyes. "The bromance is back in full bloom."

Larry snickered. "Jealous."

Abraham laughed.

Larry seemed to be coming out of his depression, and it was high time. Nearly four years of drinking himself into oblivion at every opportunity had just delayed his processing everything. He'd been stuck in the anger stage of the grief cycle. Abraham knew it wasn't a linear process, but for the first time since Duringer, he had hope that Larry was headed toward acceptance.

It felt good to know he had his best friend back.

The briefing room had become a second home to Abraham by the fifth week. They spent so much time in those office chairs, Portals on their laps, listening to endless lectures from Ghost cadre members...it was what Abraham imagined college was like.

Agent Sairus, a woman in her forties whose specialty was on the Nine Nations and interstellar diplomacy – Abraham wasn't sure he even believed that – gave them several hours of lectures on exactly what the Nine was. This included everything from the perceived pecking order as far as diplomacy was concerned, as well as the actual military capabilities of each nation. Abraham was surprised to learn that humanity was considered at the bottom of the political realm, but was solidly at the top in the military sphere of influence. He thought the Ghost's assessment might be biased, considering they were a human entity.

Agent Zerb, a bald, tan-skinned man whose scarred face did nothing to tamper his confidence, taught Abraham's favorite class; the basics of espionage. A solid month of video tutorials via projection window gave them a rudimentary understanding, and this was complemented by walk-through exercises in Los Agua, the Society's mock city block in the heart of Singularity. Abraham learned what the Ghosts considered best practices for blending into your surroundings. Techniques that could be applied to urban and suburban environments, ranging from evading authorities to creating distractions to get the focus off agents in the field.

"We're called Ghosts for a reason," Zerb would always say in his deep basso voice.

"Your best shield against suspicion is to be easily overlooked. The Corps should have taught you to operate in austere environs. We teach you how to operate in non-permissive ones. Deep inside hostile territory. Our missions dictate the need to penetrate, assimilate, and operate without being detected. Once the objective has been accomplished, we disappear. You'll know a mission is a success if you do this without a single soul realizing you were ever there."

Savony's favorite class was the advanced weapons course. Abraham did all right in it, but it wasn't his favorite because he didn't understand the need for it. So what if it took him a little longer to swap a heat sink on a CLR while he was at a dead sprint? And was it really a life-saving skill to be able to completely assemble and disassemble an L-pistol and a CLR with a blindfold on? He burned his fingers every time on the LCG – or Lens Carrier Group – portion of the CLR. In basic, the Marine Corps had left this part alone; you just removed it as one big piece and set it aside. Ghosts took things further; they had to actually slide the LCG out of its sleeve, which would expose a strange electrical phenomenon Abraham did not understand, and required a magnetic device he called a toothpick to disable.

"It's not a toothpick," Agent Sarin laughed at him. "It's a decoupler. It absorbs the magnetic field, which disables the charge on the lenses. So now you can take the lenses out and clean the carbon scoring off of them. You'll be doing this a lot more often than you think, especially if you're doing long range work. Any minor imperfection in your LCG can greatly affect the function of your weapon."

Abraham reached out, unable to see through his blindfold. His hand brushed against the disassembled barrel and a pile of what the Ghosts called CLR components – Abraham called them puzzle pieces, because the order and arrangement of them made no damn sense – and fumbled until he found the toothpick.

"Okay, now –"

He shrieked as a coil of electric shock bit into his finger. He heard a small glass-breaking sound in front of him, and knew it was his LCG, the most expensive part of the entire CLR, that had just fallen from his grip.

"Damn, Abraham, what is wrong with you?" Myles lamented. "That's two thousand digits every time you drop one of those. Keep doing it, and it's coming out of your paycheck."

Abraham pulled his blindfold off so he could look at Myles'...not eyes, but the Ghost Bar where his eyes should be.

"I've been meaning to ask you about that."

Myles laughed. "You mean you haven't gotten paid yet?"

Abraham shook his head. "No, it's not that. It's just...when I was in the Corps, I basically saved all my money. Like, nearly a hundred percent of it. I just never found a lot of stuff I felt was worth spending money on. As a Ghost, what do you spend your money on, Myles?"

Myles showed his teeth in something like a smile.

"I don't spend my money, Abraham. I invest almost all of it."

That surprised him. "Invest it in what? Are you a market watcher or something?"

"Exotic metals, probably," Larry said with the decoupler between his teeth like a toothpick. He finished sliding the reassembled LCG into his rifle, folded it back together and locked it in place with a slap. He ripped off his blindfold and sighed. "Money is boring. We're mastering this blindfold stuff, no problem. When are we going to move on to something challenging?"

"Poplenko," Sarin said wearily, "you'll be happy to know you're already at the top of this class, but that can change without notice. Confidence is an essential part of the operator mindset, but bravado is the easiest way to get yourself killed."

"Whatever." Larry turned his CLR over to look at the other side. Satisfied he had put it back together correctly, he let it rest in his lap.

"Larry," Myles said with a tone of warning, "Agent Sarin and I have been in the field as operatives. We're speaking from experience. There is an internal component and an external component to your presence. You can be a disorganized mess on the inside, but your outside better advertise that you know what you're doing. The flipside is if you know what you're doing on the inside and you let that bleed off you in waves of arrogance, it attracts attention, and that's precisely the last thing you want in the field. Incognito is the optimal condition for an operator in the field. Anything else just makes your job more difficult. Sometimes, even one person who notices something off about you is enough to put the whole operation in jeopardy."

Larry's expression softened.

Abraham could feel the awkward tension descending on the room. Myles was saying what needed to be said, but he was softening the reprimand a bit, probably because he personally knew Larry. Still, Larry's embarrassment was tangible. Abraham returned his rifle to its fully assembled state, slipped his blindfold on and started the breakdown process over again.

Ghost Academy, if you could call it that, continued to be nothing like basic training in the Marine Corps.

Abraham had the feeling it was more like a Special Operations schoolhouse. Having never been through Special Ops training, he was just making his best guess, but there were plenty of indicators he was on the right track.

Singularity's internal real estate came in at about the equivalency of half a Beijing-class starship. Everything in space, whether it was a ship, a station, or an escape pod, was built with triple redundant systems, at least one of which was automated and powered by physical backup power sources like stored solar energy or canisters filled with various types of alternative fuel. A station the size of Singularity required an unbelievable amount of power to operate at full functionality – usually a fusion drive nestled inside a mirror box with enough shielding to contain a small supernova, which is exactly what happened in the case of a fusion reactor meltdown.

Abraham thought the Ghosts might have named the station because of its resemblance to a galaxy. The central body was a massive sphere where most of the training areas, living quarters and administrative offices were located. Several hallways kilometers long circumnavigated the main body and served various functions essential for semi-permanent living conditions. The outermost ring was the hydroponics section that kept the galley stocked. The middle ring contained empty compartments with adjustable layouts for training purposes. The innermost ring was off limits to students, but Abraham speculated it comprised permanent living quarters and offices for the Ghost cadre. Spaced at intervals along the ringed compartments, thruster vents controlled by a limited A.I. managed propulsion output to maintain the universal standard one-third G. This kept personnel on station with their feet on the ground, toward the center of spin at the base of the station.

He appreciated the spin gravity, although he preferred planet-side gravity. Traveling as much as he had during his years in the Corps, Abraham had developed an absolute, burning hatred for zero G. It wasn't as fun and effortless as they made it look in films. He thought of it as swimming with no resistance, and without holding your breath. Holding a fixed position in zero G was a subtle art that he had never mastered. It took a lot of practice and a lot more patience than he ever cared to devote. As a marine, especially since he made the rank of corporal, there was always something more important to worry about. Studying tactical manuals, checking in with his fireteam, cleaning his kit, reviewing the mission briefing slides, familiarizing himself with ships and weapons technology – human and otherwise – and that didn't even cover studying the star charts. He could have devoted a lifetime to studying the star charts and never gotten a complete understanding of stellar topography. There was just too much to it – too many stars to accurately count, new planets being discovered all the time; and that even after the hundreds of thousands of years that the Nine had been exploring, the Interstellar Registry showed only thirty-one percent of the galaxy. The same registry claimed a much higher eighty percent had been charted through long range sensor scans and thousands of years of analysis. Abraham couldn't fathom star charts spanning ten million light years of space being charted with any reliable accuracy, regardless of the technology used.

This is what David should be doing, he thought. *He should be at college right now, learning all this stuff. I'm sure he'd be correcting his professors and making a name for himself. Probably running up the water bill, too.*

That was gone, though. Everything was gone, and he was here, in a viewing room on a top-secret installation in a forgotten part of the galaxy. Too busy staring at slides and text on his Portal to enjoy the view for more than a few minutes a day. No one could find him here. If anyone was even looking. Piebold wasn't, and Vase certainly wasn't, either. Those two were the only people left who even cared about him, besides the marines he'd brought with him.

He dropped the Portal on the coffee table and sighed. Studying star charts put him in a sour mood; he spent as much time learning the locations of nebulas and star systems as he did battling his own cosmic insignificance. The cold indifference of the grand vista that swirled and burned out in the emptiness bothered him.

Why? What's the point of all this?

He didn't get time to delve into the meaning of life.

The door to the viewing compartment slid open and the girls entered.

Tayla and Savony, two riflemen from his company. Tayla had been a part of Larry's fireteam, Savony had led her own. How had he convinced them to follow him on this crazy journey into the unknown, with no guarantees? They walked away from solid careers in the Corps just to follow him. Did people normally do that?

"Smithers wants us in the briefing hall," Tayla said.

Larry stood and followed her out.

Savony stopped at the threshold and shot Abraham a raised brow. "You coming?"

Abraham said, "I was hoping for a break from Smithers, honestly."

Savony replied, "Yeah, jerk-off was reminding us we have knowledge checks coming up, and if we don't pass the first time, we're basically done."

Abraham nodded and heaved a heavy sigh. "I know, I've been going over the material. This is a lot to try to cram into my brain. Don't get me wrong, I've always wanted to know how to hack networks and break into locked doors, but the technical side of this is...it's just a lot."

Savony patted him on the shoulder. "Buck up, buttercup. You ready?"

Abraham chuckled. "Of course."

He let her help him up with a hand and followed her to the briefing hall.

Larry and Tayla were already sitting down making small talk. Abraham and Savony sat next to them. Abraham caught Larry's attention, threw him a raised eyebrow.

"I dunno, man," Larry shrugged.

Smithers cleared his throat.

"All right," he said, clapping his hands together. "You all know the knowledge check finals are coming up in two weeks. I trust you're all prepared for them?"

No one spoke, drawing a smile from the Ghost.

"Right. The purpose of this little meeting is because your security clearances have come back, and all of you qualify. Due to that fact, I'm now at liberty to offer you the chance to volunteer for an incredible opportunity."

Savony made a snorting sound. Abraham knew the rest of them were thinking it, but she was one who had no problem throwing out the unspoken thoughts of the group. He really liked that she could bear the brunt of the awkwardness without caving in to the pressure.

"Is this the same kind of incredible opportunity I volunteered for in the Corps? Because I ended up guarding an Ichthid algae harvesting route for three months. I smelled like fish guts for weeks after that."

Smithers made a *hmpf* sound.

"There are no undesirable opportunities in the Society. You need to recycle that brain space you took up with Marine Corps idiosyncrasies and start filling it with tenets of the Society. I'll tell you this: there are two paths to becoming a full-fledged operative. You're all here under one path called 'star'. This gives you the basic Ghost Operator status. The other path – 'blood' – comes with certain privileges and distinctions."

Smithers raised a hand and tapped the side of the black bar that covered his eyes. A red stripe lanced across it, glowing faintly.

"This is the blood tab."

"Damn," Larry whispered behind a hand, "that looks badass."

"I want one," Tayla whispered.

Smithers continued as if he hadn't been interrupted.

"This is more than just a fancy addition to the Ghost bar. This is one of the highest distinctions you can obtain as an operator, and it comes with a hefty price. The blood tab is a mark of unquestioned loyalty to the society."

Abraham didn't bother raising his hand. "What do you have to do to get it?"

Smithers smiled. "That's the correct question. And unfortunately, none of you has the clearance to know that."

Larry guffawed. "You just said our clearances came back approved!"

Smithers nodded sagely.

"I'm only going to say this once, so listen closely. In the Society, there's always more. The rabbit hole you find yourselves in right now does not go up or down; it goes through. Through everything you think is real – we make our own reality. There is a ladder to the uppermost reaches of human intelligence and understanding. Intelligence is compartmentalized, and you will never know the full extent or implication of the things you do for the Society, unless you attain higher positions. If you do, by some miracle, attain higher positions, you will be in the know and out of the field for good. In case you have delusions of grandeur, you can forget ever seeing these higher positions if you do not have the blood tab."

Abraham was getting the picture. Star and Blood were colloquial terms the Ghosts used for enlisted and officer ranks. So why couldn't they just call them that, why did they have to make it all mystical? The more he learned about the Society, the less he understood it.

"Okay," Tayla said with a frown, "so if we can't know how to get it, what do we have to do to get it? Is it like a secret award, or what?"

Myles poked his head in the room, saw Smithers was giving a brief, and tried to dip his head back out.

"Agent Lannam," Smithers stopped him.

Myles strode into the room and asked, "Yes, Agent Smithers?"

Smithers gestured toward the marines. "The kids want to know about the blood tab. Care to fill them in on it?"

Myles nodded. "Sure. The blood tab is one of the Society's most closely guarded secrets. It's the highest mark of loyalty to the society, and it is earned on a voluntary basis only. If you volunteer to undertake the blood tab path, you can't turn back. You either earn it, or you leave."

Abraham scoffed. "So, after teaching us how to be the best spies in the galaxy, if we find out what we have to do to get this thing and refuse, you just let us go?"

Myles snorted.

Smithers kept his face perfectly still for a moment, then said, "You'll just have to find out yourself. You have until graduation from phase two to make up your mind which path you'll take. Remember, you may be a team now, but once you're wearing the bar, you'll be on your own."

That is definitely a no, Abraham thought. *I'm not swearing undying allegiance to an organization I can't trust.*

Even if they know what you are? a small voice whispered in the back of his mind.

Not for the first time since arriving on Singularity, he had no clue what he was doing.

CHAPTER 12

I'm seven years old.

Haven't had my first period.

Or kissed my first boy. Or girl.

"She's hard to read," a gravelly voice offered in the darkness.

A shifting sound, like papers or clothing. Someone adjusting in their seat.

"That doesn't mean anything. Remember who her father is."

It was cold. She felt like she was on ice. She tried to open her eyes, but they refused. Her nose itched, but her hand would not lift to scratch it no matter how hard she tried.

I'm paralyzed.

"Try the delve again."

"It hasn't worked the last fourteen times. You really think a fifteenth will?"

A shifting sound. Maybe a shrug.

"Here goes..."

The pain behind her eyes was like a burning stake shoved through the top of her head. It wasn't real – pain like this couldn't be real – but it felt real. Felt like her skull was penetrated, her left and right brain spread apart by an unseen force.

Violence.

Invasion.

The metaphysical sensation burrowed into the gap between physical and mental, furrowing into the quantum layer of her brain where electrical impulses registered as images. Thoughts. Feelings.

They were flaying her mind. Whoever they were.

Somewhere in the minefield of pain, images coalesced in strange colors on her eyelids. She couldn't stop them. She was alive, but she was not in control of herself.

The missing star. Her father always talked about the missing star in his first case.

A missing marine. Abraham Zeeben.

Emily's hot breath on her neck. She missed that.

A scornful glare from her mother.

"We don't need her life story, Sarin. For the love of Earth, get to the present day."

Oh, no, Djet thought with a grim smile her paralyzed lips couldn't make. *You're not getting anything from me, whoever you are.*

She let the drifting train of thought continue in her mind, meaningless thoughts she tried to shout inside her head. Whatever she was doing, it was working. She just had to keep it up long enough to get her captors to give up.

The coffee cup with too many marks on the side.

Exhaled vape fumes in the cab of her sky runner.

A man with a laser bolt to the neck, the flesh scorched and hollow.

"Axel, it's pointless. Psychologically speaking, she's a mess. I just keep getting old memories. It's like..." The female voice trailed off.

"Like what?" a second man's voice, deeper, interjected.

"It's like she's been trained to resist the delve."

"That's impossible."

"Should be," Axel agreed with disbelief, "but that's what we're seeing."

A daring kiss that shouldn't have been.

A different marine with a cold countenance, and something lurking deep in his eyes.

Too many mysteries for one detective to solve.

"You think he would..."

"I don't know, but unless you have a better idea, we need to try a memory wipe and just dump her somewhere. If he finds out, the settlement's coming out of our paychecks, I'm sure of it."

There was some rustling and a grunt. Djet couldn't open her eyes, but she recognized the sounds of a struggle. Were they fighting?

"Give me that!" Sarin snapped.

Fighting over something, not with each other.

Djet's morale sank. It was too good to be true, thinking they would try to kill each other and give her an opportunity to escape.

You can't even open your eyes. How're you going to escape?

I'll think of something, part of her mind argued. *Fatti told me you don't give up till the bars lock or the case is dropped. Far as I know, I'm not in a cell yet.*

Stars exploded behind her eyelids. The image of a chandelier shattering against the ground played in her mind's eye. Fractals of pain lanced through her head. Her arms and legs twitched in short spasms. She could hear her flesh slapping against the cold surface she was lying on. Her chest ached with an animalistic scream that could not break through the paralysis that imprisoned her.

"You're gonna kill her."

"It'll be easier to dispose of her body than to have her turn up a vegetable on his doorstep. He'll know it was us, either way."

"Ballsy move, brother," said the deep-voiced man.

Djet tried to resist the reel of images surfacing in her mind, but she was tired. Mentally exhausted. She was reaching her limit. They were going to get what they wanted, or they were going to kill her if they didn't.

Something unlocked inside herself, and she let go.

The paper with the symbol flashed in her mind. She heard herself whisper inside her head: *Pathfinder*. The green door. The strange man behind it. The flash of red light.

She heaved a sigh, deep and long.

The pain subsided.

"Hot damn," Sarin whistled. "That was close."

"Still doesn't tell us much," Axel grumbled.

"It's all she's got. We're one step behind him."

"We're always one step behind him."

"So we haven't given up any ground. He'll make a mistake, and when he does, we'll stop this war before it starts."

Sarin laughed gravely. "War's been going on for a long time, Axel."

"It doesn't have to be a public affair, Sarin. We can stop it before it goes mainstream. We've gotta get this back to HQ. They'll know what to do."

"What about her? Reintegration?"

A pause for several seconds left Djet enough time to wonder what that could mean.

The other man replied, "Yes, that's for the best."

The invasive force inside her head withdrew, leaving a pounding migraine in its wake. Djet couldn't flinch with each throb, though she desperately longed for some way to physically shake off the pain. Her captors spoke in hushed tones for some time. It could have been a few minutes or an hour. She wasn't in a state to assess with any kind of accuracy.

And then, blissfully, her brain switched off.

"I'm sorry, Miss, I don't tink we have da volume ya looking for."

Djet blinked. She inhaled a dust-ridden odor, something that smelled like an air vent two cycles overdue for cleaning.

An elderly woman was leaning against the counter. Thin curls of gray hair framed a look of concern on her wrinkled face. She tapped at the Portal on the counter and clicked her tongue.

"I'm not sure," the woman continued, "but it looks like da only copy was checked out four days ago. It is not due back until the seventeenth."

Djet reeled on her feet. She steadied herself on the counter, battling a wave of light-headedness. Her body felt heavy, like she had just done a full day's work and a crushing two-hour-long gym session. She took a few deep breaths until the dark spots cleared up. When she looked at the woman again, her face was more concerned than it had been the first time.

"Ya all right, Miss? You look a bit...well, ya look like ya bout to trow up. We have restrooms in da back if ya not feeling good."

She was in a large atrium, with vaulted ceilings with painted artwork. The space around her was filled with tall and wide shelves stuffed with books. A few people were milling about, carrying books or browsing the shelves. A few tables to her left were unoccupied except for some very old looking books abandoned on them.

Library...

"Miss?" the elderly woman prompted.

Djet ran a hand through her hair. It felt smooth, but her fingers smelled citrusy. If she just got off work, or had just left the gym, why did she smell so good?

I don't remember going to work...

"I'm fine," she said.

The woman nodded. She didn't believe her, but she turned her attention back to the Portal in front of her.

"Wait," Djet said, "what volume? What was I asking about?"

"Oh," the woman seemed to relax, "ya asked if we had any copies of *The Collision: One Day That Changed Humanity*, by Retired Colonel Jason Cole. I'm afraid we only have da one copy, and it's checked out."

"Who has it checked out?"

She didn't know why she asked it. The question came naturally.

"Miss," the woman smiled apologetically, "dat's privileged library information. I'm afraid..."

Djet stopped listening. Library. Why was she at the library?

She reached down to her thigh pocket, found her Pulse.

When she opened it, she found her personal data files inside.

Her schedule showed blank. It was like she'd never used that app before. But when had she –

Her skin felt tight. Her mouth went dry.

Djet swooned, catching herself on the counter.

"Oh, Miss! What on Destin is going on wit ya?" The woman tapped at her Portal and said, "Security to the front counter. Security, to the front counter, please."

The rustling of turning pages, the footfalls on carpet between bookshelves, even the tapping of Portals, all stopped at once. The commotion at the front counter shattered the library's number one rule of *Shhh.* The people were not happy about it. They dealt with it in the universal way of experts exerting their expertise in their particular sphere – deadpanning a collective glare that said, *don't you know the rules here?*

Follow the rules, you uncultured cretin, or get out!

"Destin?" Djet thought aloud.

A chime came from her Pulse.

It was a message from Vase:

I heard about Destin. Come see me when you can.

"What happened on Destin?" Djet asked aloud. Her head hurt. She couldn't think.

"Ma'am," a male voice came from behind her. "Is there a problem here?"

Djet turned to see a burly security guard standing a few paces away with his arms crossed. His palm rested on the butt of his handgun, but he spread his fingers out and away from it. Perhaps as a means of drawing her attention to the weapon without communicating his intention to use it. Or, he was an inexperienced security guard and hadn't taken the time to make himself comfortable with the weapon, and this was his way of distancing himself from the need to grab and use it.

Where do these details come from? Djet thought.

"I can't..."

Djet pushed herself up from the counter and ran her hands down her C-skin. She wanted to tell him, but she didn't know him. Couldn't trust him. He wouldn't care if she suddenly found herself incapable of remembering what she was doing here. Or how she got here.

She needed to get out of here.

Instinct took over. She smiled and said, "No sir, I was just leaving."

"I tink dat's for da best." He nodded to her, but kept his thumb hooked over the pistol grip.

Djet shuffled out of the library, aware of the security guard following her the whole way out. Once she'd exited the building and stepped onto the street, he took his hand off his weapon and gave her a wave.

"Take care uh ya'self, now."

Djet smiled and held her breath until the door shut behind him.

She brought up the map feature on her Pulse and programmed it to direct her to Vase. She needed to hit the Accel/Decel loop, which was on the other side of the ward. She could follow the guidance system on the Portal, which she considered her life preserver. If she hadn't received that message from Vase when she did...

I'm scared, she admitted to herself. *I'm in deep, deep shit.*

Djet tried to think, but it hurt too much.

The last thing she remembered was...two arrows in a circle. A yellow crate in the back of a sky puncher. Her partner talking his conspiracy theory nonsense. She remembered the grenade and the safety vent, the explosion that decimated the couch. The uncomfortable squeeze on her lungs from the smoke inhalation. That symbol...the one her father drew...it seemed like it should be important, but she couldn't remember why. She decided to focus on getting to Vase. Vase could sort this out for her.

The symbol meant nothing to her now.

CHAPTER 13

Abraham stumbled down the hallway, feeling drunk.

He steadied himself with a hand on the wall as he jilted step by step, unsteady from lack of sleep. His leg muscles were cramped and pinched as he tried to stretch them out. Sore wasn't the right word. They were stiff. Painfully stiff. He had just spent eight hours in a very small box. Stiffness was to be expected.

It wasn't the Marine Corps. This Ghost stuff was much different.

It was mental torture designed to break you.

Cracking is fine, Smithers would say, *but if you break completely, it's over.*

The Society operated with a mindset that it was pulling candidates from the ranks of battle-tested military members, most of them special operations types. The standards assumed peak physical conditioning, unbreakable mental strength, and an aptitude for emotional intelligence. Abraham felt a bit cheated on that; he wasn't special operations but he was in great physical shape, and he knew he could be tenacious when given an objective. It was the emotional intelligence part of the triangle he felt himself most lacking. He hadn't exactly been the social type growing up.

The time in the box was horrendous. He did not consider himself claustrophobic, but anyone who spent eight hours in a one meter by one meter box would feel suffocated after a few hours in total darkness with barely enough room to scratch your neck.

"You're absolutely certain this is necessary?" Abraham had asked.

"Shut up and get in the box. Once the lid is sealed, do not exit until exactly eight hours has passed." Smithers sneered with that crooked smile Abraham hated.

"Great. Sure. No problem."

He had clambered into the box and tucked his chin against his chest, hugged his knees. The lid closed over him with a hiss as it sealed.

Rule one: don't panic.

Rule two: control your breathing.

Rule three: don't lose focus.

Abraham struggled with the third rule almost immediately. He tried counting the seconds, extending a finger every time he counted to ten, then adding a hash mark in his mind's eye every full minute. One second he was counting, the next he was humping it through the jungle of Duringer, riskar dragging screaming marines into the dense red overgrowth.

The box was dark and cramped. The lack of space began to feel like a physical thing, as if the air was thickening to the point he could feel it pressing in on his skin. There was no sound aside from the thundering of his blood circulating. In the tense quiet, he felt the little twitches of his pulse in his arms and legs. The twitches, which were probably not as exaggerated as they felt, reminded him of horses. Horses he'd seen on Veranda. Flies would buzz around and land on them, and after a second or two of delay, the horse would twitch the skin under the fly and send it on its way. The process would repeat until the fly got bored and darted off. David had been scared to death of horses and refused to ever ride one. He always kept a comfortable distance of five meters between him and the animals. It was one of David's many peculiarities that Abraham had been greatly annoyed by as a kid. As he got older, that annoyance matured into an understanding that his brother couldn't help the way he was; not any more than Abraham could help his anger issues.

And what was that, anyway? Why were people supposed to conform themselves to some arbitrary societal standards? Who made those rules? How long ago? Obviously, some rules were needed. People couldn't go around stealing and murdering and all that, sure. But why were certain behaviors looked on with disdain while others were celebrated? Abraham's anger was considered a problem, and maybe it was to some extent. Fistfights in school usually aren't a good thing. That same anger channeled into the tobacco field had been good for him. Anger eventually made him a good marine, once he learned to control it.

Maybe that's the difference, he had thought in the dark. *Control.*

Control. Why had he lost control of his mysterious riskar gravity control?

That bothered him. When Tayla had shot him – how the hell had he actually convinced her to do that? – he fully expected his gravity wave power would throw up a field and stop the bullet. Instead, for the first time in his life, he felt what it was like to be pierced with a projectile at close range. The advanced medical suite on Singularity had patched him up in a week, no scarring or anything. He liked that, but he worried that something was wrong with him.

Something *was* wrong with him. Or maybe not wrong, but *off*. Weird. Abnormal.

Some part of him, however small, was not human. Avoiding that fact as he had done for the last few years, other than making stupid jokes with his buddies, was not getting him any closer to the answers. Even the Ghosts weren't helping him get any closer to answers. They were monitoring him, compiling their data and taking blood samples every other day, but they weren't sharing whatever analysis they were making. The carrot continued to dangle, always out of reach.

They kept asking questions he did not have answers for. Questions they promised to answer for him. It was almost entirely the reason why he decided to join the Society in the first place. A small part of him, maybe smaller than the amount of riskar DNA he possessed, was curious. Could he do it? Could he pass the training, would he be a good Ghost Agent, did he have what it took to master this new career field of cat-and-mouse? He was doing okay in the training so far, but the Corps taught him that training and the field were very different.

In a way, it felt like the Marine Corps had been like school, and the Society was like being an adult and moving out on your own. According to Agent Sarin – with very few exceptions – agents worked alone. You were given an objective, and it was up to you to use the technology given to you and your own knowhow to achieve that objective at any costs. The only rule was that you do so discreetly. If an agent gets exposed, they are immediately branded a political extremist. Records are fabricated. News stories ran to corroborate.

If an agent fails in the field, they're thrown to the wolves with no means to redeem themselves.

*Oh, shit...*his mind was wandering. He'd lost track of his count. Time distorted when you lost your bearings. The tight emptiness in the box, devoid of sound, light, and motion, gave no hints as to how much time had passed. Sweat made his underarms feel hot. He shifted slightly to get some air between his arms and his abdomen, but he couldn't move more than a centimeter or two in any direction. He took a deep breath and made his best guess.

It felt like four hours, so it was probably less than that. He guessed at three hours and twenty-five minutes. His legs were cramping and starting to lock up. The skin on his elbows was starting to burn from rubbing against the box. Around the four-hour mark, as he saw it, something pinched in his neck.

It was surprisingly difficult to stay focused on such a simple task. He counted and breathed for an eternity, but he was only estimating his time at six hours when the claustrophobia started to set in. His knees were tight. He wanted to bounce one leg by the ball of his foot, a nervous habit he'd been notorious for in high school because it would shake the desk and distract whoever was sitting near him. The urge for stimulation of any kind became a powerful one that was hard to ignore. It threatened to pull him out of his counting down the painfully slow seconds and minutes. Breathing was getting harder. He told himself he wasn't running out of oxygen. These last two hours were going to be much more mental than physical. He just had to tough it out.

The smell of his stale breath and the sweat that clung to his body was messing with his breathing, too. Strangely, it reminded him of his last night on Veranda. The night he got drunk for the first time and had his first kiss. The first kiss that ended with him puking in a girl's mouth. The embarrassment had branded him for life.

Focus, he thought. *One-one thousand, two-one thousand…*

That night, Digger kicked his ass. It wasn't the first time, and it wouldn't be the last, either. His mind flashed to basic training during a war game exercise, when Digger had used him as a human shield. It was a neat trick that got Abraham blasted with sim rounds. Digger was able to take down the surprised enemy team and walk away unscathed.

Focus…seven-one thousand, eight-one thousand…

When the opportunity presented itself on Duringer, roles were reversed. Abraham copied the move against his most hated enemy, the general of the riskar royal navy. Digger was able to fire off a bolt that blew off Rictor's foot. The only reason Abraham survived trading fist and claw with the alien was because of Digger.

*I can't believe…*he let the words trail off in his mind. How many things had happened since he left Veranda that caused him to say that same phrase? Too many unpredictable events that piled up, stacked higher than he could see, and he had lost himself somewhere along the way.

That's why I'm here. I'm not here to be a Ghost. I'm not here to help Larry, or to spite Vase. I'm here to get answers. To find out who the hell I am.

Abraham was here for the sole purpose of learning more about his origins, and that had a lot to do with finding out more about his father. He made the decision right then that the blood path was not for him. He didn't have unquestioning loyalty to the Ghost Society. He didn't have unquestioning loyalty to anyone but himself.

As fond as his subconscious was of throwing quotes from his father at him, it hit him with something he had forgotten until this moment. Something his mother said after his first day of school:

"Question everything. Forget nothing."

Pretty direct advice for a six-year-old, he thought.

Abraham stopped counting. For an hour he had lost the ability to take deep breaths. He inhaled sharply three times, placed his hands on the lid and pushed it open.

A downdraft of cold air swept over his face and under his clothes. He was drenched in sweat. A shiver ran down his spine, made more uncomfortable by the pinch in his neck and the cramps chewing at his muscles. His whole body felt like an electrical current was running through it.

Smithers stood at the back of the room, arms crossed, black bar covering his eyes. The most frustrating thing about Smithers wasn't his demeanor; Abraham had accepted the fact that he was an asshole from the first time he met him. The frustrating thing was that damn censor bar. It was impossible to get a read on someone you couldn't look in the eye.

"Impressive, Abraham. Seven hours, fifty-eight minutes and forty-one seconds."

Abraham rested his arms against the sides of the box, taking in deep breaths of clean air. He still smelled himself, and it wasn't pleasant. At least he passed the plus or minus eight-minute threshold. Even losing track of his counting a few times, he was still more accurate than he thought he would be. He hoped the next test wouldn't be tomorrow. He stretched his legs up over the lip of the box, groaning at the raging pins and needles in his quadriceps and feet. If he had to do anything physical right now, he would certainly fail.

Smithers cleared his throat. "You know, most people fail this at least once. Maintaining discipline in an environment like that isn't easy."

"Nothing you Ghosts do is easy," Abraham said between breaths.

"You need to start thinking of yourself as a Ghost. There is no you or I. In the Society, there is only 'we'. And we are many bodies with a single mind."

Abraham rolled his eyes. "Yeah. Got it."

Another box lid popped off. Tayla sat up, breathing raggedly. Her face was panicked. Her tan skin glowed with a light sheen of sweat, but as she took steps to slow her breathing, she relaxed.

"Tayla," Smithers said. "Seven hours, fifty-nine minutes and seven seconds. Very good."

Tayla pulled the tie out of her hair, which fell to her shoulders. She mussed it up a little with a twist of her neck.

"Yeah, it wasn't fun, but I can do it. That's good to know I can hide in Abraham's locker long enough to watch him get in the shower in the morning and he'll never know I'm there."

Abraham laughed. "That's creepy."

Tayla smiled mischievously. "You think that's creepy, wait till I wake you up one of these nights."

"You're joking, right?"

Tayla shrugged. "Does it matter? You wouldn't turn me down if I was all hot and bothered, would you?"

"Tayla, stop. You're like a sister to me."

She laughed like he'd just made the funniest joke in the world. "You wouldn't think that if you woke up to me on top of you. Naked."

Smithers coughed uncomfortably.

The thought popped into Abraham's head, and he wished it hadn't.

Tayla was attractive, but he didn't want to lose his focus. He wasn't here to screw around with his teammates. He was here to get answers. That was what the box had taught him. Bide his time. Focus. When the time is right, that's when you make your move.

He was going to have to make a move against the Ghost Society. He just had to wait for his moment.

"Whatever you do, I don't need to hear about it," Smithers said.

Tayla stuck out her tongue at the Ghost. "Jealous, much?"

Smithers didn't respond, other than to shift uncomfortably on his feet.

The lid of the third box popped open, and Larry sat up. He wasn't breathing heavily at all, but his hair was stuck to his forehead with sweat.

Smithers nearly shouted, "Larry, incredible! Eight hours and seventeen seconds. How did you manage...?"

Everyone stopped and stared.

With a wide grin, Larry held up his arms like he was showing them the answers to a test. They were covered in tiny red scratches. Hundreds of them. The scratches on his left arm were scabbed over. It looked like his arm hair wrapped around the underside of his arm and continued over the inside, where one would expect to see bare skin. Some of the micro cuts on his right arm were scabbed over, but the ones closer to his wrist were still bright red. They were hardly bleeding at all – the cuts were just deep enough to break the skin.

Larry showed off his handiwork like a star student who figured out the answer to the bonus question.

"Eight hours is four-hundred and eighty minutes. I counted the seconds, and marked down every minute, that way I wouldn't forget. You said we couldn't use the razor blade to mark the box, because that would give away that we were ever in it. You said there were only two ways out of the box, the razor blade or coming out on time. I used it to ensure my way out was on time."

Smithers smiled. "That is exactly the way a Ghost would do it. Congratulations, Larry. You beat the record by thirty-two seconds."

Larry beamed with pride.

Abraham didn't know whether to be happy for his friend or concerned. How the hell would you think to do that? It was smart, sure, but it was also...a little too much. Marines liked to broadcast how tough they were on any given occasion, but this was something else. Larry cut himself four-hundred and eighty times just to pass an evaluation?

That's crazy, Abraham thought. *Larry is certifiably crazy.*

Tayla, Smithers and Abraham continued to congratulate Larry for another minute, and then Savony's lid popped off. She swung up to catch her breath, big hair looking wilted.

"Did we get it?" she asked.

Smithers nodded. "Savony, eight hours, two minutes and thirty-eight seconds. A little too far over, but you passed. You all passed."

The Ghost clapped his hands together and rubbed them.

"Mental evaluations are over for today. Be ready for your physical finals tomorrow."

Abraham groaned inwardly as he stretched the tightness out of his back.

The only rest for a Ghost was death.

One step closer, Abraham thought, stumbling into his room.

He collapsed onto the bed, fatigue overpowering his racing thoughts. The blissful release of sleep pulled him into the void.

Abraham woke to the sound of an alarm.

In the military, there were different alarms for different reasons. A tone of a single note, for example, was a sign for impending attack or natural disaster, and was cause for preparation, but not necessarily – odd as it might seem – cause for alarm. The wavering tone was the one that separated the warfighters from the civilians: a wavering tone meant that an enemy attack was actively in progress. Wavering tones were usually difficult to hear over the mortar explosions, small arms fire, and shouted commands – the ambiance of war.

The alarm that woke Abraham that morning was neither a single endless note nor a wavering tone. It sounded like a ringtone on a Portal. It was a funky jazz riff on some kind of electronic instrument, most likely with keys or push-buttons, overlayed with a beet-beet-BEET of a horn instrument.

It was annoying as fuck.

"What in the hell –" His complaint was cut off by a loud thud.

"Ow, dammit!" Larry shouted.

He was lying on the floor, rubbing his head. Abraham didn't need the lights on. He could see his buddy's silhouette well enough to feel his pain. The low G of Singularity was nice, but the deck plating was reinforced durasteel. That had to hurt.

"You all right, Larry?" Abraham asked on his way to his wall locker.

"No, man, that shit hurts!" He stumbled over to the wall panel and flipped the lights on. "Is this Smithers' playlist?"

Abraham pulled on his black pants and shirt.

"What would make you think that?"

Larry threw on his pants and was trying to pull his shirt over his head.

He paused to say, "Smithers is a weird guy. Sounds like the soundtrack to a barnyard orgy."

Abraham shook his head, but couldn't hold back the laughter. Larry was damn near his old self again. A tang of uncomfortable feelings hit Abraham for a moment, but he let them flow through him without acknowledgment. Larry's mood swings had to be part of his recovering from his time in the Corps. Everyone had good days and bad. Maybe Larry's bad days were behind him now.

"You keep talking shit, Smithers is gonna kick your ass, bro."

Larry plopped onto his bed and slipped on a boot. "No way, man. That dude's like a hundred and fifty years old. He couldn't kick the shit out of a shit can."

Larry was referring to a Waste In-Suit Containment Capsule, or WISC, a component integrated into every space-rated suit. The brass loved their acronyms almost as much as the enlisted loved their licentious nicknames. WISCs were notorious for rupturing during combat. The military didn't see the need to waste weight and materials on reinforcing the structure of a component unnecessary for survival. They saved that for the oxygen tank, helmet and body.

"I just hope this is an exercise," Abraham muttered as the noise continued. "Actually, it doesn't make sense that Singularity would be under attack. It's a Ghost facility. No one knows it exists outside the Society."

"Sure, whatever, man." Larry slipped his other boot on and ratcheted the buckle until it was tight. "I'm going for all the records today."

That revived the issue Abraham had been trying to ignore – Larry's mental state. He passed the psych eval, but everyone lied on those. He had been instructed to lie on them ever since basic. Psych evals were the Human Collective's intrusion on the military's right to screen and select its members as they saw fit. That's what Corporal Nichols had told him, and she didn't seem disingenuous when she said it.

No one who wants to go to war is sane, recruit, she said. *Takes a little bit of crazy to be a warrior.*

Smithers' voice came from the ceiling speaker:

"Ghost cadets, report to the fitness facility. You have sixty seconds to be in place for evaluations, or you're redlined."

As soon as the words 'sixty seconds' were out, the station shuddered. Abraham's stomach leapt into his throat, and he was suddenly weightless.

"They turned off the spin gravity," Abraham said, kicking on his boot magnets.

Larry did the same. "Good thing I got these on fast enough."

"All right, we're wasting time. Let's go."

Abraham's bed sheets wrinkled and started floating upward. He ignored them and ran into the hallway with the awkward stumble of his boots sticking and unsticking from the deck. It was a two-minute walk to the fitness facility in one-third G. He was going to have a hell of a time running down the hallway like this.

"C'mon, man, we gotta move!" Larry said. He sailed past Abraham in the absence of gravity, having catapulted himself from the bulkhead.

"Ah, damn. I hate zero G," Abraham muttered, as he steadied himself against a bulkhead and jumped. His stomach lurched as the orientation switched from gliding above the floor to falling upward. He passed door after door, almost losing his bearings as he glanced down to see the bulkhead he launched from shrinking from sight.

Larry landed on the ceiling with a gentle tap and an electronic ting as his boots magnetized to hold him in place. He waved a hand to encourage Abraham to hurry up. The alarm continued its insane wailing. Abraham found it mildly distracting as he was trying to orient himself for a stable movement.

He had given himself a half-strength boots-off-the-bulkhead jump because he knew zero G was not his forte. As Larry impatiently waved at him, Abraham came sailing in and slammed his shoulder into the ceiling. Larry grabbed him and spun him around. Abraham clicked his magnets on, sticking his boots to the ceiling, which was now the floor. His internal positioning thrown off, Abraham tried to ignore the vertigo.

"In you go," Larry said, pointing at the open door to the airlock for the fitness facility.

Abraham, steadying himself on Larry's forearm, demagnetized his boots and let Larry toss him into the airlock. He engaged his boot magnets again, sticking to what was normally the floor, and felt himself calming down. He held out a hand for Larry, who waved him off and executed a perfect maneuver to plop down standing perfectly upright.

"Where's the girls?" Larry asked.

"How do you do that?" Abraham asked.

Larry scrunched his face. "Do what?"

"You float through the air like a hummingbird, man. You're perfect in zero G."

Larry shrugged. "It comes natural, man. It ain't that hard. Hit the wall panel, the girls are late, and I'm not getting kicked out for them."

Abraham stiffened. "No, Larry. We're a team."

Larry crossed his arms. "Abraham, you heard Agent Sarin. We can be part of a team, but we primarily operate solo. I helped you because you were here, but I'm not trying to have my record ruined by two ladies who –"

"Who *what*, Larry?" Savony asked as she maneuvered herself into the airlock.

"Where's Tayla?" Larry asked, annoyed.

"I'm right here, sourpuss. What's with the attitude?"

Abraham hit the wall panel to cycle the doors as soon as Tayla was inside. All in all, they still had fifteen seconds to cross the threshold into the fitness area. They were going to make it no problem. Larry shouldn't have worried.

"I just thought you guys overslept," Larry chuckled.

Tayla batted her eyelashes at Larry. "Not this little girl, Lair-Bear."

Larry put a hand on the wall and leaned his chest toward Tayla. He gave her a double eyebrow lift and said, "You keep up that attitude and I'm gonna have to straighten you out, girl."

Tayla threw her head back and laughed aloud.

Abraham and Savony shared a look.

"Freaks," Savony mumbled.

Abraham checked the Portal on his wrist. It was 0345 on Singularity, and his stomach was growling. He had eaten a light dinner at the DFAC before falling asleep in his bunk. Even though that was hours ago, he was regretting it now.

Smithers stood at the front of the room, talking quietly with Myles. Agents Sarin, Zerb and Sairus stood in a huddle off to the side. It was possible they were bored, impossible to confirm because of their hidden eyes. Sairus and Zerb were speaking softly to each other. Abraham wondered if the Ghosts ever turned their bars off, or if it was just to remind the cadets they had yet to earn their own. Part of him did think the swirling black and gray mist that danced over their c-skins looked cool. Another part of him wondered what the point of a cool pattern was if you didn't wear it where other people could see it.

The gravity inside the fitness facility was remarkably close to one solid G, and after getting comfortable in the one-third G of Singularity, it felt heavier than normal.

Abraham liked the Ghosts' gym. It was a large compartment, maybe twenty square meters, which was a massive amount of real estate on a space station. It still didn't make sense to him how the rest of the station could be kept at a different gravity than this, but he refused to waste the brainpower trying to puzzle that out. As he spent more time in the Society, even as a cadet, he was getting the impression that the Ghosts ignored laws of physics and the universe at large.

The four cadets walked into the center of the room, stood in line and faced the cadre. Mirrors lined all four walls floor to ceiling. Dozens of exercise machines were bolted to the deck along the inboard wall across from several dumbbell and kettlebell sets that rested on magnetic racks. Jutting out of the ceiling and running the length of the room on the far wall was one long pull-up bar, under which the water basin rested. The water basin was a glorified wake machine, which allowed the cadets to remain within the small confines of the basin, but still swim. Sensors in the basin monitored their motions and kept track of the distance. The center of the room was a hard cushion, like impact mats used for combat sports or wrestling. Everything was black, gray or white, including the icon in the center of the floor mat; an angry white ghost with an open mouth and a black bar over its eyes. Unlike the gyms in the Marine Corps, there was no flag draped high on a wall. No motto displayed. *Does the Society even have a motto? Probably not, or Smithers would have mentioned that on the first day of training.*

"Damn," Tayla yawned, "I hate losing my beauty sleep."

Savony looked annoyed. "You're fine, girl."

"No, I know," Tayla said, "I'm just saying. Why couldn't we do this at like, zero seven, or something? Waking up this early is barbaric."

Savony stretched her neck until it popped. "How did you ever make it in the Corps?"

"I batted my eyelashes and asked for help a lot," Tayla replied, her tone loaded with sarcasm. "There was an abundance of men lined up to do just about everything for me."

Abraham said, "I've always been of the opinion that as long as we do what we're told, we're allowed to bitch about it."

Larry chuckled. "Why do I feel like this is gonna be the easy part?"

Savony started patting herself down, smacking some adrenaline into her muscles. It was a common thing Abraham had seen athletes do as part of their warmup. Savony was a big girl. She weighed as much as Abraham did, and she was a good half meter taller. Her muscles were well defined from hours in the gym. Abraham loved having her on his fireteam. She was a solid heavy gunner, and she never complained. He wondered how she would manage the clandestine nature of the job ahead. Savony was one of those people who turned heads wherever she went.

"My favorite part of all this is the lack of information," Abraham complained. "We don't know what the grad standards are, so how do we know if we are where we need to be?"

Larry scoffed. "That's gotta be intentional. They want us to exceed the standard. Even the high standards of an organization so powerful they don't exist."

"And," Abraham replied, "one that doesn't seem to value human life all that much."

"Oh, come on, are you still on that?" Larry groaned. "They caused the Collision. That was a shitty thing to do. We all know it. But," he held up a finger, "maybe we'll learn that there was a good reason for it."

Tayla, normally Larry's biggest fan, gasped. "Larry, what are you saying? You think anyone has a good reason to kill two billion people?"

Abraham barreled toward Larry, fuming.

"You take that back, you son of a bitch!"

Larry put his hands up in a defensive gesture, his face flipping between disdain and confusion.

"Woah, man, all I'm saying –"

Savony stepped between them.

"Hold up now, boys," she said, "we don't need to do this."

Abraham bared his teeth and spat, "*We* don't, no." He glared at Larry. "You and I do."

Larry frowned, but Abraham read right through it. Larry wasn't upset at Abraham's reaction. He was annoyed that Abraham didn't see things the way he did.

"I'll never allow for what they did," Abraham said.

Larry stared at him for a moment, eyes glossy. Whatever reverie he slipped into, he came out of it despondent. When he replied, it was in a low, morose tone.

"We had a good reason for what we did on Duringer."

Abraham's blood froze. How many riskar had died on Duringer because he set off the HY/DRA weapon? An entire planet and a sizeable portion of the Riskar Royal Navy...that had to be millions of souls. His survival and that of the remaining members of his platoon required he make that decision. But were a few human lives worth millions of another species?

He still wrestled with that. He couldn't take it back, had never once wished he could. Morality in war was a gray area at best. Survival of the fittest at worst. All he learned in his four years in the Corps could be summed up with a single sentence: kill the enemy before the enemy kills you. Anything else was compartmentalized and shoved to the side. It was up to you, if you survived, whether to reopen that box. Abraham was the kind who could never leave the box unopened. He always had to sift through those contents, evaluate them and more often than not the things he learned about himself were less than flattering.

That hasn't changed since I was a kid, he thought. *I still can't let things go.*

Smithers cleared his throat, as he always did to signal to the cadets to pay attention.

"Physical evaluations are going to begin shortly. The standards are posted on the wall behind you. We'll give you thirty seconds to review the numbers, and then we'll begin."

Abraham spun around and saw a holographic square of light – a floating screen – with the letters **HTGT** above two columns.

Pull-ups	30
Push-ups	100
Sit-ups	100
Flutter Kicks	100
4000M Swim	80:00
10K Run	40:00
5K Zero G Course	2:00

"Okay," Savony breathed a sigh of relief, "that doesn't look too bad."

"Speak for yourself," Abraham said. "I'm not the best at sit-ups."

Larry slapped him on the back. "My buddy here's got a pretty weak core."

Abraham shoved him off. "I do all right. I'm just saying I don't like sit-ups."

"Nah, bro," Larry laughed. "You hardly ever do any core workouts."

"What are you talking about? When did you become a fitness instructor?"

Larry put his hands on his head and started bucking his hips. "I enlist the help of plenty of young ladies to help me get my core stretch on."

Tayla covered her mouth and snickered.

Abraham looked at her, confused. "You think this asshole's funny?"

"He's kinda cute, yeah," she said, still smiling.

Savony was already standing under the pull up bar, rolling her ankles and rubbing her hands together.

"Line it up under the pull-up bar. Let's go!" Agent Sairus said in his guttural tone.

Abraham took his place under the bar. It was a little over three meters up, and he hated it. To reach it, he had to jump just about as high as he could, and typically after spending a solid minute or two knocking out pull-ups, by the time he dropped to his feet he always got a nerve shock from the impact.

"Cadets ready," Sairus called.

Abraham leapt up, hands smacking onto the bar in a wide grip. He let his back muscles stretch in the dead hang position. It felt good.

"Go."

Abraham surged, brought himself up high enough to touch his collar bone to the bar, then let himself drop back to a dead hang.

"One," Smithers counted.

Abraham increased his pace, counting the reps in his head right before Smithers announced them. He was at fifteen when he started to feel the burn in his shoulders, twenty-three when that burn spread to his back and his muscles started to tighten up with fatigue. He risked a glance down the bar to see Larry swinging up and down at a ridiculous pace. There was no way anyone could maintain that speed and expect perfect form and a high rep count.

"Thirty-seven...thirty-eight...thirty-nine..." Sairus counted Larry's reps aloud.

How the hell is he doing that?

Abraham gritted his teeth and finished his thirtieth rep. He decided to go for forty even as his muscles begged him to stop. Minimum standards were frowned upon, he knew. As soon as Smithers counted his fortieth pull up, Abraham released the bar and slapped to the mat. The expected jolt of discomfort spiked in his feet and ran up to his knees. He caught his breath as he watched Tayla and Savony still knocking out reps.

"Twenty-three...twenty-four..." Sarin counted Tayla's pull-ups with a look on her face like she smelled something unpleasant.

"C'mon, Tayla, you got this!" Abraham encouraged her.

Smithers turned his head. He might have been glaring, but the bar hid his eyes.

"What are you doing?" he asked through gritted teeth.

Abraham balked. "Oh, is a little encouragement frowned upon, too?"

"Keep your mouth shut, Zeeben."

Abraham rolled his eyes.

Savony was the picture of sophisticated grace under pressure. Her face was tight but did not reflect the pain she must have felt. Her biceps tightened as she pulled herself up, letting a light jet of air between her lips. She touched her collar bone to the bar and lowered back to a dead hang.

"Thirty-six," Agent Zerb counted.

Tayla was small and didn't have as much weight to lift as the rest of them, but because she was small, she also didn't have as much muscle mass. She puff-puffed through her lips on her way up to hit her collarbone on the bar and dropped, bouncing awkwardly at the tail end of her shoulder's range of motion.

"Twenty-nine," Sarin counted.

Abraham decided not to call out more encouraging words with Smithers standing right next to him, but he moved to stand just behind Agent Sarin where Tayla could see him. He smiled and nodded to her. She looked back at him with wide eyes and tight lips. He wanted to shout something, to offer some kind of motivation. If she didn't get that thirtieth rep, she was done.

Smithers' words came to his mind. Words he'd said at least once a day for the last several weeks: *In the Society, there are no second chances.*

Abraham glanced at the Ghost, annoyed. Smithers watched with a blank expression as Tayla continued to struggle. It made no difference to him whether she passed or not. Or maybe he was hoping she would fail, since she was having a hard time meeting the minimum standard.

Abraham despised him.

Savony dropped to her feet. Her cold focus transformed into a smile.

"Forty-one," Agent Sairus said with approval.

Larry was slowing down. He exhaled explosively as he guided his head up over the bar.

Agent Sairus practically shouted as he counted, "Sixty-five!"

Abraham was impressed and irritated at the same time.

Tayla got her chin up over the bar. Her arms quaked and tremored. Tendons in her neck flexed, wrinkling her skin.

"Collar bone has to touch the bar or it doesn't count," Agent Sairus warned.

Abraham gave Tayla a thumbs-up and nodded. She may or may not have seen him. Her gaze was fixated on something over his head, or behind him. She probably wasn't even focusing her vision, instead putting all of her attention into completing this last pull-up.

The tiny marine emitted three quick sputters from her lips and smacked her collar bone on the bar. An explosive sigh followed as she dropped to a dead hang for a split second before falling to her feet.

"I guess that's thirty," Agent Sairus muttered. "Barely."

Tayla smiled as if she hadn't heard him. The sweat on her forehead glinted in the light, and she breathed several slow and deep recovery breaths. Abraham felt himself breathe again, too. He had been nervous that Tayla wasn't going to get that last one, or that Sairus was going to be critical of her form and refuse to count it.

Thankfully neither happened.

Larry was the last to drop with a slam to the mat. He let out a screechy "whoo!" and patted his lat muscles a few times. He sat down, spread his legs into a V and extended his arms to stretch. The smile on his face was so wide it made his eyes look small, and he still had bedhead from being woken up in the middle of the night. He looked like a wild man, and for the first time since joining the Corps, Abraham recognized the boy he'd grown up with. He was still in there, just older and with a little more baggage than he should have to carry at his age.

"Seventy-one," Agent Zerb said with a smile. "That beats the standing record of sixty-nine."

"Nice, Larry!" Abraham held out a fist and Larry bumped it.

"Thanks, bro." He accepted Abraham's hand and stood up.

Smithers cleared his throat.

"We'll move on in sixty seconds. The breaks between exercises will all be sixty seconds exactly. You'll get a five-minute break before the swim, a ten-minute break before the run, and a five-minute break before the zero G course. Rest up and when you're ready, take your position on the blocks."

The blocks Smithers referred to were near the entrance of the gym. They were in clusters of three, spaced so that a person could put each hand on one block and both feet on the third. This way, no one could rest during the push-ups; if you let your chest sink too low, you'd fall between the blocks, and that was a good way to break your nose. The floor padding was soft, but not that soft.

This is off to a rough start for Tayla, Abraham thought. Larry and Savony were killing it, and Abraham felt like he was holding his own. He hoped they'd all be able to pass; there was a certain comfort in knowing people when you were entering a new environment. He didn't want to go on to Phase Two of the training without all three of his buddies.

But he would if it came to that.

Nothing was going to stop him from getting the answers he came here for. If the Ghosts didn't have the information, he didn't know who did. As far as he knew, this was his only shot at discovering the truth, and he wasn't going to give that up for anything.

CHAPTER 14

Djet was just stepping off the transit platform in Dominicus Dorsi when she got a high priority message from Captain Spitzen:

[PRIORITY=RED]
MESSAGE BODY:
//ALL THIRD WATCH LONGARMS REPORT TO HQ IMMEDIATELY
/[END OF MESSAGE]
////

Djet was already dressed, so she set her Pocket to close orbit, double-checked the L-pistol on her C-skin belt, and headed out with adrenaline sizzling in her veins. This was the second all-call of her career. The first was when a prominent CEO's son had been abducted.

Hundreds of man-hours and millions of digits later, the case went cold. No demands for a ransom. No proof of life offered. The kid was just gone.

Djet walked the streets with Portal in hand, refreshing the feeds every few steps, but nothing was popping up on the evening news. Just your standard political updates, a statement from the Commandant of the Marine Corps about operational exercises a few light years from the Aldebaranzan system, and an entertainment headline about a local heart-throb actor whose first role was smashing streaming records. Whatever the all-call was about, it wasn't good – which, oddly enough, meant it was probably interesting and she wanted in on it.

It chafed her to have to sideline her investigation into Abraham's disappearance, but she wasn't doing that on the books. Favors didn't pay bills. She was still a real detective with real cases to work, and she had to remember that.

I still don't know what happened. I might never know.

That didn't sit well with her. Someone had fucked with her memory.

The green door beckoned in her mind, but it remained firmly shut.

Did I go in there? Did I even really see it?

She tortured herself the whole way to the station, failing to recall memories she no longer possessed.

The briefing room was packed with fifty-three of the fifty-five longarm detectives in her division. There weren't enough seats to go around, so most of them were posted up against the wall, leaning back with arms crossed and annoyed expressions. One detective reported in sick, and the other was on an undercover assignment and couldn't be pulled in without blowing their cover.

Captain Spitzen slid the door shut and locked it.

Immediately, power to the room cut to emergency lighting. All devices switched off, including Portals. All eyes went to the captain.

She cleared her throat. "Thank you all for reporting in promptly. I'm going to dispense with the bullshit and get right to the point."

She gestured at the wall behind her, bringing up an image of a middle-aged man. He had a distinguished air about him, and his nose was broken once in the past but never fixed properly. That was odd, Djet thought. He bore the Liberty House crest on his C-skin.

"This is Liberty House Representative Russolial. Those of you who are up to snuff on your political game should recognize that he has a brother, Ivanlial. What you are now cleared to know is that the Navy has deployed a detachment of Marines to escort Ivanlial on a diplomatic mission to Aldebaranzan. The details of that mission are not important, so I'll skip over them. What is important, is this."

The image on the screen changed to a crime scene photograph. The politician, Russolial, was slumped back in his chair, mouth agape. His eyes...the empty sockets were a bloody mess. Written in blood above him on the wall was an alien script that Djet couldn't read without a translator. As if on cue, an overlay translation popped up.

Barbs of Justice.

A circuit connected in Djet's brain, unloading a flood of information. Everything she knew about the Barbs of Justice, the torind people, their home world of Nea Nia, the rough history they had with any member of the Nine Nations, including their holy war saga that stretched back close to a thousand years. *That recent assassination of another politician, what...fifteen years ago?* She thought all of this in a single second.

Captain Spitzen continued. "At twenty-one hundred hours this evening..." Djet checked her Portal, realized it was still powered down so she couldn't see how long ago that was. "Representative Russolial was seemingly assassinated by the torind gang known as the Barbs of Justice. The crime scene has been canvassed, mapped, and digitally preserved. The physical location has been scrubbed, the body removed, next of kin notified. However," the captain slammed a fist on the podium, "Liberty House does not want this information coming out until after the deceased representative's brother returns from his diplomatic mission. So that's now top-secret information. Any loose lips on this subject will be thrown in Terra Sky without trial, understand?"

A firm response of *yes, ma'ams* circulated the room.

She nodded. "Good. You all have the digital map of the crime scene on your Portals. Do not, and I must emphasize this point because we have some mavericks in our ranks that I haven't been able to weed out," she locked eyes with Djet, "regardless of past missteps. Do not be the person who leaves their Portal unattended in a public space, or accidentally breaks encryption protocols by sending any of this information over unclassified channels. Is that understood?"

Another round of acknowledgements.

"I don't need to remind you all that this is a high priority case, and that Liberty House is torching my ass to get it solved right now. That's why I want all hands on deck for this. Whatever you have going on, it can wait for the next three days while we dig into this."

"Three days?" Nelson, one of the senior detectives, asked from the back of the room. "Is that when the brother's returning?"

The captain shook her head. "No, he's not scheduled to return for another month. Three days is the time we've been allotted to have this case solved. And we will have it solved."

She stared daggers at everyone in the room.

"Ma'am?" Blaze asked.

"Detective Sisneros. Yes?"

"This looks like the work of the Barbs of Justice. It's got all the calling cards of their standard MO. What needs to be solved, here? Why aren't we building a snatch-and-grab team to track down the torinds that did this and bring them in?"

"I'm glad you asked that question." The captain leaned on the podium and lowered her voice. "Every square centimeter of the room was combed, analyzed, tested several times over. There is a glaring anomaly that the crime scene bot can't figure out, which requires some human intervention."

"What the hell sort of anomaly?" Nelson asked. He was a surly recluse whose reputation for sarcasm was legendary.

Djet thought she knew. Why else would Liberty House want every detective in the district on this high-profile case, if they already had all the pieces of the puzzle? It looked open and shut. No one would argue that this was anything but what it looked like: a textbook assassination by a rogue terrorist element. Whoever had done this wanted people to assume the torinds were responsible, and that meant they were highly trained and intimately familiar with the Barbs of Justice tactics and methodologies.

They want us to think the torinds did this because they don't want the negotiations to lead to anything, which means...they want that situation left unresolved. Why? Who benefits from Aldebaranzan being destabilized?

The Pathfinders have a cell on Aldeberanzan, a whisper in her mind said.

Djet stiffened. Her head started throbbing.

Who are the Pathfinders?

Captain Spitzen opened her mouth to answer Nelson's question, but Djet cut her off:

"Nelson, think about it. Our high-grade crime scene bot scrubbed and scanned the entire molecular composition of that room. Crime scene investigators looked at that data and determined this was, in fact, not a Barbs of Justice hit. That could only be because one piece of the crime scene doesn't fit. The deceased is a politician. Manner of execution is in the style of the torinds. Timing seems politically motivated. All that checks out. The only logical thing left to turn all of that on its head..."

Djet was suddenly aware of the fact that everyone was staring at her. She continued. "The only thing that makes sense is that the bot did not find any trace of torind DNA at the crime scene."

Whispers and side conversations broke out as the other detectives gave each other their two cents on the matter. It seemed like half the room was on her side, the other thought she was completely wrong.

"They could have been wearing S-skins or B-skins, Rincon. Come on!" Nelson snapped.

Captain Spitzen cleared her throat, silencing the speculative voices.

"Detective Rincon is, regrettably, correct."

It felt like everyone in the room was holding their breath.

Nelson scoffed. "Of course she is," he muttered.

Djet was indignant. "Curb the sarcasm, Nelson. This isn't a high school class and I'm not the teacher's pet. Any dumbass who knew the first thing about crime scene investigation should have arrived at the same conclusion. The question isn't what the bot didn't find. The question is whose DNA was also found in the room."

All eyes panned to the captain.

"You don't have to be such a smartass." Captain Spitzen sighed. "We did find trace DNA on the representative's body, but it was contaminated with his own DNA. We have no way to match it to anyone in the Human Collective Database. All we know is that it's a human male."

Djet clapped her hands together. "That's the starting place. We're looking for a human male, someone who was never in the HCD in the first place. Or if he was, his records were erased."

Nelson scoffed. "You can't erase files from the HCD. It's blockchain with more quantum encryption than a Halzenti casino vault. No one has ever hacked it, because no one can."

Djet raised an eyebrow. "You believe everything you're told?"

The man puffed his chest out and huffed. "Not at all, sister. That's common knowledge."

"Common knowledge isn't always fact."

The man put a hand up to signal he was done talking. "Keep telling yourself that. You're not always right, Rincon. Remember that."

Djet laughed. "I don't always have to be right. But in this instance, I am, and until you can suggest another valid theory, mine makes the most sense." She thought about it for a split second, then decided she wasn't going to take any more shit from him. "Matter of fact, why don't you just take some vacation days. When you come back, I'll give you the full VF-5 on how I solved this case. You might learn something."

Whatever his snide reply was, it was drowned out by the other detectives making *ooh* noises. Djet almost, *almost* blushed at the response. She hated being on display like this, but she wasn't going to back down. She wouldn't be viewed as a coward. It was as much a reflex as it was about protecting the honor of the family name.

"That's enough!" Captain Spitzen spat. "Detective Rincon, my office. Everyone else, get to work. You're dismissed."

Once she was alone in the captain's office, Djet seated herself and opened up the screen on her Portal. She was already starting to process the case file when her boss entered, fuming.

"Detective Rincon..." she started.

"Ma'am, I already know what you're going to say, and I can save you a lot –"

Captain Spitzen slammed her fist on the desk. It was loud enough to zip Djet's lips shut instantly. The glare from her boss was not unfamiliar, but it was unpleasant. She looked like she'd just caught Djet in bed with her daughter.

She doesn't have a daughter. Just a son. High school age, with a low grade-point average. Why do I know this?

"Detective Rincon, I am this close," she held up two fingers, nearly touching, "to firing your ass. If I didn't need you for this case, I probably would have after that little display back there."

Djet frowned. "Display? I was connecting dots and filling everyone in on it. You can't present us with questions like that and expect us not to discuss it."

"It's not that!" The captain's voice was shrill. "It's you. Just you. If any other detective had announced preliminary conclusions they were drawing, people would have just nodded and grunted in agreement. You just have...you're just...frustrating, I guess would be the best word. You're crass, uncouth..."

"Blunt?" Djet asked.

"Yes, blunt. Too blunt. I don't know how you can be effective with witnesses at all in this line of work, disrespectful and inane as you are.

That being said," she spoke through her teeth, "I need you for this."

"I know you do, ma'am."

"That's not a statement of your abilities," she snapped. "It's because of your last name."

That threw Djet for a loop. "You don't think I can solve this case?"

"No, I'm sure you can, as much as it pains me to admit it. It's because Liberty House found out that you're your father's daughter. They've specifically requested you as lead investigator."

The floor fell out from under her. Seated in the ergonomically responsive chair, Djet suddenly felt a wave of vertigo. She was requested, by name, by Liberty House itself? How often did that happen?

Never, she thought. *Well*, the other part of her mind said, *not never, just rarely. Almost never.*

This had to come from someone who knew her father personally. That meant the person requesting it had either worked with her father, was an informant, or was a family friend. Djet ran through the list of the latter and came up with no viable names. Informants she would not know about, because her father kept work at his level separated from her, but prior co-workers...she could think of a few, one of whom was a senator. That had to be it.

"Did Senator Gorsky request this?"

The captain threw her hands up. "Honestly, Rincon, do I even need to tell you the message he sent, or have you read that already?"

Djet shrugged. "I'd like to read it."

Captain Spitzen angrily flicked her finger across her Portal. Djet's Portal chimed in response.

"Read it, follow it to the letter, and get back to me when you have identified the perpetrator. Do not...Rincon, look at me when I'm talking. Thank you, now listen. Do not attempt to make contact with or apprehend the perp without getting clearance from me. Do you understand that?"

Djet nodded. Unable to contain herself, her eyes slipped back down to the letter on her Portal.

"Rincon, one last thing."

Djet didn't bother to look up.

"Go read that letter somewhere else. I don't want to see you in my office again until you've found him."

Djet nodded, stood and exited the office as she read the letter. One line in it stood out to her:

To ensure the fastidious and complete resolution I so desperately seek, we are respectfully requesting Detective Djet Rincon be assigned as the lead investigator on the case.

Her brain itched at that line.

To ensure the fastidious and complete resolution I so desperately seek...

Something about that was odd. She wasn't sure what, but it didn't sound right.

Djet headed back to her flat. She needed to talk to her father. She needed to talk to Vase. And then she needed to get to work. Three days was not a lot of time.

Sometime soon, I need to get my memory back, too, she sighed.

Djet stuffed her Portal into her leg pocket with a huff.

"Fatti, why ya always gone when I need ya?"

Three times she tried to call him, and three times it went straight to message recorder. He had his Portal switched off. She sent him a quick text message asking him to call her, but that wasn't likely to hurry him up. Chief of the Watch on a terra-city was a never-ending job.

The dark expanse shrouded the upper levels of Vatican with the illusion of a night's sky seen on most other worlds. The stars shone with a certain indifference Djet felt keenly. She returned the indifference, annoyed as she navigated the narrow alleyway clogged with a meandering crowd of mixed species. The path to the hangar where Vase's ship was docked routed through a pub district that relied on the ambient lighting of business signs and advertisement posters. Grated gutters ran the sides of the smooth streets, clogged with trash – and probably contraband – unable to remove the sporadic puddles of spilled drinks, human waste and drug paraphernalia.

The average person wouldn't be caught dead walking this area at this hour, but Djet had never thought of herself as an average person. She had her L-pistol, and failing that, her Capoeira. That, and she was in a hurry. Three days wasn't a lot of time to solve a high-profile murder.

Djet crossed out from under a walkway and entered the docking bay apron.

The crowd thinned out in the additional space, but it still seemed to be a high amount of foot traffic, even for Vatican. She shrugged off the observation and took a step toward the hangar when she was yanked back into the alley by the neck of her C-skin.

She had her L-pistol drawn before her back hit the street, already forming a sight picture on her attacker.

"Alan?" she asked with surprise.

He held his hands up in mock surrender.

"Detective. I didn't mean to scare you."

Djet holstered her weapon and held a hand out. Alan pulled her up to her feet, wrapped his arms around her and started rubbing her back. He wasn't hugging her, he was cleaning off the street funk she had fallen into…which somehow made sense.

"Ya didn't scare me, Alan. Just confused me, really. You always say hello by grabbing a lady's collar?"

He leaned his back against the alley and gave her a smirk.

"Captain Seneca's not taking any visitors."

Djet leaned back against the alley, brushing her shoulder against his.

"What're you like her bodyguard now or someting?"

"Hardly." He looked away, as if considering what he was going to say next. "I'm a platoon sergeant now. Just means I'm the point man on the missions from here on out."

"What's the mission this time, Alan? I thought you were supposed to be a part of this diplomacy tour in the Aldebaranzan system?"

He narrowed his eyes. "You know, for a detective, you really don't know as much as you pretend to, do you?

CHAPTER 15

They finished the calisthenics portion of the evaluation. Everyone passed.

Tayla struggled with the push-ups, netting herself a hundred and three. Everyone else ended in the hundred and twenties except for Larry, who was able to get a hundred and forty-four, which was – surprise – a new record by six reps.

This guy's gotta be on steroids, Abraham grumbled to himself.

When it came to the sit-ups, Tayla surprised everyone by finishing with a hundred and fifty-one. She even beat Larry, who handled that news with all the grace and dignity Abraham had come to expect from him.

"What? That's bullshit!" he shouted, ejecting spit. He slammed his fist against the mat. He must have liked how it felt because he did it again three times in rapid succession.

Abraham glared at Larry. To his credit, he apologized to Tayla, but he was clearly still upset. He grumbled something about how important proper form is, until he got quiet when Tayla's counter, Agent Sarin, looked in his direction.

Tayla, looking pleased with herself, asked between breaths, "What…no new record?"

Agent Sarin crossed her arms. "Standing record is a hundred and fifty-five."

Tayla whistled. "Damn, I was close."

Larry visibly relaxed at the news.

They rested for their full minute, then knocked out four-count flutter kicks, which no one had trouble with. Abraham finished last, but he was able to clear a hundred and ten before he stopped. Smithers threw out a handful of his reps because he bent his knees. Abraham forced himself to slow down and focus on his form until he hit the mark plus a little extra cushion over the minimum.

The swim came next. All of the cadets needed the full ten minutes to rest up. They were in great shape, having had nothing to do but study and work out, but after pushing themselves to the limit, they were feeling it. Abraham knew he was. He hadn't been this sore since…he couldn't remember ever being this sore.

"Swimwear on," Smithers said.

Myles tossed the gear in a tangled mess near the pool. It was a cluster of masks and fins with overlapped straps, and two female one-piece suits and two tight briefs for the men.

Abraham worked furiously with Larry to get the mess untangled. They had two minutes left on their rest timer when he finally divvied up everybody's gear. He held up his briefs on a finger, looked down at his black shorts, then cast a glare at Smithers.

"You really just wanna see my dick, don't you?"

Smithers scoffed. "You are obsessed with yourself, Abraham. It's embarrassing."

Larry was already naked and stepping into his speedo, completely unashamed.

In the Marine Corps, everything was co-ed, so men and women showered together. Everything was monitored with security cameras and the marines knew it – a fact that was uncomfortable to accept, but also helped drastically cut down on incidents of sexual harassment. It did not, however, cut down on incidents of ogling, which male recruits were notoriously incapable of resisting. It was a sort of unwritten rule in the Corps that as long as you didn't get caught gawking, sneaking a peak wasn't a crime. Abraham had trained himself through extensive exercise of willpower to keep his eyes focused on what he was doing in situations like this. He had showered with Tayla and Savony, Larry and Piebold, and a ton of other enlisted men and women over the last four years. He could count on one hand the number of times he'd showered solo in the same amount of time.

So it caught him completely by surprise when he noticed the girls had their backs to him as they transitioned into their swimming gear. Neither of them so much as glanced his direction, but being girls in this situation, they probably felt eyes on them. He felt a pang of guilt that he had looked, but then, he was a dude, and they were girls, so he couldn't exactly blame himself. He thought of Vase in that moment, and before he could stop himself, he wished she was here, getting dressed in a swimsuit next to him. Fortunately, before he could take that thought any further, the clock blinked overhead with less than one minute to go time. He stripped down and donned his swim briefs.

He balled up his shirt and chucked it at Smithers, who smacked it away with the back of his hand.

"Don't push it, Abraham."

Abraham was nervous about the swim, mostly because he never swam laps before arriving on Singularity. If he was able to pull this off, he would have gone from first learning the combat recovery stroke with fins and a mask a few weeks ago to being a proficient combat swimmer. That was an achievement worth noting on its own. He doubted the Ghosts, and especially Smithers, would see it that way.

Abraham sat on the gunnel, the small trough at the edge of the wake pool, and slipped his fins on. He let his feet slide into the cool water. Goosebumps crawled up his legs, ending in a shiver up his back. The worst part about the pool was never the swimming. It was the transition in and out. Wet skin attracted the airflow in the room and felt like wrapping yourself up in a blanket of ice. Muscles in his back and arms flexed against the chill as he pulled his single-window mask over his eyes and nose, cinched down the straps and ran his fingers over them to make sure they weren't twisted or snagged.

Down the line from him, Tayla, Savony, and Larry were seated on the gunnel, double-checking their mask straps. Abraham was satisfied they were all primed and ready to go, so he raised his left fist above his head to indicate they were ready.

"Fifteen seconds," Smithers announced.

The tension in the mask straps across his temple and above his ears distorted his hearing. Smithers sounded like he was further than a meter behind him. The wake machine started with a groan, churning the water into a steady flow toward him. Ghost cadre took their positions next to each cadet.

Larry clapped his hands a few times and shook his shoulders. Inside the mask, Abraham could see his buddy's focused gaze. He was in the zone. Abraham looked down into the depths of the pool, at the frothy churn on the surface, and mentally prepared himself.

"Three...two...one...go."

Abraham slid off the gunnel with his right hand pressing his mask into his face. He plunged into the chill. Tiny air bubbles caught in his arm and leg hair or crawled up his body and popped on the surface. The cold was all over him in an instant. The only way to warm up was to swim. As his body floated to the surface, he raised his left fist as he'd been taught, caught a breath above the water line and started right away with the combat style stroke. Flutter kicks weren't considered a go-to exercise in the Marine Corps; he had only done them at basic and on Singularity, but their application in swimming was obvious.

He led with his left arm out in front of him, exhaling slowly as he kicked his legs in medium strides for a four count, turned his face to the side for a breath and followed with an arm stroke with his right hand. Over and over he did this until his brain was numb, and his body warmed up. After a few minutes he was no longer cold. His quads and calves burned with exertion.

As the minutes crawled by and he saw his distance displayed in light on the floor of the pool beneath him, he switched lead arms. Leading with his right, he could look down the pool and see Tayla, who was closest to him. She was small but her core and legs were powerful. For some reason, Larry's comments about core workouts came to mind, and he tried not to think about her in that way. Watching her was a great way to pass the time, though. Abraham had no romantic interest in Tayla, or Savony, or any of the other females he'd served with, except for Vase.

There was something about Vase that kept him in her orbit. Kept him thinking about her even though he was light-years away from her, and he had broken up with her. Over the last few years, he hadn't figured out exactly what it was, but he knew he wanted to be with her. He strongly suspected she wanted to be with him, too. The problem was, ever since they first met, she had been holding something back. As a person who claimed to value honesty – she never missed an opportunity to remind him of that – she sure liked her secrets. Abraham hated secrets. Especially when he was the one in the dark about them.

He watched Tayla's smooth legs flexing as she swam. She was a dichotomous blend of athletic and the classic feminine – toned muscle, not bulky. The counter below her indicated she was a solid two hundred meters ahead of him. He was on track to hit the mark, but just barely. Abraham needed to quicken his pace, but not too much that he would burn out. He stretched his flutter kicks out to a wider range of motion.

Tayla flipped over to lead with her left arm. Suddenly she was making eye contact with Abraham, and he gave her the okay sign with his hand.

She gave him the okay sign back and winked. Before he could blink, she pulled down one strap of her swimsuit and flashed him.

Abraham spewed his entire breath in a cloud of bubbles. He turned his head to the side, grabbed a lungful of air and switched to leading with his left arm so his back was to her. He did not need distractions like that to take his focus out of his swim. The fact that she was probably laughing her ass off at making him uncomfortable just made the embarrassment worse.

Eighty minutes is a long time, and Abraham had to switch lead arms to give his other arm a break. When he did, Tayla was still facing him. She pointed at him, pinched her fingers together and moved them below her waist.

Abraham shook his head.

I'm not flashing you back, he thought in disgust.

The stream of bubbles leaving Tayla's mouth stopped. She pouted her lower lip as she continued to swim. He couldn't help but gush up a few bubbles of air in an underwater laugh.

The rest of the time passed in a slow crawl of discomfort. Physical and mental.

Tayla was a flirt. Every night Raven platoon had been shipboard on the *Patton's Treads*, Tayla would always be found at the *Port of Call* – the only bar onboard – usually surrounded by several male marines who vied for her attention. She would laugh and whoop obnoxiously, let them buy her drinks and dance for hours. Savony would pal along with her sometimes, but not often. And now that Abraham thought about it, he had never seen Savony dance. There had been many nights when Tayla stumbled into the room reeking of booze, and she would flip the lights on long enough to collapse onto her bed with a groan. Abraham had found her to be extremely annoying.

Now he was having second thoughts. He did find her attractive. He just never connected with her in any way to make him think of their relationship as anything more than friends and comrades. She made suggestive comments, but that was just her way. She hadn't changed at all in the two years he'd known her. So why was he thinking about all this now? Because he broke up with Vase? Or because he had been on station with her in close quarters for the last two months?

The timer blinked on the floor of the pool. He had about five hundred meters to go and thirteen minutes remaining. He was in the clear if he kept his pace going, and he was confident he could do that. His shins hurt, his legs and his core were on fire, but he had gotten used to doing PT the Ghost way. Get comfortable being uncomfortable. Agent Zerb said that constantly.

When the timer finally went red with zeroes, Abraham surfaced and let the wake machine push his back against the gunnel. He finished the eighty minutes at 4235 meters, well beyond the minimum. He looked over at Larry's numbers and was pleased to see his buddy only swam a little over a hundred meters further.

Savony was next, and Tayla had beaten them all with a total swim of 4502 meters.

"Impressive, Tayla," Smithers said in his customary monotone. He didn't sound impressed at all. Abraham continued to hate the man.

Larry pulled his mask off and swished water out of his hair.

"That was fun."

"Didn't go for the record on that one?" Savony breathed next to him on the gunnel. She leaned forward, wringing water out of her hair.

"Nope. I know where my strengths are, and swimming ain't one of them."

Myles clapped his hands together sharply.

"Well done, cadets, so far everyone's passing. The zero G course is next, and we have about nine minutes to get there. Dry off, suit up and we'll head to the *Bermuda*."

Tayla leaned in close enough to rest her arm against Abraham's.

"Didn't want to return the favor, eh Sarge?"

Abraham suppressed a shiver. He replied without looking at her. "I, uh..."

She sidled up next to him and put her arm around his waist. "Didn't like what you saw?"

He stood up abruptly and started toweling off.

"You had your chance to get a peek when I was changing," he said defensively.

Tayla let out a high-pitched laugh. "How do you know I didn't?" She made an exaggerated gasp, and her voice lifted into a tone of mock surprise. "You weren't…watching me…were you?"

She laughed again.

Abraham felt his face heat up. He didn't know what to say, so he kept his mouth firmly shut.

The *Bermuda* was a scuttled *Manhattan*-class ship the Ghosts used for zero gravity training. Usually kept in Earth's orbit on the other side of the planet from Singularity, someone had docked it with the station while the cadets slept, filled it with oxygen as a safety precaution and presumably set up an obstacle course on the inside. Abraham had done zero G simulations in his off time from classes and the gym, but this was going to be his first time running a real obstacle course on a real ship. By this point in the day, his nerves were already shot; it was hard to stay in a state of nervousness for an extended period. Now, he was more settled into a state of resignation.

I'm either in, or I'm out. Just gotta do the best I can and hope it's enough.

Standing shoulder to shoulder with his team in full S-skin suits, Abraham waited as the airlock hissed to equalize pressure with the ship. The wall panel blinked green and an automated voice in his helmet said, "Pressure normalized."

The door opened with a creak, revealing a small hallway that led into a hangar.

"Hot damn. I don't know if I'm ready for this," Savony said.

Smithers' voice boomed from the ship's internal speakers:

"Cadets, take your places on the marked spots. The course will begin in exactly one minute. Be advised: the ship is thirty thousand meters stem to stern. Parameters for this evaluation is five thousand meters in less than two minutes. You each have a color designation that will be marked by waypoint in your HUDs. You will encounter obstacles common to ships disabled in the field. Your objective is the colored sphere that corresponds to the sphere you're standing on. Follow your waypoint and touch the sphere within the allotted time to pass. If you are rendered unconscious, if your suit is breached, or if you do not reach your destination in two minutes, you will be redlined."

"Got it," Larry said.

"Okay, this should be fun," Tayla said. "It's like dancing, but faster."

"Speak for yourself, girl," Savony said through clenched teeth.

Abraham cleared his throat to break up some of the knotted adrenaline. He was tired from the previous evaluations being so close together, but he was excited to get this over with. If he passed this, he was ready for Phase Two. They all were.

He stepped up to the red circle. His counterparts took their places at the remaining colors, and everyone made eye contact as they looked up and down the line.

"We should have a team name," Savony said. "Cuz if we make it through this, we're basically in, and we're going to need a name."

"Darksiders," Larry suggested.

"Moonlighters?" Tayla asked.

"I was thinking more military," Abraham said. "Something like Shadow Platoon."

"Yeah, but we're not a platoon. We're four people who aren't even going to be part of a team after this," Larry said. "We're going solo."

Savony surprised everyone when she said, "Tetsubishi."

"What?" Abraham wasn't sure she had said a real word.

"Tetsubishi. Four-pronged iron spikes. They're made in a way that no matter how they're thrown, they always have one spike facing up. That's us. We don't have to be a team, but we'll always have each other's back."

"Where did you hear about that?" Tayla asked.

Savony smiled. "It's part of a family story I heard all the time as a kid. My brother's favorite story."

Larry snorted. "Touching. Tell the story later. We're not done for the day yet."

Abraham interjected to smooth over Larry's retort. "Tetsubishi it is. Us four, we're the Tetsubishi Alliance. No matter what happens from here, as long as one of us is able, we'll never leave each other hanging."

Abraham held out a fist.

The four once-marines-soon-to-be-Ghosts bumped fists.

In one of those rare moments of inspiration, Abraham felt words pop into his head, and he spoke them without thinking.

"Contemno logica."

"Wow, I like that!" Tayla said with too much enthusiasm. "What's it mean?"

Abraham looked at her and said, "It's a dead language, but it means 'defy logic'. Something my brother said once. I feel like it sums up our being here against all odds."

Larry mumbled, "David said that? Kinda cool, I guess."

"Quit your bullshitting and pay attention," Smithers said. "We're going in ten…nine…"

Smithers continued to count in his droning voice.

Abraham double-checked the integrity of his S-skin out of habit. He knew the HUD would flash a warning if anything was amiss, and it wasn't doing anything right now. It felt weird to be in a civilian space suit, rather than the battle armor variant he was used to in the Corps. Part of him wondered if the Ghosts had their own suits, or if they just made do with these stripped-down versions. If he made it through this, and Phase Two, he intended to learn as much as he could about the Ghosts.

He stepped onto the red circle.

Immediately the circle flashed red in his visor. A waypoint appeared in the depths of the ship somewhere in front of him at the same time as a two-minute clock appeared in the upper right corner of his visor. The bulkhead door hissed. Oxygen vented in small clouds at the door's seams, and then it slid into the wall.

"Go!" Smithers said.

The other side of the door led into an air- and spacecraft hangar. Normally, this was the largest open space area of any ship, with movable maintenance catwalks along the walls and crisscrossing over the central docking bay. One would expect to find a few dropships, a few single-seat fighter craft, and maybe a few caskets – storage lockers filled with tools and replacement parts – but none of that was visible.

The moment Smithers said go and the timer clicked to 1:59, Abraham jolted forward. He made ten awkward mag-boot steps to the railing, assessing the hangar as he moved. His waypoint was on the far side of the hangar, probably through an access door and all manner of obstructions. He saw the red dot only as a digital circle through a sea of debris. Destroyed computer systems, blown apart dropships and catwalk frames bounced to and fro, glancing off walls and each other as they spun on all three axes in an uncoordinated maelstrom.

If Abraham had been in a situation like this on an HMC vessel, he would have declared the area an impassable hazard and ordered his fireteam to find an alternate route. A painful reminder edged into his awareness: *the closest distance between two points is a straight line.* He spent the entire ten steps to the railing looking for a clear path, but only saw severed support beams and wall panels tumbling in the fragmented remnants of computer screens.

Larry leaped off the balcony railing, spinning in slow circles as he drifted into the tangle of garbage. Savony hopped the balcony and threw herself toward the lower deck. Tayla was right behind her.

Everyone has a plan except me, I guess.

It wasn't just his mag boots that kept Abraham stuck to the catwalk – he vacillated for a long moment. The lack of safe, reasonable options kept him there at the same time the panic coursed through him. He did not have time to do anything but navigate the shifting debris. Just diving into it was going to hurt, if not kill him. He could be pinched between a beam and the wall; or catch a fragmented component to the head with enough force to scramble his brain. There had to be a way through, but he couldn't afford to wait for an opportunity.

Abraham thought up a plan on the fly – wasn't sure it was going to work, but he was willing to risk it. Judging the distance from his current position to the far side of the hangar as three hundred meters, he followed Savony and Tayla's first move and vaulted over the railing, holding on long enough for his momentum to swing him toward the hangar floor.

A green status light flicked on in his HUD when his boots locked with the floor. Abraham took a few steps to place himself under the questionable safety of the catwalk five meters above, and dialed his magnetism down almost all the way.

He took off at a dead sprint for the far side of the hangar.

It would certainly have been faster to launch himself and free float through the vacuum. It would certainly have been more dangerous, too. As he did the awkward high-knees kind of running across the tiled floor, the only way to run in magboots, he had to slow down twice to avoid separate clouds of wire bundles and large pieces of glass. His worst nightmare happened right when he reached the halfway point of the hangar.

A broken girder his suit measured at ten-point-three meters long and one meter thick slammed into the wall in front of him. It bounced back from the wall and should have sailed completely away, but a red halo of light slammed into it. The girder swung toward him with blinding speed.

Abraham had one thought. Riskar.

He knew gravity control when he saw it, and that was it.

So how did he activate his own? He tried for a split second with no results.

It was like a kid learning to use the bathroom for the first time. They didn't know exactly how the muscles worked, so it took them a long time to figure it out. Maybe a couple of times of the process happening naturally for them to realize where the muscles were and how to manipulate them.

He strained his eyes, his neck, made weird faces and waved a hand, but nothing happened. Nothing ever happened when he tried to make it happen. The power was innate, a reflex. Something he did without thinking. Maybe it wasn't even something he did, it was just something that happened.

Realizing he was screwed, Abraham jumped, pushing hard on his right foot while he leaned slightly to his left. He wasn't Larry Poplenko, but he hoped in that split second he could pull off the zero G maneuver well enough to keep out of harm's way.

The girder passed underneath him and slammed into the side of the hangar at the same time his boots hit and sealed to the underside of the walkway. His mind flipped the picture in his head so that he was upright and the hangar was upside down. He had pulled it off. He didn't have a second to celebrate, but the adrenaline dump in his bloodstream was enough.

Without making a sound, the girder dragged across the wall, which peeled and crumpled inward a mere two meters away. Shockwaves vibrated through the bulkheads, shearing bolts and wrinkling panels. There was no sound in a vacuum, except for the tiny vibrations that ran from the wall to the floor, up his boots and across his suit until they tickled at his helmet. The result was a sound so soft it could have been imaginary, a sound that did not match the force of the impact he saw.

And then the bulkhead was there. He had run across 300 meters in about thirty seconds. That was damn good considering the mag boots, but he still had a long way to go. Abraham reversed his jump and spun to land on the floor. The danger of the rogue girder was gone, but he still had to cross another three hundred meters to get to the access door. He knew he had wasted a lot of time and needed to make some up, so he prepared himself for a floating jump to cross the congested hangar.

A wall panel drifted by slowly, tapping three corners against the wall before gently floating away again. Abraham instinctively reached out and grabbed it, not sure why he felt like he needed it. The panel was large enough to cover his whole body and weighed basically nothing in zero G, but it wasn't going to fit through the access door.

It could shield him from the debris, though.

It'll be like a magic carpet ride.

Abraham held on to two sides of the panel, faced it toward the swirling debris and dove toward the door. He pushed a little too hard with his left foot and entered a lateral spin. As his suit indicated he was nearing the hundred-and-fifty-meter mark, something smacked into his back and knocked him off course.

He heard and felt the thud of his helmet contacting the wall. He heard his breathing as his pulse quickened. Unsure of how to recover, he let go of the wall panel and followed the red line in his HUD to see the waypoint.

In the confusion, he had floated ten meters above the floor. The impact of him slamming into the wall had shoved him three meters and counting away from the wall, leaving him floating helplessly as life support equipment and other random ship components danced around him.

Well, that's it, Abraham thought, a spike of rage hitting his gut. *I'm not passing this.*

He stewed in the frustration for two full seconds. The countdown was approaching one minute remaining.

Something slammed into his back hard enough to knock the wind out of him. He was suddenly sailing in the right direction. His lungs felt like pancakes. He wheezed, only able to take small sips of breath. Frayed wire strands passed over his visor, but he didn't swat them away. He didn't want to mess with his trajectory with an errant hand wave.

Abraham impacted on the deck. His neck pinched. He rolled from his belly up to a standing position, but there wasn't time to lock his mag boots. He coasted along the floor, grabbed the edge of the bulkhead and propelled himself forward as hard as he could.

The distance meter in his HUD clicked down, down, further down as he rocketed down the hallway, tracing the red line that led to his waypoint. He tried to ignore the velocity ticker in his HUD, but trying to ignore it made him glance at it, which brought a pang of nausea because it was showing thirteen meters per second and climbing.

Too fast, he thought.

The floor panels were an indistinct gray blur a meter beneath him. It was like looking out the side of a car at a hundred miles an hour, trying to see individual squares of sidewalk. He passed the destination waypoint, which meant it was somewhere below and behind him now.

And up ahead was an empty lift shaft. The red line that only existed in his HUD made a sharp ninety-degree turn down. At his current trajectory, Abraham was going to splatter against the wall of the shaft before he could even think of trying to negotiate a hairpin turn like that.

He clambered for the wall closest to him. Stretching as far as he could, he managed to get his fingertips on the wall enough to push himself away. He made sure the magnets in his boot were turned off, then kicked off the opposite wall. He did this jumping back and forth until his momentum slowed to a more manageable five meters per second, and then two, and then one.

Just in time, Abraham pulled his knees up and landed a little harder than he liked against the wall of the shaft. The jolt in his knees was slightly more painful than falling from the pull-up bar in the fitness facility. The countdown timer was dropping below thirty seconds when he pushed off the wall, coasting downward for a hundred and fifty meters to land on the same deck level as his waymarker.

He could see it. It wasn't a red circle, but a red ring floating in the corridor two hundred meters away. The corridor was wide enough for an aircraft to fly through; so it wasn't a corridor, it was a docking tube that led to the hangar floor. Spaced out along the corridor on either side were the Ghost cadre.

In unison, they pulled CLRs from their backs and aimed at him.

Am I in the right area? This has got to be a joke.

Abraham did the only thing he could do. He tucked and jumped.

The Ghosts lit off with their weapons. Sim rounds ripped through the air in bright, soundless flashes. Abraham tried to spin, like Larry had done earlier, by waving his hands. He succeeded in spinning himself, but with no predictable pattern, and he got lit up.

Bolts bit into his visor, which blacked out. The arms and legs of his suit were hit and locked up. He floated through space toward his ring, for all intents and purposes of the evaluation, dead.

CHAPTER 16

Djet knew Capoeira, but that didn't mean she was comfortable giving up her gun.

She sighed, tucking the L-pistol into the end table by her bed.

She didn't go anywhere without it. Not if it could be helped. She was a law enforcement officer, and that came with some privileges not afforded ordinary citizens, not even military on shore leave or stationed in an on-world garrison.

Bringing a gun into the Dominicus Domini district of Vatican, the beating heart of politics and intrigue on humanity's surrogate home world, was not one of those privileges.

She took a deep breath, brushed her fingers along the slide of her weapon, and said good-bye under her breath. Her need for the weapon was probably remote – Dominicus Domini was the most secure sector on the entire planet. In an odd counterpoint to common sense, it was the gun capital of the world, more guns than citizens.

Since she wasn't one of those holding a gun, she still felt less than safe.

An hour and a half later, she exited the sky taxi onto a sprawling platform in the uppermost reaches of the atmosphere. The darkness of space hung large and imposing overhead, making her feel like she was standing on the peak of a very tall mountain, perhaps the tallest point of land on the planet. Starlight glinted overhead, casting a wide ray of simulated moonlight over the walkway. Oxygen mist coiled at her feet, snaking up and into the air in thick clouds. She breathed it in with a shiver. This high up, the wireless electricity couldn't heat up the thin atmosphere.

Up ahead, the platform ended in an empty circle with park benches and a circular patch of grass with a statue of a planet. It was wrought with glass, exotic metal, and the smallest fusion reaction Djet had ever seen. She stared at it as she walked closer, realizing it wasn't a fusion reaction at all.

The odd artwork was a focusing chamber. The glass pieces that were supposed to be continents were catching stray rays of light given off by Starlight and focusing them into a central point, creating a ball of pure light. Djet paused to admire it. Constructing something like this was well beyond her comprehension, but it was a marvel to look at.

Beneath the statue was a laser-etched inscription in a plaque of silver, or something like it:

EARTH, circa 5-089: WE WILL NEVER FORGET

Djet mentally chided herself. She should have recognized the layout of the continents from her history books. As she had grown up, she realized Earth was one of those strange things that created two very different opinions: you either spoke the name of humanity's original home planet in a hallowed whisper, or you never mentioned it and tried to ignore that it ever existed in the first place.

"Fifth millennia, year eighty-nine...that was, what...four thousand some years ago?" Djet muttered aloud.

"Four thousand twelve, to be more precise."

Djet scoffed. She hated being corrected. She turned to face the speaker, and immediately choked off her intended reply.

Thessaly Coup De stood before her.

She was the most powerful political figure in the Human Collective. Djet had seen her on the news almost every day for the last nine or ten years. Since she was in middle school, when she won the election against...someone she forgot. Djet didn't hate politics – they just didn't interest her.

"Ma'am," Djet gave her the Longarm salute, palm facing outward.

"Thank you, Longarm." Ms. Coup De saluted back with an intense smile. "I believe you're here to speak with my son, Thalex?"

Djet was starstruck. Maybe that was the wrong word; she was shocked, startled. Caught off guard. She was in the planet's capitol, so why hadn't she considered the possibility of running into the Collective's Executor? She was going to interview her child, for Earth's sake.

"Ma'am, y-yes, that is correct."

Ms. Coup De gave a gentle nod. She had a mesmerizing air about her. Like she knew she was the most powerful and important human being, but she played it off like it was an inside joke.

"I thought so. I've taken the liberty of vacating the First Office for the two of you. I trust you'll only be an hour or so."

The tone should have been snarky, or insistent. That's how politicians were on camera, or in movies, but Djet detected none of that. Ms. Coup De was a genuine person, or she was very, very good at hiding her political guile. Djet had never met someone so difficult to read.

"Yes, Madame Executor. It should not take long at all. It won't be an interrogation, just gathering a bit of information about –"

Ms. Coup De cut her off with the slightest raise of an eyebrow. "I know why you are here, Detective. Between you and I," she leaned in slightly and lowered her voice, "this place has more leaks than a torind sunship." She leaned back and gave a polite laugh. "You wouldn't think it, but sometimes the more security a place has, the less secure it is."

Djet nodded. "I hear that, Madame Executor. I'll head in now. I promise to be thorough and prompt."

Ms. Coup De nodded graciously. "Of course, Detective. I'll enjoy a brief stroll by this lovely artifact, here. Earth," she indicated the statue, "holds a special place in my heart, as I'm sure it does for all humans. A lot went wrong there, you know. We almost destroyed ourselves. It took the sacrifice of our home and a harrowing journey across the ion trails of an unforgiving galaxy to bring us together. I do hope we live to see the day when the Nine Nations can set aside their respective past quarrels and embrace a collectivist ideology. Human or not, we biological beings are better together than we are apart."

Djet was relieved to hear someone in her position echoing the way she felt.

"Absolutely, Madame Executor. Thank you for the encouragement."

Ms. Coup De smiled, showing the whitest teeth Djet had ever seen. She could not help but like the woman.

"I'll not keep you here any longer, Detective. Please do send my secretary the full report of your findings once you've concluded the interview. I appreciate your tact in this matter."

Djet smiled, shook the Executor's hand, and headed for the capitol building.

Hot damn, that was intense, she thought. *That woman is actually everything they say she is. Kind, intelligent, and driven to do the best for humanity that she can. Politicians like that typically end up assassinated, don't they?*

Don't tempt fate, her analytical side warned. *You know that can happen at any time.*

No, Djet corrected herself, *I don't think it can. This is the most secure area on the entire planet.*

Someone could destroy the planet, her mind argued.

Ah, Djet, stop being petty and let this go. Focus. Interview Thalex. Get info on Abraham while you're asking about Representative Russolial. Don't forget you're investigating Russolial – add Abraham as a side conversation.

She mounted the steps, passing between obsidian girders that made her think of old school pewter busts she'd seen in a museum once. Well, in pictures of a museum. The building was three stories tall, boxy and relatively unassuming. It was hard to believe the hundreds of years of history contained in this building.

Four Centurions, the special guard for Liberty House, stopped her at the threshold.

They were dressed in ceremonial garb, cuirasses gilded with a shiny orange and gray exotic metal; and they each had enough weaponry to facilitate a small armory. Two of them let their rifles hang magnetically from their armor while the other two kept their weapons low ready, casting death glares beneath their helmets. The faceplates, usually transparent during face-to-face interactions, remained full black.

They could have been cyborgs, or full-on robots for all she knew. There was no whirring as they moved to pat her down, but who knew what technology the core of humanity's government had?

"Clean sweep. Citizen is permitted access," one of the guards said through his helmet speakers.

"Enter, Djet Rincon of Destin. Make a left and head all the way down to the door at the end of the hall," the other said, gesturing with his rifle toward the double doors.

Djet took a deep breath and pushed the ornate doors open. They swung open, an antique design that she had not encountered before on Vatican. It was a hallmark design, something that recalled mankind's old way of doing things on a world they had rendered uninhabitable by their own failures. It was a statement, a reminder that they would be forever vigilant, aware of that existential failure, striving forevermore to atone for their past sins.

Djet shivered. The weight of that reminder was so heavy, she felt emotional when she crossed the threshold to walk on red spongy carpet. The world she entered inside the political underbelly of the Human Collective was mind-numbing.

The red carpet stretched out across the entire floor. Dozens of spinning spheres floated around the ceiling, spitting tiny puffs of air, holoscreens popping and shifting feeds constantly. Some of them blinked with red or green lights, and a few of them chittered as they changed course at the last moment to avoid colliding with another.

Terminals were stationed in seemingly random places, but these didn't function like terminals Djet had used at cafés. People walked up to them and placed their hand on a sensor pad, before the terminal and the person disappeared suddenly in an egg-shaped shadow. Djet wouldn't have believed it if she hadn't seen it herself, but the domes looked otherworldly.

Those must be very high-security terminals, she thought drily.

Images, plaques and memorabilia of and from humanity's past hung on the walls, rested on wall-length shelves, or in the case of the ancient marble statue collection, flanked the doorways that led out of the main room. She didn't know who these people were or what they had done to deserve their likeness being memorialized in statue form, but she felt a tingle in the air that was unlike anything she'd experienced before.

Just being in the room gave her a sense of purpose, like what humanity was doing was important, it mattered, and it was in the pursuit of what was right. She liked that feeling, and she reminded herself to pass that along if she ever swapped stories with any other detectives or girls at the bar.

She passed through the main area, took the left as instructed, and walked down a surprisingly sparse hallway to a large brown door at the end. She placed her hand on the golden handle, but the door swung open of its own accord.

The Centurion that opened it gave her a curt nod but did not speak.

Seated at the First Desk was a punky teenager with blue hair, spiked in a style Djet hadn't thought was in fashion for...she didn't think it was ever in fashion, actually. He had his hands behind his head, elbows out, and his feet on the desk. His nonchalant manner was in such contrast with everything she had just seen, she felt herself getting pissed.

"So, you're the detective," he noted curtly.

"That's correct, Mister Coup De. I'm Longarm Detective Djet Rincon with the Dominicus Venti precinct."

The kid snorted. "Good for you. What do you want?"

Djet blinked. This wasn't going to go well. How could this arrogant asshole possibly be related to the Madame Executor herself?

Then again, she thought, *rich and famous and powerful people tend to have real assholes for kids.*

That, or they create miniature versions of themselves.

Cleary, Thalex was the former.

"I want you," Djet kept herself from snarling, "to answer a few questions."

Thalex laughed. "I already talked to the longarms on the scene, lady. If you're here to grill me about doing something wrong, you can stuff it. I didn't do anything wrong, that bitch-ass marine did! He assaulted me, and he killed some of my friends!"

Djet blinked. "You're friends with torinds?"

Thalex shrugged. "What's it to you?"

Djet felt herself redlining. She wasn't going to tolerate much more of this kid's bullshit. She just had to play it cool, get the answers, and move on. The way the kid was talking, it didn't seem likely he knew Abraham Zeeben at all. Something clicked in her head just then, and she switched gears.

Striding over to the side of the desk, she stood next to Thalex, leaned in close and gave him a mischievous smile. He looked uncomfortable, but not disinterested.

"Thalex," she said in a low voice, "can we talk about what really happened?"

He grunted. "I don't know what you're talking about, lady. I already said –"

Djet held up a finger. "Ah, Thalex, this only works if you don't lie."

"I'm not..." His voice died halfway through the sentence. "You know what, fuck it. I hate marines. They're low-life, two-bit thugs that parade around like they're the greatest thing ever, like we should all kiss their asses because they know how to shoot a CLR and blow stuff up." He mimed pulling a pin and tossing a grenade over his shoulder. "How hard is that, really? Anybody could be a marine. They don't deserve special treatment, and they definitely shouldn't be kicking around our local bars."

Djet nodded, forcing herself to show a healthy amount of empathy.

"I understand that, Thalex. Military's meant to be deployed, fighting wars far away from settled systems. They're too loud and obnoxious when they're landlocked on a developed world for longer than a few weeks at a time."

He nodded emphatically. "That's what I'm saying! Fuck those HOGs."

Djet made a mental note to look that one up. HOGs? It must have been an acronym...

"Okay, so can you tell me what exactly happened, then?"

Thalex shrugged. "I'm sure you've seen the video."

"Of course. But that's just one angle. I need to know what you saw."

He gave her a sidelong glance. "Why're you so interested in this?"

"Because I'm looking for one of those marines." Realizing she had to make it worth his while, she spun a tiny lie to sweeten the deal. "He's got a warrant, for this and another incident he was involved in. I'd like to bring him in, but I don't have enough to go on."

Thalex sighed and drummed the desk with his hands.

"That's a good sign this interrogation is over, sister. I don't know anything about the guy."

Djet placed a hand on Thalex's shoulder to keep him from standing up.

"Thalex," she said, leaning in even closer, trapping him with her eyes as much as with the hand on his shoulder, "you saw something. The same thing I saw in the vid. What was it?"

His eyes darted back and forth, like he was looking for an escape. When he didn't find one, he said, "That freak of a marine, he stopped a bullet in mid-air. Don't ask me any more questions, because I don't know anything else!" He shrugged out of her grip and stood. "The guy's probably not even human. I hang out with some...different kinds of people. All types. And no one I know, regardless of what they are...no one can do that."

Thalex rushed out of the office, leaving Djet standing there in a daze.

She snapped back to awareness when Thalex's mother entered.

"Ma'am." Djet snapped a salute.

"At ease, Detective, please." Ms. Thessaly Coup De waved a hand, indicating Djet should step around to stand in front of the desk.

Djet hastened to comply as the Executor took her seat. She took a slow, deep breath and laid her arms on her desk, folding her hands together gracefully.

"Detective." Her tone was still gentle, but there was a seriousness that Djet hadn't heard earlier. "I understand the normal procedure here is for you to ask questions regarding Representative Russolial and the suspicious circumstances of his death. The crux of the matter is, we already know who is responsible for it. The only thing I need from you is to file this VF-5 that we have here, and to sign this affidavit."

The forms projected into the air between them. Djet scanned the document thoroughly, not believing her eyes.

"How...Madame Executor, how are these two cases related? If I may ask."

Ms. Coup De smiled, and Djet couldn't put her finger on why.

"Officially, Detective, we've already had our best people on it. We're handing you an early promotion to Lieutenant, with a guarantee of Watch Captain in two years after you've proven your loyalty to the Collective."

Djet felt herself getting dizzy. Like she had taken a few too many hits from her father's hookah, leaving her lungs filled more with smoke than oxygen. What exactly was the endgame here, and what the hell had Vase not told her?

Djet stammered, something she never did. It went to the core of just how rattled she found herself.

"Madame Executor, I don't understand."

The old woman nodded, but her smile held strong. "I'm going to brief you on something that requires your rank be elevated, so as of now, you can consider yourself a lieutenant. That said, Hyperion-Level information is extremely damaging to galactic security if it ever gets out. We do not ever let information of this level leak to the public. What I'm about to tell you may come as a shock, although from what I know of your father and what I've read of your career files, I don't think it will catch you off guard at all."

Djet swallowed. She resisted the urge to wipe the sweat off her palms.

Ms. Coup De cleared her throat. "There is something rotten in the state of Denmark."

Djet let out a breath she didn't know she was holding. "Uh...what? Ma'am?"

Ms. Coup De let out a polite chuckle. It was an odd sound...dignified, but...mischievous? It didn't fit the woman that held the entire Collective in her palm, a finger poised over the big red button that would initiate humanity's arsenal of planet-killing weapons on a dozen star systems.

The sound, innocent as it was, made the hair on the back of Djet's neck stand up.

"Forgive me, Detective. I'm a student of ancient literature, and that line seemed fitting. I'll be concise. There is more than unrest brewing in our ranks. The Human Collective is not as imperialist as the news outlets like to suggest. Our military presence and actions are almost always reactionary. We have earned an imperialist reputation for the simple fact that we do not tolerate harassment. If one of us is mistreated or killed on an alien world, even if that world is a capitol of that foreign entity, we do not sit idly by without a response. We have the strongest military this galaxy has ever seen. Maybe some of the other Nations have superior technology, but we have always been warriors. I know of no other society in the Nine Nations that can fight and win the way we do, where only seven percent of our people are in active military service."

Djet forced herself to take slow, deep breaths. Her blood felt cold. Something big was coming, she could feel it. She could feel it like she was atop the gallows with the noose tightened about her neck – all that was left was for the switch to be thrown and she'd be hit with a world-altering revelation.

"Indeed, there is a lack of contentment seeping through the rank and file of the Collective. The tendrils of this discontentment, it seems have begun to form...let's call them problematic entities. Having solved this case, the assassination of Representative Russolial, that should get you high marks and a stellar career in the Longarms. You would outshine even your father. But I offer you something far greater than that. I'm offering you the chance to become a legend not just in Longarm circles, but across the galaxy. You know who is behind this assassination. You know the report I just showed you is false." She held up a finger. "But, you also know about the biggest threat this Collective has ever faced."

"The Pathfinders." Djet didn't have to guess.

Ms. Coup De nodded. Her smile finally slipped away.

"I need you to be my forward observer. I need you to do what no one has done before, and I need it done now. When you are done – and this office will notify you when that time comes – you can retire or have whatever post you like in any Longarm Watch. Djet Rincon," she leaned over the desk with a penetrating gaze, "I need you to infiltrate the Pathfinders."

Djet was lightheaded. She had to convince herself over and again that this wasn't a dream. None of this made sense. It couldn't possibly be real.

"The Pathfinders are planning to destabilize this government. To attempt a coup. They are too fractured, each cell isolated from the next. It is a compartmentalized rogue agency the likes of which we have never seen. They are a dire threat to the Collective, and I need you to get in there to stop them."

"Ma'am, I…I wouldn't even know where to begin."

"If you accept, we will provide everything you need. If you accept, you will begin right away. All record of your existence in the HCD will be expunged. You will be given new credentials, a new identity, an elaborate backstory, and you will play your part to get close to the man at the top. This man."

Ms. Coup De swiped a finger across her desk.

The documents floating between them were replaced with a photograph of an old man.

The same old man Djet had run into on Destin.

"His name is Bayson Dahlee. And he is the head of the viper nest that is the Pathfinders."

Djet shook her head. "I don't understand. You want me to assassinate him? Don't you have trained killers, far more skilled than a detective, that could do this sort of ting?"

Ms. Coup De's smile returned. "I don't want you to kill him, no. I want you to replace him."

Djet's blood froze. This was too much. She was in over her head just hearing about it.

How could she possibly infiltrate an organization like this? Veteran servicemen who had an axe to grind against the most powerful military-industrial complex the galaxy had ever seen? If they were willing to take on that system, they were certifiable. The compartmentalized cells gave her enough of a clue to get a sense of them; they were an organization built on distrusting everyone around them. Each cell was vulnerable, therefore none of them could have a centralized communication framework. How did they operate efficiently without a nexus funneling information back and forth?

She knew two things immediately.

One, she was hopelessly underprepared.

And two, impossible as it seemed, she couldn't refuse the opportunity.

"I accept, Ma'am."

Ms. Coup De, Madame Executor of the Human Collective, giggled.

"Jebsic," she said with a finger on her desk, "escort Mrs. Clause to the situation room."

The door opened in a flash, and a young Centurion, his helmet removed, stood at parade rest in the threshold. He locked eyes with Djet and gave her a slight nod.

"This way, Mrs. Clause."

"Mrs. Clause?" Djet asked under her breath.

"Yes," Ms. Coup De said, "you are my title fifty option under the elastic clause, so I thought a play on words was appropriate. Mrs. Clause is what you will go by when you communicate with this office. We will be in touch."

Djet followed the Centurion's gleaming orange armor as he led her back down the hallway, through the red carpeted open space in the main area, and down another set of corridors until they ended up in a three- by three-meter room with a keypad.

"Stand by for magnetic acceleration." The Centurion's voice was frank, but not gruff. He hadn't seen enough action, Djet estimated, to give him that world-weary layer to his tone.

"How did you get selected for the Centurions?" Djet asked.

The box clanked and shook. Djet gripped the handrail that ran along the sides of the room, which she now realized was a maglift. A very large maglift.

Centrifugal force pulled her hair up off her shoulders, but other than lightness in her knee joints and the feeling she was being forced to stand on the balls of her feet, the transition was smooth. It freaked her out. She could hear the roar of air rushing around them at blazing speed.

"I was appointed," the young man said with a shrug.

"Your bearing is remarkably disciplined for such a young man. Were you in the Corps, or the Navy?"

He smirked. "No, Mrs. Clause. But my father was. Navy, that is."

Ah, Djet thought. *He grew up with a strict military father. Explains the rigidness.*

"He was killed in action ten years ago. The Riskar War."

Well, that kills that theory.

"Is the selection process difficult?"

"Prepare for deceleration."

"I'm curious. What does it take to be a part of the Ninth Nation's elite honor guard?" she asked as her hair slapped against her back.

All at once, the lift she felt in her knees and the need to stand on the balls of her feet dissipated. The maglift issued a loud clank, and then all was still. The door slid open without a sound, revealing utter darkness beyond.

"It was...intensive. I enjoyed it."

The kid didn't smile when he said it, but Djet believed him. He made no motion to enter the darkness.

"Interesting," she said. "Are you not leading me anymore?"

He shook his head. "I'm not permitted access to this level. The shadow you're seeing is a security field. Whatever's on the other end of that is classified at some level I don't need to know about. Enter, and someone will direct you to the situation room."

I'm never gonna get used to this, she thought.

"Nice to meet ya, then..."

"Centurion Aldo Lin. My friends call me Rack."

Djet was about to take a step forward, but that caught her off guard.

"Rack? Where the hell did you pick up a name like that?"

He smirked. "I'm tall and lanky, like a coat rack. Or so they tell me."

Djet laughed. "Those are some nice friends you have there."

He nodded but didn't make a reply.

Djet took a deep breath, brushed down her C-skin, and stepped into the shadows.

The solid dark consumed her, and then vanished in a blink.

She was in a hallway. The walls were bare, everything the same black and gray, only distinguished by weak overhead lighting. She couldn't see the end of the hall; it ended in a white smear of light.

Where the fuck am I?

"Hello, Mrs. Clause."

The speaker was male, and he was a meter to her right. She almost jumped when he introduced himself. She hadn't seen him approach. Another thing she would never get used to, being snuck up on.

"Hello..." she offered her hand, but the stranger shook his head.

"We're a little...uptight about our security here. No physical contact between anyone. Not a handshake, no hugs, no high fives. Just...keep a one- to two-meter distance from everyone and you'll be okay."

Djet followed the man, who was in his late sixties by her guess, down a hallway where every doorway was covered in black security fields. She had only imagined she was in the heart of the place upstairs – this was the working floor.

"Feel free to look around," the man said idly, "there's not much to see until your security clearance is updated. That's the first step. Second step is to brief you on your assignment, and final step is to get you loaded up for transport."

"Transport?" Djet asked as they turned a corner. "Where exactly am I going?"

The man chuckled. "I don't know, Mrs. Clause. That will be between you and your handler."

"Handler...I'm a spook, now?"

The man stopped in his tracks so fast Djet almost ran into him.

"We do not have 'spooks', Mrs. Clause. This is the Office of the Madame Executor. We have employees, representatives and senators, and then we have field assets."

Djet could guess which one she was.

"Got it."

The man nodded curtly and resumed his stride. Djet followed closely. She knew he wouldn't let her get lost, but this maze was overwhelming. If she took a wrong turn and got separated from her guide, she would never know which security field led back to the maglift.

"Here we are." The man stepped up to a darkened threshold and walked right in. Djet followed him, unsure what to expect on the other side.

It was a rectangular room, brightly illuminated by screens along the walls. A large desk with fourteen seats was the main feature. The screens showed so many images changing rapidly that she couldn't follow them. Tactical maps, sensor readings, scans of a planet she did not recognize. It looked military. Like an upgraded version of Captain Spitzen's office at the Domincus Dorsi watch station.

Seated at the end of the table was the last person she expected to see.

"Hello, där."

"Fatti?"

CHAPTER 17

Smithers refused to speak to him. The silence, coupled with the fear of failure, made a prison cell of the airlock.

I took some hits, Abraham thought, wincing as he massaged the stiffness in his ribs. Space was cold, always cold, yet he could feel the heat from the sim-round hits, his flesh swelling inside his suit. Probably first-degree burns. Hopefully just first degree.

"That was a bitch move, camping out on my waypoint." Abraham tried to goad Smithers into a response. "You're gonna keep me in suspense though, huh?"

The Ghost pretended not to hear him. The airlock continued to cycle.

Abraham swallowed a lump in his throat. He needed water.

If I don't make it...what do I do?

He wasn't going back to the Corps, not for anything. Could he go back to Vase? Part of him wanted to do exactly that. Another part would have been just fine never seeing her again.

The thought transported him back to the flat. The sizzle of cooking oil tickled his ears. A swirling aroma of spiced meat and fresh hydroponic vegetables made his mouth water. Long and easy conversations about everything and nothing. A beer and a glass of wine. The limitless depths of her glacier-blue eyes so close he could see right into them.

What will you do? Vatican's not exactly hiring combat veterans to maintain bots or fly star skippers around.

The cold kiss of indifference. She had kept too many secrets. *Did she ever...*

He didn't finish the thought. She was an officer. He was enlisted. It was a dream. She couldn't have ever...genuinely...cared for him. Which meant she lied every time she said –

I love you, Abraham. Blonde and brown hair parted over a radiant smile.

The warm tingle under his skin dissolved into an icy knot in his gut.

No, you don't. I don't believe you ever did.

He didn't meet up with the others until they were back on Singularity, out of their suits and back in the black garb of Ghost cadets. Ten minutes later they were lined up on the dais in the briefing room. The seats were packed with Ghost cadre. An awkward silence gripped the room.

Abraham wondered if it really was awkward, or if it was just his nerves. A chill snaked up his legs. He needed a long, hot shower.

He stood at parade rest on the dais next to the rest of his friends. They all stared straight ahead, eyes locked on Smithers. This was it; they were either moving on to the next phase, or they were packing their bags.

An electric pop broke the silence.

The Ghost cadre stood in front of their seats.

The results of the evaluations blinked onto a hologram above them.

"Here today, gone tomorrow," Smithers said. "That is the Ghost Society motto."

That was the meaning of the **HTGT** atop the graduation standards hologram. It was a decent motto, Abraham thought. He liked the Tetsubishi Alliance's *Contemno Logica* better. Maybe just because he came up with it. Maybe because it was a link to his brother.

"Only when you've graduated and earned your bar are you able to use this motto. But now you know what you're working toward. We go in, accomplish the mission, and get out. Infiltrate, destabilize, fade. Every mission is no fail. That's the meaning behind the motto. It is incumbent upon you as a member of the Ghost Society that you live and die by these words."

Abraham locked eyes with Larry's. They nodded, communicating more than mere acknowledgement of each other's accomplishments.

We're ready for anything.

"There are no more physical requirements or evaluations. It is your responsibility to maintain peak physical condition in addition to the skills portion of training. This is the final phase, which will culminate in a field test. If at any point during this phase a cadre member determines you are incapable of performing your assigned tasks efficiently and competently, you will be redlined, no questions asked. We are beyond the black and white of pass or fail. From here on out, everything is gray. Your fate in the Society is completely in our hands. Impress us."

Smithers held his hands up. "That's it. Any questions?"

Abraham braced himself, sure that Smithers was about to launch a scathing rebuke in his direction.

It never came.

Myles clapped his hands once and said, "Congratulations, cadets. You're one step closer to earning your bars. Anyone considering the blood path, see me after this."

The cadre filed out of the room, leaving Smithers and Myles alone with the cadets.

"You," Smithers stepped up onto the dais, pointing at Abraham, "like your three friends here, have crossed the threshold into Phase Two of training. I'll give the course breakdown tomorrow morning, and we'll begin next week."

Abraham's legs turned to jelly. He steadied himself on Larry's shoulder.

"What?"

"You passed, Abraham. You're in for Phase Two next week."

"You mean... you're allowing me to pass, even though I don't deserve it."

Larry raised an eyebrow.

Smithers shrugged. "Sure. Think of it that way if you like."

"I don't like it. I think you're making a mistake. Making an exception for me. You shot me. Multiple times. For all intents and purposes of the evaluation, I was dead when I crossed through the ring."

Smithers shook his head with a wicked smile. "No, Abraham, the Society makes exceptions for no one. You passed not because we wanted you to, but because you outperformed our expectations. Given your history of zero G mishaps, you pulled it off. The sim rounds were just for fun."

Larry let out a roar of laughter. "Damn, Smithers, that's messed up!"

A twitch of a smile started at the corner of the Ghost's lips.

"Surprises are part of the game," he replied in his gravelly voice.

"Of course they are," Abraham scoffed. "I should have known you Ghosts would take the opportunity to kick me in the dick just because you could."

Smithers nodded. "You are correct. I would do that. Each Ghost is different. We are not a military organization. We don't tell you how to achieve your objectives. We just tell you what the objectives are and leave the execution up to you. We all meet the requirements and have the same qualifications, but in the field, we're as different as humans and aveo. There is rarely one way to achieve a desired outcome. Obviously, mission success is vital to what we do. Sometimes, the price for success is your life. You've proven to us that you're willing to die if that's what it takes. A vital quality, Abraham."

Abraham felt the floor fall out beneath him. They liked that he was willing to sacrifice himself because they might *need* him to sacrifice himself at some point. That didn't sit well with him. The possibility of giving his life in the line of duty while serving in the Marine Corps had seemed right. It was just what soldiers and marines did to accomplish the mission or to protect their people. Dying for an ambiguous goal to achieve a mission he wasn't sure was even moral just wasn't him.

"I understand all that, Smithers. I still don't feel like I deserve it."

Smithers put a hand on Abraham's shoulder.

"You don't need to tell me about that."

He touched two fingers to his chest. The smooth display of his C-skin popped on with a digital pulse. A medal swirled into view. It looked like it was pinned to his chest. It was silver and bronze with three stars in the center. As Abraham studied it, more pulses ran across the uniform.

Abraham counted seven medals in total.

"I've been there and back again so many times it's become second nature. In the Society, we get to do the craziest shit. There is nothing like it. Sacrifice is the price to enter. It costs you everything, up to and including your life, if it comes to that. But it's worth it."

Abraham was amazed. He didn't know what to say.

"So you have no regrets?"

Smithers smirked but did not reply. He touched two fingers to his chest. With a single pulse, the medals disappeared in a swirling gray mist. The uniform returned to its usual flat black display.

Smithers walked out of the room without another word.

He had just gotten out of a blissful twenty-minute shower, patted down the sore spots on his ribs and back and collapsed onto his bed when he was attacked.

"Abraham, we made it, we made the cut!" Tayla jumped on his bed and practically screamed over him.

She was shaking his bed so hard he almost fell off. How a little girl like her – maybe a hundred and thirty pounds – could rock a deck-magnet bed, he didn't know, but he found it unsettling. Tayla was a lot more capable than she looked. A lot more dangerous, too.

"Okay, that's good," he said, rubbing the dryness from his eyes. He stifled an intense yawn. "So, are we celebrating? Do they have a place for that around here?"

"We're just going to go to the dining facility and get some cookies and cake." Tayla plopped down on the foot of his bed. The force rippled and popped his head off the pillow.

"So much for sleep. Why don't you get out of here so I can get dressed and I'll meet you guys there?"

"Oh, stop it. We're not in the Corps anymore. Besides, I've already seen you naked, and I'm not interested," she said dismissively.

Abraham's cheeks grew hot. "Well…thanks for that."

He pulled the sheet off and dug through his wall locker for a pair of pants.

Realizing what she said, Tayla hastened to correct herself. "No, it's not like you're small or anything, I'm just –"

"Tayla!" Abraham shouted. "Just stop. C'mon, I don't care about all that."

In the dim lighting of simulated early morning, Tayla batted her lashes at him.

"What's wrong, Zeeben, don't you think I'm cute?"

He pulled his pants on in a hurry. He just wanted this conversation to be over. He needed Larry and Savony to divert her attention.

"It's not that, Tayla. I just don't think sexual innuendo is appropriate for teammates, you know what I mean?"

Tayla threw her head back and laughed.

"Oh, Zeeben, you're such a prude."

"I am not!" he protested, pulling on a black shirt. "I'm principled."

"More like a stick in the mud. If the stick was your –"

Abraham threw up a hand and stopped her. "Okay, this is going too far."

The door to his room slid open and Savony braced herself against the threshold.

"Oh, sorry, am I interrupting something?"

"Yes!" Tayla said at the same time Abraham said, "No!"

Savony raised an eyebrow. "Abraham, it's only been two months. Can you not control yourself at all?"

Abraham knocked the back of his head against his locker. "This…is ridiculous."

Tayla giggled. "I'm just screwing with you, Zeeben."

Savony made an exaggerated gasp. "You guys are screwing? Abraham, you shouldn't abuse your former rank like that. I knew you were a horndog. I just didn't think for a minute you would take advantage of an innocent little Ghost like Tayla!"

Abraham exhaled a deep breath as the girls laughed at him. When they finally got themselves under control, he looked them both in the eyes a few times and deadpanned, "You done yet?"

They laughed all over again.

"Hey, uh, this has been fun and all, you guys intentionally trying to make me uncomfortable, but has anyone seen Larry?"

The girls shared a confused look. Abraham pointed to Larry's empty bed. It was made with military precision, hospital cornered sheets and everything. Abraham couldn't remember hearing Larry get up in the middle of the night. Where could he possibly be? On a station this size he couldn't have gotten lost.

Tayla said, "Did he go to the DFAC early?"

"You didn't hear him get up last night?" Savony asked.

"No. But that doesn't mean anything. I think I would have heard the door open, but maybe not."

Savony rolled her eyes. "You're just full of information. Let's go check the DFAC."

The meal was good, and while Larry was there, he wasn't forthcoming about his disappearance. Abraham wasn't in the mood for conversation, anyway, and he returned to his dorm room to enjoy the peace and quiet.

He was in. He could relax, at least for tonight.

The Phase Two training wasn't going to start until the day after tomorrow, which gave him plenty of time to rest his muscles and let his overtaxed brain operate at a lower level for a while. For a blissful thirty hours or so, he didn't have to worry about passing tests involving complicated procedures for hacking or reprogramming shipboard systems. He didn't have to hit the gym and work himself into a puddle of sweat and nausea. He did not have to see Smithers at all.

But what *was* he going to do?

Several things came to mind. He could watch a movie. One of those old shows he and David used to watch when they were teenagers, after their father finally let them get a TV. Skim the galaxy net and catch up on some news. Hit up the galley for midnight chow, maybe. Or he could just lie on his bed and stare at the ceiling, which was what he had been doing for the past two hours. He was hovering in that fuzzy state between awake and asleep, a comfortable warmth building under the sheet. For the past two hours, he hadn't moved much.

But his mind wouldn't quiet down.

It was like that part of himself – the part that made all the decisions, packaged them into electrical signals and shipped them off to the rest of the body – that part was on edge. The quiet stillness let things float to the surface of his awareness that were typically hidden beneath the messy noise that was life. Vase came into his mind. He tried to make her leave. She plopped down on his cerebellum like it was a couch, stretched a pair of pale, slender legs and rested them on his brain stem like it was a footstool.

He keyed up his Portal and thumbed the video message tab.

"Hey Vase, it's me, uh...Abraham." He smiled sheepishly and ruffled his hair. It was a hopeless mess, and longer than Vase would have ever seen on him. He wondered how he looked to her, then and now.

"I uh...you know, I just wanted to make sure you're doing okay and that you know I still care about you. This isn't..." He looked away for two uncomfortable seconds. "I'm not just messaging you because I'm lonely. I made my choice, and I'm sticking to it. I miss you, though. I wish there was some way to let you inside my head so you would know I'm sincere. Sure, you probably think I'm an asshole and I deserve to feel alone. I don't blame you."

His thumb hovered over the end record button. What else could he really say?

He talked before he could stop himself.

"Vase…I still love you. I hope you're staying safe out there, wherever you are. I'm safe, for now, so don't worry about me. If all goes well, I'll send you another message in a few weeks. Until then…take care of yourself, okay?"

He ended the message and sent it.

Maybe he would regret it, but for now, it felt right. She probably wouldn't reply. At least she would know he was doing okay. It wasn't an apology, but it was the next best thing. That was all he was willing to give her. He didn't feel like he owed her an apology. Okay, maybe an apology for blowing up on her in front of the Navy's highest-ranking officer. Maybe. Finding out from the Navy's highest-ranking officer that he was Vase's father was a betrayal of trust, and for that, she owed *him* an apology.

Screw it, Abraham thought. *I don't know what she's got on me, but I can't let go. I can't let her go. I've never felt this way about anyone.*

That was the scary part. Scarier than anything he had encountered on Singularity. Scarier than Duringer. Abraham had lost so much in his life, he desperately wanted one thing to hold on to, and for some reason his mind had settled on Captain Vase Seneca. And he had kicked her to the curb.

The door to his room opened, and he thought it was Larry.

"Hey bro, I…"

Tayla stood in the doorway, resting her forearm on the door jamb. She was wearing a tight black t-shirt and shorts so short they followed the curve of her hip up and over her thigh. Her dark hair was down. It flowed in gentle waves almost all the way to her butt. She bore a look of feigned innocence, her lips pursed under her big green eyes. She rested the bare heel of one foot against the door jamb as she leaned into the room.

"What's up, bro?" she giggled.

Abraham sighed. "Tayla, I wasn't expecting you."

She pouted. "You weren't?"

Abraham sat up in his bed and reached for the wall panel to turn up the lighting, but Tayla stopped him with a pointed finger.

"Ah! Don't do that. I like the dimmer setting. Sets the mood."

She walked over to the viewport between his bed and Larry's, bent slightly at the waist and pretended to stare out into the stars. The motion hiked her shorts up even higher.

"Okay, this is weird," Abraham said. He grabbed his shirt and pulled it over his head.

"Weird?" Her voice dropped to a half-whisper. "Abraham, you're hurting my feelings."

Moving with defensive speed, Abraham popped his arms in and pulled his shirt all the way on. He reached under his bed, found his pants and placed them on the bed. He wasn't sure if he should try to slip them on under the sheets or just stand up quickly and dress himself. Since he wasn't sure, he sat there staring and stammering.

"Tayla, I like you. Don't be like that," he said, struggling. He had no idea what to do in this situation. "Look, I just don't think this is the right time for something like this. You've gotta be tired after the evaluations. I know I am." He rubbed his sore abs. "We've got a lot going on. I don't want to complicate things and I have to figure out something else, too."

She looked at him, and it was weird. Normally when someone was standing in a window – or at a viewport – they'd be illuminated by the light source on the other side. Abraham's room was orientated away from the sun, so the darkness of space kept Tayla's features shadowed. Abraham could not tell if she was pissed, confused, or indifferent to his remarks.

"You know," she said, walking over to him, her soft feet padding across the floor, "I think you're scared."

His heart thundered in his chest, equal parts anticipation and the fear she had so accurately detected. He couldn't let her know that, though.

"Scared?" he scoffed with as much derision as he could muster. "I ain't scared. But think about it. We start…being intimate…" *Why do things like this still make me uncomfortable?* "…and then we have to figure out what that means for us while we're also trying to get accepted into the Society. And if we do get accepted into the society, we may be – probably *will* be – tasked with separate assignments, and then who knows when we'll ever see each other again?"

He started off stumbling, but as she got closer he found himself talking rapid fire, words flying from his mouth like belt-fed ammunition, hoping the sheer amount of the verbal assault would stop her in her tracks.

It didn't.

To be fair, it was a small room. By the time Abraham finished his perfectly sound reasoning, Tayla had arrived at the edge of his bed, plopped herself down by his feet and stretched out with her arms behind her, slightly arching her back. She flipped her hair out of her face and cast a suggestive look at him.

"You can't say no if I don't want you to," she said.

Abraham's heart hit the floor. His body rushed with adrenaline, the fight or flight response as old as time itself, but there was a third response that was a result of inexperience or complete shock, and that was what gripped him: he froze.

Tayla pounced on him. She pinned him to the bed with her powerful core muscles, wrapped her legs around his and locked her hips, grabbed his wrists and shoved them to the bedsides. Her face was in his face so fast his shocked gasp filled his nasal cavity with the blossomy fragrance of her damp hair. Her lips pressed into his, and he felt bombs going off under his skin. The fight went right out of him.

She must have sensed it, because her grip loosened on his wrists and she pressed herself onto him, her kiss becoming more intense. He felt her exhale against his cheek like a smooth whisper.

"Surprise, dirtbag!" Larry's voice came from the doorway, and it was followed by a camera click noise. The flames under his skin dissipated in a flood of embarrassment.

Tayla flipped onto her side immediately, and Abraham saw her face in a microsecond before he looked over to the doorway. She was equal parts embarrassed and…giddy? A tiny hand that had been powerful enough to pin his arm to the bed a moment ago suddenly seemed fragile and innocent as it rushed to cover her open mouth.

Larry stepped into the room, snapping more photos on his Portal.

"Wow, you were right, Larry. I guess that's twenty digits I owe you." Savony sounded genuinely surprised.

Savony's here, too? Abraham thought he would die right then.

"Got ya, Abraham," Larry laughed hysterically, "I knew you were giving it to Tayla the minute we got here." He held out a fist for Abraham to bump. "C'mon, you old dog, you!"

Embarrassment quickly morphed into rage. Abraham slapped the hand away and sprang up from the bed ready to unleash a torrent of insults at Larry, until he realized he was standing up in his underwear. Right after Tayla had been kissing and rubbing herself on him. Given the fact that he was not wearing pants, it was obvious how his body felt about that. He hastily snatched up his pants and angrily shoved one leg in.

"Larry, I'm gonna kill you!" he growled.

"Yeah, that'll be the day." Larry snapped a few more photos.

"That's it, bro, you're dead!" Abraham tried to stuff his other leg into his pants and tackle Larry at the same time. He flopped to the floor, trailing a wave of more camera clicks as Larry and Savony laughed.

Tayla was laughing, too.

Abraham pulled up his pants and whirled around to jab a knife-hand at her, just like his old drill instructor had done countless times. It had been pretty intimidating at basic, so he hoped the motion translated the exact amount of pissed off.

"Did you do this on purpose?"

Tayla bit a finger and rolled her eyes. "It was supposed to be a joke. I didn't know you'd actually be into it, Abraham. Now I kinda wish I had just followed through with my threats."

Abraham nearly screamed in frustration.

"That's it. I'm done. I'm done with you people. You're all assholes!"

He stormed out of the room, ranting. No point in trying to save his dignity now. He let all his anger out, punched the bulkhead a few times and strained his throat with a string of curses, mostly directed at Larry.

They hadn't played pranks on each other since basic. They'd been thrown into the thick of it too fast, and it took a long time to recover from something like what they went through on Duringer. Larry had been the absolute master of pranks. Maybe this was a sign he was coming around to his old self much faster than Abraham thought.

He stopped at the dead end of the hallway where the spin gravity was lightest on the station. Abraham leaned his back against the bulkhead, letting the surface cool his back through the thin material of his shirt. He crossed his arms and rubbed a tooth with a thumbnail, something he did when he was thinking. He couldn't remember when he started doing that, or where he picked it up.

Maybe he was taking it too seriously. Maybe he could flip this around on them somehow. Set them up as perverts who went too far, something like that. The longer he thought about it, the more his mind was clouded with thoughts of Tayla. How far had she been willing to go to pull this prank? Pretty much no limits, it seemed. And was that her usual flirty, joking self when she said she wished she had known he'd be into it?

Abraham decided in that moment that he spent too much time thinking.

All that thinking had not saved anyone. It had gotten him nowhere. In the end, all the anxiety and headaches had brought him to the same place. A place where he did nothing.

I'm not overthinking things anymore.

Abraham spun on his heel and marched back to his room, determination granting him peace. He knew why he sent that message to Vase, and he knew why she wasn't going to reply to him. It was because he was stalled. Locked up in his own mind, not free to let life in and change him. He tried so hard to be the influencer, the decision-maker to the extent that he could be as a marine. He had been the protector and the enforcer for his brother before that. Now, he had the opportunity to adapt with the circumstances, rather than to resist them and eventually succumb to them.

He returned to his room to find his three comrades still laughing amongst themselves.

Tayla was laying on his bed now, wiping tears from her face.

Larry was showing Savony the photos he'd taken.

Abraham cleared his throat, and the laughing ratcheted up a notch.

"Larry, Savony, would you excuse me, please? Tayla and I have something we need to talk about."

Larry guffawed. "Sure, bro. You guys," he smiled wide and raised his eyebrows twice, "talk it out. Just try to keep the noise down, I'm sure Smithers doesn't want to hear what you sound like when you org–"

Abraham grabbed Larry by his shirt, stealing his reply, and shoved him toward the open door.

Savony put her hands up in mock surrender. "Wow, Sarge. I've never seen you like this."

"You may leave now," Abraham said, his face red again.

Savony shook her head and walked out, muttering under her breath, "I hope she fixes him up, cuz I do *not* like him like this."

Tayla rested her head on her hand but didn't move to get up at all.

Abraham locked eyes with her as he hit the wall panel. The door shut behind him.

"What did you wanna talk about, Abraham?" Tayla asked him innocently.

CHAPTER 18

"Everything is a learning opportunity."

Heard ya say it a thousand times, Fatti...

Djet asked, "What the hell is this?"

Warin Rincon, Djet's father and the Chief of the Longarms of Vatican, looked old.

Older than when she had seen him on Destin a few weeks ago. His hair wasn't any more gray. His skin wasn't any more wrinkled. It was not a physical aging that she could quantify with changes in his appearance. It was like his affect, his breathing, his emotional presence, was heavier. Grave.

It scared her.

"Djet, I need ya to listen to me. This is perhaps the most important ting I can tell ya, and I only get a little bit of time to say it. So listen. Can ya do that?"

For reasons unknown, she felt hot, stinging tears in her eyes.

"Okay."

Warin interlaced his fingers on the tabletop.

"Sit. Good. Now, I haven't been honest wit ya about my past. The incident on Singularity. The big case that earned me these chevrons." He indicated his Chief of the Watch rank insignia on his uniform. "I didn't help the Navy, and I didn't help the Watch, either. I did what I was told, because I thought it was going to help. I stumbled into a mess, and I thought cleaning it up was the solution. If I had known better at the time," he looked away, face locked with emotion – or the effort of holding it back – and said, "I woulda ran this shit straight to ground. Instead, I've obtained too much notoriety in my twilight years. So, the burden I should bear has to be cast onto you."

Djet shifted in her chair. It didn't squeak.

"What are ya talking about, Fatti? What's the mess? What happened on Singularity?"

Warin continued to avoid her gaze. He muttered through clenched teeth, "I should have...I could have...wouldn't be like this if...damn that man..."

Djet reached out and touched her father's hand. His eyes snapped to lock with hers.

"The reason for all this...it's because of Singularity. I made a mistake, and I got promoted for it. Djet, you've always been just like me."

She smiled, a jolt of pride swelling in her chest.

"Too much like me." Warin sighed and pulled his hand back. "Because of that, they want you to do what I could not. They want you to step in and clean up the mess that I left. It wasn't my mess. Soon as I walked into it, it *became* my mess. That was my mistake. I thought I could handle it, and där, I cannot."

Djet's stomach was in a bind. Her heart alternated between fluttering and pounding. There had been times in her career when she thought she was going to die. When scatter rounds flew by on a routine traffic stop. When she entered the flat looking for Blaze and a grenade detonated in the room with her. When her mother found out she was into girls.

But this…this was fear.

Cold, paralyzing fear. Her throat was so tight she had to swallow twice before she regained the ability to speak.

"Fatti…what does this have to do with the Pathfinders?"

Warin's lower lip quivered. He wiped furiously at his eyes with shaky hands.

"Djet, I know ya tink highly of me, but ya hafta understand, I was a rookie back then, I didn't know…I couldn't have known what I was doing. It's no excuse, but I…I failed, the biggest way a longarm can." He slapped at his rank insignia with a balled fist. "And they promoted me as an insult. To keep me quiet, to keep me…to make my mistake an eternal reminder that if I stepped out of line at all, they could ruin me by leaking that story."

Djet recoiled from her father. Not out of fear or disgust or disappointment, but sheer disbelief.

"Everyone makes mistakes. This can't be so bad as all that."

Warin met her gaze. His bloodshot eyes swollen with tears made her cry, too.

"Aye, Djet. It's every bit as bad as all that, and then some."

He sniffed.

"The man you're going to replace," he made air quotes. His voice cracked as he said, "I killed his son."

Djet went rigid. Her brain had been trapped in a hyperloop. Information and questions swarmed her. Physically taxing her strength until he said those words. Now, it was like time itself stopped.

She looked at her father, not comprehending.

"So what?"

Warin covered his face with his hands and sobbed for a few beats. He inhaled sharply, rubbed his eyes and slapped his hands on the table. He looked like he was about to have a heart attack.

"I murdered a ten-year-old child. Because I thought it was the right thing to do. How fucked is that?"

Djet felt it, now. Or rather, didn't feel it. It was as if her heart had stopped beating. She didn't feel like she was breathing. It seemed like all the oxygen had been vented from the room. She was going to pass out.

He's an old man, just regretting the biggest mistake of his career.

He's a murderer. Who kills a child?

How could killing a ten-year-old child ever be the right thing to do?

Fatti is a bad man. Evil.

Nothing makes sense. Your life, your whole damn life*, Djet, is a lie.*

She tried to speak. She couldn't form the words in her mind, let alone get them out.

Warin shuddered. Part of him seemed to get lighter. Like sharing the burden of this terrible secret had given him the tiniest shred of peace. Or maybe he just hoped that his daughter, the most precious thing in his life, would be the one person who could accept this part of him. Possibly even understand it, since they were both longarms.

"The back..." Warin cleared his throat. "...the background is that this Bayson Dahlee is the head of an underground movement to overthrow the Collective." Tremors wracked his voice, but he found his stride as he continued. He started to sound more like his old self, like the father Djet had known. "If the Collective falls, there will be a void that all other Nations will rush to fill. Our military dominance has been acknowledged for over five hundred years. But we're in a fragile state right now, and the average citizen doesn't know this.

"We have two agendas. Two paths being put forth. The Collective is wary of artificial intelligence. The self-aware kind, at least. We are also steadfastly against post-humanism. These Pathfinders see our position on these issues as a dire threat to the progress of humanity. Their chief arguments are not important. What *is* important is that they utilize the legal and political process to further their aims. Organize a protest. Lobby a senator. Not plot to violently overthrow the establishment. If they were playing by the rules, we could, too." His eyes shimmered. "Sometimes, the only way to stop a criminal is to become one."

Djet was listening, but she felt disconnected. Like she was watching this whole thing unfold from the outside. She couldn't handle the revelation he had just dumped on her. Everything in her life suddenly made more sense: why her parents were constantly bickering and why her father seemed to go out of his way to keep his temper in check. Why her mother was constantly babying him, telling him what a great job he was doing all the time.

She knew. Mutti knew, and never told me.

It was like tearing the initial wound open again, and it hadn't even stopped bleeding yet.

"Djet," her father said, "ya following me?"

She gave him a wooden nod. Her eyes watered. She refused to let the tears fall.

"Okay." He turned to the wall between them. The screen displayed the man in question: Bayson Dahlee.

"This man claims that the Collective is running experiments on kids. That the government itself is trying to achieve post-humanism for the elite, while keeping the rest of society out of that loop. Because he believes this, he has been conducting experiments on willing volunteers to try to achieve their post-human vision for the future. Djet, I saw this. I saw this man open a door on Singularity without a voice command. Without a device, without physically touching it. Whatever he's doing, it works to some extent. And that's the problem. We need someone to infiltrate the Pathfinders, cozy up to Bayson, but not kill him. We need you to win the hearts and minds of the Pathfinders so that they will want to follow you more than they want to follow Bayson."

Djet couldn't think. For the first time in her life, she felt she couldn't put a coherent thought together. She was acting robotically, just going through the motions. The detachment she felt – from reality, from herself – she had never felt like this before.

Nothing made sense.

Everything is a lie.

"How do I...do that?" she managed.

The corner of Warin's mouth twitched. Under different circumstances, it might have passed for a smile.

"You'll be going undercover. A simple injection will make you post-human enough that they'll accept you. The effect is temporary – it will only last for seven or eight months. But it should be enough to get you in and close to Bayson."

Djet sighed and leaned back in her chair. Her brain expected a squeak; all chairs squeaked when you leaned back in them. Not this one. It bothered her that it didn't. Like an itch she couldn't scratch.

"So, what...I'm going to be able to move things with my mind?"

Warin shook his head. "I don't have the details on that. I do know that whatever it is, it will be something the Pathfinders can't resist. Something Bayson doesn't have, but desperately wants. And when you tell him you've found it, he'll bring you right in."

"It's too late for me to say no, isn't it?"

Warin's face was a stone mask. He nodded.

"I, uh...okay."

Her father wrinkled his brow. "Okay? You're okay with...everything?"

The leading question dangled in the air and died.

Djet shrugged.

"All right, där." He stood and moved across the table to hug her.

She allowed him to wrap his arms around her. She did not hug him back.

"I love ya, Djet." He looked down at her. She refused to meet his gaze.

"And I'm sorry." He left the room.

As soon as she was sure he was gone, the dam of her emotions burst open.

For the first time in her life, Djet Rincon cried.

Djet did something she almost never did. She went to the bar.

Her past outings of this sort were usually to prowl for ladies looking for a good time. She was always in the mood for that, but recent events had boxed up those impulses and shoved them far back into a storage locker in the deep recesses of her mind. It felt like she'd swallowed a grenade and spit out the pin. Her insides were a jumbled mess, her emotions the tattered shreds of revelations too terrible to accept.

Yet, they're real. Your father murdered a child.

You're going undercover. Something you would never have had the opportunity to do before.

I don't think I want to do this. But I have to.

Someone had to atone for her father's evil. The balance of the universe – maybe just the tiny slice of galactic real estate owned by the Rincons – depended on that. Justice had been pounded into her by her parents every day of her life. One of those people had perpetrated the greatest injustice against the natural laws of the universe. That stain could not be allowed to fester. It had already ruined her father. She couldn't let it take her down with it, and her mother...*poor Mutti bears the shame, too.*

Djet left the simulated moonbeams of Starlight and entered the bar. Trading one darkness for another.

Perhaps that was what Fatti thought he was doing...stopping one evil with another.

The end result was far worse, though, she thought as she skirted the dance floor and its overhead neon strobe lights. She was in the mood for friction, but dancing wasn't the right kind. She didn't know if she could step outside of the maelstrom in her head right now, anyway. Better to drink until she was numb. She needed some cold introspection. Affixing a gulf of alcohol between herself and these tormenting thoughts wasn't just a good idea; it was essential to her survival. She couldn't live with herself. Crushed by embarrassment. The disorienting shock of her childhood hero being unmasked as a man with no limits.

Where she came from, they called people like that evil.

She observed the room without trying. It was a skill that had developed into a habit and was now embedded into her psyche.

Thirty to forty people bumped and grinded to a complicated slap metal beat loud enough to drown their conversations. A few people stood off to the side, drinks in hand, casually observing. The bar, a meter-and-a-half tall slab of clear crystalline that wrapped around three walls, was packed. A fleeting thought of the time – 0117 – passed through her mind as she squeezed herself between two men whose haircuts and fit bodies screamed off-duty active military.

"Help yourself, there, ma'am," the one to her right grumbled, freckles dancing on his face in a sneer.

The one to her left, red face indicating he was a little more drunk than his friend, said, "Eh, Gary, cool your tits." He leaned in just at the edge of Djet's personal space and said, "You're now a rose between two thorns, Miss. What're you drinking?"

Djet waved for the bartender, a stick-thin quivarien. Seeing Djet's raised hand, she bowed her head to the floor and hustled over without making eye contact.

"What can I provide you, miss?" The voice was shy and hard to hear over the dance floor music.

"Red Fir Whiskey, two blood oranges."

The quivarien shivered, shaking the flesh fold on the back of her head. It looked like a backwards bonnet. She poured, worked the glass under the counter; and when she brought the finished beverage up – a red-gold liquid with two peeled blood oranges skewered on a toothpick – the soldier on her left placed a hand on the quivarien's.

The alien froze in place. Djet wondered if they knew each other, or if the quivarien was just scared.

"Put that on my tab." He glanced over his shoulder. "And add two more Earth Ales for the marine in the back."

"Of course, sir." The quivarien's voice shook. She still hadn't moved a millimeter.

"Thanks, darling." He released her hand and she sprung into action at a frenetic pace.

The soldier on her left chuckled. "Damn, lady, I didn't figure you for a Risky Whiskey drinker."

Djet knew a little about a lot, but drinking was not one of them.

"Risky Whiskey? Never heard of that."

He smiled, showing a gap in his front teeth.

"Yeah, those red fir trees on the label, they're from Duringer. Riskar make better whiskey than they do war."

"Good for us, I guess."

The soldier on her right, Gary, laughed. "They got something we want, or we wouldn't have been at their throats for the last fifteen years, Bronx."

"I don't talk politics, especially over drinks."

Djet picked up her glass, swirled it and downed half of it in a single swing. She sucked air between her teeth to ease the burning on her throat.

"We don't, either." Bronx leaned over the bar to shoot his buddy a glare.

Djet crushed a blood orange in her teeth. The bitterness soured her expression, but it accented the flavor of the whiskey. Made it harsher. The discomfort was therapeutic in a way, bringing the mental anguish and physical discomfort closer together.

"That one of your friends?"

Bronx shook his head. "Just a marine on shore leave." He pointed to a patch on his C-skin sleeve. It was a falling meteorite with wings. "Once a marine, always a marine."

"Semper Fi, oorah!" Gary slapped his shot glass on the bar and swallowed the whiskey expertly.

"Semper Fi!" Bronx shouted and gulped a few swigs of his beer.

Djet smiled. "Ya military types are all the same."

Bronx set his bottle down. "I know you're not military, but you're something. The way you carry yourself. You've got your head on a swivel. Higher SA than most."

SA. Situation Awareness. The military loves its acronyms.

"Longarm," Djet said offhandedly. "What's the story on the guy drinking alone back there?"

Bronx shrugged. "He didn't say. I suspect, from the look of him, he's nursing some wounds. Physical scars heal. You can even have them removed if you want. But the emotional ones…those are hard to heal."

Djet knocked back the rest of her drink and patted Bronx on the back. "I'm going to talk to him."

"You a shrink, too, longarm?"

Djet ignored the comment. She made her way across the dance floor, ignoring the people. Something in her gut told her she needed to be over there. She came here on an impulse to get drunk and forget herself, to try to rebuild her understanding of her life and her place in the universe with a safety shield of alcohol-induced distance, but this…maybe swapping sorrows with a stranger was what she really needed.

The marine was in the corner when the quivarien dropped off two Earth Ales and cleared away a cluster of empty ones. She murmured something in her soft voice and disappeared quickly. He didn't react, just kept staring at the half-empty bottle in his large hand.

Djet stepped up to the edge of the table, and her heart almost stopped beating.

She couldn't take any more surprises. This was a twist of fortune so ridiculous, she had a millisecond to wonder if she should start believing in fate.

"You planning on drinking both of those, Corporal Piebold?"

Alan Piebold looked up with a scowl.

"If you don't have any updates, get your own drinks."

Djet sat down across from him, scooped up one of the beers and took a swig. For such a light golden sheen, it was surprisingly bitter. It soothed the singe in her throat from the Risky Whiskey, though.

"I don't have much time before I'm taking the plunge on this case," Djet said, "so let's not waste each other's time."

Piebold shrugged. "I'm not here for a social call."

"I thought you were on assignment. Isn't your unit headed to Aldebaranzan?"

He nodded and ran a hand across his buzz cut. "Yeah. They already left. I'm delayed for another thirteen hours."

"Delayed? What for?"

"Bereavement leave."

Djet's stomach sank. "I'm sorry."

Piebold smiled, but it wasn't a smile. It was an expression of pain.

"No, you're not. You wanna know who died. And that's none of your business."

Djet nodded. "Perceptive as always, Corporal."

"I'm off duty. Call me Alan."

"Okay, Alan. I still need your help. I'm no closer to locating your friend, or your sister. And as I said, I had something come up that may or may not be related to them. I want more information on the –" she looked around to make sure no one was listening. "The Ghosts."

Piebold finished his beer, swapped the empty bottle for the full one and took a healthy gulp from that one before answering. "I already told you everything I know."

"Maybe you did, maybe you didn't. Point is, I'm not going to be able to solve this case on my own. Alan," she reached out to touch a finger to his beer, "we're going to have to work together to get to the bottom of this."

He didn't move, but his eyes roamed over her. Assessing her, sizing her up. She could detect that now, unlike their previous meeting. He wasn't checking her out, he was determining if she was a threat or not. Alan carried himself differently than Bronx and Gary. He was a killer.

Maybe the other two had been, once, but they weren't any longer. Alan was different.

Reluctant resignation. He didn't enjoy it.

There was no hesitation, no chink in his armor. He was a professional.

He reminded her of her father. She found it irritating one second, endearing the next. The storm inside her mind was gone, replaced by this new puzzle: what was Alan Piebold's deal? Who was he, exactly?

"Don't know how much help I can be, like I've already said." He pulled out a can of tobacco from his C-skin leg pocket and tapped it a few times, "But I'm gonna be here for a few hours. Enjoy the lack of responsibility before I gotta get on the FTL can, back to the platoon."

Djet waved a hand for another round.

"I'm buying tonight, Alan."

"That's my kind of lady." He tipped his bottle toward her in a salute.

Djet flinched. He hadn't said it in a flirtatious way. It was...like he was letting her know she was okay. That he was willing to talk, or just share space with her.

She tipped her bottle back for a few swigs to cover. Hopefully he hadn't noticed. If he did, he didn't say anything.

They spent the next few hours in start-and-stop conversation. Djet learned about his father's job as a janitor with a Hyperion-level security clearance. She told Alan about her father's job as Chief of the Watch. The drinks flowed and the empty bottles began to fill the empty space between them. As the time pressed on, the awkward silences became less and less, and Djet felt like she may actually have a friend in Alan.

He was concerned about his sister, obviously. She had been missing for twelve years. Alan confessed to her that he had written her off as dead because it was easier to think of it that way, but in reality he had just shut off that part of his life. Tried to forget his entire childhood. It wasn't until – he must have begun to trust her, because he started getting personal – his father had died yesterday, that Alan realized he had never given up hope that Seelie was out there somewhere.

"She had to have escaped," he slurred after his thirteenth beer. "I'm telling you, even though she was nine when they took her, she was a tough kid. Parents couldn't control her, said she had some hyperactivity disorder or something." He snorted. "That's not a real thing. Kid just had a lot of fight in her. Maybe, on some genetic level, she just knew she'd need it one day. That fight. I know if she could have helped it, she'd have escaped from 'em. Kicked those sick bastards in the 'nads and just tore off for somewhere."

Djet felt warm on the inside, and not just from the beer.

She got a peek into the depths of who Alan was...if this were a case, she would have said she'd cracked it wide open. Alan had never dealt with what happened to his sister. He'd been avoiding it, ignoring it, hiding it for so long that he never went through the grieving process.

Alan cleared his throat. "I suppose I can trust you, then. What with you being an officer of the law and all that." He chuckled. "Captain trusts you. To her, you're like a Jane Eyre or something."

Djet gut laughed. "I ain't no Earth cowgirl, Alan."

He beamed at her understanding the reference. "You got good taste in entertainment. That's enough for me." His voice softened – no, it hardened, dropping to barely above a whisper. "I want to get this off my chest. Something I haven't told even the military shrinks."

Djet couldn't help but scoot to the edge of her seat.

His eyes glazed over. *It's a war story, then.*

Djet kept her face neutral, though she braced herself internally.

"The thing you gotta understand about Abraham Zeeben is that he's not exactly human." Djet's blood ran cold, but before she could ask anything, Alan continued. "I've seen him do some impossible shit. Stop bullets. Go toe to toe with the General of the Riskar Royal Navy. And if you know anything about the riskar, you know they have some weird anti-gravity tech. Abraham has that, too. Only it's not tech, it's...it's like it's inside him. He told me he wasn't sure about his parents, not exactly. But I knew his father, a little bit, and he was a weird guy. That's not what I wanna talk about, though.

"I wanna talk about Duringer. When Abraham and I got separated and...that's when shit got real. Too real. We had already crash-landed on the planet. Still don't know how they found us, I never understood orbital mechanics all that well. We came in hot. An unplanned high orbit to ground drop...that's what I mean by crash landing, I guess. Our ship disintegrated in atmo. We tumbled down to the surface, and by the time we rendezvoused with the rest of the company, we were already operating at reduced numbers. I had no idea that the casualties were just starting.

"We had S-skins, no weapons, no supplies. We were stranded. It was the worst few days of my life, and I thought for sure we weren't getting off that planet alive. LT and the staff sergeant did their best to get us a game plan. We did some recon. We were in the middle of all that when we got this mysterious delivery from nowhere, outfitting us with B-skins and CLRs, some additional weapons and grenades. A full company loadout. Was it too convenient? Yes. Did I question it? There wasn't time for that. I just loaded up my kit and got ready to do whatever needed doing. After our recon, we realized we were on Duringer, the riskar home world that had been eluding the Navy for over a decade.

"Long story short, I guess, and this is where it gets real bad – we got attacked. Riskies came from the jungle, snatching up marines one by one. Their weapons threw tiny spits of flame that turned to glass on impact. Nasty stuff. LT – that's Captain Seneca, now – made the call to make for cover in the jungle. It was the only call to make. We were getting slaughtered out in the open, exposed with no cover. So into those red firs we went, running, gunning and dying. Abraham and the Staff Sergeant – Digger, too – they all fell over the side of a dead man's drop, and I thought they were KIA on the spot. The film left out my side of the story, for which I'm grateful.

"See, Staff Sergeant Demarius Hinton had been our drill instructor. You've heard of him, right? Medal of Honor recipient, he had that wicked purple scar around his neck like a permanent bowtie, courtesy of the torinds? Yeah, everybody's heard of him. He was our drill instructor at basic on Juno. We were supposed to be in transit to A-school on Mattox. Got told infantry was no longer needed, we were all gonna be Starfighter mechanics. Probably a knee-jerk reaction by NAVCOM, since the Riskar War officially ended while we were in basic. Anyway, Staff Sergeant Hinton had himself a girlfriend named Sergeant Nichols. So the LT and the sergeant, they were leading us through the gauntlet in the woods. Riskies had us surrounded. Slaughtering us like fish in a barrel. I saw a lot of my buddies go down with window-sized panes of smoking glass stabbed clean through them. Come to think of it, it probably wasn't glass the way we know it, because a lucky shot could stab right through a B-skin.

"So, we made our death march through the jungle over the next ten hours, getting picked off one at a time. I was just a private. It was my first combat action. I was damn near pissing my B-skin, I was so scared. I can still hear the riskies shouting and the glass shattering...marines' screams being choked off by glass rounds. We thought we were safe. Thought we'd finally outrun the riskies when the jungle got too thin for us to hide in. That's the thing about combat, you gotta have cover or concealment, and we found ourselves with neither. That was when Sergeant Nichols got it. This is the part I didn't tell the Navy about.

"She got a wicked blade of glass in the back. I tried to get it out, but it was poked clean through her solar plexus. I knew she wasn't going to make it, but I tried to talk her through it. I carried her, had Private Eilson...Amory, she didn't make it, either...she covered me so I could sling my CLR and focus on carrying the sergeant, but we all knew she was on her way out. That was when she told me – as she was bleeding out in my arms – that she was pregnant. Had just found out she was seven weeks along. Now, I don't know anything about pregnancy and babies or anything, but that...when she told me that, it made everything worse."

Alan choked up. The tears in his eyes were real.

"She should have never been there," he whispered.

Djet was locked in place, unable to move. She realized she was holding her breath and slowly let it out.

He cleared his throat. "That more than anything has been the hardest thing I've had to deal with. Knowing that we weren't supposed to be there, and because we were, the greatest marine I ever knew, Staff Sergeant Hinton, was gone. His pregnant girlfriend and their baby..." his lip quivered, "murdered by those animals."

Djet put a hand on his and said in a soft voice, "That is one of the worst tings I've ever heard." She cleared her throat. "But, Alan, that's war. War isn't fair, and it isn't fun. It's not fortune and glory. It's hell and it's the worst ting in the galaxy."

She thought about her father murdering a child because he thought it was a good idea at the time. Maybe war wasn't the worst thing, but it came close.

"I just..." He sighed. "That broke me. Duringer broke all of us. I'm not saying I'm special or anything, just...I haven't been able to put myself back together. It's like the pieces of me I picked up are all different, and they don't fit together the same way."

Djet smiled. "Alan, they're not meant to. Fit the same way, I mean. The pieces are shaped different because *you* are different. When you get them back together, and you will, because you're a good person and the toughest man I know – I can tell that about ya even though we don't really know each other – the picture of ya will be different, too. You'll see. You'll be a better person for going through someting like this and coming out the other side intact."

"Refined in the fire?" he asked with a smirk.

"Someting like that."

She was about to check her Pulse to find the time, but Alan slapped her hand lightly and stood up. He stretched his back with a groan and stepped out of the booth.

"You from around here, Djet?"

She rocked her hand side to side. "Sometimes."

"Me too. Before the Corps I hadn't been back here since my parents split up, about a year after my...well, you already know."

Djet clapped him on the back. "I do know. And I'm gonna do someting about it, Alan. I promise ya."

Alan nodded. "Good. Take me someplace fun. I got about five hours before I'm headed out, now. Let's make a memory. A good one. I've been collecting shitty ones for years now."

Djet finished her sixth – or was it seventh? – beer and left the empty bottle on the table. She followed Alan out of the bar and into the warm air of the street. Exhaust fumes from the air traffic tarnished the beautiful light displays with their oily clouds.

"There is a place not far from here. Vase and I used to call it the Green Mast. Up there, you can see the curve of the city, the orbital traffic coming and going, and most times you can see Starlight even if it isn't shining on this sector. It's worth a look."

Alan laughed. "Let's do it."

Djet felt like she was a teenager again, sneaking out of the house to prowl the constant motion of the city that never stopped moving. She considered taking him up the maintenance access path, hand and footholds that scaled the side of a few levels to arrive at the Green Mast. As they stumbled along, Alan humming a tune off key and she feeling like dancing – something that could only come from alcohol, for Rincons did not dance – she decided they weren't sober enough for such a daring route.

Kids were falling off those buildings every night. Djet had been to the scene of several of them. Falling a couple levels down to an instant but gruesome death did not appeal to her.

They took the stairs, working off some of the buzz. Dodging passersby of all types became a game. By the time they reached the square, Djet had only shouldered through two grand pleaides and a human couple that refused to stop holding hands. She hadn't been keeping track of Alan.

Taking in the oxygen mists of the upper level and the sprawling spires that marched slowly toward the curved horizon, she breathed deep. The extra oxygen sobered her a little, like a splash of cool water on her face.

Alan joined her on the garden level, a smile on his face. He wasn't out of breath. His C-skin stretched across his large frame. Standing next to her, he was significantly taller. He looked out at the cloud cover and the towers that pierced them.

"So much glass," he said.

Djet wondered if that was a good thing or a bad thing in his mind. If he was seeing the duraglass or the riskar glass. The smile on his face could have been taken as genuine or a mask. It was irritating that she couldn't tell which was real.

"Took over a thousand years for us to build up this city," she said, "and now it's the heart and soul of humanity."

Alan laughed. "I'm not sure humanity, like the Human Collective, has a soul. These Ghosts, whatever they are, there's no chance they can get away with what they do without someone at the top knowing about it. Profiting from it, at least."

Djet had to give him that. "I thought we were supposed to be making a good memory, here?"

"Well, how's this? There's a path I used to take, level-dropping. You've shown me this, I'll take you down that, and we'll call it a night."

"Alan, I'm drunk. I'm not in the mood to battle against gravity, and I don't have any equipment, either."

Alan shook his duffel bag. "First rule of being in the military, Djet. Always come prepared."

He smiled. He was serious.

"You live dangerously. There's a lot of shit-talkers at the bar, any bar on Vatican. But you're the real deal, Alan."

He gave a modest bow that was anything but. "Of course, my lady. I live for the thrills. I'm not against humanity, I just didn't join the Corps to become a killer. I wanted to jump out of spaceships. To feel the fires of breaking through atmo, taste the fear and chase the adrenaline."

Djet gave him a flat stare.

"Okay," he laughed, "so I'm a weird guy. But at least I'm interesting."

Djet shook off her nerves. She wasn't going to let him get the better of her, not in something like this.

"All right, Alan. Lead the way."

CHAPTER 19

Caution was thrown to the wind. A hurricane-force gale ripped the sails of destiny clean off the mast. Abraham let the storm take him.

Tayla sat on the bed, chewing a fingernail with a mischievous smile.

"I'm in trouble, aren't I?" she snickered.

Abraham sat down next to her. He put his arm around her and looked directly into her eyes. He inhaled the fragrance of her hair and smiled.

"You're in big trouble, girl."

She wrapped her arms around him. His pulse raced.

He kissed her. She kissed him back.

Abraham leaned over her, hands moving over her body.

She pulled him closer, pressing against him. He could feel her breath on his neck.

No more words. It was just the two of them. Alone.

And then it was over. Feelings that had been thrown around like two kids playing hot potato with a grenade...detonated. It was over. Abraham didn't need to do a deep-dive analysis. He shared something with Tayla. Something intense and potentially dangerous.

But he needed it.

After so long feeling disconnected from everything, he finally found something that made sense. The next few weeks of training went by in a blur. Early mornings spent working out, the days filled with studying and practicing new skills taught by the Ghosts, and late nights with Tayla. They would give each other massages and quiz each other. Swapped stories about what their lives were like before the Society and before the Corps. Abraham realized they had almost nothing in common, but somehow that didn't matter.

Larry had taken to staying the night in Savony's room to 'give the lovers their alone time'.

Abraham didn't mind the digs from Larry and Savony. Tayla didn't seem bothered either. Every time Larry would say something, she'd just shrug and say in her most innocent voice, "Are you sure you're not jealous, Larry?"

The group dynamic was different, but it still held strong. The four of them were the only familiar faces on the station. As deep into the training as they were, the Ghosts were still a big unknown. The former marines had passed the halfway point of their evaluations, but Resurrection Week was coming up. The final exam.

One of those late nights, Abraham lay in bed slowing his breath. Tayla wrapped herself over him. Her nakedness was natural. Comforting. He ran his fingers down her bare back with a contended sigh.

"Abraham?"

"Yeah?"

"You know it can't always be like this," she whispered.

He nodded in the darkness. "I know."

"You still think about her?"

He stiffened.

"I don't want to talk about her."

Tayla kissed his chin. "I know you still think about her."

"I don't want to think about her," he said.

"I know you don't," she said softly. "I hope I'm able to help you forget her."

Something tightened in his chest. *Is she sad? I've never heard her sad before.*

"Tayla, I –"

"Abraham, stop." She covered his lips with a finger. "I know I'm convenient, because I'm here. I've always been a flirt. But I like what we're doing here." She kissed him and looked into his eyes. "I like it a lot. I just don't want it to be about anything – or anyone – else."

"Okay."

She fell asleep with her head on his chest.

Abraham lay awake for some time, fighting the urge to think.

He fell asleep, trying to forget the hospital room after Duringer. The first time a woman had told him she loved him. As he slipped into the void of sleep, a horsetail waterfall broke into dancing moonbows that cascaded down the dark, reflective rocks of a mountain.

I should have never walked away.

Abraham sat in the escape pod, which was barely big enough for him and the gear he was allotted for the final exam. Field Week, he liked to think of it. The Ghosts had a name for it, but it was pretentious and hollow, and he hated using it: Resurrection Week.

So what, they were going to kill him and bring him back to life?

He had heard the stories about the special operations community. Specifically the Marine Corps Raiders. How they would drown their recruits and resuscitate them as part of their graduation standards. Supposedly this process, called flatlining, made them less afraid of death because the big fear of dying was the unknown. The idea was that once you died and came back, you knew what to expect. Therefore, having died once, you'd be less afraid to die again. Until now, he thought the stories were exaggerated. When humanity had their first contact war with the avian Nordo Che, the Nordo Che came under the impression that all members of the HMC were required to kill a family member to gain admission. This rumor was not discouraged by the Commandant of the Marine Corps, and it led the Nordo Che to avoid engaging with infantry forces at all costs. This fear ultimately cost them the war.

Insofar as Abraham could determine, the galaxy was a strange place with strange things happening all the time. The Nine Nations were constantly developing advanced technology – technology that was magic to a simple man like himself. Weapons of war so devastating they could destroy entire planets or consume whole stars. Starships the size of small moons that could break the light barrier several hundred times over. But nothing changed the one immutable law of the universe.

When someone, or something, died, it stayed dead.

So no, they weren't going to kill him. The power of the metaphor was not lost on him, though. Five months and three weeks into the training, he knew the Ghosts pretty well. They weren't going to put a bullet in his skull, or disembowel him, or make him walk out of an airlock without a suit. Whatever special brand of hell they cooked up, it was sure to make him wish he was dead.

That was how they played their little games.

Head games inside head games, designed to burrow deep inside the psyche, sniff out any scraps of weakness in you and drag them out into the light. Once exposed, you had to own it. Hold it under the water until the bubbles stopped. Don't let it up until you feel that last, final twitch inside your grip. Only then, when you realize it is a brand of suicide by degrees, only then do you understand what it takes to join the club. Not all of you – because you just spent the last six months slowly killing parts of yourself they didn't like – but enough of you remains to respond when your name is called.

A tattered ruin of a person, albeit the most dangerous and capable version of yourself, you stand at attention until they patch those tatters together with seams of their own making, stringing you back together with the unbreakable bonds of oath, duty, and a willingness to die for the greater good. The definition of the greater good is provided to you by them.

The final piece of this process is the realization that *them* now includes *you*. There is no longer a separation between the two. In truly oxymoronic fashion, the whole being made up of individuals, you are all one and the same.

Abraham did not know what to expect from Resurrection Week.

But he was as ready as he would ever be. Ready for it to be over.

The inside of the pod wasn't exactly cramped, but he could barely stretch his arms without brushing his fingertips against the sides. His standard loadout was locked in a storage locker behind him. One B-skin, a CLR, several heat sinks, HE grenades, two MREs, an L-pistol, and one plant mine he had called the enemy's welcome mat in the Corps. Carrying the gear in his B-skin wasn't going to be too much trouble. The movement assist was built into the suit. He was unsure why he needed all this equipment. He had never seen any of the cadre in full kit. He had been given a singular objective: survive the week. He would be pulled out by dropship on the seventh day at noon. Knowing that this was going to take place on Earth, or the Ghost Planet that had once been called Earth, was a strange feeling.

There were no viewports on the escape pod. A screen the size of his Portal linked to the external camera feed showed the view of the planet below. The photos of Earth were always blue and green covered in swirls of white clouds. The planet below was not that same planet. The blue was a murky gray like stagnant water. There wasn't a single discernible patch of green. Smears of mud brown alternated with yellowish rock. Earth was covered in craters and canyons similar to the surface of Luna.

Humanity's original home planet, he thought without emotion.

People died to protect it until those same people destroyed it.

Milune was destroyed by people, too. Not the riskar as the news stories ran. Ghosts.

His people, now.

Harsh turbulence shook the pod. He caught himself against the cold metal handrails, then settled down into his crash couch and buckled the safety harness. If his descent didn't end in a crash landing, he would be surprised.

"You are experiencing entry turbulence now," Smithers said over the speakers. "Expect a rough landing."

Called that one, he thought.

The view on the screen became obscured by the red-hot glow of entry fire for a few miserable moments until it was completely whited out with flame. Abraham clenched his jaw tight, rocking back and forth as the pod succumbed to gravity's pull. The pod descended toward the dead world below at terminal velocity.

A few minutes passed with the pod jostling and shaking mercilessly.

He held on to the hope the rust bucket he was in would hold itself together. A shriek emanated from the craft as the reverse burn started to slow his descent. He felt himself pulled toward the floor with a massive force. Flames fled the screen, exposing the first hints of the famous Earth that held such reverence in humanity's collective consciousness.

A sand-covered continent spread across the screen, growing larger with each passing second. He spotted two or three patches of green, very far apart from each other and indistinct at his current position. It would be interesting to see the same kinds of trees his ancestors had seen thousands of years ago. The number of people who could say that were probably limited to the number of cadets who had been through the Ghost Academy.

The turbulence started up again as Smithers came over the speakers with a warning to prepare for landing. Abraham rolled his eyes but got himself set. He hated crashing. If he had a choice between redoing his Phase One evaluation and going through a crash landing, even if he was guaranteed to survive unharmed, he would not have picked the crash landing.

It happened anyway.

The bear hug of gravity pulled him to the ground too hard. Screeching metal twisted and buckled. Mass impacted mass, belching aftershocks of kinetic energy through the pod. Safety harness straps dug into his C-skin, grinding against his collar bones.

The screen became a useless black rectangle, about as informative as a Ghost Bar. One of the panels sheared and slammed into the bulkhead next to him. A lancet of sunlight stabbed the opening repeatedly as the pod careened wildly in its struggle to find a resting spot gravity and Newton's Third Law could agree on.

When the wreckage that was left of the escape pod finally settled, Abraham allowed himself to relax. He survived the crash landing. Check that box off his graduation requirements list. The straps to the safety harness hadn't fused, so he kept his knife in its ankle holster and unbuckled them.

The storage locker was a little warped, but everything inside was in the right place. He opened it up, donned his B-skin quickly, and loaded up his equipment. Once the helmet sealed to his neckpiece, the HUD flashed to life in a frenzy of beeps and warning lights.

The tactical map loaded a few seconds later.

Several red triangles were approaching his crash site from the southwest. Too many to count, or a few that stood too close together for the suit to separate them as individuals. Either way, his first five minutes on Earth were shaping up to be a firefight. The topographical overlay hadn't come up yet. He was looking at a two-dimensional scope of a five-kilometer radius from his suit. What his suit flagged as enemy combatants were already within five klicks.

I have a feeling this is going to be a shitstorm.

Nothing to do now but assess the situation, and he couldn't do that inside this shitcan of an escape pod. He slapped a heat sink on his CLR, charged it, and tucked the L-pistol into the internal leg holster of his B-skin. It closed and locked as he slipped the equipment bag over his head and shoulder. The egress hatch blew out with a kick on the red handle.

His visor dimmed to ward off the invading sunlight. He climbed up and out of the escape pod. Everything was distorted with heat waves. He dialed down the environmental controls in his suit.

Abraham hit the ground at a dead sprint.

The terrain was grasslands as far as he could see. A few gentle rolling hills here and there, but his target was a copse of deadwood trees three and a half kilometers to the northwest. He hoped to find some cover there, although his black and silver B-skin would probably glint in the sunlight.

Gonna have to dig a foxhole just to stay hidden, he grumbled.

The red triangles on his tactical map were drawing closer, but they were moving slow. It had to be foot soldiers. Judging from their rate of approach, they weren't wearing an armor system with a power assist. Whatever low tech beings they were, he hoped their weapon systems mirrored their armor. He couldn't stop himself from casting a glance over his shoulder every minute or so. Every time he did, he saw nothing.

The grass was spongy under his boots. Recent rain was a possibility, but more likely his B-skin was heavy and his wide running stride was hitting the ground with excessive force. A thought occurred to him then: *I might be pounding the ground hard enough for the enemy to feel my steps. I'm sure I'm leaving tracks in the dirt.*

You can only worry about one thing at a time.

If the enemy was low tech and didn't have power armor like he did, he could just stop here and smoke them as they poured in, but the marine in him was hard to let go; he needed cover or concealment, and preferably at an elevated position so that he could be in defilade over the enemy.

In land warfare, straight up infantry against infantry, the high ground was still a massive advantage.

He skidded to a halt at the line of deadwoods. Just on the other side of the leafless limbs was a one-meter drop. On the other side, the land rolled down at a gentle decline before leveling off in a yellow gradient of grass all the way to the heat-lined horizon. A chill like a tiny breath of wind passed down his spine. It was too convenient. He had himself in defilade up to his chest, which checked the box for cover, and the deadwoods over that, which checked the box for concealment. It was almost like it was built for exactly what he needed in this situation.

Maybe it was, he thought drily as he ducked through the branches of two trees, *and I can add geoengineering to the never-ending list of magic tricks the Ghosts have up their sleeves.*

Somewhere in the distance, he heard a peal of thunder. Casting a furtive glance at the sky, Abraham wrinkled his brow. He found no answer in the grayscale cloud overhead. The barometer in his suit was reading high, which meant there shouldn't be any significant weather systems rolling in this way.

No natural ones, anyway.

He didn't know what to expect. This was Resurrection Week, and the Ghosts could do anything. Until he was shown different, Abraham operated like there was no limit to the power of the Ghosts. Next to the ability to instantaneously transit from planet to planet without a starship, manipulating the weather on a planet seemed like child's play.

Settling himself down against the drop-off, he shirked his equipment bag and pulled his CLR off his back. With a twist and a yank, he telescoped the barrel to marksman mode and dialed the laser intensity up to match. The weapon emitted a droning whine, powering up as he rested the barrel against a deadwood root. The visor of his B-skin projected the scope into a window directly on his HUD so he had a full-screen view down the sights.

A blackened impact crater gouged a small trench through the grass and dirt right up to the escape pod, which rested at an odd angle and looked like a cracked egg. It was easy to find, given the plume of smoke emanating from it. The swirling clouds had shifted from black and gray to mostly white, which meant the fire was no longer burning. Abraham remembered that from an unwanted science lesson David had given him one summer back on Veranda. Active fires burn dark. Fires that are simmering down or out exhale white smoke.

Status lights on his HUD were all green. Rounds counter on his CLR had switched from one hundred to twenty. Twenty high-powered bolts of death, a third of a meter thick and deliverable at lightspeed. Abraham enjoyed the physical feedback of kinetic weapons, but there was an elegance and grace to light-based weapons that kinetics just couldn't match.

If David had the opportunity, he might compare them to a rapier and a battle axe. Both lethal, but one was a gentleman's weapon, the other that of a ruffian.

Although railguns were fun, too. On second thought, he grabbed a magazine loaded with thirty rounds of 10-mil slugs and slid it into the bottom of his CLR. Carrying the extra weight wouldn't be a big concern because of his B-skin's power assist, and if he exhausted his heat sink, he could use the kinetic rounds to cover his sink swap.

Abraham had been down range. He survived the near-death experience on Duringer. He'd done patrols and search-and-destroy missions on two other worlds in his four years in the Corps. There was no second-guessing his tactics because he had gotten comfortable in the field. He still had the on-and-off twitch in his fingers and eyes, but that was just the adrenaline. Life or death experiences provoked that response in the body. He didn't think any amount of combat would rid him of the pre-combat jitters.

The pealing thunder never subsided. It grew louder.

He glassed the horizon, searching through his enhanced view via the CLR's marksman scope. When he scanned over the northeast section, distinguishable by a more brownish patch of grass, he saw the red triangles on his HUD scope in the flesh, and his stomach did a flip.

Headed toward the escape pod, a line of horses clobbered the ground with hoof beats. The source of the thundering he'd been hearing. He guessed their number at thirty or more, but what really freaked him out wasn't the horses – it was who was riding them.

They were human.

CHAPTER 20

Djet was tipsy. Perhaps drunk.

"Social area up there." Alan pointed to a cluster of tables at the end of the street.

"Looks good."

Djet stumbled over an imperfection in the street.

Definitely drunk.

Alan caught her, pulled her against him as they walked.

"Watch your step now, lady," he said with a grin.

He was drunk, too. She could tell by how happy he was.

"Y'know, Alan," she said with a chuckle, "I don't think I've ever seen you actually smile before."

The grin grew wider.

"I don't usually have fun, Djet. That's why I don't smile. There's not a lot of vacation time in the Corps. Plenty of down time, but I spend most of that trying to forget shit."

They walked across the street under the gentle glow of Starlight. The neon lights on the buildings were starbursts that bounced with her every step. Djet knew she was probably four or five beers over her limit, but she didn't care. She needed this. Needed to let loose, to forget about all the terrible shit of the last few weeks.

"I know what you mean, Alan," she said, looking up at him. "You just bottle it all up inside, hoping the day won't come when someone shakes it up."

He nodded. "Trick is to learn to blow your top at the right time. In the right setting. Channel that angst into something positive."

Djet laughed. "Yeah, like kicking ass in a bar."

He winked. "Or blasting a drug dealer."

They laughed until they made it to the social circle. Alan sat across from her and packed his can of tobacco with a few slaps.

"Is that a military thing, or...?" Djet asked.

He slid a pinch into his lip and snapped the can closed.

"You still investigating, Detective? I thought this was supposed to be an off night."

Heat rushed to her cheeks.

What the hell? I'm blushing? I don't blush!

"Oh, of course not. I'm," her brain glitched for a second, the alchohol swirling her thoughts, "...I'm...just asking."

Alan nodded, his lower lip now bulging slightly. "Well," he paused to spit, "it's more a small-town thing. Stony Ridge, Veranda."

Silence fell over them both.

Djet shattered it. "That's fucked up."

Alan wrinkled his brow. "How do you figure?"

"Is there nothing going on in the galaxy that doesn't have to be heavy, soul-crushing bullshit?"

Alan nodded. A shadow seemed to pass over his face, his eyes glazing over for a moment. He blinked and leaned forward, his voice soft.

"There's some serious shit going on. Not just here, but everywhere. Whatever's going on, you're in the thick of it, Djet. I've got about two hours until I gotta ship out on the chase ship, but before I go, I want you to promise me you're gonna be safe."

Djet shivered. "I'm always safe."

"No," Alan stood suddenly and sat next to her. He wrapped his burly arm around her and pulled her to him. "You're not. I know you well enough to know you put your job ahead of your well-being. Captain wouldn't have picked you for this if you weren't that type. Djet, this is serious."

He smells like tobacco, she thought.

"I don't meet a lot of people who are willing to go the distance with things, ya know? I get the feeling that you're different. I like that about you."

Djet wanted to recoil. To throw his arm off her. To shove him away. Something about this felt...wrong. Why was he being so...weird?

"Okay..." she dragged the word out. "So what do you suggest?"

"I suggest," he said, "you keep me and the captain posted on what's going on. If you need anything, if we can help you at all, you just let us know."

"You're gonna be halfway across the galaxy, Alan."

"I know." He smiled. "But I don't make friends easy. After tonight, I consider you a friend. That might not mean anything to you, but it means something to me. I want answers, don't get it twisted. I want answers. But not if it's gonna kill you to get them. You're unique, Djet."

Djet felt her strength go. She was drunk, but that wasn't it.

She was warm. Calm.

It was the same feeling she used to get when she was a child, when her father would talk with her before turning off her night light. Soft, strong words whispered into her ear.

You're one of a kind, Djet. Don't ever let the world force you into a box.

"Alan?"

"Yeah?"

"Thank you."

He didn't respond.

She wrapped her arm around him, laid her head on his barrel chest, and fell asleep.

He woke her with a gentle nudge.

"Djet, I gotta get gone. You have somewhere you need to be, don't you?"

Her head was already hammering from the booze.

"I'm sure I do."

"All right then." He stood and offered her his fist.

She bumped it and said, "I'll see ya around, Corporal."

"Actually, it's Sergeant, now. Take care of yourself, lady."

Djet watched him walk away. Nothing made sense anymore.

But that was just her life now.

Thankfully her hangover was almost gone when she reported to the medical facility in the basement of the capitol building.

It wasn't a big operation. Surprisingly it wasn't a big needle or a big syringe, either.

A tiny little prick and a zap.

"If I knew becoming post-human was so easy, I'd have done it sooner."

"You don't mean that."

The room was quaint. Djet sat on the patient slab, trying not to think about what the injection was going to do to her. Next to the slab a medical tech pivoted on a rolling chair to drop the empty syringe into a sharp-safe container. The woman swiveled around and put a hand on her hip, gearing up for a lecture.

"Humanity has been schizophrenic about post-humanism since the public health scandal on Earth way back when. If you know medical history at all, the pharmaceutical companies tried to force that transition on the people without their knowledge."

"I heard about that in school. There was an uprising and they had to back off. Delayed globalization of the earth for a hundred years."

"That's right. Stopped us from getting to the stars earlier, too."

Djet rubbed the injection site. It itched.

"Don't do that."

Djet stopped, not because she wanted to, but because she felt like the tech knew what she was talking about. She didn't need an angry welt forming at the injection site to delay her departure. Now that she was on assignment from the highest office in the galaxy, she just wanted to get in and get out. She had the weight of the Collective on her shoulders, and that was a burden she didn't think she could carry very far. She was doing her best to keep it together after the conversation with her father...when he admitted to slaughtering a child.

How could he do something like that? My Fatti...

You can't be a good man and do things like that. Some lines, once crossed, change you forever.

Am I about to cross a line? She shivered.

The itching sensation spread into the rest of her arm. She felt it, like microscopic ants crawling under her skin. She tried and failed to block that mental image.

I have to be insane. No rational person would take this kind of risk.

Stakes are too high, girl.

The words were her own thoughts, but they came colored in Blaze's voice. Her old partner. Set up as a patsy for a political killing. The people that now had her doing their bidding.

The wages of being married to the job; once it's done, so are you, I guess.

Is that what's going to happen to me? she wondered. *I get pulled in too deep, can't separate my identity from the job, and then...what? I get fired, or retire with honors, and the tedium of life apart from the longarms kills me?*

Djet had never given a moment's thought to what she would do when her career was over. The tech started talking. Djet wasn't listening. When the conversation started into the possible side effects, a deluge of uncomfortable thoughts began to poison her mind.

"So, what exactly is going to change?" Djet blurted. Anything to distract herself. "What does this stuff do?"

The tech shrugged. "I don't know. I'm just a phlebotomist."

Great, Djet thought. "I'm not going to grow any extra appendages, am I? Are my eyes gonna glow in the dark or someting?"

The tech sighed. "I'm just waiting another three and a half minutes to make sure you don't have a reaction. After that, you're free to go."

The time passed in awkward silence. Her stomach did flips.

She told herself it was just nerves. Made herself believe it.

The itching was everywhere now. Not painful, but resisting the urge to scratch took concentration. When the creepy crawly tingles made their way up to her neck, she felt the injection site go numb.

She touched it with a finger. It wasn't numb, after all. It just didn't itch anymore.

"All right, you're not going to die from the injection, so we can check that box." The tech gave a half-hearted smile, tapped a few things on her Portal and gestured to the door. "You're free to go."

Djet stood up and took a deep breath. Her neck itched now, but the rest of her body was starting to calm down. Whatever was in the injection, it wasn't going to kill her. At least not right away. She had to accept that and move on.

She had a paramilitary domestic terror organization to infiltrate.

I'm in over my head.

But longarms never back down from a challenge. Especially not when their last name is Rincon.

The lower level of Vatican was not where she expected to end up. It was the last place she thought she'd find the Pathfinders.

I work these streets. I know the people, the shopkeepers, the workers and their families. How could one of them…or more than one…be a domestic terrorist? Operating right in my own fucking neighborhood?

"This is where we part ways," Jebsic said, handing her a small purse. Digits jingled inside, small coins of precious metals accepted as currency.

Djet took the handbag, curious. "I didn't know I'd be needing this."

Jebsic was a Vatican Centurion, but no one who looked at him would have known. He was dressed in a plain C-skin, a basic digital pattern that was popular on Destin. He could have been from here. That was the look his clothing suggested.

"Actually," he said as they entered an intersection, "I'm gonna need that back."

Djet stopped walking when she felt a jab in her ribs. She glanced down and saw the barrel of an L-pistol in Jebsic's hand. Pointed at her.

"What the –"

The laser blast ripped through the din of Destin's streets as it bit into Djet's ribs.

She dropped the purse on the ground when she collapsed to her knees.

Her hand flew to the wound and flinched away. It was hot. Her C-skin was on fire.

Black spots swirled in her eyes, eating at her view of the startled people on the street pointing. Someone screamed.

It wasn't Djet. She couldn't gather enough air to make such a sound. Every inhale was like a sip of fire in her lungs. The pain spread from her ribs to her gut. The street was empty now, except for two shopkeepers who were pointing and shouting. One of them had a Portal in their hands, filming her.

Djet's eyes rolled into the back of her head. She wasn't giving up, but the pain was so intense she momentarily lost the ability to think clearly.

And then she got a stark blast of clarity; a splash of water fell over her. Steam rose from her in thick clouds.

"Get her up," someone said.

She wanted to resist. To fight.

But her pain was…it was going away.

It was going away.

Her ribs felt cool. Not cold, but cool.

A siren warbled somewhere. It drew closer.

The man that had picked her up was struggling to carry her. She could smell his breath. Onions and spices.

"Grab her legs, dipshit!"

Suddenly she was floating. Carried by two men she didn't know, to who knew where.

CHAPTER 21

The humans weren't like humans Abraham had ever seen.

Scratch that. They weren't like humans he had ever seen in real life.

They wore black berets atop their heads and thick, straggly beards over green and brown camo-patterned fatigues with dark brown combat boots. They were odd colors, too. A few of them were very pale in skin tone, others very dark, and their facial features were wildly different. Some of them had rifles slung across torsos with crude fabric straps. Others held their weapons aloft, stocks in shoulders. When Abraham zoomed in with his scope, he could see they were ancient black rifles. Small-caliber slug-throwers.

Did I travel back in time, or what the hell is this?

Absent a clearly defined objective, the only thing Abraham had to go off was the crash landing and the fact that his HUD automatically identified these *soldiers* – he thought of them as soldiers because he had seen humans like them in historical war films – as enemy combatants. The Revised Geneva Conventions stated that arms and intent were the only qualifiers to designate a person as an enemy combatant.

So far, they seemed armed, and as for intent...the Society could sort that part out later.

He watched them, finger resting on the kinetic magazine well. Trigger discipline was ingrained in him.

Finger off the trigger till you're ready to shoot.

The soldiers approached the crash site, fanning out. One of them could be seen barking an order before dismounting. The soldiers still on horseback began circling the perimeter until they reached the side nearest Abraham, where they began to dismount. They encroached on the escape pod, weapons up, fingers...on the mag well of their rifles.

This is freaking me out, Abraham thought.

The leader stood back, holding his rifle unslung at a low ready, observing his men as they scouted the area. Abraham watched them with a curious eye. He was just as interested to learn who these people were as he was to find out if they were genuinely hostile. Then again, this whole thing could be a simulation like the one at basic training, and he wouldn't realize that until he woke up or saw some really unbelievable shit.

Like jumping from one planet to another without a spacecraft?

Okay, fair point, he answered himself. *But if flaming unicorns fall from the sky, I'm calling bullshit on this whole thing.*

Damn Ghosts. You never can tell what they're capable of.

Secrets don't make friends. Vase's words flowing through his stream of thought.

Rather than rehash that old argument with her in his mind for the thousandth time, he shrugged her away. He wanted to dwell on those words, on her lips forming those words, on her in his arms by that stupid, beautiful waterfall and all the things that should have been…

He couldn't afford the distraction.

Still, he couldn't shake the tingling scent of vanilla and honeydew that lingered between his skull and his brain.

Focus, marine.

No. Focus, Ghost, he corrected himself.

My life is a mess.

The leader barked another command, drawing the troops back onto their horses. The lone soldier who did not dismount pointed at the ground, then waved a hand in Abraham's direction.

They had found his tracks.

As one cohesive unit, the soldiers oriented their horses into a wedge formation, bringing their rifles around and holding them at a ready state. They moved westward, headed directly for Abraham's position. The soldier who had pointed out the tracks was a few gallops ahead of the rest, acting as scout. He periodically pointed to the ground as the horses moved at a light trot, keeping the noise down but moving with respectable speed. Abraham's HUD marked the distance at two kilometers, which gave him – he glanced at the mission clock in the lower left corner of his HUD…they would be on him in less than five minutes.

He thumbed the safety off.

The scout trotted his horse back to bring himself alongside the leader. He indicated with a knife-hand the copse of trees a few meters to the right of Abraham's position. The leader asked him a question, to which the scout's response was lost as his head exploded.

Boiling blood and blackened brain matter sizzled centimeters from the leader's face and hit the grass. A thick laser bolt flashed in and out so fast the lead soldier barely had time to register it before it pierced through his chest and back. His feet locked securely in the stirrups and prevented him from falling off the horse. The body slumped onto the creature's back.

The sudden loss of two of their own caused chaos to erupt in the formation. Horses reared, whinnying and shrieking, and chucked their riders to the ground. The animals that had successfully cleared their saddles of soldiers took off at a brisk gallop in random directions.

One one thousand…two one thousand, Abraham counted, giving the CLR's barrel an appropriate cool-down period between trigger pulls. The audio scrubbers in his helmet filtered out the shrieking *pyow* of each laser bolt. Sound waves shook the deadwood branches above him. He had grown so used to firing the CLR in its various modes that he didn't even think about the fact that his eardrums would be liquefied mush running down his cheeks without the protection of his helmet.

Abraham saturated the target-rich environment with well-placed shots. Bolts reached out and tore clean through the ancient plate carriers – primitive tech like that couldn't really be called armor – and blew right through the tender flesh beneath. Men died not with screams and shouts, but with choked gasps as superheated light burned holes through their insides. A few died with a pair of *thunks*. One for the headshot, one for the body hitting the ground.

The soldiers were in full-on retreat mode now.

Three of them had formed up into a sort of slapdash quick reaction force and charged the deadwood tree line. Abraham made quick work of them. The rest were turning tail and running to try to catch their escaping horses. Two mounted soldiers steered their horses toward one or two of their buddies that were still standing and tried to pull them up behind the saddle. Abraham prioritized these targets. He couldn't let any of them get away; if they were part of a larger force, he did not want them making it back to their base and raising the alarm.

One of the soldiers regained his footing and started limping away. Another came by and sent a volley of inaccurate fire in Abraham's general direction, then stooped to pick up his wounded comrade. Once he had him slung over his shoulders, he stood and started marching westward. Abraham's twentieth shot cut through both men. The soldier collapsed with his buddy on top of him. Neither of them moved to get up.

"Swapping sinks," Abraham said before he could stop himself.

It was automatic. He must have said this a thousand times in the field.

This time he wasn't speaking to his fireteam, or his squad. He was talking to an empty comm net that perhaps Smithers or some of the other Ghost cadre were monitoring. He shrugged off the embarrassment, popped the smoking heat sink off his CLR and kicked it down the hill before slapping a fresh one onto his weapon and priming it with a yank on the charging handle.

The downside to the CLR's marksman mode was the possibility of it torching the barrel and rendering it useless. If he let it overheat, he'd be out a primary weapon. This generally wasn't an issue when you were in a sniper's roost or moving between firing positions to take precise shots. Now, though, he had just lit off twenty shots in a little over two minutes, and the enemy was on the move. Nine triangles still blinked in his HUD. He had to do some legwork to prevent the enemy escaping.

Pausing only to collapse his CLR to standard firing mode and to sling his bag over his neck and shoulder, Abraham clambered over the ledge and took off at a dead sprint for the crash site.

The sink monitor in his HUD automatically switched from twenty to one hundred shots.

The soldiers broke into two teams of four and headed off in different directions. The ninth turned to face Abraham, rifle up. Abraham knew the varmint rounds those ancient rifles fired weren't going to harm his B-skin at all – likely they wouldn't even make a dent – but it still chafed him that he was going against sound tactics by rushing out in the open.

The soldier gave a fierce war cry and opened up with his rifle. The blowback from the weapon ruffled his beard, but his sunglasses stayed firmly in place. Brass shells arced out and past his shoulder, glinting in the overcast sunlight. He would have cut an intimidating figure if he was matched against an opponent with similar capabilities.

Abraham skidded to a standing position two hundred meters from the crash site, bringing his rifle up before the skid stopped and brought the soldier into his sight picture.

Two, then three rounds plinked off his B-skin.

It wasn't enough to even throw off his aim.

He registered shock that his body hadn't thrown up a gravity shield, but he didn't have time to analyze why his mysterious riskar power seemed to have vanished.

Abraham double-tapped the trigger.

Two modest laser bolts bit into the soldier's torso and neck. The antique black rifle fell from the man's grip, dangling uselessly on the sling. Thin white trails of smoke followed him to the ground.

A ticking clock chimed in Abraham's head. It wasn't real, but he felt it like the bell that rang at the end of the school day. He needed to stop the fleeing soldiers before they got too close to whatever base they had come from. They arrived on scene at the crash within twenty minutes; they couldn't be too far from home. Unless he caught them when they were doing a patrol, but he dared not hope for such good luck.

Abraham opened his bag and rummaged through it until he felt the portable plasma tube attachment. He took a knee, slapped the rectangular launcher onto the bottom of his CLR and latched it to the body of his weapon. As soon as his thumb was on the launcher and it was secured to his CLR, his HUD automatically switched reticules to the plasma launch rangefinder. He held the rifle out in front of him, stock against his hip, and angled the weapon up forty-five degrees. A blue line painted itself in his HUD, showing a small circle where his suit predicted the plasma grenade would land and indicating its effective kill radius.

He took a deep breath and exhaled slowly, placing the circle right in the path of the four-man fireteam fleeing to the south. Satisfied with the trajectory arc, he pulled the trigger.

WHOOMPF.

A sphere of white-hot plasma arced up and out from the launch tube, sailing through the air like a fireball. Pressed for time, he did not sit and watch to make sure the plasma found its mark; he would check his HUD after the impact. He detached the launcher and stuffed it back in his bag.

Abraham turned his attention to the north and took off at a sprint.

His rate of respiration was increasing with all the start and stop sprinting. In his experience, the heightened sense of danger was what got his heartrate up, but this...this was almost like a PT exercise. Shoot, run, shoot, run. Launch a plasma mortar, run. Shoot, run, shoot.

Part of him felt bad for the soldiers. They didn't stand a chance.

But then, he also felt like there was a high probability that this whole thing was a simulation. He wouldn't know for sure until it was over. In either case, he needed answers from the Ghost Society, and if this was the only way to get those answers...

Nothing's gonna stop me.

The remaining four soldiers had crested a knoll in the rolling grass and disappeared from his immediate line of sight. Abraham hoofed it at breakneck speed – the suit clocked him at fifty KPH – much faster than any human could run unassisted. Augmented running was a strange thing; easier on the joints, like using an elliptical, but your lungs still worked at normal capacity like you were running on a hard surface. It took some getting used to, and if you were out of the habit for a few weeks, like taking a break from B-skin wear on station at a secret facility that did not officially exist, you could get rusty. Rusty enough to, maybe, lose your rhythm or trip yourself and fall flat on your face at a blurry fifty kilometers an hour.

Which is what happened to Abraham...

He looked into his HUD radar scope as he was running. He was just outside three hundred meters from the hill between the soldiers and himself, and then his heel slammed into his shin and he started seeing the sky chase the ground like a revolving door as he tumbled head over heels, shoulders and knees bouncing off the slick grass until he skidded onto his back.

It was a miracle that he clung to his CLR.

Black and gray clouds trundled overhead, indifferent to his blunder.

Abraham cursed to collect himself. Some mistakes were unavoidable, but this wasn't one of them. This was a stupid mistake that could get him killed. If Staff Sergeant Demarius Hinton were here, he would have skinned Abraham's ass alive for making such a potentially lethal mistake.

As it were, the hill separated Abraham from the still-fleeing soldiers, so it was a 'no harm no foul' situation. He could not hope to get any more lucky breaks, though. Especially since this was the Ghost Society's final entry exam. Things were definitely going to get a lot tougher before the end.

Abraham ran up to the peak of the hill, CLR at the ready.

The plasma mortar hit with a buzzing thud in the distance. All four triangles winked out a few seconds later. He didn't need to turn around to see the emulsified remains of that enemy fireteam to know they were KIA. Through the increased magnification of his visor, he saw the remaining enemy break formation, taking off individually in different directions.

The hill rolled down for fifty or sixty meters and then levelled off to the horizon, with a few minor hills and several patches of waist-high grass intermixed with sections of shorter, yellowish brown field. A couple of clusters of deadwood trees sprang up haphazardly out of the short grass, gray-barked branches adorned with small heart-shaped leaves in shades of pale green. Beyond the trees lay a large body of water circled by a swathe of mud and trampled grass. Several animals, funky looking horses with black and white stripes, large lumbering yellow and brown spotted things with massive necks and small heads, and a variety of smaller four-legged creatures with thin black horns on their heads were congregated around the water.

David could've probably named all these things, Abraham thought.

He didn't care about the creatures because they weren't tagged as enemy combatants on his HUD scope. He kept his peripheral on the motion tracker as his eyes roamed the field, trying to get an actual location for the approximations his suit made. He figured two enemies were behind or near separate tree clusters, one was prone in a patch of tall grass, and one might have slipped into the muddy area near the water.

Abraham made a snap decision and ran to the nearest patch of tall grass and went prone. These soldiers didn't appear to have technology comparable to anything like he was working with, but it didn't make sense to stand out in the open as an easy target. He peered through the break in the grass blades at the waterline, zooming in with his visor to search for enemies hiding in the herd of creatures.

The visor shook. Abraham held back his confusion, but he could only see the horned creatures and the spindly legs of the spotted animals. There wasn't so much as a breeze; the grass stood tall, proud, and undisturbed. And then he saw it. A black beret in the heart of the creature huddle. Abraham propped himself up on his elbows and grabbed the barrel of his weapon, preparing to telescope it into marksman mode, when the ground shook again.

He stopped, lying as still as he could.

The tremor happened again, a dull thunder that sent vibrations across the ground and up through his B-skin, causing little shakes in his visor. He didn't have time to form the words in his mind before he saw it.

A squad – he automatically designated it a squad because he counted twelve units – of mounted soldiers marched onto the scene atop massive beasts that erupted with bleating shouts. They looked like statues he'd seen in some restaurants on Milune when he was a kid. The ones that smelled like saffron and allspice and served hot tea in kid-sized cups, even to adults. He remembered the gilded statues out front of the marble pillared entrance, imposing with their graphene tusks and a long dangling nose that looked strong enough to knock a man's head clean off.

These weren't statues; they were much larger. Dirt and grass clods flung from massive feet as they pounded into the animal huddle like plows. The smaller horned creatures darted out of the way first, zigzagging with hurried elegance. The long-necked creatures lazily stepped closer to the water to make way.

Angry sounds blasted from the long-nosed behemoths, scaring even the long-necked ones away.

Seated on a thrown-together saddle atop each beast was a soldier, but these were different from the soldiers his HUD tagged as enemies. For one, they were all a more homogenous shade of dark skin, and they wore cloth over their heads like bandanas. Most had bandoliers lined with small caliber rounds and brandished rifles similar to the antique black rifles carried by the other soldiers, except these were metal and wood and looked much older.

Abraham watched as one of the beasts stomped straight over the black beret, crushing it into the mud. He was too far away to hear, but he could imagine the unlucky soldier's bones crinkling like a ration bar wrapper under the extreme weight.

That triangle winked out in his HUD. Three enemy left, and he wasn't sure what to make of the newcomers. The IFF system in his suit didn't register them at all. As far as his suit sensors were concerned, it was like they weren't even there.

"Okay, I need to just get this over with," he muttered under his breath.

Abraham jumped to his feet, sighted in on the closest copse of trees and fired as he walked, moving toward the high grass. As he predicted, grass started flying up in shreds as the prone soldier sent a burst of fire at him. He pivoted to bring the soldier into his sight picture and lit him up.

Five, six laser bolts blasted into the man. The incoming fire stopped immediately.

The remaining two soldiers, probably sensing the futility of their situation, opted for a frontal assault. They barked a few words at each other before sliding out from cover to simultaneously dump their mags.

Incoming fire plinked against his armor without enough force to throw his aim off. Abraham sighted in and fired. Pivoted, sighted in, fired.

The second soldier raced to beat the first to the ground, both with smoking holes in their faces. At that exact moment, Abraham realized he'd made his biggest mistake of the day.

The beast riders weren't tagged by his suit.

He had not assumed they were friendlies, but he thought they might have been a hunting party after some of the animals that were making a pit stop at the local watering hole. When he lowered his rifle after cleaning up his last two marked enemies, he had just enough time to look to his right before one of the beasts was on him.

B-skins augmented the user's movements to just under the level of superhuman. Abraham could catch a fly just by thinking about it, or sprint in a straight line in excess of fifty klicks an hour, but he was not fast enough to move completely out of the way.

A thickly muscled snout swiped him off his feet and tossed him right onto his back. He hit the dirt as a foot bigger than his whole body slammed him into the ground. Alarms and lights flashed like fireworks in his HUD, too many for him to make sense of. Even through the stellar construction of plates impervious to a direct hit from a .50 caliber round, he felt the air pressed out of his lungs. The B-skin groaned and squished tight enough to prevent him drawing a full breath.

The panic hit him like a bolt of lightning to the chest.

Holy shit, I'm dead.

The CLR smacked into the grass an arm's length away. He went to reach for it just as a foot came down and crushed it with a thunderclap that made the HUD go skitz for a second.

Ghosts don't die, Abraham. Smithers' words in his father's voice.

Fat jiggled in loose flaps of skin on the belly of the beast that towered over him. The skin drew taut and the pressure on his chest doubled. The HUD went dim.

Then his visor exploded.

Instinct pulled his eyes shut and turned his face away at the same time. Heat stung his eyelids, face and neck with hot sparks. Sound rushed in through the hole in his helmet, a discordant cacophony of animal noises and the shouts of men.

His mind was racing. His heart pounded against his sternum.

He slammed his fist into his leg panel, snatched up his L-pistol and aimed it blindly at what he hoped was the vulnerable underside of the creature.

He squeezed the trigger as fast as he could. The whole world was swallowed up in the *skree-skree-skree* of laser bolts discharging. Smoke shot out the sides of the weapon, choking his already desperate lungs.

The pressure relented enough for Abraham to rapidly squeeze a few short sips of air. He threw himself to the side, but his suit didn't move.

The suit was completely unpowered. He was stuck in a very expensive, very useless iron maiden. It would be his coffin if he couldn't move.

The animal reared on its hind legs, flailing and bleating.

Abraham's hearing was dialed down to a dull, indecipherable roar. A tinny ringing from discharging a laser weapon without hearing protection. He fired several more shots at the underside of the creature's chin until one lucky bolt slammed into the open maw.

The trunk came windmilling around and smacked into him with enough force to roll him three meters off, face down. He tasted coppery dirt and grass.

How had he gone from having an unfair advantage over primitive and underequipped soldiers to being in a fight for his life?

He popped the useless seal on his helmet and rolled it away. With his head clear, he turned his neck to watch his surroundings as he worked the latches on his chest piece. They came free, with a little extra persuasion given that they were mangled.

Abraham slipped the chest section of his B-skin off just in time to see the rock come sailing through the air at him. He didn't recognize it at first, not until he saw it up close. By the time he realized it, the primitive projectile cracked against his forehead.

Lights out.

The wall of waves crashed against a granite rock face with a gurgling splash. High tide really packed a punch.

The moon was close. Too close.

The sky was red. Blood red.

The sun…there was no sun.

The red was gravity, and the gravity was everywhere. It should not have been so bright, but the proximity of the encroaching moon was wreaking havoc. The red surged just like the waves. The entire sky surged with it. All sense of body and feeling was gone. There was only the looming sense of imminent destruction. A distant whirring percolated everywhere at once, registering at a decibel that skirted the limits of human hearing. The emerald moon wreathed in red shimmering sheets of gravity, flared and pulsed in its losing tug of war with the gravity of the larger planet that was its unintended destination.

The forested surface of the moon anthropomorphized to sneer at the much larger planet below, as if to say, *you really wanna do this? Well, then, I'm gonna make it HURT.* Long held prisoner by the planet's gravitational pull and now forced to sacrifice itself by joining the planet in a cataclysm it had never intended, the moon exercised the only form of control it could: it embraced its death. It taunted the planet with a hateful sneer.

The moon fell. It fell fast, and it fell HARD.

PART 3: GHOST PLANET 001

Knowledge becomes evil if the aim be not virtuous.

- Plato

CHAPTER 22

Djet woke up on a cold concrete floor in a dark room.

It wasn't pitch black. Weak light from a candelabra on the wall brought the floor into view, covered with a thick layer of dust.

This room must not see much traffic.

"She's awake."

For a moment the disorientation was getting to her. She couldn't remember who she was, or how she ended up here. Her ribs itched.

A groan escaped her lips. Her abdomen was sore, like she had just completed a core workout. Too many sit-ups or something. She rubbed a hand, gently, across her right side. When she examined the hand in the light, it was covered in soot and dried, scabbed blood.

I got shot...

That's right. That Centurion, he shot me. I'm undercover. Supposed to be infiltrating the Pathfinders. Why would he...

"Hey, Miss..." A raspy voice emanated within the room.

She stirred. The man was speaking from just outside the light's reach. She couldn't see him, but she could tell his position from his voice. She looked into the unbroken darkness and glared at him.

"Now, look, Miss, you're probably disoriented. I understand that. I was gonna give you some time to rest, but..."

He stepped into the light. He was a tall human, coffee-colored skin covered in tattoos. His hair was long and greasy, tied in the back. He had facial hair around his upper lip that ran down past his chin in thin straggles. He gestured with an open hand toward her.

Djet sat and up and turned her itching side toward the light.

Her C-skin was damaged. Her ribs and a small portion of her right breast were exposed. Smooth, unblemished, undamaged skin. It itched.

"You look pretty good for someone who just got blasted a couple hours ago."

Djet's head swam. *How the hell...*

...she remembered in a flash. The meeting with Ms. Coup De.

The assignment.

She looked up at the man again, taking in the tattoos. Vague symbols, like crossed swords over a shield, a skull with an arrow through the forehead and blood running out of it...that didn't make sense...

...and on the neck, a half circle with two bent arrows pointing up beyond the arc.

Pathfinder.

She was supposed to find them, link up and infiltrate.

But they had found her.

"Now," the raspy voiced man said, "I see you don't have any signs." He ran a finger down his arm, indicating his tattoos. "But your miraculous recovery tells me something different. What cell are you with? What trouble did you get yourself into?"

Djet crossed her arms to hide her shaking hands. She was supposed to say something…like a code phrase…

She couldn't remember it.

"I'm not…" she stammered, trying to think of what to say. "I'm just looking for a place to stay."

It sounded weak, even to her. She had a cover story, she just couldn't remember it. That shot to the ribs had taken her by surprise. It was hard to remember all the details she'd been briefed.

I'm gonna kill Jebsic.

The man laughed. It sounded like a cough, but he was smiling. "Why don't we start with your name?"

Oh yeah, she thought. *I'm not myself anymore. Can't afford to be. I have to be…*

It came to her in the moment. Her survival depended on it.

She inhaled her last breath as Djet Rincon.

When she let it out, her hands stopped shaking.

She smiled. When she spoke, it was different. Her accent was gone. Extra emphasis on the vowels as her voice propelled the words from a deeper part of her throat. She tried to project a confidence she didn't feel.

"You can call me Miss Katana. My cell. We infiltrated Liberty House. They know…not everything, but enough. They know about Aldebaranzan. What we're going to do."

The man crossed his arms. "Is that so? Who says we were planning anything, Miss Katana? Can't blame me for not trusting you. I don't know you from an under-level call girl."

Djet shook her head. She pointed to her bare ribs.

"This isn't enough for you? I've been on the inside for five years. And," she touched her own neck, referencing his tattoo, "signs don't make us friends. Info I got is for Bayson Dahlee only."

The man nodded a few times and tapped his foot. He mulled this over for a moment and then said, "You know Bayson?"

Djet nodded. "Know of him. Know that he's the only one I can trust with the results of the last five years of my work."

The itching was almost unbearable. Djet wasn't sure how long this accelerated healing would last, but she hoped it would be long enough to keep her out of trouble. If things went south, she didn't expect the Pathfinders would let her live very long.

"Sebek." The man offered his hand to her, and she stood with his help. "Stevin Sebek. The road to Bayson is a long one, so if you're hoping to stop us walking into a trap, that timeline's already expired."

"No," Djet said, "not stop it. We can still make this work."

Sebek raised an eyebrow. "How do you suggest we do that?"

Djet leaned slightly to the side, trying to stretch her rapidly healing wound. She gave him a mischievous look.

"Call it a tactical adjustment. Details are for the man. Only him. He can decide who needs to know what, and how to flip this around on the Collective."

Sebek, to her amazement, nodded.

"Clearly you been in this a while, Miss. You don't suffer fools. I like that. As much as I'd like to help, I've got my hands full here." As he stared at her, his pupils dilated once, shrunk back to pinholes, then dilated again.

Drugs or cybernetics? Genetic modification? she thought. *I'm in too deep now.*

"You still haven't told me why you ended up in an alley with a blaster wound. Even if it wasn't fatal. If Liberty House made you...your intel is about as good as the tallest shitpile in the gutters down here."

Sebek reached behind his back and pulled something out of his waistband.

It was a pistol. A slug thrower. Large caliber. The barrel was pointed at her face.

Her stomach sank so low it could have hit the floor.

She had no idea where to find Bayson. The plan was for the Pathfinders to bring her in and lead her to him. How could she convince them to do that? She couldn't let him, this Sebek guy, know that she was afraid. These thoughts blazed through her mind at lightning speed. She did not let it show on her face.

Her hands wanted to shake. She told herself it was all in her head.

Sebek was posturing. Just trying to figure her out.

But *his* hands weren't shaking.

"You can kill me and pass the message along to Bayson. Maybe he'll thank you for it. Maybe you'll get a pat on the back. Or, you can help me get to him, and I can help blow this shit wide open."

Djet stared into Sebek's eyes. They were cold, but not lifeless. Dark brown. Just like hers.

"What intel you got that's so particular I can't be let in on it?"

She remembered the man on Destin, the stranger the Ghosts were after. He told her she needed to get to Aldebaranzan. She knew then what she had to say.

"I've hit the prime factor," she said, finally remembering something from her briefing. "The one thing that can turn the tables on the Collective. I can find him on my own, of course. But it'll be faster if I have help. We all know *of* each other, but we don't all *know* each other. You message a friend who messages a friend…links in the chain that get me to him."

The gun clicked.

She didn't flinch.

It took everything not to.

She allowed herself to blink.

The click wasn't the trigger. It was the slide hitting the man's palm.

He waved it toward her.

"I've been running this cell on Vatican for thirteen years. Too embedded to uproot. I can't go with you." He smiled. "But I can get you a lift out of here. That's the best I can do."

She took the weapon, ran her fingers over the stippling on the grip, the slots on the slide. It was solid. Dangerous.

And now she was, too.

CHAPTER 23

Abraham's skull rang like a bell. It felt like when you held a solid steel bar and smacked it against something solid, something really hard, how the vibrations traveled up the solid steel and into your arm and you felt your bones vibrating.

His skull felt like that.

He opened his eyes without meaning to, because even though he was having a hellish nightmare that he did not want to continue, the realization that he was alive and awake could only be worse.

He was in a dark place, wearing only the undersuit of his B-skin. The armor plates, wherever they were, were too dented to be of any use. His visor was busted…that was one of the last things he remembered before the rock hit him square on the forehead.

It was musty and smelled like dried blood and stagnant water. His face itched at the creases of his nose. It was probably broken, but he couldn't tell without use of his hands, which were tied behind his back. His hair stood out straight from the top of his head. His head pulsed with heavy, staggering beats. Heat wafted off him as he realized he was suspended upside down. A few drops of sweat fell from his hair and rippled in a puddle below him. It was too deep to be a puddle of sweat. It must have rained while he was out. The smell indicated he hadn't lost control of his bladder; it was a rank, mossy kind of odor, thick enough to taste in his throat with every breath.

These indigenous soldiers must have knocked him out, dragged him to a camp of some kind and strung him up from a tree. Or the side of a building, or something. If he thought the weird gray overcast sky was something to wonder at, the sky he could see beyond the rope and whatever he was tied to was something else. He craned his neck to see it better. His undersuit creaked with the motion. Overhead was an endless black with big, fat white and blue and yellow stars everywhere. Even on Milune, Abraham had never seen stars like this. The milky way itself was visible in a purplish, greenish swirl of light tricks with matter that he couldn't begin to comprehend, but for just one second the beautiful sight held him together. Staved off the imminent collapse that was about to hit when he faced the futility of his situation.

Someone shouted. Maybe it was the someone who hit him. Maybe it was someone worse.

Grass shifted with the sound of approaching footsteps. Abraham peeled his eyes off the marvelous view above him and snapped back into himself. The one thing he remembered clear as day, and no matter how many times he got hit on the head would never forget, was what Agent

Sairus had said about POW situations: every interaction is an opportunity.

Tears beaded in his eyes, but they weren't emotional tears. They were being squeezed out of his eyes as the pressure on his head increased with blood continuing to pool there. He imagined his face looked like a fully ripe tomato by now. If it was this dark, how long had he spent dangling like a prized trophy in this camp? Long enough to damage his brain's processing power at least. That dream he was having was disturbing, to say the least.

He tried...he didn't know how to try, but he willed in his mind for gravity to reverse its grip. Let him float gently around to right side up, and maybe snap the limb off the tree he was dangling from. If that worked, he would never need to use the gravity thing again, he swore to himself.

Just this one time, universe, please? C'mon, cut me a break here!

There were no more lucky breaks to be had.

A soldier...the guy wasn't exactly a soldier – he wore a denim button-up shirt, khaki pants and flip flops and had sunglasses on his head which seemed weird because it was almost pitch black outside. But he carried one of those gray metal and wood rifles, and he had an unlit cigarette dangling from his lips. The man reached out a hand and slapped Abraham across the face.

He shouted something Abraham couldn't understand.

Dangling like a fish out of water, Abraham groaned.

"Will you at least let me down? My head hurts."

The man pointed two fingers at him and moved them quickly across his own throat. He shouted some more, lit his cigarette and put his hands on his hips. The rifle dangled by his side, and Abraham wanted nothing more than to snatch it off him and show him the business end.

Two more men, similarly clad but not wearing sunglasses at all, stepped into Abraham's field of view. They, too, carried rifles like the first man. They wore stoic expressions, as if this was just another Tuesday night thing they had to do. Abraham's emotions went through an intense knee-jerk shift.

He was briefly overwhelmed with fear: exposed, vulnerable.

He didn't have any weapons. He didn't have his B-skin, and he didn't even have...

Amory's dagger.

He still had that. He forgot to take it out of the portal pouch in the waistband of his undersuit. Perhaps after the hellacious day he'd had, there was a little luck left in his jar after all. Abraham wasn't one to believe in luck, but it was that or fate was watching out for him. He wasn't one for fate, either. So maybe it was just the universe's way of apologizing for all the bad shit that had happened, all the times his life had been irrevocably damaged by things that should be impossible. He slid his bound wrists across his back and located the dagger with his knuckles. All he needed was one of the three enemies to come within arm's reach, and he...

Every interaction is an opportunity.

...let his hands fall back to a natural rest position. It hadn't come to that, yet. If he could get through this with negotiation or guile, that would be preferable to killing more soldiers. More humans. He still couldn't believe that there were humans on Earth. Smithers was going to get hammered with a thousand and one questions about that if Abraham survived this and made it back to Singularity.

"This one!" Sunglasses shouted.

Abraham's ears perked up. He understood that, but the words weren't meant for him.

The other two started rapid-fire discussing something in a language Abraham didn't know. The leader waved a hand emphatically, silencing the other two. He took a long drag on his cigarette and held it aloft with his elbow resting against his abdomen and a perfectly straight wrist. Smoke spilled out the cherry end of the cigarette, collecting beside his face while he stared. And stared. He took another short drag and let out a ridiculous laugh, smoke stutter-firing from his lips with each new peal of laughter.

"This one," the man explained, and Abraham understood, "this is precious. We have finally captured one of the Djinn."

"Djinn?" Abraham asked.

Rifles clicked and clacked in response. Two barrels aimed right at him, safeties off, fingers on the trigger. The man in the middle snorted a plume of smoke and waved his men down. They lowered their weapons, but not without protesting in their native language.

Sunglasses slapped them both on the back of the head, knocking their berets crooked.

"This one is a youngling. He aspires to be a Djinn. But he is not, yet." The cherry glowed brighter when Sunglasses took another drag. He stepped up less than a meter from Abraham and leaned in to look him straight in the eyes, exhaling smoke in a slow, measured column.

Abraham tried not to cough, but his already moist eyes burned.

"What're you talking about?" Abraham asked. He couldn't keep the pain out of his voice, as much as he tried.

The man spoke with a thick accent. He was using the right words, but they had different vowels. Almost like he was drunk.

"We know what you are, Djinni. You want to be Djinn. Tell me this, Djinni. The people of Kalahari assist you in your quest to become Djinn.

I," he slapped his chest three times, "Mustafar, assist you. You become Djinn, you grant me my three wishes."

Oh, shit, Abraham thought. *I'm about to be tortured.*

"What do you mean by...Djinn?" he asked, fumbling for his waistband.

Sunglasses, or Mustafar as he called himself, smiled. The cigarette was almost burned down to the filter, which he made apparent by rotating his hand to look at it from multiple directions. It might have been a whim, or it might have been his intention from the start, but he stepped up to Abraham and touched the cherry to the exposed skin on his neck.

It was a searing heat, and it did hurt, but Abraham had been through much worse. He didn't even flinch when the pain bit at his neck. He kept his gaze deadlocked with Mustafar's, telegraphing for all he was worth that he did not feel the pain.

His fingers wrapped around the diamond hilt.

The two men who stood a pace away on either side of Mustafar made excited noises, like college kids that had convinced one of their peers to make good on a dare. They looked at each other and started play punching each other on the shoulders.

Abraham saw his opportunity, and he took it.

Mustafar, for a brief moment, flicked his eyes to his peripheral and opened his mouth to tell his cohorts to knock it off. That was when Abraham slipped the dagger from his waistband and slit the rope around his wrists in the same motion. The ratty old rope came flying apart with a snap, like it was under opposing tension on both ends.

The blade flashed for a moment in the light of the fire. It sank into Mustafar's neck, severed the carotid artery with an eruption of blood. The two jackasses stopped their horseplay immediately, and they noticed Abraham with his hands free.

Abraham shoved Mustafar toward them.

The dying man stumbled into them, choking and coughing. The confused pair caught their leader and tried to hold him up. Blood spurted between the fingers of one of Mustafar's hands. The other pointed weakly at Abraham.

Adrenaline overrode the slamming, throbbing pain in his head long enough for him to cut his ankles free of the rope. His body squished into the puddle and the mud that surrounded it, but he was already scrambling for the darkness beyond the reach of the fire.

The rifles barked. Shouted commands chased him into the tangled brush.

He crossed a line of thin-branched, sickly trees, and cleared them.

He could have taken the two by surprise, duked it out in a fight for his life, but he no longer had his gravity shield mystical riskar bullshit, so he wasn't taking any chances. He had to soldier on like the rest of his fireteam had in every deployment and mission they'd ever been on. He wasn't special anymore. If nothing else, this Resurrection Week day-one experience had taught him that he was not invincible.

He stood in an open clearing. There was no cover save the darkness of the night. He sighted a patch of tall grass and made for it, heart beating hard and fast. Lungs burning like he was inhaling acid. His stomach roiled. Survival instincts clamped the impulse to vomit long enough for him to dive into the grass and hope that it was enough.

The endless dark above him, the thick grass blades around him, and if he could get his breathing under control...all that might be enough to keep him alive until he could think of a better escape plan.

Until he did, he was alone with a knife in the middle of hostile enemy territory.

Gray clouds backlit with the weak light of the sun roiled across the sky.

Abraham heard the patrols rustling through the tall grass. A few times they fired salvos into patches of grass before they entered them. His ears rang every time they did that, which meant they were getting closer.

He knew he couldn't stay in one spot for long. It didn't take a B-skin and a motion tracker to find a man hiding in the grass. The soldiers would find him eventually. He popped up on his knees and elbows and shuffled to the edge of his hiding place, parting tall green strands with a hand.

A vehicle rolled through the area with a large machine gun mounted on the back. The barrel bounced as the vehicle sped across the uneven terrain. The gunner standing behind it held onto a rail that separated him from the driver's seat, and he looked bored. Abraham sighed, unsure of how to proceed. He needed a distraction of some sort, but he had no equipment. His bag had to be somewhere back at the camp, which was a lost cause at this point.

Or was it? If they were out patrolling right now, how many people did they have back at the camp? The opportunity would never get better than it was right now. He switched gears in his mind and shuffled to what he thought was the north side of his cover and scouted ahead.

It was clear. Not a single soldier in sight. The camp was a cluster of wooden shacks and a few makeshift tents that stood on a heavily trodden patch of mud and flattened grass. It looked like nobody was home, which gave him hope that they had left his bag in one of the shacks.

After nearly being crushed to death by the massive creature

yesterday and being held captive last night, he was very aware of his mortality. He unsheathed Amory's dagger from the waistband of his undersuit, took three deep breaths, and made for the camp at a sprint.

He was ten meters from the edge of the camp when a soldier came out from one of the tents, headed straight for him.

Abraham committed. He leaped through the air. The dagger flashed.

His body slammed into the soldier, tackling him to the ground. His knees pressed into the man's belly, knocking the wind out of him with a groan. He stabbed the soldier in the neck, twisted the knife to open the wound and turned his face to avoid getting the blood spray in his eyes.

The man closed his eyes like he was just going to sleep.

Abraham wiped the blade on the soldier's uniform and took a few steps toward a nearby tent, trying to cross the open space before anyone else could detect him.

Two more soldiers came out of the same tent, ancient rifles at the ready.

Adrenaline hit Abraham's gut. He was about to make a break for the tent, but something held him stock still in place.

The men shouted to each other and rushed to their fallen comrade. One of them tried to stop the bleeding, but it was clearly too late. They looked around, confused.

Abraham watched them, equally confused.

He was standing two meters away from them, exposed in the open.

But they looked right through him.

He glanced down at himself...and saw mud and grass.

He couldn't see himself. He was invisible.

Because his life was on the line, he didn't question it. He slowly stalked around the soldiers as they shouted at each other, panic filling their voices. Another soldier, probably the last one in the camp, pulled open a creaky wooden door to one of the shacks and rushed out to see what the commotion was.

Abraham hustled up as quietly as he could, caught the door before it slammed shut and stepped into the shack.

It smelled like a fire had recently been burning inside. The only light source came from the gaps between wood planks, but it was enough for him to see a small table with the contents of his equipment bag spread out. He ignored the CLR heat sinks, instead snatching up his L-pistol, three heat sinks, two ration bars and his B-skin belt. The belt was dented at several attach-points, so he could only affix one heat sink to it, but it latched around his waist without a problem.

Abraham unwrapped one ration bar, snapped it in two pieces and shoved both into his mouth. Next, he snatched up the canteen bladder and filled his mouth with precious, clean water. It took him almost thirty seconds to down the ration bar and half of the canteen bladder. The instant lift he got from the nourishment was worth the risk of discovery.

His brain started working again.

He ran through his situation at the speed of thought – maybe another two seconds.

Alone, in the middle of unknown enemy territory and with no objective other than to survive, Abraham decided this little shanty town was of no significance. He needed to find the base the first patrol of soldiers had come from. Resurrection Week was supposed to test all skills required of Ghost Operatives, so he was sure there would be a high-security facility that he would need to break into to figure out what the hell was going on.

Armed, nourished, and somehow invisible, Abraham felt like he had everything he needed to get that done. He searched the shack but didn't find anything else of use. Someone had his plasma launcher tube – it wasn't here. Nothing so useful as a crude paper map of the area, either.

He exited the shack and headed west. That was the direction the soldiers had come from to explore his crash site. It was his best guess for where the base would be.

It took Abraham three days to find the base.

He ran out of water on the second day, and he had to backtrack to the watering hole under the cover of darkness to refill his canteen bladder. The enemy didn't seem to be a fan of night patrols, which didn't make sense but suited him just fine. Maybe they didn't have NVGs or any other kind of tech that made night operations possible. Driving around in vehicles, or riding around on wild beasts, probably didn't help locate escapees in the deep dark of night.

The base was exactly what Abraham thought it would be. An actual hardened structure, with a large parking area for vehicles, a long stable that probably housed close to a hundred horses, and several barracks near a small building next to a firing range. The building that was probably the armory looked small. He scouted the area for hours, counting upwards of two hundred soldiers. A fence surrounded the perimeter about eighty meters from the structures inside the base, but it looked thin and frail. The top had some serrated wire wrapped around the top, which he absolutely did not want to tangle with.

This was going to be next to impossible. Even in class, Agent Sairus had said surveillance and intelligence gathering were the primary functions of a Ghost agent. It was ill-advised to act on incomplete intel.

But since Abraham had already burned four days just surviving after the debacle of his day one and two experience, he only had two days left to accomplish whatever the mystery objective was.

That didn't exactly fill him with confidence.

He had the benefit of more than ten hours of surveillance, during which time he felt like he had the general routine of the base firmly established. The commander strolled around the base with an entourage of six soldiers as he went building by building, probably checking in on his people. Abraham figured he was the commander because of the dedicated six soldiers who never left his side, and because anyone who came in contact with him saluted first. Also, the first time Abraham saw him, he came out of the largest building in the camp on the northwest corner of the camp, the only building with a flag out in front.

The only question was, if there was valuable intel to be had, would it definitely be in that building? It seemed too obvious to Abraham, but then, if there was a CIC anywhere on this base, the only logical place to set it up would be where the highest-ranking officer was located. About midday, maybe around noon, two young soldiers showed up and entered the building through a side door by sliding a keycard to gain entry. Abraham waited for the better part of an hour before they came back out and headed off to the barracks section. He didn't have a scope, or his high-tech B-skin helmet to zoom in, but he was pretty sure he could pick out one of the soldiers in a room; he had short-cropped red hair and was a tall, pale, lanky build that reminded Abraham of Larry, except for the hair color. Abraham designated him Little Red.

Abraham decided he would find Little Red, incapacitate or kill him, snatch his keycard and gain entry to the building from the side door. Once inside, he would have to search around for some kind of secure storage area, maybe the commander's office, and see what intel he could gather.

He didn't want the alarm raised, so incapacitation was his primary option.

Once again waiting for the cover of darkness, Abraham passed the hours by downing the remaining half of his last ration bar and stewing in his own thoughts. The invisibility trick had faded, and he wasn't sure if he could count on it a second time. He didn't remember feeling any different at the time, other than being a little nervous that he couldn't see himself. There was no explanation for why it happened, either. Riskar could not make themselves invisible. Abraham was admittedly not a scholar, but he didn't think any alien race had the ability to completely render themselves invisible to the naked eye. He wasn't sure if this was part of a simulation, or if it was real life. He knew that he was tired of accumulating questions he had no answers to; the frustration was getting to him, building into a rage that was harder and harder to control.

He tried to bite it back and keep it at bay, if only until he got himself out of this mess. He couldn't get answers if he was dead, and worrying himself to death about things was going to affect his judgment. He just had to get through Resurrection Week, and then...

There was always something else. Some reason he had to put things on hold.

He was tired of that, too.

The thin sunlight that failed to break through the cloud cover started dimming. The lighting was almost like a lower hanging cloud over the base, a flat gray and white that felt like looking through wispy layers of fog. Foot traffic slowed to a trickle, and then to just a few stragglers.

Abraham almost dozed off, but then the door to the barracks opened and a dozen soldiers came out, talking and laughing. One of them was Little Red.

Time to move, Abraham thought. He checked his L-pistol, made sure the riskar dagger was still in his waistband, and started a slow low crawl up to the fence. Once he was through the barrier, he had to cross eighty meters to get up to the barracks, and from there, he had to try to get Little Red's card without anyone noticing.

CHAPTER 24

They never used the word 'Pathfinder'.

This maxim was implied and mutually understood.

Sebek rapped his knuckles on the cell door.

There wasn't time to process relief. She had sold her backstory, but that was only the first part. To dwell on the mission she had been forced into would have overwhelmed her. She needed to think about it one step at a time.

Step one: convince them I'm a Pathfinder.

Check.

Step two: convince them to take me to Bayson.

Check.

Step three: get to Bayson.

"You coming, Princess?"

Djet blinked. She was standing in the cell, holding the slug thrower at her side. She tucked the weapon into the waistband of her C-skin with a smile.

"Just wondering when I'm going to get a chance to clean up."

She gestured over her side. Smooth, dark skin unblemished from the wound she'd sustained in the alley. Her C-skin had failed to stitch itself back together. The edges were still blackened coils over her ribs.

"In due time." Sebek waved for her to join him. "I want to introduce you to the rest of the cell. They'll appreciate seeing you in your...current state."

Djet followed him, biting back the disgust that caught in her throat.

That's just what I need. A room full of violent dudes groping me with their eyes.

The lighting in the hallway came from the floor in tiny emergency lighting strips like those on spacecraft. Recessed doors to her left and right every four meters...must be the crew quarters section...*but how big are they? Is this a club or a force?* The ceiling was low enough to make her feel like she was in a cave, or deep underground. For all she knew, they were. The Collective knew a lot about the Pathfinders, but they didn't know everything.

Djet walked in silence, matching Sebek's pace. She wondered at the man. His long, wavy black hair was pulled into a ponytail that shook as he walked. It might have looked feminine if it weren't for his thick mustache and chinstrap. The weathering of his face – like a wood carving – exuded masculinity. Here was a man who had seen and done things that left scars on his psyche.

I've arrested many such men, she thought.

Now you're working with them.

"So," Sebek coughed, "through these doors ahead is the mess hall. I'll have one of the new kids get you a room. Introduce yourself and make friends. Once you're on the path, all who walk alongside you are your brothers and sisters."

The door creaked open, leading into an open room with a vaulted ceiling.

Djet immediately thought of prison.

Tables and chairs were arranged in a perfect grid, exactly four chairs to each table. Everything was gray and black metal. No cushions. No aesthetics. No pictures on the walls and no devices in sight. The kitchen was tucked in the back of the room, separated by a counter covered in plates stacked with pre-made meals wrapped in clear plastic. An assembly line of people, maybe ten or fifteen, were making their way across the line, stacking their trays with plates. Djet counted three women among them.

No one wore the same outfit. The popular mode of dress was threaded clothing, dark colors, and wild hairstyles. Longarm regulations did not exist here, not that Djet expected them to. They were every bit the rag-tag army the Madame Executor told her they were. Which begged the question...*how much does the Collective know about them?*

Sebek led her to a table with two open seats. He gestured for her to sit.

"Hanson, Grip." Sebek nodded at the two men seated opposite her. "This is our new arrival. You can call her Miss Katana."

The two men considered her for a moment.

The tension in the air was thick. They measured her. Djet felt her stomach tighten.

"Where's that new kid?" Sebek grunted.

"He's checking the post," Hanson replied, eyes darting between Sebek and Djet. He was skinny and had reddish blond hair, with a deceivingly youthful face. Worldliness lingered in his eyes. It could be felt when he spoke. He'd seen things. Maybe not a lifetime filled with the horrors of war, but Djet sensed that he wasn't exactly new to the Pathfinder lifestyle. He trimmed his nails with a curved knife. The only word Djet thought to describe the blackened blade was *sinister.*

"Grip," Sebek called on the guy seated next to Hanson. "boot in ass. I want that kid in here five minutes ago."

The man grunted in a deep basso from his barrel chest. His biceps were as large as Caldwell's head. The table groaned when he rested his hand on it. He stood, towering over them by a good measure, and left without speaking.

"He's the strong, silent type," Sebek explained. "Not like the new blood."

"Aww, come on, sir!" Hanson complained. "He ain't that bad."

Sebek crossed his arms and said with a scoff, "He ain't that good, neither."

Djet scooted her chair in so she could lean back without looking like she was trying to distance herself. She wanted to distance herself. This was already too close, too familiar. She didn't want to get to know these people. She did not want to become like them.

But that was exactly what she was supposed to do.

Become one of them. Replace their de facto leader.

An impossible task.

An awkward silence stretched between them for a minute or so, and then the door to the mess hall was thrown open with a loud clang. In walked Grip, stooping to fit through the door. He dragged in a stout, short man with close-cropped hair. A thin white line, razor-straight, ran from above his left temple to the nape of his neck.

The squat, burly man struggled to remove Grip's massive hand from the neck of his C-skin. It was a futile effort. The look on Grip's chiseled face broadcast it clearer than words: he wasn't getting out until Grip decided to let him go.

Grip let him go by tossing him halfway across the room.

"Caldwell!" Sebek shouted so hard his voice cracked. "Pick your ass up!"

Caldwell brushed dust off his chest, grumbling under his breath. When he laid eyes on Djet, he froze. Slowly walking his eyes up and down her body, he let out a shrill whistle.

"Dayyum, Ma'am! You lookin' good enough to eat."

Grip slapped the back of his head. Caldwell's knees buckled.

"Yow! Cool it, sir, if you please!" He hurriedly stood up, rubbing the back of his head vigorously. "You don't know your own strength there, Grip."

Sebek cleared his throat.

"No, Caldwell. Grip knows his strength, and he's using it appropriately. Miss Katana here ain't no street bird. She's the newest temporary member here, and you're making an ass of yourself by way of introduction."

"That's a proper introduction for Caldwell," Hanson chimed in from the table.

Caldwell drew in a deep breath. His jaw flexed and his eyes bulged.

Sebek stole his rebuttal with a shake of his head.

"Enough dick dancing, kids. Katana crossed our path today. She's in need of some assistance. We will provide that assistance. Hanson, get Lenkford and the rest of the hopefuls in here."

"All right." Hanson slid his blade into a sheath on his pants. The customary *shring* of metal-on-metal Djet expected never happened. The shape of the handle blended in with his pants. He made hardly a sound at all as he left the room.

These guys are professionals.

Bottling up the fear was not easy. Her skin crawled every time Sebek spoke.

It feels like I'm in prison. I shouldn't be here, she thought.

Caldwell asked, "We got a mission, boss?"

Sebek ignored him.

Djet covered her exposed skin by crossing her arms. The stares from these hardened killers were starting to get to her. It was different on the streets. When she was a longarm, she had her partner to watch her six.

Here, in the belly of the beast, she was on her own.

Hanson returned a few minutes later, finally breaking the extended silence.

Three more Pathfinders followed him into the cafeteria. Sebek prompted them to introduce themselves. Djet catalogued the names. It was a welcome distraction from the awkward silence.

Lenkford was in his late thirties. He had a neck tattoo – the same as the man that had tried to kill her a few weeks ago in that flat – and rough, yellowed skin. Maybe jaundiced from advanced stages of alcoholism. Simon and Abernathy were younger, maybe in their early twenties. They both wore disheveled longer hair, their bodies skinny and wiry with signs of malnourishment. Djet wondered if they had been street dwellers on the lower levels.

Sebek cleared his throat.

"Now we all know each other." He jerked a thumb at Djet. "Hanson, I want you to take Lenkford and Caldwell for Miss Katana's inprocessing."

Djet's blood froze.

Hanson ran a hand through his shaggy red hair and clapped Lenkford on the back.

"You got it, boss. Miss Katana, follow me."

Djet stayed stock still. Electric static clung to her skin.

"You deaf, woman?" Lenkford smiled, revealing yellow and blackened teeth.

Djet took a deep breath. She balled up her fear and shoved it deep down. It was one of the hardest things she'd ever done. Inprocessing sounded ominous; for all she knew they were going to torture her. She couldn't dwell on that. She was on a mission. She'd never considered herself a Collective loyalist, but now…knowing what she knew about the Pathfinders and the Collective, she realized she'd lost control of her life ever since she met Vase in that coffee shop. Something big was pulling her, guiding her down this new path. Her life had come down to one guiding principle.

"I'm ready for anything," she said. She stood and walked over to Lenkford, wrapped an arm around his shoulder like he was an old buddy she hadn't seen in a long time. Lenkford was caught off guard. He smiled, until Djet leaned in close and said, loud enough for everyone to hear, "But I'll tell you right now, kid. Katana ain't no one to fuck with."

The Pathfinders around her let out a chorus of jeers. Grip slapped his hands in a drumroll on the table. Hanson smirked but gave her a slight nod.

"She talks the talk," Hanson said. "Time to see if she can walk the walk."

CHAPTER 25

Once Abraham arrived at the fence, the idea struck him that he was doing this all wrong.

He did not have time to come up with an alternative plan; he was already committed. But he did make a promise to himself that he would, in the future, at least try to think things through instead of bullshitting his way along on instinct. Instinct had gotten him through his four years in the Corps, and it had carried him through the Ghost Society selection program up to this point, but it wasn't without its shortcomings.

If he had been smarter, he could have sent a plasma mortar into the enemy soldiers at the crash site and taken them out with one or two launches. He could have rigged a proximity explosive in the escape pod. He could have relied on his CLR's marksman mode when he chased down those last four soldiers, rather than rushing out into an ambush. Of course, he had no indication there could be an ambush, but that's why they were called ambushes. He needed to start considering more possibilities and put some contingency plans into place. It was different, operating solo. He didn't have a fireteam to use as a sound board for ideas and suggestions. All he had to go on were his instincts and guesses based on experience.

The wind picked up, rattling the chain links against the fence poles. Abraham unsheathed the dagger and slid it down through ten or eleven links. The blade parted the thin metal with almost no resistance. A crude spotlight finished passing over the fence and rounded the corner to the north. Abraham slipped in through the gap and folded the chain links back together. The cut was so clean, he was able to take almost a full minute to rest the severed ends of each link together. It would take a stiff gust of wind to pry those apart, and a diligent eye to spot it.

He probably bought himself another couple of hours thanks to that.

The eighty meters to the barracks was mostly grass and dried mud until it gave way to a gravel moat that wrapped around the building. Several rocks flanked the rear entrance to the building, where a sidewalk extended out and wrapped around the side of the building to join the main thoroughfare that led to the rest of the base.

Abraham crossed the grass with extreme discipline. It helped that his B-skin's undersuit did not have shoes; the bottoms of the feet were hardened, but flexible. His steps barely made a whisper as he moved. He felt a tiny jerk in his chest, and it was familiar. It felt like when he and Larry had snuck out of the Raven platoon tent during basic training. The imminent danger of what he was doing wasn't on his mind; he felt like a kid sneaking out of his parents' house at night. Like it was a game, and the consequences of discovery weren't as grave as they actually were.

When he finally stepped across the gravel, slow and light on his feet, he sidled up against the cinderblock wall of the barracks. The roaming spotlight scanned the fence. He held his breath as it passed over the portion he had cut and stuck back together, but the light passed over it without lingering. *So far, so good.*

A clatter arose from the other side of the building.

Maybe Little Red will step outside for a piss, Abraham thought.

He knew it wasn't going to happen, but he held out hope. Why not?

The door around the corner, the main entrance that was bathed in the main bank of lights inside the base, opened with a creak. Several soldiers were chatting it up and laughing. Abraham didn't know what Little Red's voice sounded like, only what he looked like, but he was willing to bet this group was the same one he'd seen head out a little over an hour ago. If so, he just needed to wait for them to bunk up and fall asleep, and then he could –

The door opened.

Abraham's breath caught in his chest. A soldier stepped out of the door, bent down with his back to Abraham and picked up a large piece of gravel and stuck it in the door to prevent it from shutting. He walked a few paces out and lit up a cigarette.

There were no bushes in sight, nowhere to hide.

He didn't know the layout of the barracks inside. It would not be a good idea to just stroll right in. He was tempted, but he knew for a fact there were soldiers inside and they were awake. He could walk into a dayroom filled with fifteen or twenty of them, and then he'd really be screwed.

Wait...why did this guy block the door from shutting?

He saw it. A keypad below the door handle. It wasn't a digital one like he was used to, but five pins stuck out of a black box with numbers beside each pin. The guy either didn't know the combination, or more likely was too lazy to input it. *There*, Abraham thought, *is my opportunity.*

He crouch-walked over to the other side of the door, pulled the large piece of gravel out and chucked it in a parabolic arc that took it over the shoulder of the smoking soldier. Immediately, he let the door shut and scrambled around the back corner of the building.

The rock he threw smacked into the gravel well beyond the soldier. He muttered something, and then the door slammed shut. The soldier started cursing, or at least making loud angry sounds while he stomped out his cigarette. Boots skidded against the gravel as he complained.

Abraham peeked one eye around the corner and watched as the soldier pressed in the pins. Just like that, he had the combination for the door.

The keypad beeped, and the soldier yanked the door open.

"Which one of you assholes threw a damn rock at me and locked the door? I'm gonna kick your ass! C'mon now, fess up, fellas!"

He disappeared inside and the door shut.

Abraham didn't have a watch, but he figured he'd give the soldiers another fifteen or twenty minutes to settle in for the night. If this military was like the one he had served in, they were early risers and sleep was a privilege that everyone took advantage of when they could. It couldn't take long, and his opportunity would come.

He counted the seconds as he had in the box in Phase One until he hit eighteen minutes.

It was now or never.

Abraham used the same pattern on the pins and was rewarded with a beep.

He entered a dark hallway with thin slits of light equally spaced on both sides of the hallway until they ended in a darkened dead end. These were certainly rooms, he knew, and the dead end must be a T that led to...bathrooms and laundry? He shook his head. That wasn't his main concern. He needed to figure out which room Little Red was in, and then swipe his keycard.

It was a long, slow process that had his heart hammering in his chest to the point that he thought he was going to give himself a heart attack. He was certain the sound would at least cause one of the sleeping soldiers to stir, but they all remained asleep and didn't so much as twitch or reposition while he snuck in and out of their rooms. The rooms themselves were small – three-meter-squared, maybe a little bigger – and uncomfortably held four soldiers in two bunkbeds.

Whether these guys showered or not, Abraham could barely hold back a cough after being in most of the rooms. They just had a smell to them, like the opposite of cleaning solution. The rooms, maybe not even the people in them. Most cleaning chemicals had this air scrubber kind of scent that smelled bad, but in a way that smelled better than whatever they were cleaning did. This was an angry kind of scent that tried to cling to and corrupt anything it touched.

After the third room, when he still smelled this odor in the hallway, he knew it had latched onto his undersuit. It would serve as a kind of cover, the smell, but anyone catching sight of him would know instantly that he did not belong on the base.

The seventh room was the right one. Abraham found Little Red had a bottom bunk and was snoring so loudly it hid the creak of the door. He found the keycard on a lanyard hanging from the upper bunk's bed post.

It was a thin white plastic square with the kid's pale face and fiery red curls on it.

Abraham didn't relax until he exited the barracks the way he had come, and even then, it was only a half sigh of relief. He still had to make his way to the complete opposite side of the base, dodging the spotlight and any patrolling guards. At least at basic training on Juno, when he snuck out of the tent to pursue a mysterious red light that only he could see, Larry had tagged along with him and watched his back.

He needn't have worried. The trip through the base was quick, and almost too easy. He only saw one patrol of two soldiers between the barracks and the commander's headquarters. All the lights on the HQ building were on out front, where the flag was still flying at the top of the pole, rippling in the stiff wind.

Abraham was confused by the setup, but he didn't question it. He needed intel, and the most likely place was inside the HQ, so that was where he was going. The keycard slid into the door with a beep and a click. The interior of the building was carpeted with a short, stiff blue and black pattern of threads. The walls were cold to the touch despite the heat outside, and it wasn't cold because of some climate control system; the stone or cinderblock, whatever they were made of, it was naturally cold, like metal, except it wasn't metal; tiny fragments of the grid came off on his hand, like little grains of sand.

This place is weird, he thought.

Everything about this is weird, the other corner of his mind shot back.

He didn't care to get into a long, drawn-out conversation with himself. It must have been because he didn't have anyone else to talk to that he kept going on these internal tangents. They were distracting and generally unhelpful. He really needed to rein in his self-control and just see this through.

Abraham followed the black markings on the carpet until he arrived at a counter. Behind the counter was a series of glass doors, through which he could see a large military crest on the wall above a set of double doors. Made of dark, heavy wood, the doors looked ornate.

That's gotta be it.

He used the keycard on the glass door. To his surprise, it worked.

Gently shutting the glass door behind him, he looked at the wooden doors. There were no keycard access slots, no pin-based physical input pad below the handles. This was something he was going to have to pick the lock on...except he didn't have a lock-picking kit on him.

This would be the improvise part of his new skillset he had to try out.

He rummaged through the desk drawers but came up with nothing but a couple of really old click-pens, in a style he had never seen outside of movies. He took one apart and looked at the internal pieces, thought he could maybe use the insert, but that only accounted for part of what he needed.

Glancing around at the desks in the area, he noticed one of them had a bunch of pink and purple flowers, and several print photos taped near the computer terminal. On a whim, he riffled through the drawers of the desk and hit the jackpot.

As he suspected, it was a woman's desk. There was a grooming kit in there, with a pair of tweezers just the length he thought would work. He snapped it in two, took one of the tangs and the pen insert he'd appropriated and got to work on the heavy wooden door's lock.

It was amazing how similar it was to the locks he'd picked in Agent Sairus' class.

Two minutes, and he had the thing open.

The office inside was ornate, three times the size of the dormitory rooms he'd snuck into just a few minutes ago. All kinds of military memorabilia hung on the walls – posters of uniformed soldiers in formation, an exploded view of one of the ancient black rifles that showed its internal parts and construction. Sitting proudly on the desk was a wooden rack with several coins resting in its slots, and a grenade that looked like a small, bumpy fruit.

This has to be a simulation, he thought. *All of this stuff is old human tech, thousands of years old…*

It couldn't be anything else. These soldiers, the people his B-skin had tagged as enemies…they couldn't be real people. How would the Ghost Society have kept an entire civilization of people a secret from the Human Collective?

When was the last time he saw an advert for a vacation trip to Earth?

You would think humanity's home world, the origin point of an entire species, would be a prime spot for tourism. But it had been designated a Ghost Planet, marked off-limits for travel for thousands of years.

The carpet, or the desk…something was emitting a pungent smell, like soap or sandalwood or deodorizing powder. It smelled like it was supposed to be clean, but it just masked the same stench he had detected in the dorm rooms. Abraham shook his head to clear it. He didn't have time for this. He just had to worry about the next thing. Whatever the next objective was, he had to accomplish it. Only after he pushed himself far enough and finished what he set out to do, then could he scrape together enough down time to try to parse and analyze.

This whole lack of clear direction was going to take some getting used to.

Abraham opened drawers, shuffled through papers and photographs, a couple of trinkets and office supplies. He was about to give up when his eyes came to rest on the photograph on the wall of the antique rifle. It wasn't simply a poster hanging on the wall; it had a wooden border, and it was perfectly parallel to the floor. That might be normal in a military office, as the military instilled the value of attention to detail with almost religious fervor, but something about it kept his attention.

He remembered an old movie David and he watched as kids, where an otherwise unassuming bookshelf had turned out to be a secret passageway. One of the books was actually a switch that unlocked the door, and with the bookshelf fastened to the door, the whole ensemble swung open to reveal the hidden passage.

It wouldn't be the first time an officer hid their secrets in plain sight.

Then-Ensign Vase's illegal violin at basic came to mind.

Not having any other leads, Abraham started messing with the frame. He felt the smooth sides of the wood, but there wasn't anything like a switch or a lever that he could see. He tried removing the frame from the wall. It wouldn't budge, so he gave it a shove instead.

The entire photograph sunk into the wall. He slid it to the side, revealing a small safe.

"Wow..." he breathed, "thinking like a Ghost is...kind of addictive."

He smiled inwardly. He could get used to this. If nobody could hide anything from him, he had all the skills he needed to track down the mysterious history of his father, and ultimately...he already possessed the key to finding out his own secrets.

Abraham decided he didn't have enough time to go searching for an augmented listening device, and he wasn't even sure where to look for one, so he dug through the commander's desk some more, until he came across the man's personal effects beneath a stack of reprimand paperwork awaiting review. The only thing he could find was a birthday card from his wife and daughter.

Passwords were almost always something easy to remember, highly personalized to the individual. There was a good probability that the commander would have used something like his anniversary date, or a birth date of his wife or daughter, as the combination to the safe. Abraham was able to snoop through the paper calendar on the man's desk and found his daughter's birthday.

He tried a few permutations, succeeding on the third try.

The safe opened with a click. A small blue light illuminated the inside.

Abraham didn't know what to expect when he looked inside. He could not have predicted it, not for all the money in the galaxy.

He pulled the photograph out, looked at it, read the text at the bottom and stared at the photograph some more.

The text at the bottom said, "Prisoner 004".

The man in the photograph had long dark hair that was pulled over one eye. He was a bit on the chubby side, and he looked absolutely scared out of his mind.

It was his brother.

The first thing he felt was surprise. Shortly following the floor-falling-out-from-under-him rush was disbelief, relief and anger.

David's alive?

It was too good to be true. It forced his mind to lock in on the simulation theory. He had never been in a simulation that lasted longer than twelve hours, but he wasn't sure if the Ghosts had technology to make simulations last as long as they wanted. They probably did. He could be in a simulation for years and never know it.

David was dead, though…wasn't he?

How could he have escaped the riskar's retaliation on Veranda?

None of that mattered. Abraham ran those thoughts through the mental shredder.

This photograph...when was it taken? How did a commander on Earth have a photograph of Abraham's brother?

Smithers' words creaked in the back of his head:

…something a little…closer to home.

"That son of a bitch," Abraham said through his teeth. "I'll kill him."

Abraham searched the safe, his hands shaking. He found a loaded antique slug-thrower pistol, a spare magazine and two documents. One document was an incident report, the other a record of findings.

The incident report explained that the Sky People had delivered one of their own as part of a deal for something the report kept referring to as 'the arrangement'. Abraham was starting to put it together now, and it was making him sick the more he thought about it. If this was real, and David was really alive, there were only two possibilities.

Either a fringe element of humanity had stayed on Earth when the bulk of humanity left, or the Ghosts brought a group of people here and started a secret, isolated civilization. They kept them here as a sort of perpetual force to test out their cadets. That explained why the second detachment Abraham encountered referred to him as a Djinn. David was into history, and his obsession had left Abraham with a few scraps of retained terms. Djinn were some kind of gods from ancient Earth mythology.

The Ghosts were revered as gods by the remaining people on Earth.

Even the commander's report that called them 'Sky People' showed that the Ghosts had intentionally kept these people in the dark about what was going on in the rest of the galaxy. The soldiers didn't have the means to get into space and rejoin the rest of humanity – because the Ghosts denied them that ability.

This is sick…

Abraham fought back the bile rising in his throat.

He skimmed the second paper, the record of findings.

They were torturing and interrogating David for information.

As his eyes devoured the words on the page, it slipped his mind that he shouldn't have been able to read whatever ancient language these humans spoke. He couldn't believe that they would torture an unassuming human, an unarmed civilian for all intents and purposes.

But then, what would he do if he were in their position?

After I get David out of this, Smithers is going to have some explaining to do.

Abraham tucked the slug-thrower into his waistband, replaced the documents and studied the picture of his brother. He was somewhere on this base. He just needed to find out where.

And that required a distraction.

CHAPTER 26

The smell of shit and rotting vegetation was so rank, so humid and pervasive, Djet had to concentrate not to throw up. Every inhale was so offensive it was painful. When she exhaled, the smell of her own breath made her eyes water. She stumbled through the darkness, following Lenkford, who seemed to know exactly where he was going.

"Do we have to do this out here? I don't know how y'all live like this."

Hanson laughed from behind her. "I wish I could say you get used to it, but...you don't."

Djet had been down to the lower levels before. She had never been to the ground level. Down this far, the foundations that held up the superstructure of three-hundred-story buildings were massive linkages many times thicker than a human body. It reminded her of the surface of a starship. Modular compartments linked together in a maze.

She messed with the settings on the headlamp she'd been given, but even the brightest setting only allowed her to see about three paces in front of her. It felt like being underwater. Every step further into the darkness she expected to walk into a wall.

"Where are we going?" she asked.

Lenkford sniffed. "That's for us to know and you to find out, Princess."

"It's a fair question," Hanson said. "But it's also privileged information. Why don't you give us some background, Katana? You know who we are. But we don't know nothing about you."

"There's not much to tell. I've been on the path for a few years. I'm sick of the Collective covering its own ass and leaving the rest of us in the dust." She stepped over a rotting log, slipping on a tangle of moss. She caught herself before she fell. Barely. "You know, I'd really like a shower at some point."

"Fair enough," Hanson said.

"It's just up ahead," Lenkford called out.

Great. Adrenaline spiked in her gut, mingling with the nauseating fumes.

As she stepped toward the sound of Lenkford's voice a shiver ran up her spine.

"Lights off," Lenkford said.

She flipped off her headlamp.

It was so dark she couldn't see her hand in front of her face. Her skin tingled with static cling. It raised the hairs on the back of her neck.

What the hell is going on here?

Her throat itched. She wondered if she was about to feel Hanson's blade cut her open.

Would her body heal fast enough to keep her alive if it did?

Someone grabbed her arms, gently.

"Steady, Katana." Hanson's breath on her neck. "I'll guide you. Walk slowly."

Her knees felt weak. Tremors ran up her legs as she took unsteady steps forward.

"There," Lenkford said.

"Hold still, Katana."

Djet opened her mouth to ask Hanson what the point of all this was.

Something heavy slammed into her back and knocked the wind out of her.

The force of the blow threw her forward.

There was nothing to grab, no ground for her feet to sink into, as vertigo yanked her stomach into her throat.

She was falling.

It was like trying to breathe through a straw. She stole tiny sips of air. The small of her back hurt. She didn't feel like anything was broken.

Where the hell am I?

She couldn't have fallen far. She'd landed on a bed of moss. It could have been the remains of a rotting tree. Whatever it was, it was moist. It stuck to the side of her face and her forearms in grainy little pieces. Dead leaves crinkled as she forced herself to her feet, chest heaving.

She tried to shout, but all she managed was a few breathy vowels.

"You all right down there, Princess?" Lenkford called.

Focus, she told herself.

The lightheadedness started to fade. She could breathe a bit easier.

"What the hell is this?" she growled.

"You don't see it?" Lenkford asked.

"That's not a good sign," Hanson said.

Panic hit like an electric shock. Djet spun around, heartbeat slamming her chest.

She saw it.

Lines crisscrossed over the wall, faintly glowing with a pale blue bioluminescence. Thousands of tiny roots protruded like stalactites, covered in dirt and small rocks. The faint glow spread over about two meters. Dozens of tiny black spiders covered in thin white hairs scuttled across it. A cluster of mushrooms spread along the base of the wall. Their caps were covered in glowing spots.

"I see it," she announced.

"Good," Lenkford said. "Now, read it."

"What kind of inprocessing is this?" Djet grunted.

"We just need to know you are who you say you are, Katana. If you're really on the Path, this will prove it."

Djet got closer to the glow and pulled out a few of the dangling roots to clear the overgrowth. Instinct told her to avoid touching the glowing lines. She spent a few minutes carefully plucking the roots until she could read the writing on the wall:

NATURE IS A LABORATORY

She repeated the words aloud.

"So, what's it mean?" Lenkford asked.

Djet was pissed. "You couldn't ask me that? You had to drag me out here and dump me in this hole to show me this? What the –"

"Answer the question!" Hanson shouted angrily.

"It's about the Path."

"Then say it!" Hanson shouted.

Djet thought about it for a few seconds. It came to her, something that mysterious stranger had said behind the green door. She had forgotten it until now. But now, she wondered, as unlikely as it seemed, if he was the one who left this writing on the wall.

"We have two choices..." Djet said, working it out as she said it. "The scientist, or the rat."

"And?" Lenkford asked.

"I ain't no rat."

Someone whistled.

"I had my doubts," Lenkford said, "but she's the real deal."

"All right," Hanson said, "get her out of there. She's earned her shower."

Djet spent a solid thirty minutes in the shower.

It took that long to wash the stink off her skin.

She slipped on the threads they provided her. Just a few days ago, she would have never worn something like this. The shorts and shirt were a bit baggy. When she walked, they swished. It was uncomfortable to feel the air flow between the clothes and her skin.

The night passed without incident. She slept. It was the blissful sleep of exhaustion. Her mind was a maze, coiled so tightly she had no hope of unraveling it. Sometimes, that's a good thing. When a problem is so insurmountable you can just ignore it. At least, for a little while. Long enough to get some sleep and re-attack in the morning.

When she woke the next day, her first stop was the mess hall.

She grabbed a tray, went through the line and filled it up with a plastic-wrapped sandwich and a bowl of something like miso soup. It was hardly more than broth and a few sprigs of an unfamiliar vegetable. She made sure to check for mushrooms in the soup. Her stomach grumbled at the smell. *When was the last time I ate?*

She took a seat at the table, joining Hanson and Grip. Their trays were already empty.

Rather than jump into a conversation, she devoured her food hungrily.

"Damn, Katana, you got an appetite," Hanson snickered.

"Yeah," Djet said between bites, "getting death-marched in the dark and dumped in a hole will do that to you."

"You took that pretty personal, huh?" Hanson laughed. "You know that was all bullshit, right?"

Djet stopped her spoon halfway to her mouth. "What?"

"You think Sebek would let you into our cell because of anything you said? You can't be that naïve, Katana."

Djet looked at Grip. He tapped a thick finger against his temple but said nothing.

"Hanson, what are you talking about?"

"We're a bunch of fringe scientists, but you know that, being one yourself. First thing we do is run DNA on any potential candidates. You're a bit of a special case, because you're from another cell. You need our help. We still needed to verify who you are."

Djet covered her shock with a slurp from her spoon. The soup tasted bitter. It needed salt. And hot sauce.

"Yeah," Hanson went on, "turns out your DNA isn't in the system."

Djet sat back in her chair, unwrapped her sandwich and took a huge bite. The only flavor she could taste was the watery chill of lettuce that had been in cold storage a bit too long. She was too hungry to care.

"That shows how much pull we've got," she said matter-of-factly.

Hanson nodded. "I don't like anyone the first time I meet them. But I had a feeling about you. I think you're legit. I asked Sebek to make sure I'm a part of getting you to the man."

Djet laughed. "So what, Hanson...you like me?"

Grip let out a guffaw. He patted Hanson on the back a few times.

Hanson flinched with each pat.

"I still don't know you from a streetwalker, Katana." He pursed his lips. "Let's just say...Sebek and I...we expect great things from you."

"How's that?" she asked.

Hanson replied, "I've seen a lot of things on the Path. Biotech being chief among those things. I've never seen anyone that could survive a point-blank laser blast to their vital organs. Whatever you got going on, if that's really what you're trying to get to the man, it's going to change things. Could be the advantage we need to level the playing field."

Djet finished the rest of her sandwich, wiping the corner of her mouth with the back of her hand. The Collective came through for her. They wiped her records from the Collective database. Which was supposed to be impossible.

I may have a shot at succeeding after all.

"So," she asked, "where do we go from here?"

Grip cracked his knuckles and grunted. Hanson looked from the big man to Djet.

"You've got an appointment with the man. We'll bring you along on this next run, and you'll get your ride to Aldebaranzan. This war's going to start, and when it does..."

He pulled out his blade and spun it by the ring at the base of the handle.

"The Collective won't know what hit them."

CHAPTER 27

The only thing Abraham wanted to do was kick in the door and melt the faces of everyone that stood between him and his brother.

But that would surely get David killed, and probably himself, too.

So instead, he rearranged the office to cover his tracks, retraced his route through the HQ building and shut the door. He circled around the base with a plan already forming in his mind. He returned to the section of the fence he'd cut and cut out more chain links, leaving a large hole. He did this in three more places along the same length of the fence and left the scrap chain links on the ground. Figuring he had about twenty minutes before the next spotlight sweep, he got himself a perch between the eaves of what he thought was the armory, and bided his time. Once he was up in a little hidey-hole he'd found by scaling the brickwork of the armory and hiding between stacks that jutted out of the roof, safely hidden from patrols and passing spotlights, Abraham had a few minutes of uninterrupted time to think.

David is alive.

Those three words repeated in his head for the next ten minutes. He tried to run through the base routine he spent the previous day observing, but he couldn't let go of the excitement and the nerves. His brother was alive. In the last four years, this was the best news he had received. A million questions shouted inside his head. It was like someone showed up to the brainstorm party and started popping all the balloons.

The only place David could be held in was inside a building in the center of the base. Abraham remembered one unassuming building in particular, a gray and white thing that no one entered or exited the entire period he was on surveillance. It did have a lone soldier guarding the entrance, and he had been tagged out by another soldier only once. So, it seemed like a twenty-four-hour guard, two twelve-hour shifts.

Most likely, prisoner guard detail.

Abraham decided the distraction he needed could be a simple one; stage a false breach of the armory, get everyone's attention fixated on that, and then allow the breach in the fence to be discovered after that. If all went according to plan, by the time the soldiers realized there was someone on the base and began their search of the buildings, he and David would be a few klicks outside the wire.

At any rate, if he didn't die trying to pull this off, he would be seeing his brother for the first time in four years. It was gonna be one hell of a rendezvous: *Hey, bro, how ya been? Oh, those sirens? Yeah, I broke into a military facility, snooped around and found out where you were, and now I'm here to rescue you.*

It had been a long time, but he still imagined David's childish mannerisms. The goofy stare he was sure to give him popped into his head, and he had to suppress a laugh.

Once he'd counted ten full minutes, somehow managing not to lose track while his thoughts raged at breakneck speed, Abraham slid down the roof and dropped to the gravel with much less sound than he expected. The reinforced soles of his B-skin's undersuit were perfect stealth shoes.

He double-checked his waistband. The 1911 slug-thrower and Amory's dagger were still there. He would have liked to be armed with more than this, but he had what he had, and he was going to make do. It was night and day from being a Marine, but in his short time as a Ghost cadet, he had started to grow used to being underequipped. It actually felt normal.

Abraham pulled the dagger from his waistband and slipped the blade into the door jamb next to the knob. He fiddled with it for a second, finding the angle he wanted, and then shoved it in and pried the door open.

Immediately an alarm began wailing from several places at once. A flashing red light strobed on the roof of the building, temporarily casting aside the darkness of the night and bringing him into full luminosity for any patrolling soldiers to see. His danger sense pegged, and he let the door swing halfway open on its hinges.

Before he could be spotted, Abraham made a dead sprint for the building he thought David was housed in.

He encountered the soldier on prisoner guard detail about ten meters from the target building, drew the 1911 and fired.

The weapon discharged with a flash of fire from the barrel. The kickback rocked his wrist back in a plume of smoke.

The soldier dropped to the ground, fully visible in the dim lighting over the steps that led up to the building's only access door. Abraham ran past him and shoved his dagger into the door jamb, same as he did with the armory door.

"Hey!"

Something in Abraham told him to move, and he obeyed his instinct without question.

He left the dagger in the door and rolled over the side of the stairs as a hail of automatic fire bit into the door, cutting through empty air where he had just been standing.

It was the soldier he'd just shot.

Damn slug throwers are so inefficient, Abraham thought. *Must have caught him in the plate carrier.*

He thought about popping out of cover and sending a few more rounds into the soldier's face, but he wasn't sure he could deadeye a shot at this distance. When he reached up to wipe sweat off his brow, he realized he was invisible again.

Abraham stalked toward the soldier, circling behind him with quiet steps. The man did not look scared; he had a big plug of tobacco in his lower lip, and his eyes were alert. If anything, the wailing alarms had woken him from his wandering thoughts while he was trying to ride out the night on guard duty.

Abraham pounced on him from behind, wrapped his arms around the man's neck and squeezed. The soldier struggled, dropped his rifle to dangle on its sling, and tried to pry Abraham's arms off, but Abraham wasn't letting go. This soldier stood between him and his brother, and that meant he had to go.

The struggle lasted for almost a full minute, and then the fight left the man. Abraham decided against breaking the man's neck; he wasn't trying to kill anyone he didn't have to – he wanted to get in and out as fast as possible.

He lowered the man to the ground and returned to the door, popped it open with the dagger that was still stuck in the jamb, and entered the building.

The only sound inside was his heavy breathing. The man he'd just choked into unconsciousness had put up a serious fight. Abraham should have stopped to catch his breath, but he was high on adrenaline. His stomach felt greasy with it. His fingers twitched as he returned the dagger to his waistband.

The lights were off in the building. That seemed wrong.

He pressed on, ignoring the open doors to his left and right. He should have cleared them, incapacitated or killed anyone inside. It was standard Marine Corps breach and clear procedure, but he didn't care. The Ghosts probably would have preferred he do that, too. But he wasn't doing this for the Ghosts anymore. He just wanted to see his brother.

The dark hallway led to a staircase. He followed it down to a locked door.

On the locked door was something that made Abraham freeze.

He had seen this kind of lock mechanism many times. He was intimately familiar with it.

It was a biometric thumblock, standard across most worlds controlled by the Human Collective. It had no purpose being on a door in a scantily guarded building on a fledgling military installation on a Ghost Planet that officially had a population of zero.

At this point, the unexpected only encouraged him that he was on the right track.

He slid his thumb down the pad and depressed the access button.

The door slid aside without a sound – it might have made a slight hiss, or a swoosh, but Abraham didn't hear it.

His attention was fixed on the Spartan interior of the room.

One table, one chair, ambient lighting from the ceiling that spilled over the individual seated in the chair.

It was David, and he was very much alive.

"David!" Abraham almost shouted.

He stepped into the room.

This time, he heard the door slide shut behind him. And lock.

"Congratulations, Abraham."

Smithers smiled from the corner of the room, where he was leaned up against the wall with his arms crossed.

"What the hell is this?" Abraham growled.

Smithers just smiled.

"I told you I had some answers. I didn't promise all of them. Surrender your weapons. This is your opportunity to prove your loyalty to the Society."

Abraham dropped the spare magazine onto the floor. It clattered by his feet. He pulled Amory's dagger, the diamond on the pommel shimmering in the light, and threw it at Smithers as hard as he could.

A red wave of antigravity knocked it into the wall beside Smithers' face. It was so close, he didn't know how it hadn't drawn blood.

Did I do that? Abraham breathed.

"Hand over that antique," Smithers indicated the 1911.

Abraham ejected the magazine and racked the slide back, sending the last round out of the chamber to tinkle across the floor. He handed the gun to the Ghost.

"Good. Now, it's decision time."

Abraham looked at his brother.

David looked up at him, eyes stretched. A line of thick drops of perspiration hung on his brow. He rocked slowly back and forth, breathing heavily through his nose. The duct tape over his mouth prevented him from speaking, and he didn't even try to make a noise.

"Smithers," Abraham said, his voice trapped in his throat, barely crawling out at a whisper. "Tell me what the fuck this is, now."

Smithers lost his smile. His face went blank as he stooped down to pick up the full magazine for the 1911. He loaded it, charged a round and flipped the gun so he was holding the barrel. He swung his arm to offer Abraham the weapon back. His reply came out like sandpaper against sandpaper.

"Your brother has information these soldiers want. Desperately need.

With it, they can gain access to the stars, and they will compromise the Society. Deny the enemy this vital intel, and you're in."

It was unthinkable. Smithers couldn't really expect Abraham to kill his own brother, could he?

Unless this was a simulation. Just a test of his loyalty.

It isn't a simulation, his mind warned.

It has to be a simulation, the other part of him insisted.

"You're out of your skull, Smithers. I'm not killing my own brother. I'll die before I kill him. You don't understand that because you never had a family. I'm not going to murder my brother for you, for the Society, or anybody else."

Smithers smiled. "That's your choice, Abraham. You either do, or you don't. I'm not going to hold a gun to your head. You have to choose, and if you choose to walk away..." he smirked, "I can't stop you."

Abraham took the gun, adjusted his grip on the weapon. It was strange how such an old thing could feel so right in his hand. He thought hard about shoving the barrel in Smithers' eye socket and pulling the trigger. Wanted to do that more than he had wanted anything in his life.

After all this time, he was in the same room as his brother. He couldn't even talk to him, and now the Ghost Society wanted him dead? None of this made sense.

Abraham pointed the gun and pulled the trigger.

Smoke emanated from the 1911 as the receiver slid back. Another round entered the chamber. The slide slammed forward. The weapon was ready to fire again.

Abraham had no intention of firing it again.

Down the iron sights of the gun, he saw David flinch.

His one exposed eye went wide, the pupil dilating from the flash of fire that snaked out of the barrel. He snapped back into his chair, his shoulders clambering against the cheap, thin metal.

Abraham blinked.

There was no blood.

David's head bobbed. He looked down at himself, then back up at Abraham with a wrinkled brow. He must have expected to be dead. But he wasn't.

He had not been shot after all.

The soldier outside the building...Abraham remembered shooting him with the 1911, but it hadn't killed him. Because he thought he was firing slugs.

Abraham removed the magazine from the 1911 and looked at the round at the top of the mag. It was a flat-faced, flimsy plastic cover in front of the brass.

A blank round.

The soldier he fired at must have been as confused as Abraham had been. He hadn't caught a round in the plate carrier; he'd slipped on his ass trying to dodge a round that never came his way.

Abraham cast a glance at the dagger stuck in the wall over Smithers' shoulder. He knew firing the gun at Smithers would have been pointless; the Ghost had already proved that with whatever anti-gravity shield he had used to deflect the dagger from burying itself in his forehead.

So, Abraham had only one choice. Shoot his brother.

"Abraham," Smithers clapped his hands and laughed. "You did it. You're in."

Abraham dropped the magazine on the floor. The antique pistol landed on the ground next to it.

"You got me, Smithers. I can't believe I was willing to do it, but you got me."

Smithers nodded. "I'll let you escort your brother to the dropship. Give you some catching-up time."

"Thanks," Abraham said, because he didn't know what else to say.

Smithers grunted and left the room.

As soon as the Ghost disappeared, David started making grunting noises.

Abraham hurried to get the tape off David's mouth.

"David, it's all right, I'm here. I'm here."

He yanked the tape off all at once.

David wailed desperately, "Shoes! Shoes!"

"What?" Abraham asked as he worked to undo the duct tape around his brother's wrists.

"Off. Off. Take them off!" David screamed. His face twitched. Abraham recognized the sign of an impending breakdown.

"Okay, just a second."

He abandoned the wrist restraint to pull off David's sneakers. As soon as he got them both off, David breathed a sigh of relief and started calming down. Abraham returned to pulling the tape off his wrists.

"Fuck!" David squealed. "I hate wearing shoes."

Abraham couldn't stop himself from laughing.

"The first time you've seen me in four years and you wanna complain that they made you wear shoes?"

David's glare could have melted steel.

"All right, that's it." Abraham pulled off the last bit of tape and crushed his brother in a tight hug. "I can't believe you're alive, David. How did you get off Veranda?"

David didn't return the hug, but he allowed it. That was a marked improvement. Abraham took it for what it was worth. It felt so good to be close to someone he knew, someone with whom he shared a history. He had spent what felt like a lifetime bouncing from unfamiliar place to unfamiliar place. Even though he was in a prison cell of sorts on a distant planet, this was the closest to home he had felt since he left.

"Abraham," David sounded surprisingly calm, "get off me."

"David, c'mon, bro," Abraham released the hug and tried to help his brother stand. "I thought you were dead! Fill me in. Is Father okay? When did you see him last? How did you get off Veranda?"

David swatted his hands away. "I should be dead. You shot me!"

Abraham rubbed the back of his neck.

"You didn't die, though. I didn't even shoot you. It was loaded with blanks."

David crossed his arms and bounced on the balls of his feet.

"That doesn't mean anything. You shot me."

"I didn't –"

"I don't know anything." David sighed. "I haven't seen Father since I left. I didn't even know Veranda was attacked until three months after, when your best friend Agent Smithers told me."

"You left? Where did you go?"

"I didn't make it far!" David snapped. "Your freaky boyfriend snatched me up and stole me right off the street. I was going to join the Navy. Just…get out of there, like you did."

Abraham felt his stomach drop. "You what?"

"I hate farming." David shrugged. "And Father was a real pain in my ass after you left. He kept trying to make me do all the work you used to do. I'm not supposed to farm. I'm supposed to go to school and learn stuff. I don't need to know how to plant seeds and water tobacco and all that. We spent years already learning that. It's boring and I hate it. So I told Father if he kept making me do that I was gonna leave, just like you did. He didn't stop me."

Abraham felt like the room was suddenly very small. Like all the oxygen inside had been sucked out. Obadiah was a stubborn old bastard, but would he really just let his disabled son waltz off to try to join the military? What the hell was going on with him?

"David, I –"

"No," David said. "No, Abraham. I'm an adult. I'm capable of making my own choices. I don't need Father, or you, or Smithers, to tell me what to do. I just want to go to school. I deserve to be at a college somewhere getting a perfect grade point average and accumulating all the knowledge of the universe. It's what my brain does. It's what I like. I don't give a shit about anything else."

"Oh. Wow. Did you spend the last four years in this room, locked away from the galaxy net and everything that's been popping off in the universe? Something is going on behind the scenes, David. Something that has humanity scared to death."

David shook his head emphatically.

"Not this room, but someplace like it, yeah. And…I don't care. I don't want to be part of what's going on. I just want to watch it all go down. I want to study it. Understand it. That's what I learned over the last four years, being confined to a cell and having to read paper books in a disgustingly underutilized library in whatever dustbin of a space station they held me in. These Ghosts are freaks, and you're a freak for hanging around them."

Abraham couldn't deny that. He was disturbed by his brother's apparent lack of interest in doing something. His aversion to doing anything to stop what was happening. He needed to try to swing this conversation off himself and get back to what mattered.

"David, I haven't told you everything about where I've been and what I've been doing. You need to hear it, and I…I need your help figuring everything out."

David snickered.

"What? Can you say that again? I couldn't hear because you were muttering."

Abraham choked down his pride and tried again.

"I said, brother, I need your help."

David beamed with elation. He threw his head back, which tossed his hair over his shoulders and showed both his eyes. Abraham was so glad to see him alive he didn't care that his brother was still the same asshole he had been on Veranda. Apparently, forced captivity by the Ghosts hadn't done much to damage his personality. Maybe that was a good thing. Maybe it meant they hadn't been torturing him all this time. Other than denying him access to the limitless resources of the galaxy net. David would probably classify that as torture in and of itself.

No serious bodily harm, though. And no straining of his mental faculties.

It was far better than Abraham could have hoped for.

"C'mon, bro." Abraham patted his brother gently on the shoulder. "Smithers made it sound like you're coming back up to Singularity with me. I'll catch you up on the ride. You can help me try to puzzle this out."

David eyed him suspiciously.

"Is this about some boy you met in the Navy? Because I don't do relationship advice."

Abraham laughed. "I'm actually in the Marine Corps, David."

David blew a raspberry.

"You're not strong enough to be a Marine. Stop screwing around."

"Well, I was. Now I'm in with the Ghosts, as you said. But I've got some serious surprises for you. Including that Larry Poplenko is with me."

David beamed all over again.

"My best buddy is still alive, and he's here? Whoo!"

David started fist bumping. It looked ridiculous.

Abraham had to admit to himself he was a little hurt to see David so excited about Larry, and only mildly annoyed that he, his own brother, was here. That was David, though. He was not in touch with or in control of his emotions at all. It was part of his peculiarity that clued people into the fact that he had peculiarities.

"I can't wait to see Larry! Hell yeah! For the first time in years, I'll be able to laugh again. And make stupid jokes. And Larry will play games with me like he used to. It's gonna be great!"

Abraham steered David toward the door.

"So," David asked over his shoulder, allowing Abraham to guide him, "what's this problem you have?"

Abraham said, "You won't believe it when I tell you, and that's why I need your help."

CHAPTER 28

Sebek let her access the vesper net. It was something even longarms were forbidden from doing except under strict supervision and only with a court ordered search warrant. The dark side of the web was dangerous if you didn't know what you were doing. Hackers were notorious for blackmailing people with crypto-ransoms and stealing personal information. While this might be dangerous for an individual, it would be catastrophic for an organization.

The level of trust Sebek was placing in Djet was not lost on her.

"It's a privilege I reserve only for the inner circle of my little detachment here," he said in his raspy voice. "If you need help finding what you're looking for, just ask Franco. He's still awaiting a background check, but he's probably gonna be the new tech brain for Detachment 13. You make yourself at home, Princess."

He'd taken to calling her that when no one was around.

The hollowness in his eyes stole any loaded emotion that might have been bottled up in that term. From anyone else, Djet would have considered it a flirtation. Sebek wasn't like anyone else she'd met, though. He was one-dimensional. His whole purpose in life was devoted to the Path, and to bringing about a new intergalactic war. That was her professional opinion on the man. It had taken her less than a week to arrive at that conclusion.

The hacked terminal was in Sebek's room. It couldn't really be called an office because his bed and footlocker were there. She resisted the urge to riffle through his things. As a detective, this kind of access without a search warrant was unprecedented. She had to balance that with the role she was playing. Caution won out in the end; she needed to get to Bayson more than she needed to learn more about the leader of this Pathfinder cell.

Djet considered trying to find information on the Ghost Society, or to look into the Pathfinders, but those ideas were wiped off the slate pretty quickly. She had only used the vesper net once before, and found it incredibly complex. She decided to refine her searches to one man.

Vase's scorned lover.

Abraham Zeeben.

She ran queries on his military records. She was able to see his service record, though much of it was redacted. She found his Port of Entry into the Marine Corps, a planet that had been decimated in the Riskar War. When she tried to access those records, she wasn't getting anywhere.

That was when she took Sebek up on his offer and brought in Franco.

Franco wasn't what she imagined a hacker would look like. He was a tan-skinned, well-built man in his mid-thirties, with a classically handsome face, and a combed back hairdo that must have taken some serious pomade to hold in place. He was more than happy to help her out.

"Vesper net sleuthing requires adult beverages," he said, holding up a bottle of fire malt whiskey. "I figured some Irdana Whiskey ought to set us straight."

Djet let out a low moan. "Oh, Franco, you know how to win a girl over. I'll pour, you type."

She snatched the bottle from him, popped the top and filled two paper cups.

"Let's see..." he muttered, taking a seat next to her at the terminal. "You're trying to find information about a specific individual. The vesper net is the best place to get the kind of records people don't know exist about themselves. Most people have a digital profile that runs off facial recognition and biometric data. It's like a permanent record of anything they've ever done, galaxy net or vesper. We should be able to find something..."

His mumbling trailed off as he typed.

"Oh, that's interesting."

"What?" Djet leaned forward, savoring a sip of the expensive whiskey. It warmed her with a fiery tingle.

"Do you know anything about his father?"

Djet stared at the holoscreen. Smaller windows popped up as Franco typed. A photograph, a small biography, topographical maps of planets on which he had passed through customs, and...

"Singularity?" Djet read aloud.

Franco whistled. "You know what that is, right?"

"No. What does it say...it's a Ghost Society installation? What are we saying here?"

Franco ran a hand through his hair.

"There's a record of him being logged into the station. He physically went there, at least once. Look at this, though."

Franco tapped at the keyboard. The photograph of Obadiah zoomed in on his face. A separate window filled with strings of numbers too fast for Djet to read. A moment later, it froze. The numbers became letters she recognized.

Next to Obadiah Ossef's name was the unmistakable symbol of the Pathfinders, and the number 7.

"Djet," Franco said, "I don't know what happened to the guy you're looking for, but his dad was a Pathfinder."

Sebek's door slid open. Djet nearly dropped out of her chair.

"Boss?" Franco asked.

Sebek leaned against the door frame, scratching at his facial hair.

"Franco. I need to speak with you. Alone."

Franco stood quickly and brushed off his shirt.

"Sure thing, boss."

Sebek turned to follow him out of the room. Djet didn't think anything of it.

Not even when she saw, at the small of Sebek's back, the butt of a pistol protruding from his waistband.

Djet stared at the image on the holoscreen floating in front of her.

How the hell is this possible?

Vase had set her on this ridiculous chase to find her scorned lover. It was supposed to be an innocuous missing person's case, just a find, locate and contact kind of thing. It ended with her career in shambles, her identity lost and rewritten to be exactly the kind of person she had dedicated to hunting down and locking up behind bars.

The man in the image looked like Abraham. She squinted at it, confused.

Bold white letters under the photo claimed the man's name was Obadiah Ossef. A green symbol next to the name, the symbol that had scared her father so much just at the sight of it, denoted his affiliation with the Pathfinders. After spending the better part of a year infiltrating their ranks, she was convinced of one fact: the Pathfinders were a group of insane criminals.

Former military, intelligence community types, and private military contractors. Some had never served, but all were dangerous. Whether through gangs peddling drugs and slaves on the streets, or through the various branches of the military, every member was well-versed in weapons, tactics, and highly skilled in the trade of violence.

She took the last swig of her fire malt whiskey and gently set her paper cup on the table. The singe traveled down her throat and percolated in her gut, and she sighed. Her nerves were on edge; a tingle of psychosomatic electricity flitted across her skin. The blanket of fear she had grown accustomed to since going undercover was rapidly blown away by the whirlwind rushing through her head.

Obadiah Ossef was Abraham Zeeben's father. Obadiah was a Pathfinder before he changed his name to Zeeben and went into hiding. There were no records of military service for Obadiah...but there was that dangling thread of his having been to Singularity. What would a Pathfinder be doing on a Ghost installation? All Ghost Society operatives were ex-military, from what little she could find about them on the vesper net. The more she dug, the more she felt like nothing made sense.

Which usually means, she remembered her father saying, that you're close to cracking a case. The nexus of confusion is a cloud; the eye of the storm holds the key to everything. The big cases, the ones that get made into films and books once they're solved and the headlines sensationalize everything...they all get solved the same way.

Djet took in a sharp breath and held it. She was right there. On the cusp of unraveling this whole tangled web that was Obadiah Ossef. If she could just figure out this man, who he was and where he came from, she could connect all the dots. Obadiah was the nexus. The crux of the problem.

All of this from trying to track down one former Marine at the request of his commanding officer and could-have-been lover. Vase's unwillingness to let him go had set off a chain reaction that had derailed Djet's whole life.

The galaxy is a big place. The absence of records on one individual was easily explained as a glitch in the system. Maybe Obadiah was from a planet outside the control of the Human Collective. If that were the case, she just needed to trace his records back to the very first time he was ever inducted into the system. A speeding ticket on some backwater world. An arrest record for public intoxication.

Or...the idea hit her and she blew out the breath she had been holding.

She was looking at this all wrong.

Obadiah wasn't the type to have been caught up by the criminal justice system at any point in his life. The history she had learned about Abraham in the skimpy, disjointed records of the Navy database, showed he had some kind of hero complex.

Like father, like son?

She should be looking for public accolades. Some kind of award.

Maybe Obadiah got third place in a science fair and made the local paper. Maybe he was on the Dean's List at a college. He seemed to have a heart for the riskar, and maybe aliens in general. A soft spot for life in any form. That had to come from somewhere; most humans had an innate fear or revulsion of alien life, and spent a good number of years dedicated to purging those biases from their subconscious. Or not.

She looked again at the Pathfinder's Detachment 7 form.

Obadiah Ossef, planet of origin listed as Yelsh. Yelsh was a metropolis, a century of development away from becoming a terra city.

Was it possible he could have been from a small town on that planet? Despite spending time on Vatican and Milune, Obadiah did not seem the big city type. He settled in as a tobacco farmer on Veranda for a few years. Djet did not know many terra city citizens who chose to give up the convenience of that lifestyle for a life of manual labor and exclusion.

She pulled up Yelsh's database and ran some queries. She started with the citizen registry list, moved to the Dean's List of every college, then to the honor roll system for the outlying school districts, but came up with no hits. She pulled up the news records for the last hundred years and ran a simple name query.

She got a hit.

Axiom Xenobiology Industries. A company that worked to catalogue and explore the genetic structure of the flora and fauna of Yelsh. A biomedical engineering research lab that collected samples in the natural environment and synthesized them to try to predict future evolutionary developments in their biology, with the intent of diagnosing and preventing negative trends. Essentially, they wanted to increase crop yields through genetic engineering and genetically damage nuisance plants, hoping to eliminate weeds and other less than desirable growths in the agricultural field.

Ninety-one years ago, an entry-level lab technician named Obadiah Ossef received an award for his help in synthesizing an antigen that increased crop resistance to pesticides by 83%. The award said that he had shown promising signs of becoming Yelsh's future authority on genome synthesizing projects.

"So," Djet said under her breath, "you were a mad scientist before you were paramilitary. Before you were a Pathfinder. Why, for the love of Earth, would you go into hiding?"

That question answered itself almost before she finished asking it.

Why would a longarm join the Pathfinders?

Obadiah Ossef did something that would piss them off.

He joined the Ghost Society.

She couldn't stop herself from laughing. She had finally figured it out. Cracked her first big case. It felt good. She didn't know everything, but she didn't need to know everything.

She needed to talk to Vase. Vase would be able to put the pieces together.

And then they could figure out how to tell Abraham his father was responsible for ruining his life.

CHAPTER 29

Larry wasn't waiting for them when they got back up to Singularity.

Tayla and Savony greeted the brothers when they arrived on station, and David was blushing like Abraham had never seen before. He was immediately infatuated with Tayla, mostly because she indulged his endless stream of questions and offered him a hug right when he crossed the threshold of the airlock.

Abraham felt beat to shit. He saw the same look in the girls' eyes as soon as they met. They had passed their final evaluation, but no one knew why Larry hadn't come back to the station. Abraham hoped that Larry had passed; he couldn't imagine Larry hitting his stride in Phase One of the training and suddenly not passing Phase Two.

The foursome spent a good two hours at the DFAC.

After surviving Resurrection Week, Abraham felt like he could have eaten a whole long-necked, spotted animal, the ones he saw by the watering hole. As soon as he let that fact be known, David rushed to correct him.

"It's called a giraffe, you ass. How do you not know that? That's like, basic Earth history we learned in second grade."

Tayla and Savony shared a big laugh at his expense.

Part of Abraham was miffed at David's correction, but the larger part of him was still in awe that his brother was alive and breathing, and sitting right next to him, nonetheless. It was like a drug, the nostalgia of being in close proximity to a member of his family after so long without hope.

"Sorry, David, I was more interested in armor tag games. I tend to rely on you for all the nerdy stuff."

He patted his brother on the head in a *good job, son* gesture.

"Oh, whatever."

Savony's third plate was cleared without a scrap of evidence it had ever been filled in the first place. She leaned back and let out a decent belch, then sighed.

"You know," she said to David, "I've always thought your brother was pretty smart, as far as Marines go. He was a fireteam leader, and he did get his squad out of a shitstorm on Duringer."

"I didn't get everybody out." Abraham sighed and pushed his plate away. His stomach was full to bursting, and the direction the conversation was going threatened to push him over the edge.

"That sucks about Digger," David remarked like he was commenting on the weather. "But he was an asshole, so…fuck him."

Tayla looked at Abraham, her mouth open.

Savony scratched her arm and found something interesting on the ceiling to look at.

That rosy image Abraham had of him and his brother back together, trying to make a future for each other, cracked right down the middle.

"Do not speak ill of the dead, David."

"Nah," David said, "I'm not excited that he's dead. I'm just glad he's not ripping ass in people's faces or punching them anymore."

Abraham decided not to press the issue, as much as it chafed him.

"Tayla," Abraham said, trying to change the subject, "how'd you do? I mean, obviously we all passed, but how did it go for you?"

Tayla sighed, took a long swig of her iced tea, and said, "You know, I don't really want to talk about it."

Abraham tried to laugh it off. "That's fair. I felt like it was the worst week of my life, bar none."

David said, "Things have changed since you left. There's actual females that don't mind hanging around you."

Tayla sputtered iced tea into her glass. Savony shot her a confused look but didn't say anything.

"Uh, yeah, David, I've been meaning to have that conversation with you." Abraham capitalized on the opportunity to flip the jab on his brother. "You see, when a man and a woman like each other, sometimes they express that in a physical way, like –"

David covered his ears and made a bunch of indiscriminate noises.

Everyone laughed.

Savony said, "This is nice. I didn't know you had a brother, Sarge, but he's a lot of fun. It's nice," she sighed, "things being light like this after everything."

"Yeah, it is," Abraham said. "So, now that we're officially graduated, does that mean we're allowed access to the Ghost Bar?"

Tayla, who had just finished wiping her face off with a napkin, made an excited grunt. "Ooh, I hope they have karaoke!"

"Screw the karaoke, girl," Savony said, "I'm gonna drink that bar dry tonight."

Abraham knew Savony was less likely to talk about her experience during Resurrection Week than Tayla was, but there was something in her bearing that told him she'd had it harder than the other two. He couldn't put his finger on it. She just took long pauses, and although most Marines who had seen combat had developed that thousand-yard stare they were famous for to varying degrees of intensity, hers seemed heavy. Much heavier than he remembered on her.

An awkward silence reigned for a few minutes as they sat, groaning over their too-full bellies and just enjoying the comfort of being out of the field for the first time in a week. They looked like it, too. The girls' hair was mussed and frizzed, and they all smelled like they needed a long, hot shower.

"So, David," Tayla asked after a minute, "what are you going to be doing here?"

David's face lit up. Getting attention from a woman was new territory for him.

"Well, Tayla, I have no clue. I've been locked in a room for four years with little free time. I mean, all I had was free time, but like I told Abraham, I wasn't allowed access to the galaxy net that whole time. So, I made do with the dusty paper books they have in the library. I read them all – twice. Three times in some cases. And in that time, I've developed an encyclopedic knowledge of myth, lore, folktales, history as the Human Collective records it, and a bunch of other useless bullshit that I'll probably never get an opportunity to make use of."

"Wow," Tayla said, drawing the word out.

David, not picking up on her losing interest, continued with his explanation.

"Yeah, it was terrible, and I wanted to kill myself almost every day from the isolation. Smithers came in to ask me questions and talk to me about once a month or so, and even though I hate that bastard...when you have no one to talk to, you kind of look forward to the interaction just for the sake of interaction. Smithers kind of let it slip one time – maybe about a year ago now I think, but it was easy to lose track of time, I think it was a year ago – he said that there were more than just agents here, and that not all operatives are field operatives. So, maybe I could be like an analyst or something. Since my brother here is under their wing, I don't think they'll be letting me go anytime soon."

Abraham was watching Tayla struggle not to roll her eyes. She did this by glancing at her palms, rubbing her right shoulder, and taking a minute to pick at a decent gash on her left forearm that had scabbed over. He felt drawn to her, like he needed to comfort her. Part of that might be the memory of her just a week ago in his room, but he tried not to think about that.

Because that was a one-time thing, and it was over. She had told him that.

As flirty and flighty as Tayla was, he knew better than to provoke a woman. Once they made up their mind about something, it was like trying to pick up a mountain by the base and relocate it to another part of the planet. Things he used to think were impossible until he joined the Ghost Society.

Now he thought he probably could find a way to make that happen, if he had to. If he was willing to possibly kill his own brother, what wouldn't he be willing to do?

That was the point, he realized. The Ghosts had him right where they wanted him.

He was willing to do whatever it took. If they asked him to jump, he wouldn't even ask how high. He'd just jump as high as he could and if that wasn't good enough, he'd jump higher if he got a second chance.

What they didn't know, at least not yet, was that he didn't hold that loyalty as an immutable fact. As soon as he got the information he needed about his father, he would re-evaluate everything. And who knows where that would lead him.

After David rambled his way to a natural pause, Abraham interjected on behalf of the group.

"Okay, this has been fun, everyone, but I need to shower. I smell so bad I'm surprised I haven't set off a smoke alarm."

David nodded with annoyance but didn't say anything.

Abraham held out his fist.

"I'll catch up with you after I get some rack time, bro."

David bumped it.

"Okay," he said glumly. "I'll probably just be wasting away in my own personal hellhole some more, so feel free to drop by. I'm not allowed to open and shut my own door, you know."

David got up and left.

Abraham gathered his food scraps onto his tray, but despite his intentions made no attempt to get up from the table. He cast his eyes at Tayla, searching for a clue of how she felt, but her exterior was a mystery concealed behind a weak smile.

Savony looked at her, waved a hand in front of her face to get her attention.

"You all right, girl?"

Tayla laughed, a little too forcefully. "Oh, yeah, I'm great. A week of hell out in the wilderness, nothing to write home about."

Savony raised an eyebrow. "You sure?"

Tayla nodded, but she had tears in her eyes. She stared at the table, her gaze locked. Her voice had the slightest hint of strain when she said, "I said I'm fine."

Savony sat back in her chair, hurt written on her face.

"All right then. I'll leave you two alone."

Savony scooted her chair out and left her tray on the table.

Abraham reached out and placed his hand on Tayla's. She yanked it back.

"Don't."

Abraham wasn't sure how to respond, so he didn't.

She didn't look away from whatever she was staring at on the table, or maybe she was looking through the table. Remembering some untold horror she had endured during the past week. After a minute she said, "Come to my room?"

"Okay," Abraham said, keeping his voice soft.

She got up, left her food, which Abraham just realized was only half-eaten, and moved slowly out of the DFAC. He followed her, staying close but not crowding her, trying to wrap his mind around just what could have happened to her out there in the wasteland that had once been humanity's home world.

She didn't speak until they were back in her room. Savony must have known more than she was letting on, because she was gone. Tayla sealed the door shut behind Abraham and collapsed onto her hands and knees.

"Tayla, holy shit! What's wrong?"

Abraham knelt next to her, tried to put a hand on her back but she swatted it away.

"Don't...don't touch my back. Can you help me?"

She indicated her shirt.

Abraham helped her pull the black t-shirt off. She wasn't wearing a bra underneath, and he would have been distracted by her nakedness under any other circumstances, but when he saw her back, he almost vomited.

The gash on her forearm was a papercut compared to the wounds that crisscrossed over the once-smooth tan. Now her entire back was a swollen, angry red. Abraham couldn't even count the number of wounds that ran from her ribs and wrapped completely over her back to the ribs on the other side. They crossed over each other several times, and some of them were infected. Tayla was once a Marine, so she had a certain level of toughness ground into her at basic. She had seen combat, killed in the name of the Human Marine Corps and to some extent, on behalf of the whole Human Collective. But this...this was torture.

This was what Abraham thought the Ghosts had been doing to his brother.

"Tayla...what happened?"

She shuddered as the cold air of the station drifted from an overhead vent and contacted her skin. Tears drifted to the floor, slower in Singularity's lighter gravity. Her hair hung in frizzed straggles over her face, so he couldn't read her expression.

"I need you..." she breathed through the pain. "I'm not going to medical. Can you –"

She let out a strangled moan.

Abraham tucked her hair behind her ear. He gently touched her chin, and she looked up at him with wet cheeks. He had never seen her so worried, and it scared him a little.

"Let's get you in the shower. I know it's gonna hurt, but if you're not going to the medical wing, you gotta let me clean them."

She nodded. Her lower lip trembled as she took in a sharp breath, and he helped her stand. He slowly shuffled her to the shower unit attached to the room, turned the water on lukewarm. He grabbed the antibacterial soap from the wall unit and smeared it over his hands.

"Okay, you ready?"

She nodded and sobbed.

"Holy shit, I can't believe you're doing this. You're one tough lady, Tayla. A lot tougher than I ever gave you credit for."

"Just fucking do it already!" she snapped.

Abraham rubbed his hands down her back as gingerly as he could.

Tayla did not scream. He had to give her credit for that.

She groaned, a deep, gut-wrenching groan that made Abraham think of a woman in labor. Her teeth creaked, she was clamping her jaw shut so hard. But she got through it. He continued soaping up her back and running his fingers through her wounds, paying close attention to the areas that looked infected. Tayla swooned midway through, groaning like an addict in the peak of relapse. Abraham tried to focus on getting the wounds as clean as he could, but some of the gashes were deep. One of them on her left side had a four-centimeter rip. He could see the pale white of a rib bone between the yellowish orange globes of fat embedded under the skin.

He had to stop for a second and breathe. The moisture in the air clogged his nostrils, and he felt like crying. He couldn't do that, wouldn't do it in front of Tayla. Part of him felt stupid for thinking about that at a time like this. He shook it off and shut the water off.

As gingerly as he could, he helped Tayla to her bed and laid her on her stomach. She shared the room with only Savony, but he draped a thin sheet over her legs and butt to preserve her modesty and because that cold air was still pouring in from the overhead vent. After he did this and made sure she was situated properly, he knelt by her head and kissed her forehead.

"You're gonna be okay, Tayla. You have a pretty gnarly tear in the skin on your left side, so try not to roll over on it. I know you don't want to go to the medical wing, but you need a nanostitch for that. Does Savony still have her go-bag, or did the Ghosts –"

"Closet," Tayla muttered.

"Okay, closet." Abraham moved over to the wall locker and found the standard issue duffel resting in a heap at the bottom. He riffled through it and pulled out what he thought was the medical kit.

It was a Portal. Savony's portal.

The lock screen had a picture of her and another Marine on the front, arm in arm like they were old pals. He didn't recognize the guy, but the name tape was the same last name as Savony: Raelis. The guy looked like he had forgotten how to smile but was giving it his best effort. It was weird, seeing something from Savony's personal life like this. He felt like he was snooping, and hurriedly replaced the device and searched until he found the medical kit.

"Here you go." He pulled out the nanostitch, snapped it off at the approximate length of her wound and placed the teeth along the edges of the bleeding gash. "This is gonna hurt, girl," he said in his best impersonation of Savony.

Tayla giggled. It sounded like a forced gesture, like it came from far away. Or like she'd done it in her sleep.

"You still with me?"

She made an affirmative grunt.

Abraham used firm but delicate pressure to line the edges of the tear close together and popped the nanostitch into her skin. The linked teeth clamped at forty-five-degree angles, sealing the wound shut. A trickle of blood spilled out and then stopped.

Tayla didn't respond.

Damn, she's tough, he thought, running his fingers through her hair.

"The worst part is over," he said softly.

Tayla grunted in dissent. "This was training." She paused to take a few shuddering breaths. "They're...prepping us for suicide missions."

"I got that feeling, too. Sorry I roped you guys into this."

She grunted again. "Didn't."

"You mean you wanted to come and subject yourself to this?" He stopped himself short of using the word torture.

"Wanna...be the best." She gave the barest shrug, hardly more than a twitch of her neck.

"Yeah...I get that. I just came here to try to figure out what was going on with me. Figured selling my soul to them was the only way to get them to cough up their secrets. Finding out my brother is still alive was an unexpected bonus."

Tayla smirked.

"You okay? I'm gonna –"

"Stay," she mumbled.

He stroked her hair again. "Okay. I will."

His chest burned. He wanted to stay. Liked that she wanted him to stay.

It might have meant something, might not have meant anything.

But he liked that, too.

He stayed with Tayla until she drifted off, then ducked out of the room quietly so he didn't wake her.

Abraham did not want Savony to pop back into her room to find him in there. It wasn't that it would have been rude or intrusive of him to be in there – they had been fireteam leaders and had seen each other in the shower, so privacy wasn't the issue – it was that he wanted to give Savony some space and the opportunity to reconnect with Tayla on her own terms. During their welcome back meal at the DFAC, Savony throwing that hurt look at Tayla spoke volumes.

The girls were close. Abraham knew that. In the back of his mind, he knew their newly formed Tetsubishi Alliance was more than just lip service to a temporary friendship.

Abraham walked back to his room and hit the shower first thing. His body was covered in bruises and cuts. He was grateful he had gotten by relatively unscathed compared to Tayla. Although, if he had the chance, he would have traded places with her.

What was that about himself, that he felt like that? If it had been Larry, he wouldn't have wanted to trade places with him. He would feel sorry for his buddy, maybe want to kick the asses of the people who had tortured him, but he wouldn't trade places. Why did he feel like that about Tayla? Abraham liked girls in his high school, but he never really had any luck with them. Vase was the first girl he ever loved, and he knew he still loved her. Always would. Something about her, he just couldn't let go. But Tayla...did he love Tayla, too?

He didn't think so. He liked her a lot, especially after that night they were together. That was something he wasn't going to forget, even if she said it was a one-time thing.

He may not love her, but he did care for her. He certainly didn't like seeing her hurt.

It hurt him that she had suffered. He didn't want to see her in pain.

That brought him around to Larry. Where the hell was he? Did he fail, and the Ghosts killed him or something? None of that made sense. Larry was the most likely to pass out of the entire Tetsubishi Alliance. The most capable, and that was a surprise to Abraham.

Until the Marine Corps, Abraham had only ever been average at everything. Until he lost his riskar powers of gravity control, he had been an exceptional Marine.

Now, maybe he was just an average Ghost, and Larry was the super star.

Abraham toweled off and threw on a shirt and some pants. He lay down on his bed, wondering where the hell his buddy was. If Larry didn't pass, there was a flaw in the system.

After a week in the field, his bed felt like a magic carpet, or a cloud of cotton. It was so comfortable he felt like he was sinking into it, and before his thoughts could wander very far at all, he let the warm folds of sleep pull him in.

Smithers informed them that the graduation ceremony was to take place in a week. They had the entire seven-day cycle for some much-needed R and R. Rest and relaxation was the military's way of giving you a little vacation after you had seen some serious shit. As the Ghosts were all ex-military, or at least the agents were, they fed him this line of military jargon and he ate it up wholeheartedly.

Abraham pilfered some nanocyte injectables from the medical wing during the first three days of R and R, and stopped by Tayla's room to administer it. Angry red wounds became wicked purple scars by the end of the third day. Savony was in the room each time he stopped by, but other than opening the door for him, she didn't really acknowledge his presence.

Abraham kept his visits brief, hardly more than a check-in and a quick shot of the medicine to get Tayla back up to speed. She recovered remarkably quickly, and it wasn't just physically. Her mental state was back to normal by the second day. A bubbly personality like Tayla's couldn't be held down in gloom forever, even if she had been tortured by the indigenous soldiers on Earth. Abraham was relieved to see her returning to her old self, and this time, things were a little different.

He never did get the full story out of her, but the pieces he did told him that the four of them had gone through very similar Resurrection Weeks. Apparently, the Ghosts had set this up to play out organically; the cadets had to go through a crash landing, scouting, evasion, capture and escape that led to some kind of personal revelation. It was still anyone's guess where Larry was, and his absence was starting to worry everyone.

Tayla never told Abraham what her revelation was. He thought he was being a little immodest, but he wondered what big secret she had going on that could possibly have made a difference to the Ghosts. Maybe that was the point, though. It didn't have to matter to the Ghosts

– it just had to matter to Tayla. It was a forced sacrifice of some kind.

Hell, he thought, *maybe she's a princess on some faraway world and had to resign her title or something like that.*

Outlandish, maybe, but it would be pretty cool. And probably devastating for Princess Tayla, if she were an actual princess. On second thought, he hoped it was something different. It wasn't until the fourth day that Tayla was feeling good enough to join him in the gym, so they did a comfortable ten-kilometer jog, lifted some weights in the fitness facility, and chatted it up at lunch.

Abraham broke away from her after lunch to go see his brother.

David was sleeping when he stopped by, so Abraham woke him up.

"Hey," David said, rubbing his bleary eyes. "It's about time you showed up. So busy with your girlfriend you waited a week to come say hi?"

Abraham sat on David's bed, stretching his tight muscles. It felt good to be working out again. It was a weird feeling, this Ghost thing. It was like being in the Corps, except you were a one-man squad. You were your own chain of command, your own gunny, your own sergeant and PFC. The only one responsible for every aspect of your fitness as an agent was yourself. You still had the company commander of sorts in Smithers, but he was rarely around.

Abraham didn't mind that.

"Well," Abraham sighed, "I was thinking. The ceremony is in a couple of days, and I'll officially be a Ghost. I'm probably going to go on assignment right away, and who knows when we'll see each other again."

David arched an eyebrow. "Or if you'll even come back."

Abraham nodded. He would have laughed, because David intended the comment as a joke, but the possibility of him dying was real. The Ghosts didn't do things the easy way, and they did not allow themselves to be discovered by the public. Clandestine or die, that was their *modus operandi*.

"Yeah, that could happen. Regardless, I'm here, and I still don't have any answers. From the sounds of things, neither do you. Have you been thinking about what we talked about, my DNA and all that?"

It was David's turn to sigh. "I have. The Ghosts poked and prodded me at least once a week since they took me, and they swear up and down I have a hundred percent human DNA. So at best, that makes us half-brothers."

Abraham balked. "Oh, come on, David. You think Father…screwed around…with an alien?"

David shrugged. "I don't know. I never really got along with him, but from the sounds of things, and what happened to you on Duringer, that's the only thing that stands to reason. You are the son of Obadiah Zeeben and some riskar babe he hooked up with somewhere. I don't know how Mom would have been okay with marrying Father, knowing he came with a hybrid freak baby like you, but apparently that didn't stop her from having me. If all that's true – and I don't see another plausible scenario – then we can't be more than half-brothers."

Abraham thought about that for a moment while David stared off into space.

"I don't believe it," he said.

David lay back down on his bed and kicked Abraham in the side.

"Get off."

"Hey! C'mon, bro."

"Don't *c'mon bro* me. This bed is the only thing I have in here. I want it all to myself right now."

Abraham slid off the bed and sat cross-legged on the floor. It wasn't worth fighting over.

"I don't think Mom would have been okay with…that. If that's who I was. She was always nicer to me than Father was, anyway," Abraham reasoned. "That, and I don't have any physical characteristics of a riskar. Or any alien, for that matter."

David hummed for a minute. His gears were turning.

"Mom was a native of Milune," David said slowly, "the daughter of a jeweler. We never got to meet grandpa, because he was pretty old when Mom was born, and died when she was a teenager. Grandma died shortly after I was born. But what do we know about Father's family?"

Abraham blinked. "I don't remember him ever mentioning his family."

David snapped his fingers. "That's because he didn't, Abraham. We know he wasn't born on Milune. He's talked about Vatican a few times, but do you remember him ever saying he was born there?"

"No," Abraham admitted. "I just assumed –"

David nodded and cut him off. "I did, too. Can you access the galaxy net?"

Abraham nodded.

"Run a query for Father's name and try to find him. Maybe he built buildings on Vatican or went to college there. If we find out more about him, maybe that will tell us something."

"Okay. I don't think I'll find anything, but I'll give it a shot."

Abraham spent the next few minutes trying to think of something else to talk about, but he couldn't think of anything. David was safe, and that was enough. His brother didn't have anything else to talk about either, and started snoring.

Taking that as his cue to leave, Abraham headed to Tayla's room.

Savony answered the door, a mischievous grin on her face.
"You back for more already, Sarge?"
Abraham blushed. "I don't know what you're talking about, Savony. I'm just –"
"Tayla's not here, but I'm sure she'll be back. You can wait for her in her bed or in the shower, if you want."
Abraham crossed his arms. "I don't know what you think –"
Savony held up a hand. "Oh, it's not what I think, it's what I know."
"What you know?" Abraham asked, confused.
Savony did the Larry thing, flitting her eyebrows twice suggestively. "Girls talk."
She glanced down rapidly at his belt and then locked eyes with him, her lips pursed like she was struggling to hold in a fit of laughter.
Abraham reflexively clasped his hands together and held them over his belt buckle to shield himself.
"Okay, that's not fair. I don't know if Tayla said anything to you, but I wouldn't –"
"Abraham?" Tayla asked from the hallway behind him.
"Tayla, I was just –"
"Coming back for more?" She giggled.
Abraham heaved a huge sigh. What could he say? They had him cornered.
"I was…"
His words fell away as his breath caught in his throat.
Tayla's grin slipped off her face. Savony looked at Abraham, suddenly serious, and the girls turned their heads to look down the hallway.
Larry was walking down the hallway with a smile so big his cheeks looked like stretched plastic. His face was clean, although he still wore the B-skin undersuit, meaning he had just come in from the field. Four days later than the other three. He had a swagger to his step that he hadn't had before; it reminded Abraham of Digger. Larry threw his arms out wide and flashed his teeth. The smile never left his face when he shouted a greeting to them.
"Oh, Tetsubishi, I'm home!"
The three rushed him and crushed him in a group hug.
Larry laughed, and the group broke into hysterics. Questions flew, and laughter, and Larry made a big show of regaling them with how well he did on his exam. Apparently, he had decimated the entire base where he was dropped in.
"Killed them all, every single one of those punk ass bitches." Larry beamed. "And when I got the instructions for the last step out of the

commander's vault – stupid sonofabitch used his anniversary for the combination on the lock – I evaded pickup for so long, Smithers had to sound off a special horn to let me know that the evaluation was over and I passed. That's why I got in so much later than you shitbags, because not even the Ghosts could find me! I'm the second candidate in Ghost history to skip the interrogation portion of the final eval because I was just too damn sneaky for them!"

"Wow," Abraham said, "that's impressive, Larry. Congrats, bro, I'm so damn proud of you I think I'm gonna be sick."

He shared a fist bump with Larry, and a puzzled look came across his friend's face.

"Why are we all gathered at the girls' room?"

He cast a suspicious eye at Abraham.

"Oh, I see..."

Abraham blushed again. "Larry, don't –"

Larry started gyrating his hips and smacking the air in front of his crotch. He howled like a wolf and shouted, "Abraham's back for some more Tayla action!"

Abraham covered his face with his hands.

Someone pulled one of his hands from his face. It was Tayla.

"I'm glad you're back, Larry, but you smell like something an animal chewed up and shit out. You should go shower." She turned and gave Abraham her best innocent wide-eyed stare. "Abraham and I have some things we need to discuss...in private."

Abraham's chest developed a light airy feeling that he thought might be the aftershock of a direct hit from a lightning bolt. The hair on the back of his neck stood on end.

Savony lightly punched Larry on the shoulder. "C'mon, Poplenko, I'll get your gear cleaned up while you shower."

Larry, still laughing hysterically, marched down the hallway crooning a raunchy tune that Abraham didn't recognize.

Tayla pulled him into her room and shoved him, hard.

The door slid shut behind her.

He regained his footing and looked at her.

She looked at him, still smiling, but there wasn't a trace of innocence left in her eyes.

"I know I said that was a one-time thing, but it doesn't have to be."

Abraham's mouth was dry. He swallowed noisily.

"Uh, well...yeah, about that, I..."

Tayla walked over to him and ran a hand through his hair. It was long now, long enough that it sometimes got in his eyes when he was working out. He hadn't realized he'd been out of the military that long. It felt good, her fingers brushing against his scalp.

"You don't have to say yes." She kissed him gently. "But you'll have more fun if you do."

Abraham's leg twitched. His body was already responding to her kiss.

He didn't offer her a yes or a no.

He put his hands on her hips and pulled her against him.

It felt good to have her this close. To be alone with her.

Between kisses, he said, "I was hoping you'd say that."

"You thought I wouldn't?" she giggled.

"I just..."

She pulled her face back and pressed her finger against his lips.

"Don't talk. No more talking."

She stole his stammered reply with another kiss.

The next few days passed by with a comfortable bliss that Abraham knew was the best time of his life.

He was either hanging out with his friends, working out the mysterious origins of his father with his brother, or he was spending time with Tayla. In between all that, he still had plenty of time to go to the gym, to scan the galaxy net for information about his father, and to catch a couple of hours of sleep before the next day. He checked his credit account, and saw that his first Ghost paycheck had cleared.

He had earned three months' worth of Marine Corps pay in one month. Those digits were listed as "Banquo Consulting Services". Abraham didn't get the reference, but if he knew the Society at all by now, he knew there was a hidden meaning to the name of the shell corporation that distributed their paychecks.

Larry would not stop bragging about his stellar performance in Phase Two. He had broken six Ghost Society records, and in his words, "Even if I get smoked on my first mission, I'm in the history books for life, man. Well, not the history books, but the Ghost Society records for sure. That practically makes me immortal!"

Savony seemed to have recovered from whatever she went through during Resurrection Week...at least, enough to convince Abraham she was back to her usual, snarky self. She amused herself by overreacting to Larry's boasting, which encouraged him to go on long tangents about how he was possibly the best Ghost in the history of the society, or by making lewd comments about Abraham and Tayla, which made Abraham uncomfortable while Tayla laughed them off.

When Graduation Day finally came, Abraham woke up with a nervous stomach. He had survived Resurrection Week, but he didn't feel like he'd died and come back to life. He kept trying to shirk this nagging feeling that something big was going to happen, that the real kick in the ass was going to go down at the ceremony. He made a point not to stay the whole night in Tayla's room, and she didn't spend a lot of time in his room, either.

It was a lot different than things with Vase. Vase challenged him intellectually, whereas Tayla and he seemed to have more in common. Maybe it was the officer/enlisted thing that separated Abraham and Vase, or maybe it was just that Vase carried an iron-clad wall of confidence that, if he was honest, intimidated him. She was never wrong, and if she was, she could sell a convincing case that she was wrong because that was what the situation demanded.

After knowing her for four years, he still didn't know her.

He had known Tayla for almost two full years, and had been with her for just a few weeks, but he felt like he'd known her all his life. It didn't make sense, but he couldn't deny the connection, either.

That made his stomach worse, thinking about the future.

After graduation they would get their first assignments, and who knew what that was going to entail. Ghosts operated solo, except under rare and extreme circumstances. He might not ever see Tayla again, or if he did, they might be very different people when they reconnected.

Anything long term was destined to fail.

He knew that. She knew that. And so they enjoyed what they had in the time they had left.

He showered, toweled off and passed Larry as he grabbed the brand new C-skin out of his wall locker.

Larry mumbled something, wiped his bleary eyes and turned on the water.

Abraham pulled up his C-skin and inspected it. No tears, no cuts or fraying of the fabric. It was fresh from the factory, and it had that new straight out of the factory smell. He pulled it on, tapped the ratchet cuffs and let them seal on his wrists and ankles. The magnetic boots were lighter than he remembered. But then, he hadn't worn a C-skin since the Navy Ball. Phase One of Ghost training was mostly classroom with a few exercises in a B-skin, and Phase Two had been a B-skin as well. It felt weird to wear something so plain, so civilian, and know that this would be his new uniform. He pulled out his Ghost-issued Portal and dialed the pattern to the billowing smoke theme that was the Ghost standard.

There were no ranks in the Ghost Society. You were either Star or Blood, and Abraham hadn't yet been told which one he was. He wasn't sure how you attained the Blood Path, but he was pretty sure Smithers would have told him if he had been given the opportunity for this distinctive honor.

Larry exited the shower and sat naked on his bed, rubbing his hair with the towel.

"You ready for this, Abraham?"

"Ready as I'll ever be." Abraham shrugged.

"Yeah, me too. I'm ready to get into some secret squirrel shit. This is so much better than the Corps ever was."

Abraham nodded. "It has a certain…there's something to it, for sure. I don't know what it is, yet, but I like it, too."

Larry stepped into his C-skin. "Yeah, bro, I wonder what kind of assignments we'll be on. Are we going to be stopping uprisings on backwater worlds, or are we going to be starting them in terra-cities? I hope I get a terra-city assignment. I don't miss Veranda at all."

Abraham slipped his Portal into the leg pocket of his C-skin and craned his neck to throw Larry a questioning gaze. "You don't miss home?"

Larry sealed his ratchet cuffs. "No way, man. I'm not excited about it being burned to the ground, the whole planet, you know. But, I kinda don't give a shit, either."

That threw Abraham for a loop.

"Woah, dude, what about your grandparents?"

Larry shrugged. He was scrolling through the Portal. He found the Ghost pattern, tapped his portal, and his C-skin blinked, suddenly covered in swirling gray mist.

"I miss my grandma, sure. But my grandfather? He was kind of an asshole."

"Larry," Abraham almost gasped, "he was a good man. He worked and put a roof over your head and –"

Larry interrupted him, "Food on my plate and he was always there for us. Yeah, sure. Doesn't stop him from being an asshole. If he had any kind of spine, he would have done a few years in the Corps, or the Navy. He was freeloading off society by dodging service."

Abraham sat down on his bed.

"Freeloading? He ran a business. He was just a private citizen, what's wrong with that? The military isn't for everyone."

Larry locked eyes with him. Something burned in them, like mini solar flares lighting off. "He was a coward. He had the physical aptitude and the mental strength to do a tour or two as a rifleman. He backed out because he was scared he was actually going to have to fight. That old bastard talked a bunch of shit about his father taking him hunting with that antique scattergun, but I'd bet my life that he never went hunting after his father died. He never took me, not once. He talked about that stupid scattergun. Hung it on the wall in the living room, I'm sure you remember seeing it, and he would show it off to everyone, but he never did take it off that wall. If you wanna know the truth, I think he was scared of it."

"Just because he had the ability to serve doesn't mean he had the obligation, though, Larry. It's a choice, and not everyone has to choose to sign their life away like we did. That doesn't make him a coward."

Larry tucked his Portal into his leg pocket.

"I think it does," he said, eyes staring at the floor. Through the floor.

"Larry, you okay?" Abraham asked.

He blinked, realized he had been staring off into space, and smiled.

"Oh, dude, I've never been better. Just thinking, you know." He patted Abraham on the shoulder. "Let's do this thing, man."

Abraham patted Larry's shoulder and said, "You know, bro, if this shit gets crazy, don't forget about TA. We've got each other's back, no matter what. I'm always gonna be here for you, Larry. You're my brother."

Larry laughed. "David's your brother. I'm just your best man."

Abraham glared at him. "Tayla and I –"

"Are getting it on, and that's gonna lead one of two places. A baby, or a wedding, whichever one comes first is up to you. I'm just throwing my name out there, so if you take things that direction sooner rather than later, I'm standing by, ready willing and able to take on the full responsibility of the best man role."

Abraham rolled his eyes. "No one's getting married or having babies."

Larry lurched his eyebrows. "You practice enough that it's bound to happen."

Abraham punched him in the arm. "Not happening, bro."

Larry laughed. Abraham laughed.

Abraham followed his buddy out of the room and down the hallway. They crossed several hallways and ended up at the forbidden access door. Tayla and Savony were already there, waiting on the other side of the door's threshold.

"Tayla," Abraham greeted her.

"Abe," she smiled and simulated a curtsy.

He thought it was cute.

"Sarge," Savony said, "we still on for the TA thing?"

Abraham crossed his arms. "Nothing's changed for me. That's still a thing, right everyone? Any one of us finds themselves neck deep in shit, just sound the alarm and we'll take care of each other. I know we're solo operators now, but I'm not planning on leaving anyone behind."

"Still a thing for me," Tayla said.

"You know I'm down," Larry chimed in.

Savony nodded. "I can't leave my Corps buddies behind. Even if we are Ghosts now."

They bumped fists to seal the deal.

The door slid open.

Smithers and Myles stood in the doorway.

Myles said, "Enter and line up."

Smithers flashed his weird smile. He and Myles stepped to the sides to open up the entryway.

Larry entered first. Abraham followed him with the girls in tow.

The room was dark.

Four weak lights, almost like torches, danced up ahead. The Ghost Society crest was partially illuminated on the wall beneath the torches. Abraham followed Larry, but the lack of light in the room made it hard to see. If he didn't have the pale outline of light around Larry's head, he wouldn't have been able to see him at all. They went about ten paces inside and mounted a set of stairs, then made their way to stand, one person beneath each source of light. Larry stood at parade rest underneath one light. Abraham copied him, heard the girls' boots clicking on the floor as they fell into position beside him.

Somewhere in the dark, Smithers cleared his throat.

"You have," he spoke in his gravelly voice, "exceeded the standards of the Ghost Society's requirements. You have entered into a pact with the Society, one that is not given lightly. You will continue to exceed the standard every day. Every action you take will be measured. Every word you say will be accounted for. Every breath you take is a gift you share with the most elite group of operators in the Human Collective. But you are no longer a member of the Human Collective. You are now dead to them. As you die to the nation you have sworn to protect, you are reborn into an elite group that is the hidden hand of humanity. The first line of defense that the Collective does not even know it has."

Abraham maintained his rigid position, but his heart leapt at those words. He didn't know that he was being erased from the Human Collective. Didn't know such a thing was even possible. That wasn't part of the contract he signed. Did that mean he was being declared dead, or that his records were simply being erased?

"It has been said," Smithers droned on, "that it is appointed once for a man to die. In the Society, we live two lives. The one before, and the one after. As of this moment on, consider yourself dead. The life you carry on into the future is that of a Ghost. You will have no contact with anyone in your previous life. Your old life is gone. Welcome to the beginning of your new life in the Society."

At once, all four light sources diminished.

The room was plunged into total darkness.

Abraham tensed. He expected to hear a series of laser blasts or feel a blade drag across his neck. He thought for sure he heard boot steps somewhere in the shadows. His heart slammed against his chest. He felt shaky on his knees, realized he had locked them, and slowly rotated his weight to the balls of his feet to loosen the joints up. His head pulsed, as if his blood pressure had just skyrocketed.

The lights came back on, and the world was different.

It wasn't just the four torches behind him; someone had cut on the full illumination in the room, and he could see everything. He could see more than everything. All the Ghost Cadre were there, standing in the back of the room, and he could see their faces without Ghost Bars. Smithers eyes were a pale red, utterly colorless, and completely devoid of any emotion.

Agent Myles Lannam, the coolest kid on Veranda, his eyes were the same as Smithers. The sclera was white, but the iris was a pale red, and the look cast by them was emptiness. Like a bottomless well, or the unending darkness of space.

"You are seeing through your Ghost Bar now," Smithers announced. "This is the greatest secret of the Ghost Society. Three of you are on the Star Path. One of you elected for and achieved the Blood Path. Congratulations are in order for all of you. Agent Lannam."

Myles cleared his throat. "You are seeing the world in two facets. The Bar is a window into a higher spacetime. A shred of another dimension that layers over this one. We have implemented this higher technology to make operations easier, and to make you harder to kill. The higher plane of spacetime will be confusing to you at first, but as you stare into the abyss, the abyss stares back into you. It will adapt to you as you adapt to it, and it will become the most important tool in your arsenal. Wear it proudly. The nature of this shred will shield your face, and hide your identity, from anyone you encounter. You can switch it off with a thought, call it up with a thought. All interactions with the higher plane are on the level of thought, because the speed of thought is the only thing in this dimension that is truly faster than light, the only thing that is detectable by the higher plane."

Myles looked at Smithers. He nodded.

Smithers said, "This concludes the ceremony. Celebration will be at the Ghost bar, Dutchman's Cove."

Abraham relaxed from parade rest. They shared fist bumps and hugs all around, but one thing caught Abraham's attention in a way he didn't expect.

Tayla smiled, her blue eyes wide with joy. Savony laughed and crushed him in a tight hug, her green eyes filled with happy tears.

When Abraham shook Larry's hand and they clapped each other on the back, his eyes were pale red. Just like Smithers and Myles. Abraham knew what that meant. Smithers, Myles, and now Larry…

Larry had taken the Blood Path.

The Dutchman's Cove was the coolest place Abraham had ever been. It was all glass. The bar area, the floor, the ceiling, the walls, the tables and the chairs. Abraham felt like he was standing on an invisible point in space surrounded by vacuum and stars and the endless stretch of nothing that was the universe.

The four of them assaulted the bar with a quickness.

"What ya got?" Larry shouted. Eyeing two tall neon green bottles, he pointed and said, "Gimme a double of that!"

The drinks, the songs, the camaraderie lasted long into the simulated night on a space station in a forgotten sector of space. Stories were told, scars compared, and in the end, it felt less like the start of something new.

It felt like the death of what was.

CHAPTER 30

I'd been down to the lower levels of Vatican before, but not like this.

It was different.

Whenever Blaze and I ventured that far down, we would always go together. Bring the team of forensic analysts with us. The crime scene replicator bot. The furthest down we ever went was the three hundred levels, and that was just to let the bot do its thing. The smashed mess of blood and gore, the red smear and tiny bone fragments the only indication it had ever been a human, would come down to DNA analysis. I still wish I could forget seeing that.

It was worse when I had to watch the security footage of the teenage boy trying to do some level drops, his Pocket recording the daring jumps and reckless maneuvers. It was one of those things where you were just waiting for the accident as you watched. And it happened. The Pocket tried to chase him as he fell, caught a distance shot of his arm breaking on a guard rail, and then lost him in the impenetrable dark somewhere around the four hundred levels.

I watched the vid without audio. Blaze told me he could hear the slam of the kid's body liquefying on impact.

I'd already been down here two weeks when they started telling me it was going to be another two or three before they could arrange passage for me.

Where am I going? Aldebaranzan. Because of course that's where the leader of the Pathfinders is – right at the epicenter of this whole shitstorm.

I didn't know if it was because I was embedded with these guys – who were every bit as dangerous as they claimed to be – or if it was just because things started to fall apart for my career by that point; whatever the reason, I could taste the desperation in the air.

It wasn't confined to the overgrown moss and creepers that had reclaimed the exterior, and sometimes large portions of the interior of the buildings that far down. It wasn't something you could smell, like a nervous sweat on Sebek when he gunned down an addict in the street a half meter from me. Left the man's brain on the moss-covered wall.

Said something like, "That'll keep the plants fed."

As if anything down there needed feeding. The whole place was a festering cesspool that needed nuking from orbit. Only, to do that, you'd destroy the foundations of the whole terra city, and then the whole planet would go up in flames.

Part of me wondered if that's exactly what needed to happen.

Maybe Vatican had become so corrupted, the parts I thought were comfortable and familiar were just a polished veneer, held afloat by the underworld of drugs and sex and death. Humanity always had this dark side. Why, though?

Because utopia's a dream. A pipedream. Utopia is not what the representatives and senators say it is. I figured, at this point, even the madame executor herself was selling an impossibility. The only real utopia was the stuff these lower-level addicts packed into their pipes and smoked every hour on the hour.

I had found myself thinking like one of them. Because to get in with them, to blend in so well that they would mistake me for one of their own, I had to become one of them. The old part of me, who I was before, had to go. Djet would have gotten me killed. Because I knew for a fact these Pathfinders hated anything government. Anything longarm. Give them a cause and they'd spout a half dozen reasons why that cause was corrupt, evil, and needed destroying.

These people just wanted to break things.

Like Hanson. He'd been a sensory operator on a navy frigate. Saw some minor action over his twenty-two-year career, had to repel boarders in one of the worst navy mishaps in Collective history. Or so he said.

"Intel was bad. I fucking hate bad intel," he said in his deep drawl, a voice that made it seem he'd earned his machismo, although I suspected the opposite was true. "And then that dumbass commander let us get boarded. Thought it was a good chess move, letting the enemy onto our vessel. We only had one kill team of Marines on board, and they couldn't stop everyone."

He sharpened his knife against his boot as he talked. Hanson was from a human-controlled world on the outskirts of the Orion Arm, a hotbed for trade between major sectors of human- and aquasian-controlled space. He told me several times that it was one of the busiest space and air traffic planets in the entire galaxy, and I believed him. I didn't believe the story he was telling me then, and I wonder if he believed any of mine.

"Torind pirates, you know. They cut their way in, fore and aft sections. Kill team takes the aft section to protect the engineering section, so they can't scuttle the whole damn ship. Fine by me. The fore section just happens to be where most of our non-infantry crew are stationed. I knew it was gonna be a bloodbath," he remarked offhandedly, scraping his knife across the sharpener on the sole of his boot. "But the armory is in the middle of the ship. I can't get there and back; torinds are already slithering through the breach. So, I just had to make do with a couple of box cutters."

He was smiling, reliving something. Whether it was real or not, I couldn't decide. His fervor for the story was clear, but if he'd watched someone do it or just completely made it up was unclear.

"Yeah, Princess, that's where I found my love for the blade," he said with an exaggerated sigh. "Never turned my back on her since. That's why I only did twenty-two, instead of thirty. Got out straight away, didn't re-up, and I went searching for the masters. That's when I found my path."

He whipped his hand in a chopping motion. The knife he was sharpening zipped through the air and embedded itself in the brick with a crack.

He watched in his peripheral for my reaction. I gave him a wide-eyed grin, just to try to win him over.

Acting as nonchalant as he could, he got up and brushed himself off, rubbed the dust from his hands on his pants and strutted over to retrieve the knife.

"Guess you could say I made the cut." He chuckled at his own joke.

I laughed, too. Strained, of course – I didn't think any of this was funny.

Honestly, I was scared. Not scared of Hanson, because I'd dealt with people like him before. I was scared that Hanson was the closest thing to tame I'd come across in that rogue cell of former military.

Hanson was the newest member of Sebek's cell.

They called themselves Detachment 13.

Det 13 because there's thirteen hard and fast members. They take in people all the time, or so Sebek told me, because they lose people all the time. I'd given him the excuse that I couldn't get a tattoo because Liberty House knew to look for it, but that didn't stop him from branding all the new guys.

I met Caldwell and Grip the first day.

Caldwell was a jokester, a prankster, and generally more of an asshole than the rest of Det 13. He was young, maybe in his early twenties, and bragged constantly about having been one basic training class from Duringer. Said he got to go to the frontlines of the Riskar War just as it was ending, killed himself a dozen or more riskies; and when he didn't get a medal for saving his platoon sergeant, he deserted.

"Knew I was never gonna get my due," he complained while we were circled up for dinner. Dinner was freeze-dried ration packs around a fire pit made of trash and pieces of crumbling buildings collected in a steel drum sliced in half. "So I said fuck it, y'know? I'm a damned war hero and they're gonna congratulate the senior enlisted people? When I pulled their asses outta the fire? No thank you, no sir. I'll take my skills and training and make them work for me. I don't wanna be contributing to a war machine that ain't paying me dividends."

Caldwell laughed, a high-pitched tremolo that raised the hair on the back of my neck. His discolored teeth let me know he was skimming some of the supply that this group was peddling, but Sebek didn't seem to have a problem with it.

Grip was a different story, and it was hard for me to figure out why he stuck around with Caldwell. Grip's nickname, or callsign as they referred to their monikers, came from his impressive physical stature. He was over two meters tall, weighed at least three hundred pounds, but he was solid. Like the difference between a steel pipe and a solid steel bar. Nothing could get through to that guy, and even when I tried to introduce myself and talk to him, he just grunted and mumbled a few one-word responses. He looked the type that should have been on the professional fighting circuit, although I doubt his strong silent personality would have generated much publicity, even if he pulverized his opponents.

There was Lenkford, Simon and Abernathy, and they all could have fit in upstairs. These were the standing professionals, people who came down to report on the goings-on in the city. Lenkford reminded me of the guy I'd shot in flat 201 a month or two ago. He had the neck tattoo, and I wondered if he was running the same game, peddling drugs and serving as a lookout.

About a week and a half into my stay with Detachment 13, Sebek had a meeting with someone, a reason to head up to the two hundred levels, and I was ordered – tasked, which amounts to the same thing – to attend with Grip.

I didn't understand half of the in-house acronyms and vernacular, but what I did get was that Detachment 13 wasn't the only cell operating on Vatican. How could it be? I chided myself after the fact, because Vatican is a terra city, and the home world of humanity.

When I got roped into helping with a 'tasking' from higher up – Sebek's words, not mine – I was rear guard while Sebek, Hanson, Caldwell and Grip broke into the storage floor of a factory. I wasn't let in on the details. I didn't know what the hell we were doing, and I was okay with that. If I had to run afoul of the law to keep Sebek on side, or at least to stay in his good graces long enough to get to Bayson, I was okay with that.

Especially because discretion seemed to be his biggest rule when dealing with the 'upper crust', as he called it. Any operations that required Pathfinders to go up to the real world were considered a catastrophic failure if their presence was detected. Pathfinders were expected to use any means necessary to avoid capture, up to and including suicide. And if they were captured...the first rule of being a Pathfinder was to never be captured.

The second rule, and I'm not military so I didn't understand the reference, but the second rule Sebek gave the new guys was "every mission is a no-fail. We don't take unnecessary risk, but we don't shy away from opportunity, neither." The concept was easy to grasp, that failure wasn't an option, but I felt like there was more to it than just that.

I got to see that play out in real time during the factory raid.

We crammed down a ration pack a piece, and then Sebek led us to the Det 13 armory.

It covered the entire office area of a particularly run-down building. Concrete fragments and dust littered the place. Several dark stains marked the hallway leading in, long dried from whoever had died leaving them on the walls and the floor. A few desks were overturned haphazardly, riddled with carbon scoring and laser bolt holes. In the back of the open floor plan, lining the entire wall, were a series of floor-to-ceiling lockers.

Sebek punched in the codes on the keypads. They swung open one by one, revealing an arsenal the likes of which I thought was impossible. Dozens of CLRs, even a few MLRs and two B-skins. These didn't look used, either. They had a factory fresh scent, like they'd never been worn.

"No B-skins for this op. Discretion, boys. Remember, discretion. Leave the heavy stuff for when we need it. Travel light, spare the fight."

Sebek's raspy voice had a casual tone to it. He was in his element. Sounded comfortable.

That made me more nervous, but I learned quickly to mask my nerves with bravado. It was a good look, especially when I was trying to come across like I knew what I was doing, when I was in fact the only person here who had no clue what they were doing.

"Rearguard's gotta have a CLR, at least," I said, snatching one off the hooks.

I'd operated one of them before, on the range. Never had to use it on the streets, as that would be more of a Special Tactics Division role, but it had been a longarm yearly requirement to maintain qualifications at the range. I preferred handguns because of the familiarity, but I knew enough to sell my competency with the CLR.

I grabbed a heat sink, slapped it on the side and primed it with a yank on the charging handle. The weapon whined as the laser keyed up. It felt like I was gearing up for war. The way Det 13 carried themselves, it wasn't a safe bet that we weren't.

Sebek gave me a nod of approval.

"That's fine, Princess." He passed me two more heat sinks and a grenade.

Holding the thing up, I remember thinking it was heavier than I'd expected.

"I thought you said we were being discrete?"

He shrugged, picking up a CLR and collapsing it to scatter mode.

"We plan for discretion, but we go prepared for all hell to break loose."

I played into this, trying to up my credibility without giving too much away.

"I like this cell already. Last one put a little too much emphasis on the 'sleeper' part."

Caldwell, stuffing a pair of L-pistols into his belt, broke into a fit of laughter.

"You wandered into the right cell, Princess. Here at Det 13, we're prime movers. We leave the sleeping to the dead."

Grip slung a CLR and stuffed spare heat sinks into his dark cargo pockets. He didn't laugh, but his lip twitched with the beginnings of a smile. He picked up a grenade and tossed it through the air like it didn't weigh a thing.

Hanson caught it by the pull-ring with an outstretched finger and slid it onto his kit.

We all wore LCEs, which I should have known stood for load carrying equipment, but we had a different term for it at the Watch. I was trying not to replace my known terminologies for these new, learned ones, hoping the unfamiliarity didn't show in my mannerisms.

I must have pulled it off, because Sebek slapped me on the back.

"Standard smash and grab, boys. I'm on point. Weapons hidden until we're inside. The new kids will be the grabbers."

"Makes us the smashers!" Caldwell practically shouted.

"I'll handle the delicate work. I'm more of a slasher," Hanson said, deftly maneuvering a butterfly knife.

"Ooh, that's even better. Team Smash n' Slash!"

Grip rolled his eyes, which made me laugh.

The men continued to jeer and cajole one another. There was a lot of backslapping and fist bumps, which I joined in on. I needed these people to be comfortable with me, which meant I had to be comfortable with them. The whole thing was so unnatural.

I was still trying to settle into my role when we hit the maglift.

I was feeling awkward, holding my CLR under a light terrelian leather jacket. The barrel stuck out, so I tucked it into my belt, but it bulged the seam of my pants awkwardly. I collapsed the CLR to scatter mode, which compacted it enough to stay hidden. I spent a moment cursing my stupidity, but thankfully the ones Sebek called the new kids behind me were too busy chattering amongst themselves to notice.

The plan was that they were supposed to serve as lookouts until Sebek gave them the go-ahead to grab whatever it was we're planning on stealing. I was concerned cramming this many bodies in a decrepit level-one maglift would be too much for it, but Vatican's reputation for great engineers and the galaxy's best architects rang true. The thing functioned without a hitch.

We exited on level 342. Significantly higher up than I thought we'd be. Not high enough that security was going to give us trouble. I thought.

Sebek walked through the doors, followed by Grip, Caldwell and Hanson. Interestingly, I noticed that we didn't have a comm setup.

How is this supposed to be coordinated without comms?

Sebek led us across the street, dimly lit by lights in the underside of the level above. I saw condensation on the walls. A steady stream of liquid was trickling down the sides of the plate over our heads, and I thought it was water until I smelled it.

It wasn't water.

"Ugh..." Caldwell groaned. "There's a burst sewage pipe."

Grip smacked the back of Caldwell's head, but didn't say anything.

"Right, sorry." Caldwell rubbed the back of his head.

We continued crossing streets, largely abandoned. I thought this odd until I realized I had completely lost track of time. A quick glance at the Pulse on my wrist revealed it was zero two-thirty hours. The middle of the night.

I recognized that this was an industrial district. No one lived down here. Or if they did, they didn't have living units here. Either squatters in abandoned businesses or street walkers too lazy to venture higher and too smart to travel to lower levels. I remember thinking I'd be surprised if we encountered any longarm presence down here. At least, until the alarms started sounding.

Sebek led us to a roll-up garage door. It was a heavy automated thing that we didn't have access codes for; or at least, I didn't think we did. I knew Sebek was well connected and well funded because of the nature of his trades, but he couldn't have –

"Caldwell," Sebek rasped in the darkness.

"On it, boss." Caldwell rushed to the keypad next to the roll-up door, pulled a cord out of his Pulse and connected it to the keypad.

Whatever he did, it was fast and quiet.

The roll-up door didn't open. Just shifted in place with a muted clank.

"Unlocked," Caldwell said, wrapping up his cord and tucking it away.

I'd never seen anything like this before. Vatican was supposed to be the pinnacle of technology in the Collective. Unless that didn't apply to the lower levels.

"No system is too complex for me, Princess," Caldwell whispered as he passed me. He was bragging, and he had a right to. It felt weird, though. Almost like he could read my thoughts.

"Think your ego's gonna fit under that door?" I asked.

Hanson snickered, but Sebek wasn't having it.

He pointed to Grip. "Manual labor assist."

Grip nodded and stepped forward. He was a massive human. Maybe the biggest I'd ever seen; and when he bent down like a powerlifter to slip his fingers under the edge of the roll-up door, I had no doubt he could move it. Even though maintenance bots were usually required for such tasks.

The door creaked loudly as he lifted it to about one meter off the textured floor. He was straining, huge muscles bulging with the effort, but he didn't groan or exhale loudly. Just bent and lifted, and suddenly we had our access point.

"Stick close," Sebek said to the rest of us.

He dropped prone, peeked under the door, then crawled through.

"Clear," he rasped from the other side.

Hanson slipped in next, followed by Caldwell and then me. Grip slid his feet under the door, bench-pressed the door a little higher and slid on his back. The door came slamming down an inch from his head.

Hanson and Caldwell offered Grip a hand. He pulled himself up, nearly bowling the two of them over.

I took a second to get acclimated to the total darkness.

How does Sebek see anything in here?

I moved my hand in front of my face. I couldn't see it.

"Sebek," Hanson whispered by my side, "he's got the sight. That was his path, and he's been leading us ever since."

That could only mean he had enhanced vision tech. A bionic implant, or something similar, that let him see in low light conditions. Or maybe even different light spectrums. If he'd paid enough.

"Nice," I said. "I'm jealous."

Caldwell whispered a hoarse response. "Not as nice as your accelerated healing. Where'd you pick up biotech like that?"

I was momentarily thankful for the darkness because it hid my blank expression. *What's the cover story? Where did I get this post-human tech?* I'd completely forgotten.

"You don't wanna know," I said, the first thing that came to mind.

I expected that to go over like a fart on a live broadcast.

Instead, Hanson sighed. "That's the one downfall of this outfit. Too many damn secrets."

Caldwell snickered. "Calm down, Hanson. It just means she stole it.

She'll let us know when she trusts us more, won't you, Princess?"

Their back and forth gave me time to think of something, something I remembered from researching Obadiah Zeeben.

"I got it from a scientist on Mattox. My father was pissed I used up my college fund, but I knew what I wanted."

Grip was making a quiet, hoarse sound next to me.

"Is he okay?" I asked.

"Ah, he's fine," Caldwell said, annoyed. "That's just how he laughs."

"Grip, you okay?" I asked with an edge to my voice. "You sound like a storg that swallowed a fly."

He grunted an affirmative, and I didn't know what to make of that.

Emergency lighting came on, silencing the snickering men. Light strips that ran along the floor cast aside some of the shadows. We were in a factory. I looked around, seeing vague shapes suddenly take the form of conveyer belts lined with uncut glass tubes of various sizes. They stood stock still, just waiting for cuts to be made at the end of the line.

I then understood why we were hitting this particular factory.

I'd disassembled enough laser weapons to recognize a focus tube when I saw one, even in its uncut form. Put that with the Pathfinders trying to start a little rebellion on Aldebaranzan, and the pieces fell into place.

Aldebaranzan was a pacifist planet. One of only a few in the Collective officially designated such. Weapons of any kind were not allowed on world, with the rare exception of military visitors on official orders, or licensed bodyguard personnel. Even they weren't allowed to have rifles, only handguns.

Sebek and Det 13 were sending their Pathfinder buddies a weapons shipment…in parts.

Every single part of a rifle could be printed or manufactured by hand with moderate skill and a decent amount of time invested. It may not have functioned like a top-tier Marine Corps CLR, and wouldn't have the same range of applications, but a rifle beat a handgun eight days a week. Especially when numbers were a consideration.

Holy shit, they can actually pull this off…

I'm actually going to help start an uprising.

Sebek returned to us, breathing like he'd run a mile.

We all pulled out our weapons as soon as we saw him approach.

"Grip, get the door and let the kids in. Hanson, I need you to solve a problem for me. Katana, you're watching the door."

Grip moved to lift the door. I telescoped my CLR to rifle mode and checked the heat sink. Hanson and Caldwell followed Sebek. Caldwell hung back at the corner to serve as an additional lookout for the loading operation, while Hanson followed Sebek into the shadows and they both disappeared.

Grip managed to get the door lifted enough for me to wave the three new guys in, and they started snatching up the tubes two at a time. I wasn't sure where they were taking them, but they disappeared around the same corner Sebek did. They returned a moment later for more.

The whole thing was playing out in front of me like a scene from a movie. There was no security, no cameras, no bots. It was eerie. Calm. So quiet it had the hair on the back of my neck standing on end.

This is too easy.

Grip pulled his CLR to his shoulder and shook his long wavy hair out of his face so he could look through the glass sight. The weapon looked like a toy in his hand. Like a marshmallow shooter I had when I was a kid.

"Watch." The big man lowered his rifle and pointed across the factory floor.

I strained my eyes. The emergency lighting was good enough to navigate by, but all I saw were conveyer belts, glass tubes, some other equipment I didn't recognize, and a catwalk that ran high over the middle of the floor.

The catwalk was what Grip was talking about. It was about five meters up and ran from a windowed office box to the other side of the room. A set of stairs criss-crossed underneath the box, but what had my attention was the middle of the walkway.

A security guard was leaning over the walkway, looking down right at us. Without vision enhanced like Sebek's, he probably couldn't make out very much. But he seemed alert to the fact that something wasn't right. He rotated his wrist and brought his Pulse to his lips.

He never got to make the call.

Hanson came from the shadows, blade high. The dark metal glinted before plunging into the man's neck. At the same moment, a swift kick bowed the knee at a bad angle.

Shick-crack!

The guard was an older man with a pot belly. He stood no chance against a hardened killer like Hanson. The gurgles and gasps lasted only a few seconds. Then everything was silent.

Hanson lowered the guard to the catwalk. The only noises we'd made in those twenty minutes were a few whispers and that wicked death rattle.

It seemed like no one knew we were here.

Grip smiled at me. He winked, and he was about to open his mouth to speak when half of his face was ripped away by a high-powered laser bolt.

I heard the report of the laser blast next.

Instinct kicked in before I could process what was happening. I was on my back, CLR in my shoulder and angled up, my cheek on the stock. My red dot was resting on the pull-door next to the closed roll-up.

“Longarms in the building!” someone shouted. “Weapons down and hands up, or we shoot!”

CHAPTER 31

Abraham stood in the hallway outside Smithers' office in the same parade rest position he had started in two hours ago. It wasn't that he couldn't move, it was that he refused to move. Smithers had called him over the station intercom, and then refused to answer the knock at the door. So, if it was a contest of wills the Ghost wanted, Abraham was not going to back down.

Off and on throughout his four years in the Marine Corps, Abraham had spent countless hours at parade rest and the position of attention. While neither was as comfortable as sitting, or even just standing at ease, the military stances offered a level of familiarity that he had grown to appreciate. It didn't stop him from being annoyed after the first fifteen minutes of waiting, nor did it stop him from being pissed off once he realized he'd been waiting for over an hour.

Once the clock hit two hours, he started to think about just returning to his room. Singularity was not a *Beijing*-class battleship that took the average person forty minutes to walk stem to stern; his room, clear on the other side of the station, was a simple five-minute walk away.

"Abraham," Smithers' voice came from the door's intercom, "what are you doing out there?"

It took everything for him not to unload on Smithers with both barrels. He sighed, took a slow, deep breath, tried to keep his voice measured.

"Agent Smithers, Agent Zeeben reports as directed. You called me here two hours ago."

There was a moment of silence, just long enough to make Abraham wonder if he was going to have to wait another two hours for a reply.

"Abraham...why don't you have your Ghost Bar switched on? You're an agent now. You should have it on at all times, unless you're alone in a secure area."

"I don't see anyone in the hallway right now," he retorted.

"Don't be a smartass. I need to speak with you, and I've been waiting two hours for your dumbass to figure out you need to switch your bar on. Do it, and enter."

Unbelievable, Abraham groaned inwardly.

He tapped the Pulse on his wrist, and the bar slid across his eyes. It was like wearing sunglasses, a gentle translucent shade of black over his vision, but filled with an overload of augmented reality information as the bar scanned everything he looked at. He stepped out of his parade rest position and looked at the door.

A blue node spun inside a red circle that spun the opposite direction. A message popped up in the augmented reality: **ACCESS NODE**

Annoyed that he hadn't thought of using the bar himself, Abraham mentally clicked the access node. The Ghost Bar blinked, and the door slid open immediately.

A strange smell wafted into the hallway. Abraham wrinkled his nose as he stepped into Smithers' office. Standing proudly atop the desk at the back of the room was the strangest plant, a stiff, half-meter tall thing that looked like a birch tree, but with burnt sections of bark that oozed a red and yellow sap. Vines rather than leaves hung from the finger-thin branches, which twisted in a crooked weave. A small, wide pot held the base of the thing, catching droplets of the ooze as they beaded up and dripped soundlessly.

Smithers stood behind the desk, manipulating a holoscreen with his fingers. His Ghost Bar was still active, which was probably for the best. Whoever said eyes were windows into the soul had never seen this man's eyes. The holoscreen had the text inverted from Abraham's perspective, but there were several images buried in the sea of text, large enough for Abraham to recognize what they were.

The Ravens platoon on Juno. His platoon, the basic training photo. He saw Amory, Digger, and so many others. Vase, too. There was an emotional tug in his chest, seeing their faces, his mind temporarily transported back to that moment in time. It had only been a few years, but it felt like a lifetime ago. The words 'back in the day' swelled up in his mind, and he understood how retired soldiers felt telling their war stories to whoever would listen to them at the bar.

"What is this?" Abraham asked.

Smithers swiped the screen with a smile. "I'm getting to the important stuff."

The screen slid over to show the face of a young man. He had dark hair, short, and was extremely fit. His black shirt clung to a well-defined physique, his skin was a generous tan, and the bottom fibers of a mustache peaked out from below the black bar that covered his eyes. Abraham studied the image. Smithers spun the screen in the air so he could see it straight on.

"Is this you when you were younger or something?" Abraham asked.

The bottom of the image proclaimed: **AGENT OSSEF**

"So it's not you. Old boyfriend of yours?"

Smithers chuckled. "Something like that. Watch this."

Smithers held out two fingers and swiped across the photo.

The Ghost Bar dissolved, and suddenly Abraham realized what he was looking at.

More accurately, who he was looking at.

"My father was an Agent?" he asked.

Smithers nodded.

"You understand I couldn't reveal this to you until I was sure you were sticking it out with us."

Abraham reeled. His entire life flashed before his eyes at lightning speed.

Obadiah Zeeben's real name was *Ossef*? When had he been a Ghost, and how did Abraham never realize it? He didn't even know what a Ghost was until he was in basic training, but still...he had never detected anything about his father that made him think he had any military background.

His father was an architect. He designed and oversaw the construction of buildings. Then, he was a farmer. He built a single seat spacecraft in the greenhouse, that was unusual...but he wasn't a spy. There was no way he could have been tactful enough for the delicate line of work that was the Ghost Society's bread and butter. The thought of his father going through physical evaluations alone almost made Abraham laugh. Obadiah was not a physical marvel, not at all. Obadiah met a girl on Milune, the daughter of a middle-class jeweler in a suburban district...but he never told Abraham if he was from Milune. His father had left him with so many unanswered questions.

"How is this possible?"

Smithers smiled again – that crooked, cruel smile empty of feeling.

"You never knew? He never told you anything?"

Abraham shook his head. He was unable to speak.

"Agent Ossef wasn't our best agent, but he was involved in some big-time operations. He did not ride the bench, and he was not junior varsity. He was one of the only agents that got on a first name basis with the big boss. His defection from the Society was devastating. We actually created the Blood Path to ensure the most sensitive missions could not possibly lead to agent defections. He infiltrated the Society, gained our trust, and did some serious damage to the integrity of the organization."

Abraham shook his head. These revelations were slamming into him like an orbital bombardment; a meteor shower of information with deep impacts on his mind. The main question he kept returning to was, *how?* How had the same man he called Father, a simple family man, how could that same person have been a ruthless assassin in the most secretive organization in space?

Smithers clapped his hands together, dissolving the screen. He stuck out a finger, collecting one of the sap bubbles from his tree and licked it. He let out a satisfied sigh and sat down in his chair.

"No questions? If this is as big of a shock to you as you claim, I'm surprised you don't want to know more."

Abraham took a minute to try to piece his life back together with all of this new information. He struggled to reconcile it with his upbringing. He was raised by a Ghost and didn't know it. His father had despised the military, warned Abraham that the military wasn't the answer to his problems. But he had also allowed him to run off and enlist. Why would he do that?

Did Obadiah know the Ghosts would find out who Abraham was eventually?

The Ghosts destroyed Milune. They killed Mom...

"Did you destroy Milune because you were trying to kill him?" Abraham asked.

Smithers nodded slowly.

"Holy shit..." Abraham breathed.

It happened again. The same thing that had happened to him in Vase's apartment.

He felt like he was sucking air through a straw. Dark spots bloomed in his vision. He was standing in the station's one-third gravity, but he felt like he weighed a ton and was balanced on the point of a needle. Steadying himself against the bulkhead, he curled his hands into fists and tried to steady his hammering heartbeat. This was too much. Nothing made sense.

"This can't be true..." he breathed.

Smithers' gravelly voice intoned, "It is the only truth about your father you've been given your whole life, Abraham. I don't know why, and it seems you don't either, but the man you called your father has lied to you. Agent Ossef was excommunicated from the society and marked for retirement because he did the unthinkable. He crossed a line that no human should ever cross, and he did it in his capacity as an Agent."

Abraham's gut was in a knot. He felt like a child again. A little boy who watched his mother die before his eyes. A kid with no family at all who grew up being bounced around between foster homes, or who found out they were adopted. He enlisted in the Corps because he wanted to find out who he was, but that had been metaphorical. Now, presented with this insane truth, he felt further from understanding the concrete reality of just who the hell his father was. If he couldn't understand the man who raised him, what hope did he have of discovering who *he* was?

"So Zeeben is not my real name?"

Smithers shook his head. "Zeeben was your mother's name. It seems to us that Obadiah took your mother's name when they were wed on Milune. Unusual, but not unprecedented. It was the perfect cover for an agent on the run. It did take us a considerable amount of time to locate him."

"And when you did, you thought the best way to go after him was to destroy the entire planet?" Abraham hissed.

For a moment, he was blasted back through time to basic, when Vase had given the Raven platoon the news that Veranda had been hit by the riskar. That Veranda was largely destroyed. An out-of-the-way world of simple farmers and business people with no military presence, suddenly delivered up to the front lines of a war it had no interest in...that wasn't the riskar, either.

"You destroyed two planets to try to kill him? Veranda was you, too, wasn't it?"

"We had to be sure. Thing is, we're still not."

"Still not sure?" Abraham echoed weakly. He dared not hope.

Smithers stood and walked around the table to stand in front of Abraham. His faced moved ever so slightly side to side, like the eyes that would never reveal themselves were searching him. Sifting him on a deeper level than the visceral.

"Agent Ossef was excommunicated for improper conduct with an alien species."

Abraham's knees gave out. He slid down the bulkhead of Smithers' office, folding in on himself. So it was true, then. His mother was not his mother? Obadiah screwed an alien on some faraway world and somehow brought the child to Milune? How had his mother been okay with that? How had the alien just given up the child to be taken away by his father?

"No," Abraham groaned, "no, I can't...I can't be half alien. I had a human mother! I don't look or think or act like a riskar."

"You have their innate ability to manipulate gravity, Abraham. Stories and books have postulated that humanity will develop enhanced abilities at some point in the future, but until you came along, that has existed only in the imaginings of artists and writers. You are the first of your kind. A union between man and alien is the only thing that could have resulted in this type of advancement."

"*Advancement*? I wouldn't call this advancement."

"No?" Smithers asked. "People have volunteered for experiments, implants, surgeries and sold their souls to bioengineers on a fledgling hope of being able to do one tenth of what you're capable of, Abraham."

"I don't want to be capable of any of this shit. I just want to be normal. I want to be human."

"You are, to some extent. We need to do further testing to figure out just how much, but for now, you need to do some soul-searching and see if this jogs anything in your memory. Anything your father ever told you, anything he ever did that you didn't understand at the time. Maybe with this new context added, you can piece it together. Solve the one problem the Society has never figured out."

"Who Obadiah Ossef was?"

Smithers frowned.

"No." He took a deep breath, like he was tired. "Exactly who and what you are."

Abraham shuddered. "I came here because you told me you could figure that out."

Smithers showed his teeth. "I've done all I can. The rest is up to you."

CHAPTER 32

I was frozen in place. I didn't know what to do. One part of me was screaming to run toward the longarms, the other panicking to get out of there.

Blood dripped from the catwalk, pattering on the factory floor.

Grip was standing there with a mottled red mess for a face. Still standing.

I'd never seen someone get shot in the face and live.

I felt a presence at my side. It was Sebek. I knew this because I could hear his breathing. It sounded like a rotary saw starting and stopping. I didn't need to see him to know the shock that must have been on his face. He hadn't been expecting company.

But Detachment 13 of the Pathfinders weren't amateurs. They knew combat. Most of them had served in the Collective's military. All had been in gunfights and lived to brag about it. I knew things were bad, but I also knew Sebek had a contingency plan in place.

He pulled the pin on his contingency plan; a Mark-V stun grenade. He let it cook for a few seconds in his hand, then rolled it toward the door. It bounced against the door jamb and arced out of the factory.

A shout of "grenade!" came from outside.

The pop-hiss of the grenade shook the roll-up door, but it stayed in place.

Grip spun on his heels, weapon up and firing on full auto. His face was a nightmare, and I only caught a glimpse of it; but that glimpse still gives me nightmares. Most of his fire hit the roll-up door, but a few bolts lanced through the open pull-door, effectively suppressing the longarms' entry.

Suppressing fire. Like warning shots. The dots connected in my head and I pulled the trigger. Bursts of laser bolts screamed from my CLR, so loud I thought my brain was going to melt. The wall next to the open door collected blisters and burns. Smoke started to percolate, obscuring the view outside.

Sebek grabbed my LCE by the handle and lifted me to my feet. My finger left the trigger immediately and I lowered the weapon.

"Go!" he shouted, shoving me toward the hallway.

I had my CLR at a low ready. I was moving as quickly as I could without swinging the weapon like a counterweight. I knew how longarms think. They already had the building locked down. They were waiting for us to try to escape out a back door into an alley. If these guys were worth the badges they carried, they'd be ready to greet us with weapons at any escape point from that building.

Full lockdown. Standard operating procedure.

I wasn't supposed to know this. I wasn't supposed to be a criminal. A fugitive. A terrorist.

I guessed that since I was there doing all that, I was all those things.

It's for a good cause.

I'm sure that's what the Pathfinders tell themselves, too.

I caught up with Hanson in the hallway. He led me to another open bay, this one with a garage door, locked full down. A couple of star skippers were parked near the door. A series of huge utility lockers lined the wall behind them. At the end with his back against the lockers, I saw Caldwell working with his Pulse. A cord ran from his device to a large box. I couldn't tell what was in it, but I knew it wasn't the focus tubes. One of the kids – the one lucky enough to already be in when the shooting started – was shutting the lid on the fourth case and sealing it.

"Hell yeah!" Caldwell raved. "Four cases, four pocket rockets. It's like they wanted us to have all this loot, you know?"

"The hell you talking about?" Hanson fumed. "Grip's got his face blown off. We gotta get *her*," he pointed a knife in my direction, "and the packages out of here. I can hold them off –"

Caldwell unplugged his cord from the box as the lid snapped open.

"No need, my friend. Pocket rockets. Didn't you ever use one of these when you were a kid?"

He reached into the box and pulled out what looked like an exercise ring, a hula hoop, with a pair of wicked-looking boosters attached. I knew what they were as soon as I saw them. On Destin, we called them hip flares. As a kid, I used to jump well over a hundred meters with one of those, and that was just a civilian model.

"I was in the Navy, Caldwell." Hanson cast a glance over his shoulder. The laser blasts were getting thicker and closer. "I'm not a wild-ass space marine."

Caldwell threw him a rig. Hanson caught it reluctantly.

"Space marines have more fun. And bigger balls."

"Whatever," Hanson said, unbuckling the belt and wrapping it around himself.

"You used one of these, Katana?"

"Of course," I said, taking one from him and belting it on. The ignition and decelerator buttons were exactly where I remembered them.

"The real question is, how well do you know the city?" Caldwell laughed with his annoying high pitch.

"Well enough," I said.

Sebek rounded the corner, Grip right behind him. I was amazed the man could still stand, let alone fight. His neck, shoulders and chest were covered in blood, but it was already drying. Bits of his skull peeked out between layers of scorched flesh. His cheek was halfway vaporized, exposing a few teeth even with his mouth shut. Which it always was, because he was Grip and he didn't talk.

Sebek looked at the three of us, then at the Grip, then back at us.

"It looks worse than it is," he quipped.

Caldwell whistled. "Hot damn, Grip. You are one bad motherf–"

Sebek cut him off. "They'll be here in thirty seconds. Grip and I will take a star skipper, run a distraction. You four, get the loot and get it up to the drop-off point."

I was confused, so I had to ask, "Where is that, exactly?"

Sebek took a half second to raise an eyebrow at me.

"In case we get separated," I pointed out.

"It's a private docking pad twenty levels up. We've got a good pilot. Came highly recommended. I don't like to work outside of our established network, but I paid extra to keep it discrete. He'll get this stuff where it needs to go. And you," he nodded at me, "it's your lucky day. One of us has to see the shipment delivered. You wanted to get to the man, and that's where these parts are going."

"I'll never complain about being ahead of schedule," I said, dropping my CLR's heat sink and swapping it with a fresh one. I picked up one of the crates, about the size of a recycling can, and strapped it to my back. It was heavier than I'd expected.

"That's our Princess." Sebek patted me on the back. "Grip, can you fly?"

The big man grinned. Or maybe he didn't and his injury just made it look that way. He latched his weapon onto his LCE and made for the star skipper. Sebek ran a hand over his goatee. He offered me the other hand, palm up.

I stared at him, confused.

"Grenade," he barked. "You're not gonna need it."

I pulled the little ball of death off my LCE and passed it over to him.

"Go on, boys – and Katana – it's time to make like we were never here."

I bit down on a laugh.

That's a distinct impossibility, right now.

Caldwell pulled one of the two L-pistols from his waist and waved a hand at me and Hanson.

"Let's break some windows."

Hanson and I followed him into the tool crib on the other side of the garage. Caldwell aimed and fired his L-pistol, knocking out a window on the far side of the room. He got a running start and jumped, making his body long and thin like a dart. He sailed through the open window, making it look easy. Hanson followed and copied the maneuver. Then me.

I landed, not as gracefully as the other two, but I made it through.

Glass fragments stuck to my forearms. I was bleeding a little, but it wasn't the worst injury I'd ever had. I brushed myself off and tried to get my bearings. We were in a street. Maybe a dozen meters from the safety barricade at the end of this level's platform.

"All right, lady and gentleman," Caldwell said, keying up his pocket rocket. "Jump's here, decel's here." He tapped his right and then his left hip. "Try to keep it smooth, and don't go for more than one level at a time. These things barely have enough juice to make it up the full twenty levels. Be conservative."

A thunderous crash got our attention.

The roar of repulsors burning on full throttle split the quiet of the night. Sebek and Grip were in the star skipper. They were making a break for it. The longarms, whom I still hadn't seen in that alley, were lighting up the airborne vehicle as it lifted off. Laser weapons would damage the hull, but they weren't going to punch through it before the Pathfinders got away.

I knew where I was going then, so I didn't wait for Caldwell and Hanson.

I dropped my CLR in the street because it would only get in the way, and I still had the slug thrower Sebek gave me in my waistband. I hit the lift-off switch as I approached the emergency barricade. A roar of flame shot out from my hips.

Airborne. G-forces pressed down on me, my lower back pinching slightly. I may have overdone the lift, but as I sailed up and over the next level and my finger feathered the decel switch, I felt the air heating up around me.

I risked a glance down. Between my feet I saw two longarms with CLRs firing at me. Their shots went wide. Very wide. Longarms didn't use rifles much, and right then I was thankful for that. Hanson was right behind me to the left, Caldwell already arcing down to the level plate on my right. I sailed over the safety barricade and executed a tuck-and-roll landing.

"Nice jump, Princess. Keep it moving!" Caldwell called and lifted off again.

We repeated this process a few more times. Each hop took a little bit longer for the pocket rocket to get up to speed; and I had to start the deceleration mode later and later. After I'd ascended fourteen levels, I knew my pocket rocket wasn't worth the risk of making another hop. I unbelted it and tossed it over the barricade, taking my chances with climbing the infrastructure.

My pulse was pounding as I climbed. Most of the buildings had maintenance access points where suction cups or carabineers could be clipped in for safety purposes, but I didn't have time for safety measures. I was just grabbing hold of irregularities in the wall tiles, windowsills and antennas, pulling myself up one grueling arm length at a time.

What we had going for us was that the longarms didn't know where we were going. They couldn't just rush up to level 346 and cut us off. They had to follow us level by level because we were going too fast.

I heard the star skipper screaming through the air some distance away and chanced a glance over my shoulder. Sebek was hanging out the window, firing his CLR at the longarms below us. He didn't have a chance in hell of hitting any of them, but he wasn't trying to. He was just laying down some suppression to distract. Incoming laser bolts were enough to distract anybody. Except for Grip, maybe. Sebek's flyby gunning was working to buy us time...buy me time. I still had the heavy loot box weighing down my shoulders.

Two longarm star skippers arrived on the scene. Red and blue lights painted the walls around me. Sebek ducked his head back inside and pulled the window up. Grip pointed the nose of the air vehicle skyward. They took off, riding a blue-blazing corona straight up at blinding speed. The longarm skippers gave chase. I was covered in shadows again.

I climbed up three levels before I was concerned that my arms and back couldn't take the strain anymore. I dropped off onto the level plate and made for the nearest escalators. Hanson was right on my tail. Caldwell, a hard-nosed former marine, had decided to climb the whole way up. Good for him, right? I wasn't risking muscle failure and a plummet down who-knew-how-many-levels to end up an ugly splatter mark.

I was out of breath and lightheaded when I stepped off the escalator onto level 346.

The landing pad was in view, maybe three hundred meters away. It jutted out from a local business; big glass panes on the front with a sign that said FRESH MEAT DELIVERED DAILY.

There were a few people in the street, but they gave me and Hanson a wide berth. A couple of people running through the street with large crates on their backs probably wasn't the weirdest thing they'd seen down there.

Hanson rushed ahead of me and kicked in the door.

As we hustled into the establishment, all hell broke loose.

Laser blasts filled the place so thick I dropped to my face without time to draw my sidearm. Glass shattered all around me, clattering by my face. Hanson was tucked up under a table, his eyes wide. He hadn't expected to encounter anybody at that stage of the game. I hadn't, either.

I drew my sidearm and blindly let loose two rounds, hoping to force the shooters to take cover. I popped up as the second round left the barrel with the weapon out in front of me, sweeping back and forth.

I saw a kid standing there, holding a full-on Marine Corps issue MLR. The thing was resting on the counter. The weapon was so big and mean he looked like a child behind it. The blue spike of hair he was sporting set all kinds of warning bells off in my head.

"Holy shit, lady, you didn't have to shoot at me," he grumbled, stepping away from the weapon with his hands up.

"What the –"

Before I could finish that expletive, Thalex opened the door and waved a hand.

"C'mon, let's *go*!"

I was too confused, and we were in too big of a hurry for me to argue.

"Hanson, up," I said, following the punk outside. The Pathfinder shuffled to his feet and followed me.

"I'll get her fired up, you load the stuff in the back," Thalex said as the boarding ramp lowered. The ship was a small one. Enough room for maybe ten crates the size of the one I was carrying. I saw seating for six people minus the cockpit.

As I was about to climb the boarding ramp, a longarm hit the landing pad, a pocket rocket decel cooling at his waist.

He levelled his CLR as I brought my sidearm to bear.

We locked eyes, and for a moment, there was hesitation.

He shouldn't have been there. He was too high ranking to go on raids.

He did this to me. He sent me here.

I saw his mouth forming a 'D' and I couldn't let that happen.

I couldn't let my cover be blown.

Even though he was my Fatti.

I pulled the trigger.

The kinetic round punched through his LCE, left a tattered hole in his chest.

He dropped his rifle, hand flying to his chest.

He stumbled over the edge and fell. I looked away.

I focused on getting the crate off my back and tucked away. Hanson copied me.

Caldwell showed up a few seconds later, red-faced and heaving.

"This is it," Hanson told Thalex.

"Whatever, bro. We're outta here."

The boarding ramp sealed shut. I was grateful.

I didn't want the temptation of peering over the edge. I didn't know if my round killed him or the fall did. I wanted to keep it that way.

I shot my…

The repulsors roared to life. G-forces tweaked my lower back. It hurt more than it should.

I tried not to think about it. Tried not to remember who I was, and what I had just done. But I knew I'd never forget it.

"Setting course for Aldebaranzan," Thalex said with a quiver in his voice. "Strap in."

We disappeared in a flash of light.

EPILOGUE

Captain Vase Seneca stood on the bridge of her starship, monitoring the approach to Aldebaranzan. The planet was growing larger in the viewport. Predominately green landmasses were surrounded by cerulean seas and covered in thin white streams of cloud. It was, in her view, the most beautiful planet she'd ever seen.

The Jewel of the Collective.

Four of the most prestigious universities in space were installed here. It was a planet for retirees, white-collar workers, and vacationers who wanted to get a feel of what the legendary Earth of humanity's heritage may have been like half a millennia ago. It was neutral territory. Since the colonization of the planet, armed conflict had never transpired upon its surface.

"That's about to change."

"Ma'am?" Lieutenant Duran spoke from the XO's chair.

"Sorry Lieutenant. I didn't realize I was speaking aloud."

Duran, her executive officer and second-in-command of the ship, grunted politely, distracting himself with the sensor station. Vase liked him because he was stiff and professional. He knew regulation inside and out, and he enforced those standards with no room for error. Many of the subordinates hated him, which was a blessing in disguise. It took the heat off her, for one.

"Lieutenant, get me the Platoon Sergeant. I want to let him know the plan."

"Has there been a last-minute change, ma'am?"

Vase took her seat in the captain's chair and let out a sigh.

"Lieutenant, get Chief Kalty and Sergeant Piebold up here, now."

"Aye aye, ma'am!" Duran fired off a brisk salute and spun on his heel, leaving her alone on the bridge.

Vase rubbed her temple. Her fingers were cold. Space was always cold. She had grown used to it in her line of work. The cold that descended on her now, though, wasn't the chill of sailing the endless dark. It was the shiver up the spine that came with doing something you knew was wrong. Her father, the Admiral of the Navy, had requested it. She knew better than to disobey a direct order from a superior officer. Even if her conscience demanded it.

It was her career on the line. She knew too much to back down now.

"Still," she wondered aloud, "I wish she would have gotten me something a little more solid on Abraham. If he's running with the Ghosts, that...complicates things."

Her mind drifted back to basic training. The hottest, most miserable planet she'd ever set foot on – Juno. How she had been given the most important assignment in her very new career. A message from her father explaining the details. Classification level Hyperion. A security clearance level so high, Vase had never heard of it:

STAY CLOSE TO ZEEBEN. WHATEVER YOU HAVE TO DO

She hadn't understood it at the time. And of course, she had to play the game, to break the rules to draw him close to her. No one would believe an officer and an enlisted marine would spend so much personal time together. There were regulations against that exact thing. Fraternization, conduct unbecoming an officer and a gentlewoman…it was nonsensical. Abraham Zeeben may have been naïve enough to disregard the regs, but Vase Seneca was not.

She hated doing it. Hated breaking the rules.

But she wanted a full career. She wanted to follow in her father's footsteps. And so far, stretching the rules behind the scenes had gotten her promoted to captain far earlier than she would have dared possible. In her mind, the success she achieved honored the memory of her mother, a woman she had no memory of, who died protecting her little girl from pirates so many years ago.

Vase was not so simple as to wish vengeance upon the entire alien race responsible. But now that she had it – now that she had helped Abraham set the riskar back to an unsustainable population level – she confessed to herself she enjoyed a certain sense of justice.

The one thing she couldn't figure out was how she had failed so miserably. She had actually started developing feelings for Abraham. If she was honest with herself, she still had feelings for him. She did not know why. That, more than the attachment itself, bothered her.

"Ma'am," Lieutenant Duran announced himself.

Vase swung her chair about.

"At ease," she said.

Sergeant Piebold stood at parade rest next to Chief Kalty. Their confusion was clearly written on their faces. It was unusual for enlisted personnel to be called to the bridge, especially on approach to their destination.

"Platoon Sergeant," Vase said, "I know you've had a recent death in the family. Are you fit to fight, should this mission require it?"

He nodded. "Affirmative, ma'am. Whatever the mission requires, I'm full-up."

Vase looked to the chief. She was in her mid-forties, close to hitting 30 years and retiring. If she survived this mission, it would probably be her last.

"Chief Kalty, do you agree?"

"Yes, ma'am. Sergeant Piebold is fit to fight."

Vase nodded.

"Then I'm going to give you the real mission brief."

Sergeant Piebold's brow narrowed. He wasn't expecting this.

"We're not here to escort the ambassador on a diplomatic mission. We're here because a certain group of rogue citizens is attempting to start a war. We must stop the war before it begins. If they succeed, the Riskar War will look like a minor skirmish between neighbors. This rogue group, they want full-on intergalactic war. They want to tear down the Collective and raise up something new."

The sergeant spoke. "How are we going to accomplish this, ma'am?"

Vase picked up a Pulse off the arm of the chair and swiped a finger across it.

Two Pulse chimes followed.

"The details are now on your Pulse. I want you to divide your platoon into four squads. Each of you will be responsible for finding and eliminating High Value Targets within your scope. Once that is accomplished, any remaining dissenters will be expunged – to the last man or woman."

"Understood," Chief Kalty replied.

Vase brought her hands together.

"This new mission comes straight from the top. I did not learn of it myself until a little over an hour ago. I'll get the clearance from Aldebaranzan Watch Command, and we will deploy to the surface in twelve hours. Make your preparations. Dismissed."

Piebold and Kalty fired off salutes and left the bridge.

Lieutenant Duran resumed his post at the sensor terminal.

Vase spun her chair around.

Aldebaranzan filled the entire viewport now. They were close. Closer than they'd ever been.

Close to securing the Collective from domestic terrorism.

Close to exterminating the cancer cells that called themselves Pathfinders.

And failing that, close to starting a war that would bring about the extinction of all mankind.

Acknowledgements

The author wishes to acknowledge the Gatekeeper and the incredible team of hardworking inter-dimensional entities at Temple Dark Books. Without the sweeping dedication and perseverance from these otherworldly types, ***By Blood or By Star*** would not exist.

Introducing a 2nd POV (point of view) character in Book 2 was a risky move. It was not a decision made on a whim. The author has a few insightful readers to thank for confirming Djet's story as a refreshing look at the universe to which Abraham is slowly being introduced. Though the full pay-off of having two characters on either side of this burgeoning interstellar affair remains to be experienced in Book 3, the stage is set for an interstellar showdown that will change everything.

The following names were integral in the process of completing this book:

Trevor Acor, Alex Acree, Kyle Baglia, Sir William Belkofer, Devin Clemmer, Eric Burnworth, Kelly Burnworth, Kyle Bryant, Donnie Jenkins, Bill Scheve, Louise Scheve, Randy Carrasco, Tiffany Carrasco, Kirk "Red" Nelson.

Glossary of Select Terms

C-skin: Civilian skin. A jumpsuit made of millions of nanofibers that functions as a wearable screen. Can be powered on or off, the display pattern changed with the touch of a button or a voice command, to suit the wearer's fashion sensibilities (or lack thereof).
Dajun: Milune's sole moon. Once lush and verdant, it was destroyed in The Collision.
Destin: industrial planet in Vatican's shadow, the place where Djet grew up.
Duringer: homeworld of the riskar, glassed by the HY/DRA weapon shortly after the Riskar War.
Ghost Society: [REDACTED]
HUD: Heads Up Display. A screen or overlay that displays information.
L-pistol: Laser pistol.
L-rifle: Laser rifle.
Longarm: police officers on humanity's adopted homeworld, Vatican.
Milune: Abraham's home planet. Destroyed in The Collision.
Pathfinders: Little is known about this paramilitary organization.
Pocket: A personal drone that can store small items; and is controlled by touch or voice command.
Portal: A civilian tablet used for mobile internet/video calls.
Pulse: The military version of a Portal, featuring upgraded encryption.
Riskar: alien race with the ability to manipulate gravity.
S-skin: Space skin. Insulates the wearer from the harsh environment of vacuum, completed with a life support suite. Commonly worn over a C-skin or an undersuit.
Terra-City: a planet whose surface is almost completely covered in man- or machine-made infrastructure.
Torind: aquatic aliens that use tentacles to choke and/or decapitate their enemies.
Vatican: humanity's adopted homeworld, a terra-city.
Veranda: Abraham's adopted home planet, the place where he, his brother David, and Larry grew up.

CPSIA information can be obtained
at www.ICGtesting.com
Printed in the USA
BVHW041033061222
653555BV00004B/23